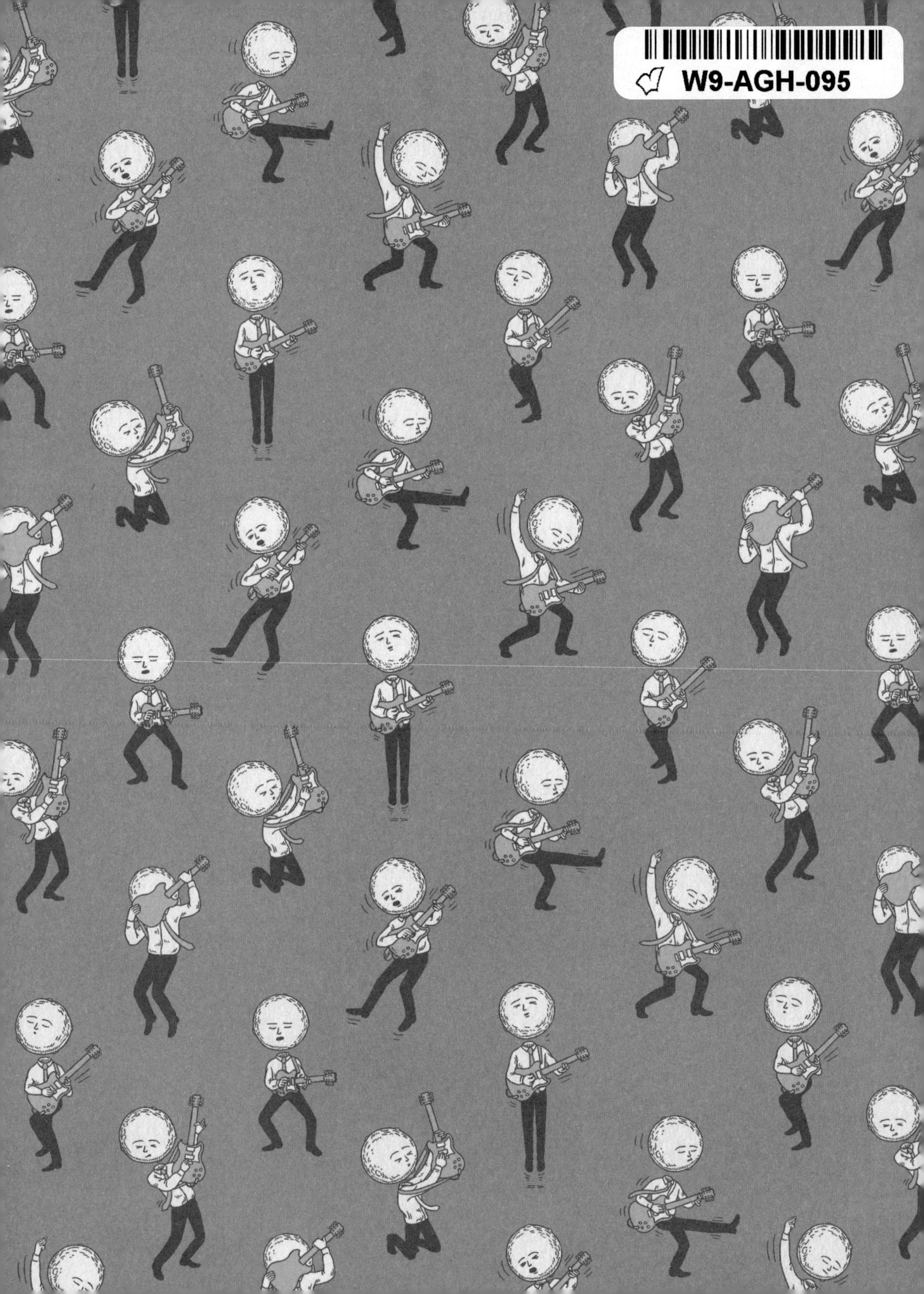

MIX
Paper from responsible sources
FSC® C101807

This is a first edition printed in 2014 by Nobrow Ltd. 62 Great Eastern Street, London, EC2A 3QR.

Published in the US by Nobrow (US) Inc.

Printed in Belgium on FSC assured paper.
ISBN: 978-1-907704-78-9

Order from nobrow.net

MOONHEAD

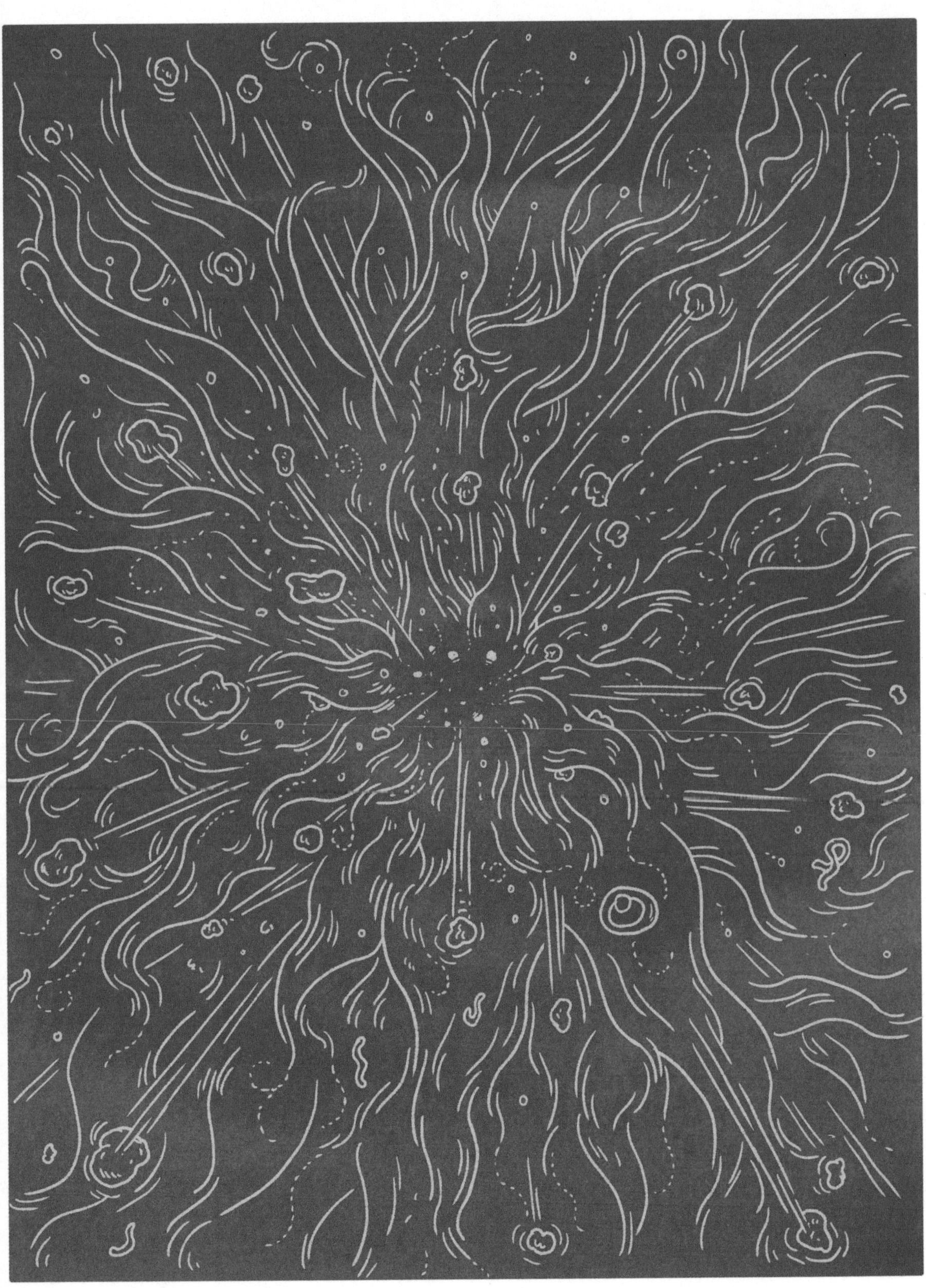

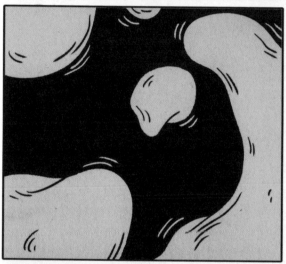
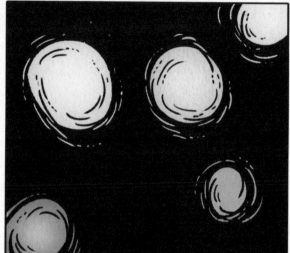

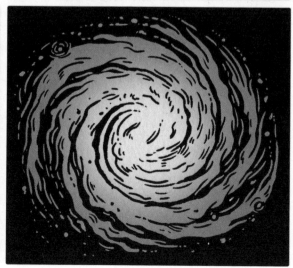

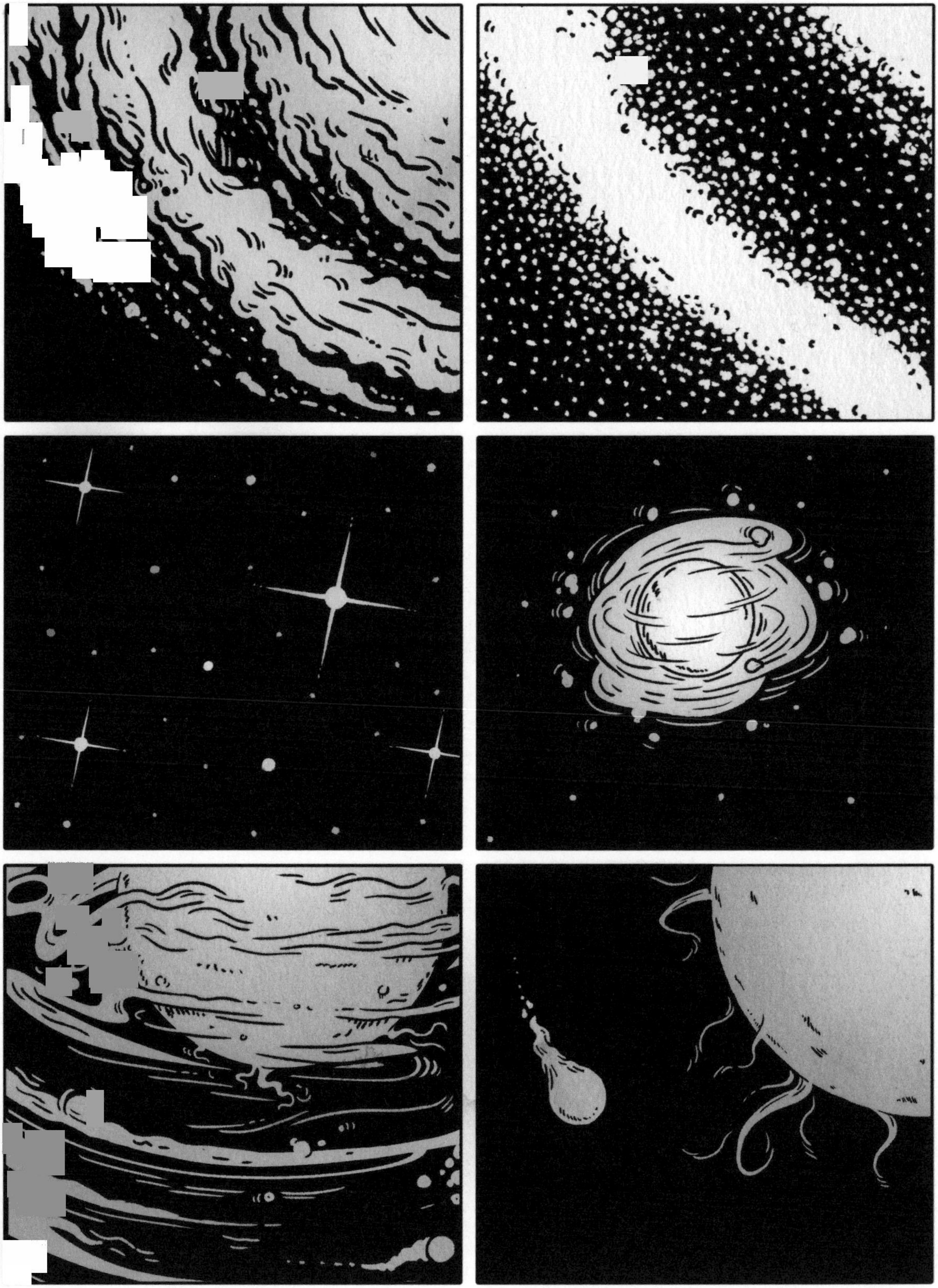

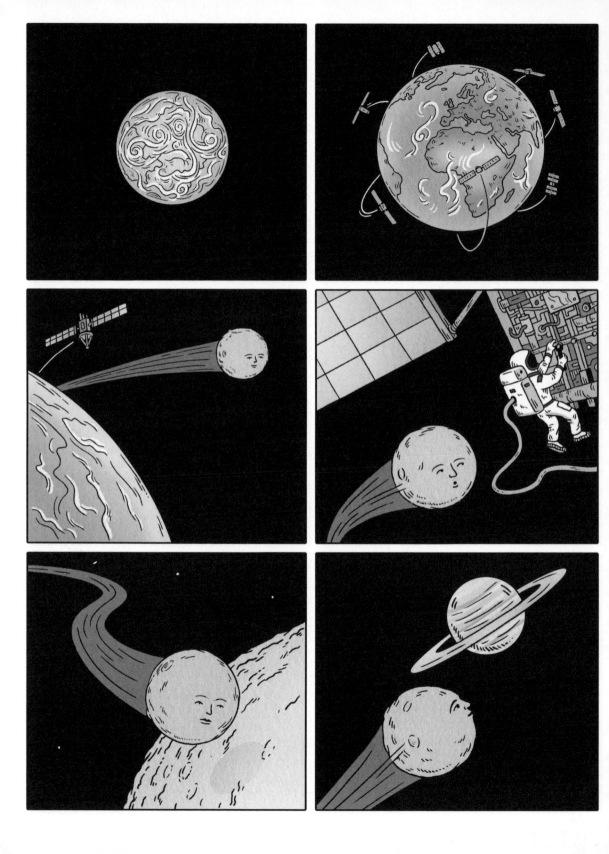

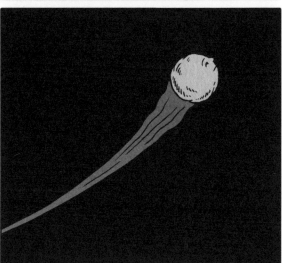

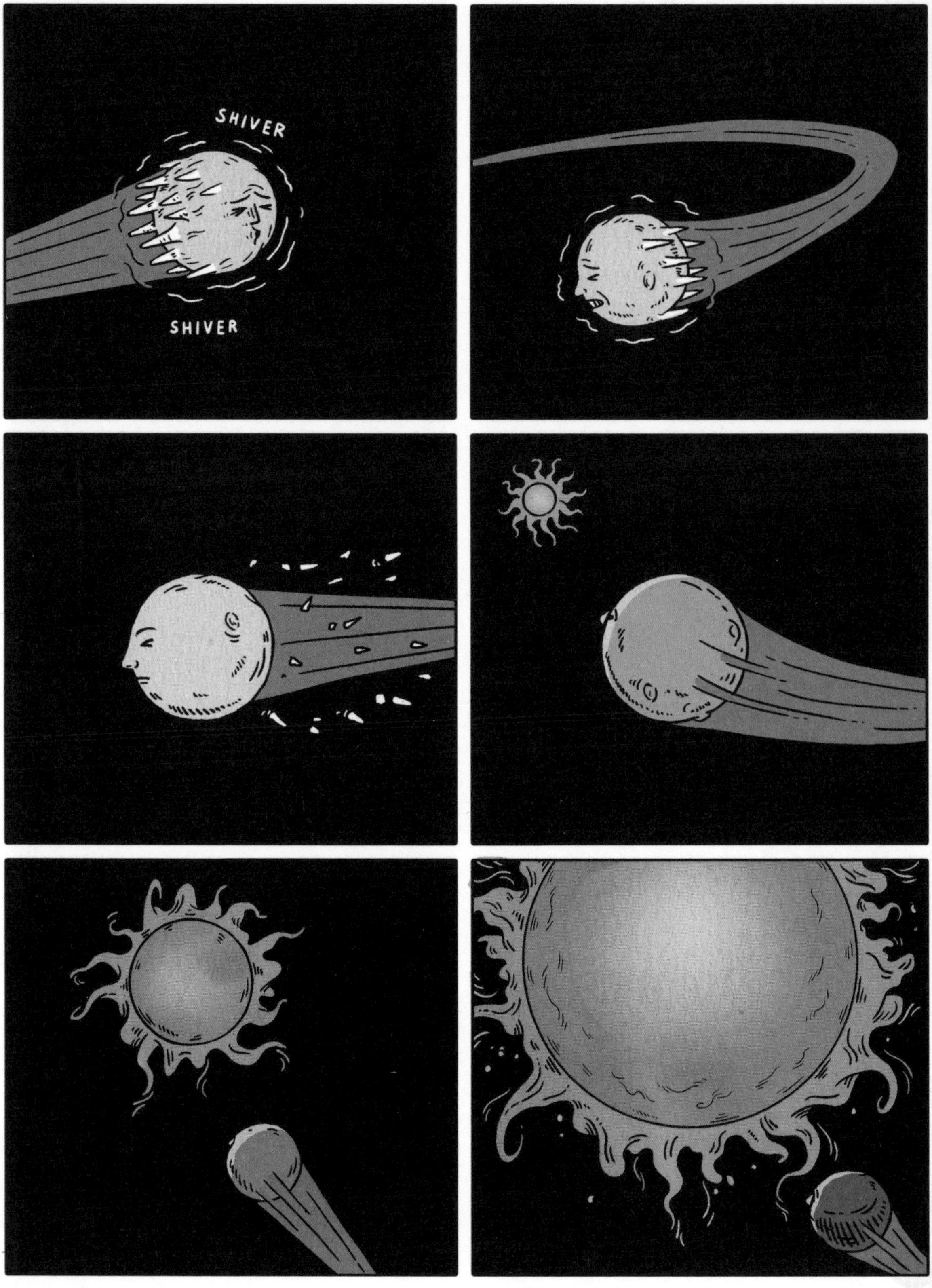
SHIVER
SHIVER

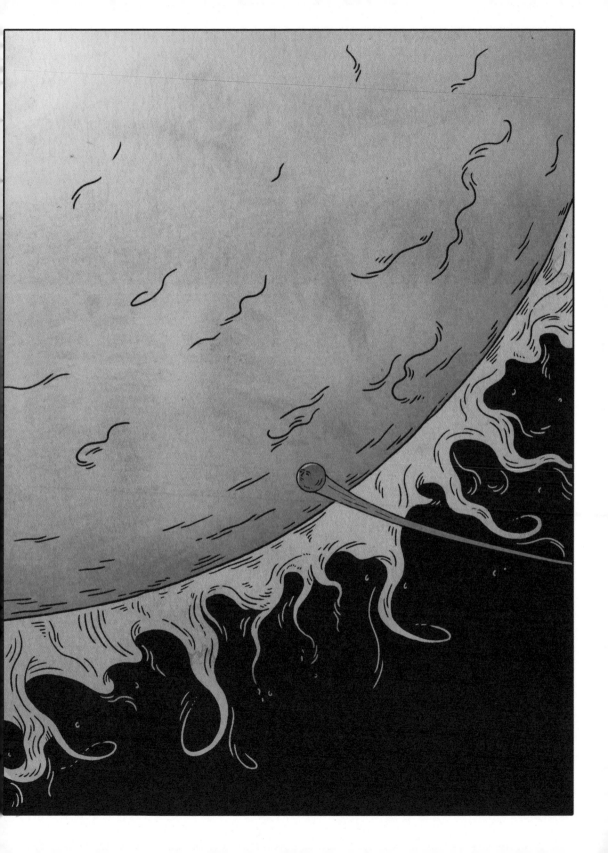

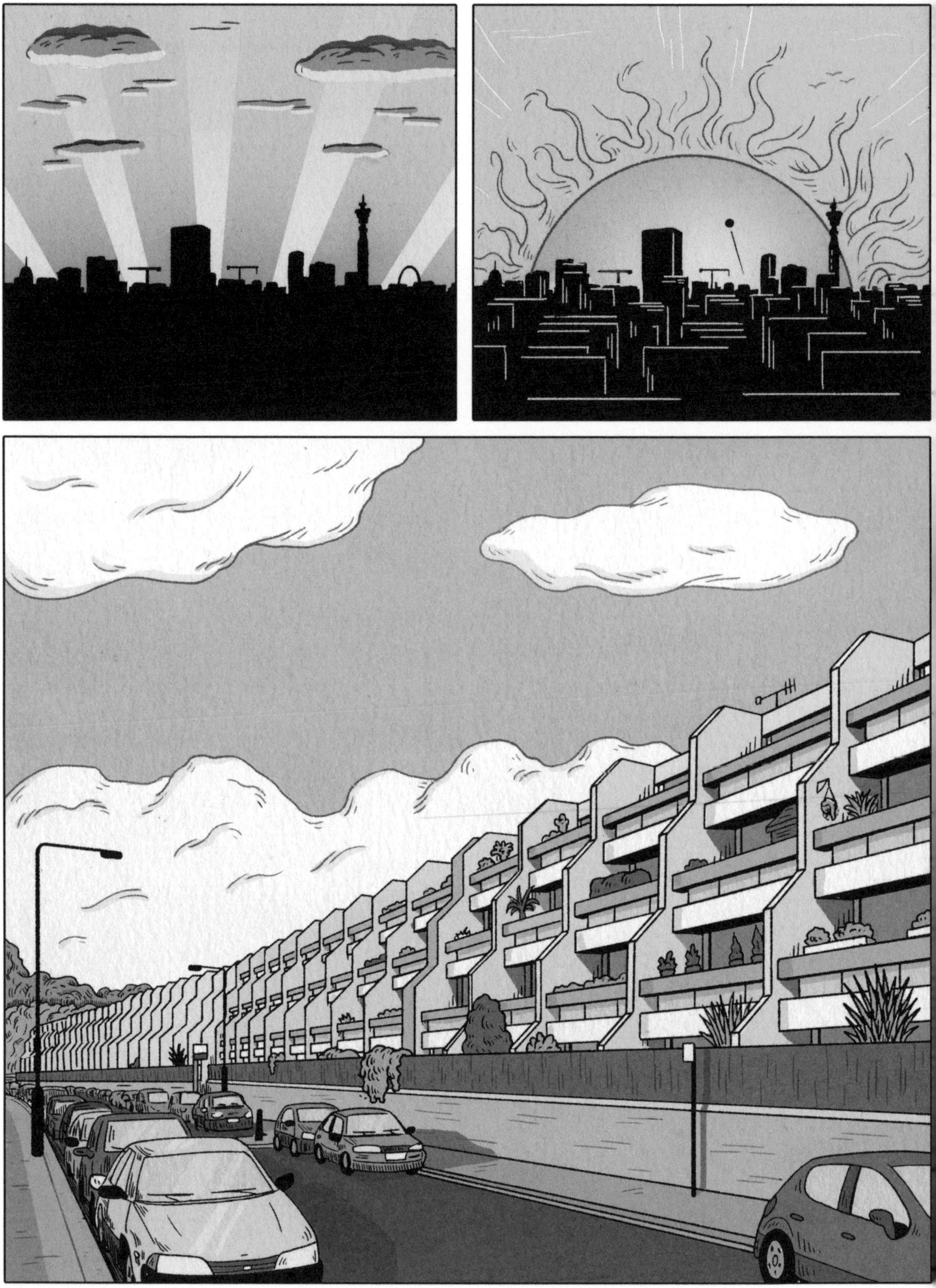

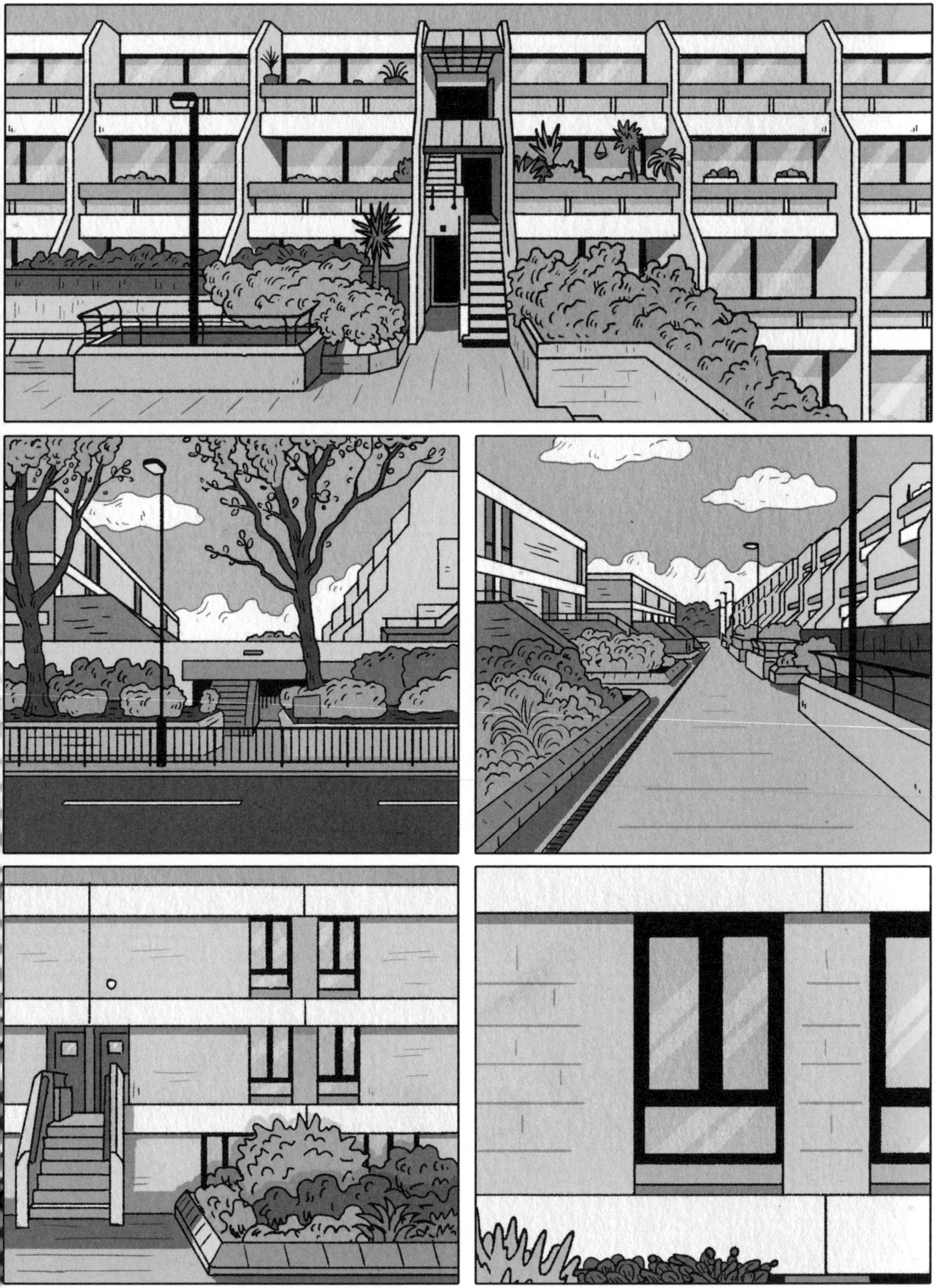

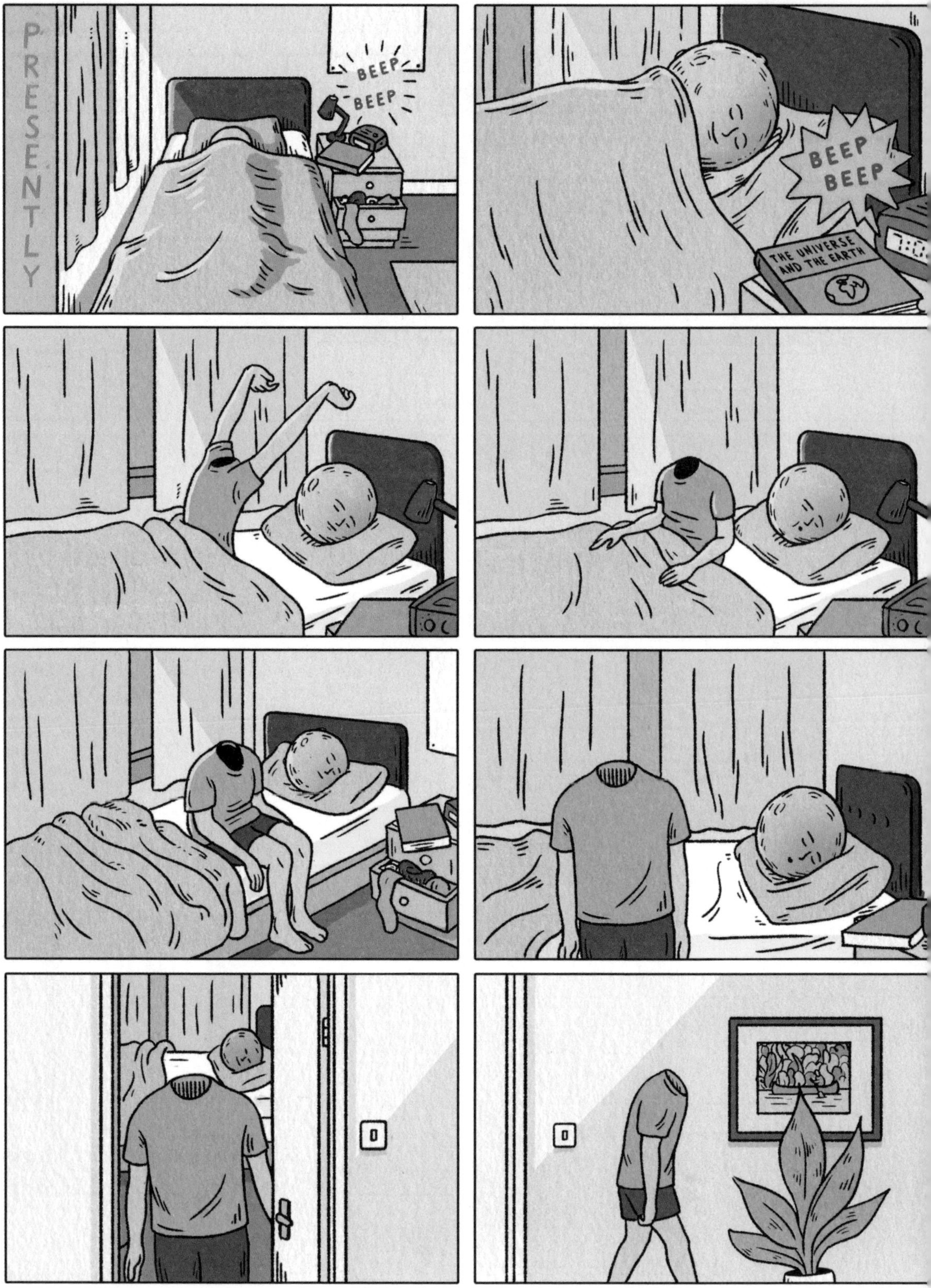
PRESENTLY
BEEP
BEEP
BEEP
BEEP
THE UNIVERSE AND THE EARTH

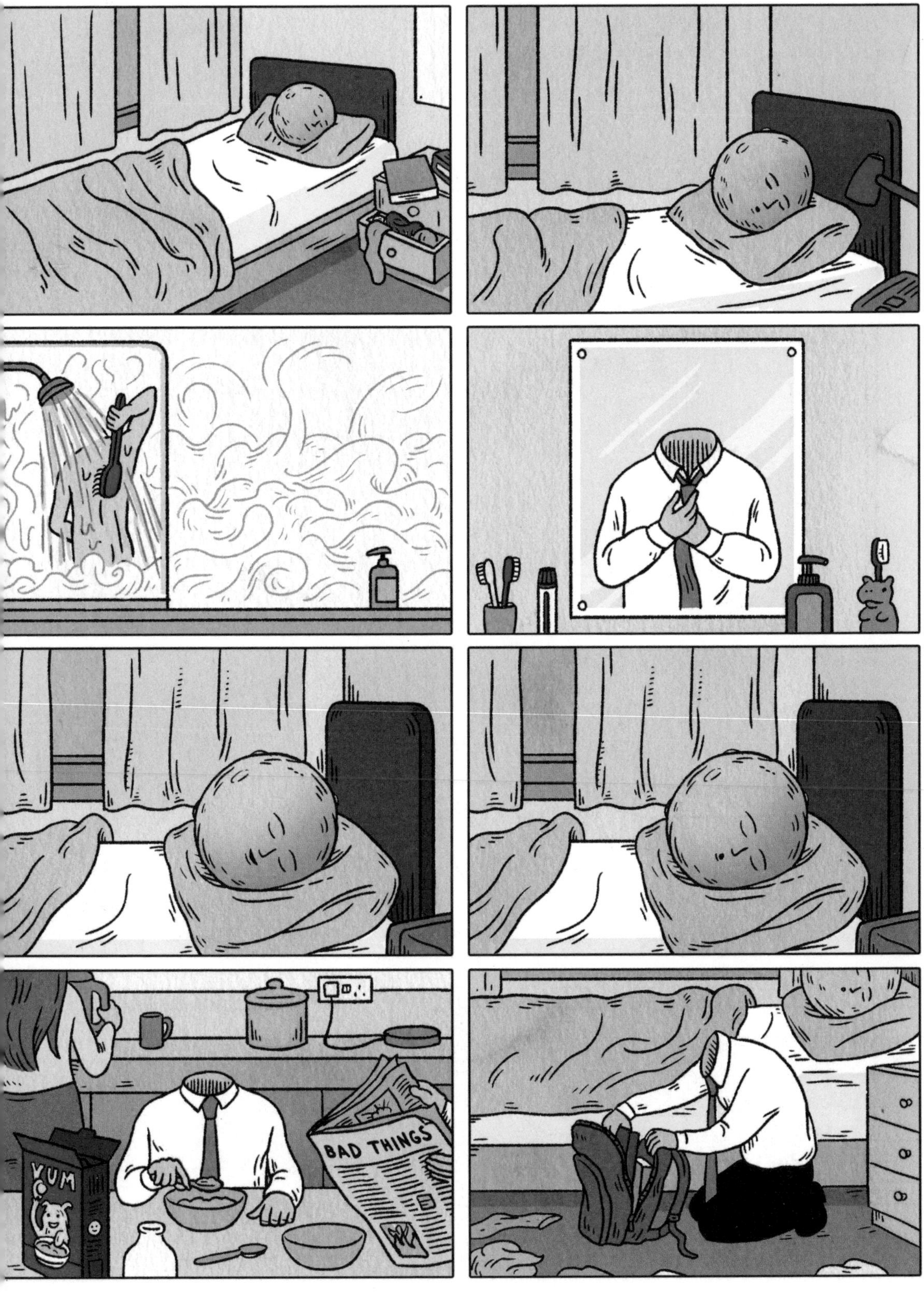
YUM
BAD THINGS

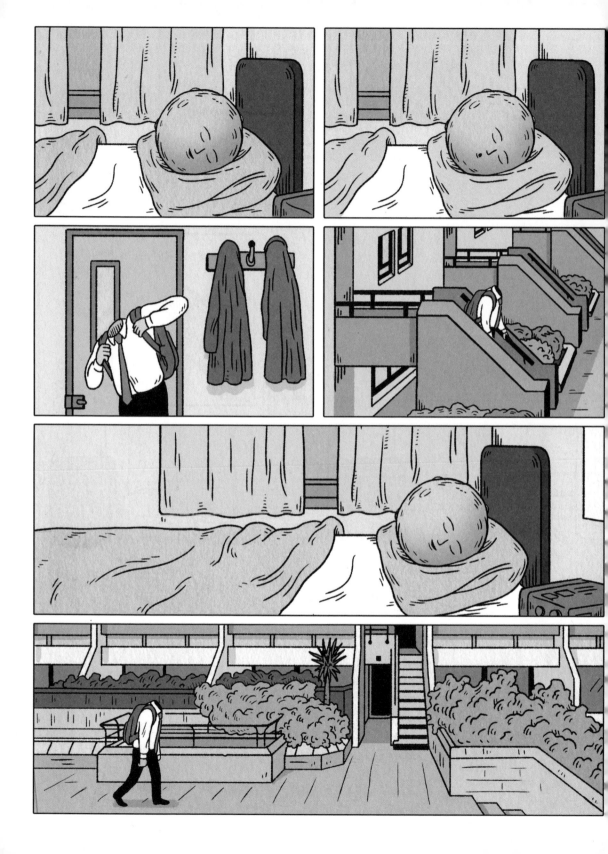

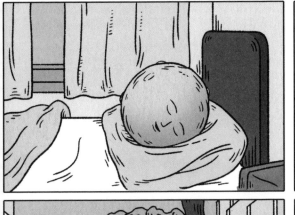

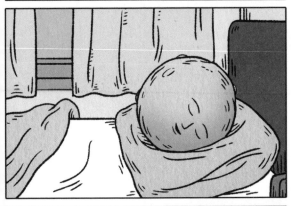

MORNING

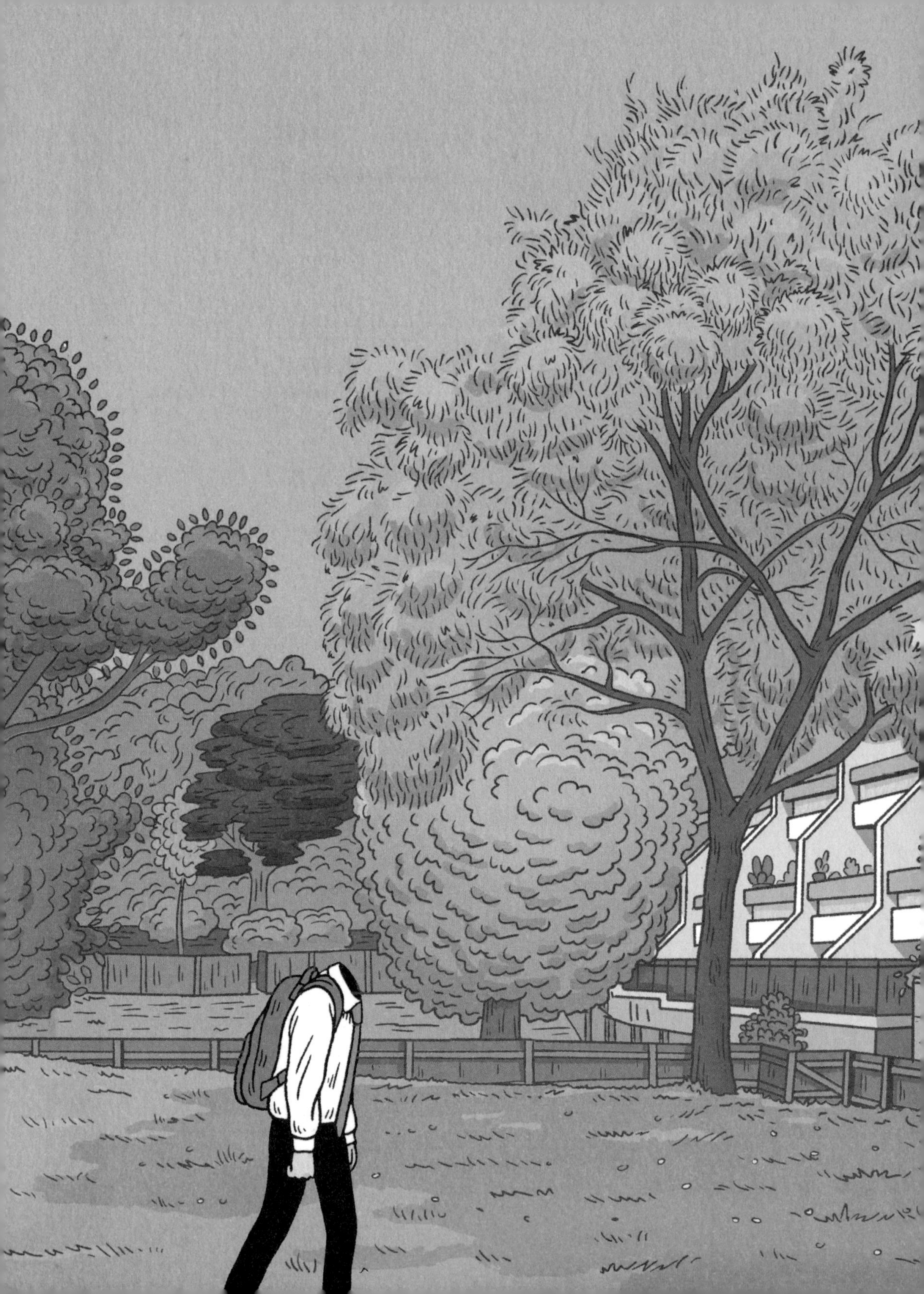

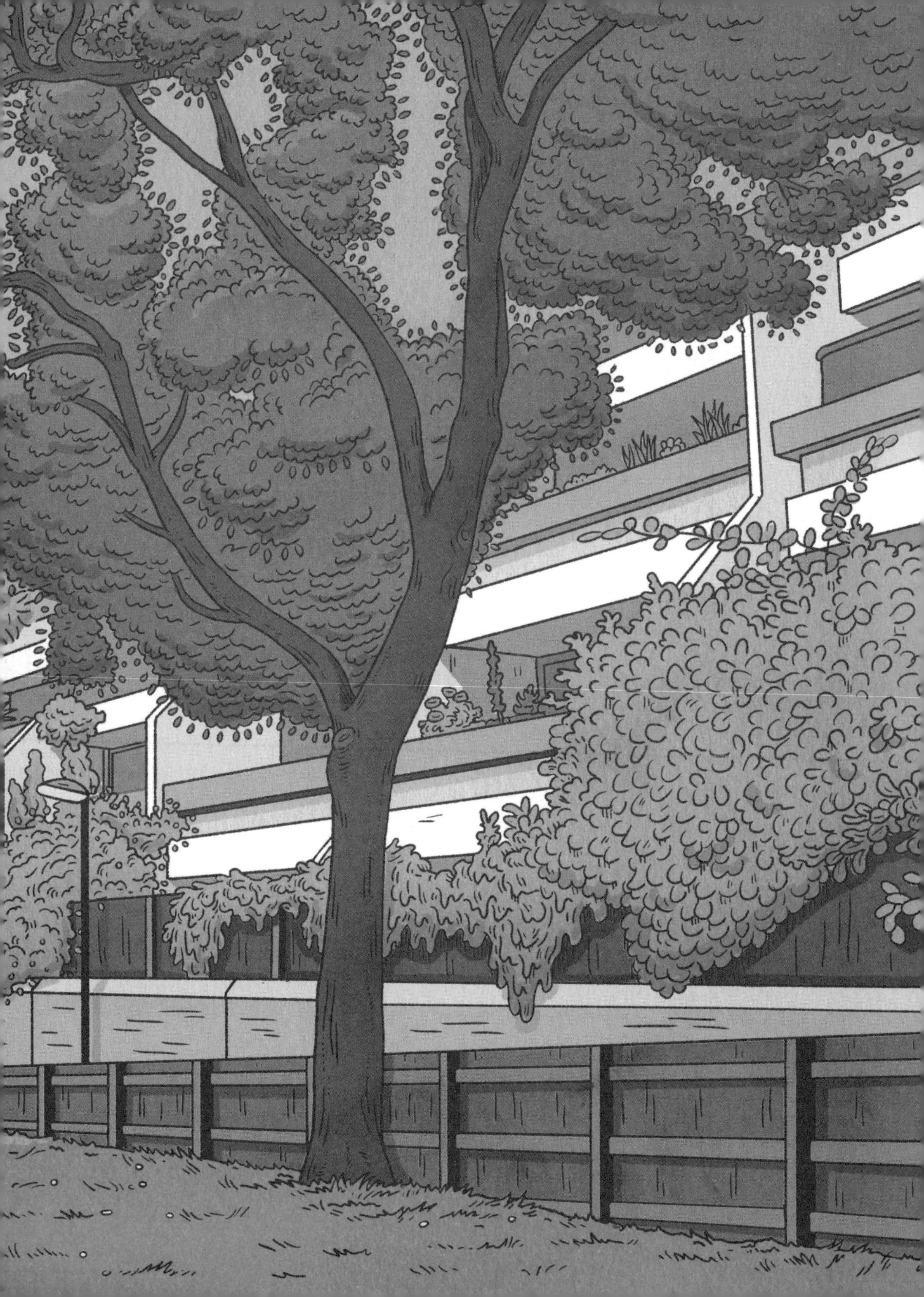

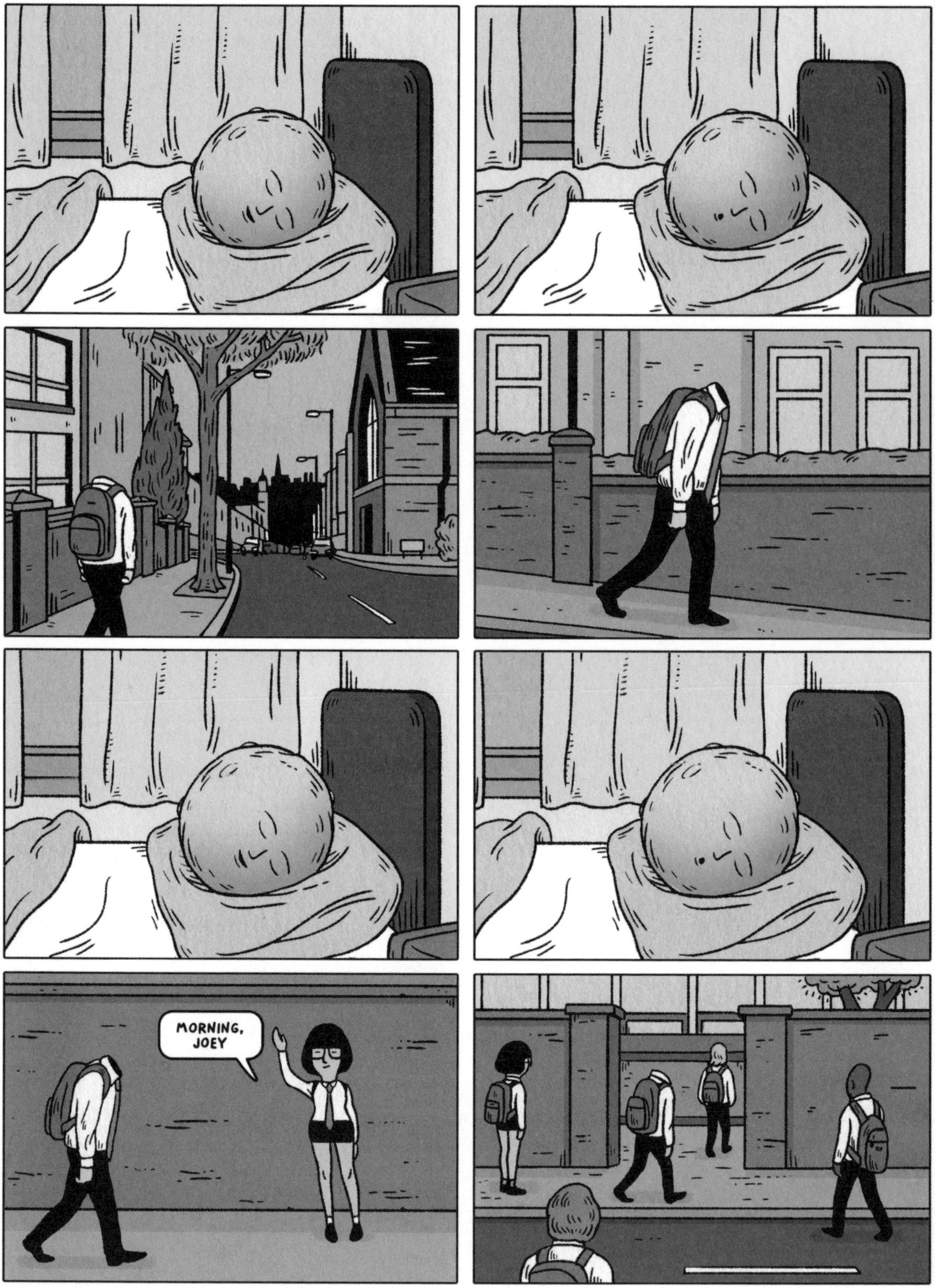
MORNING, JOEY

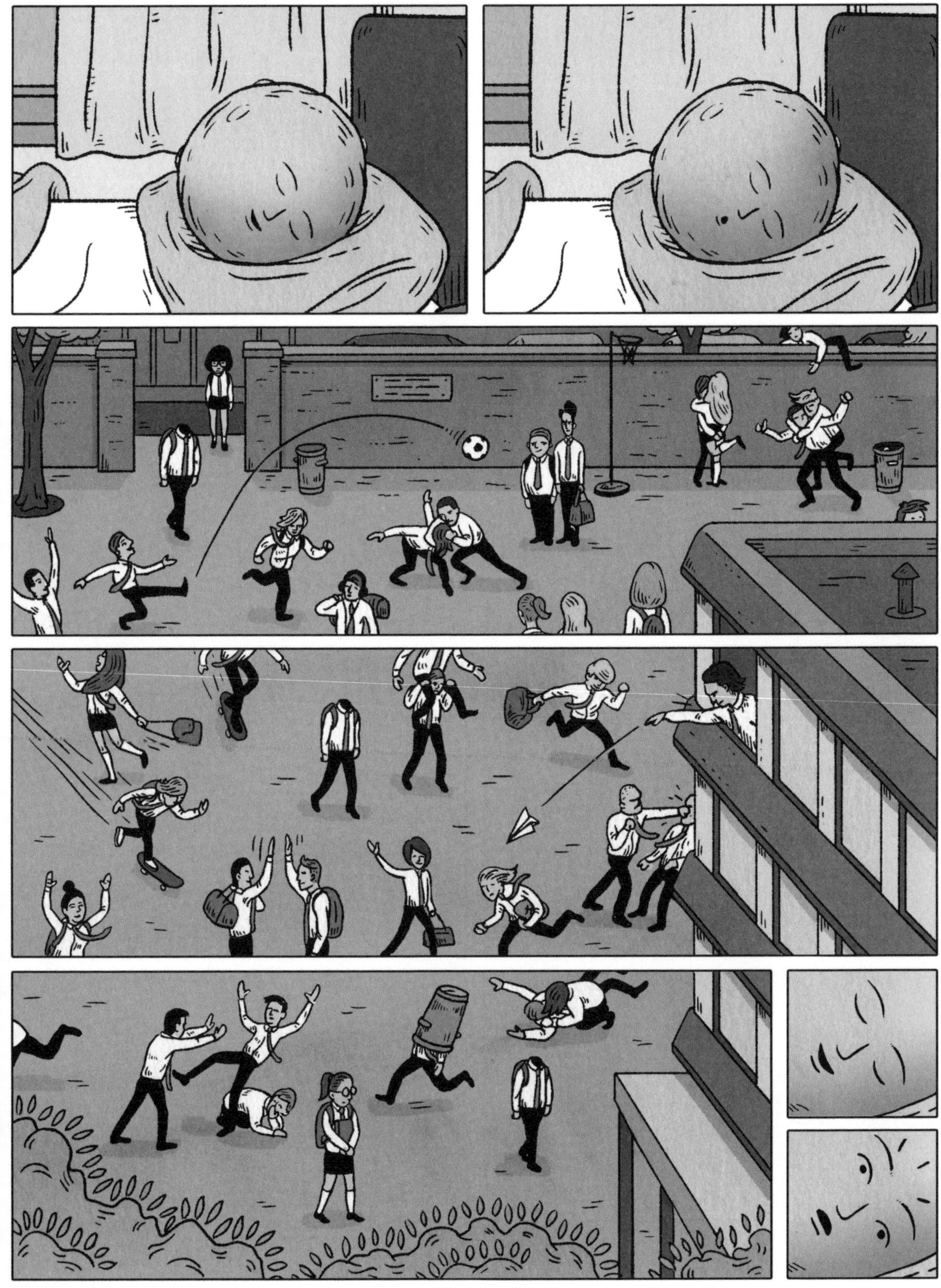

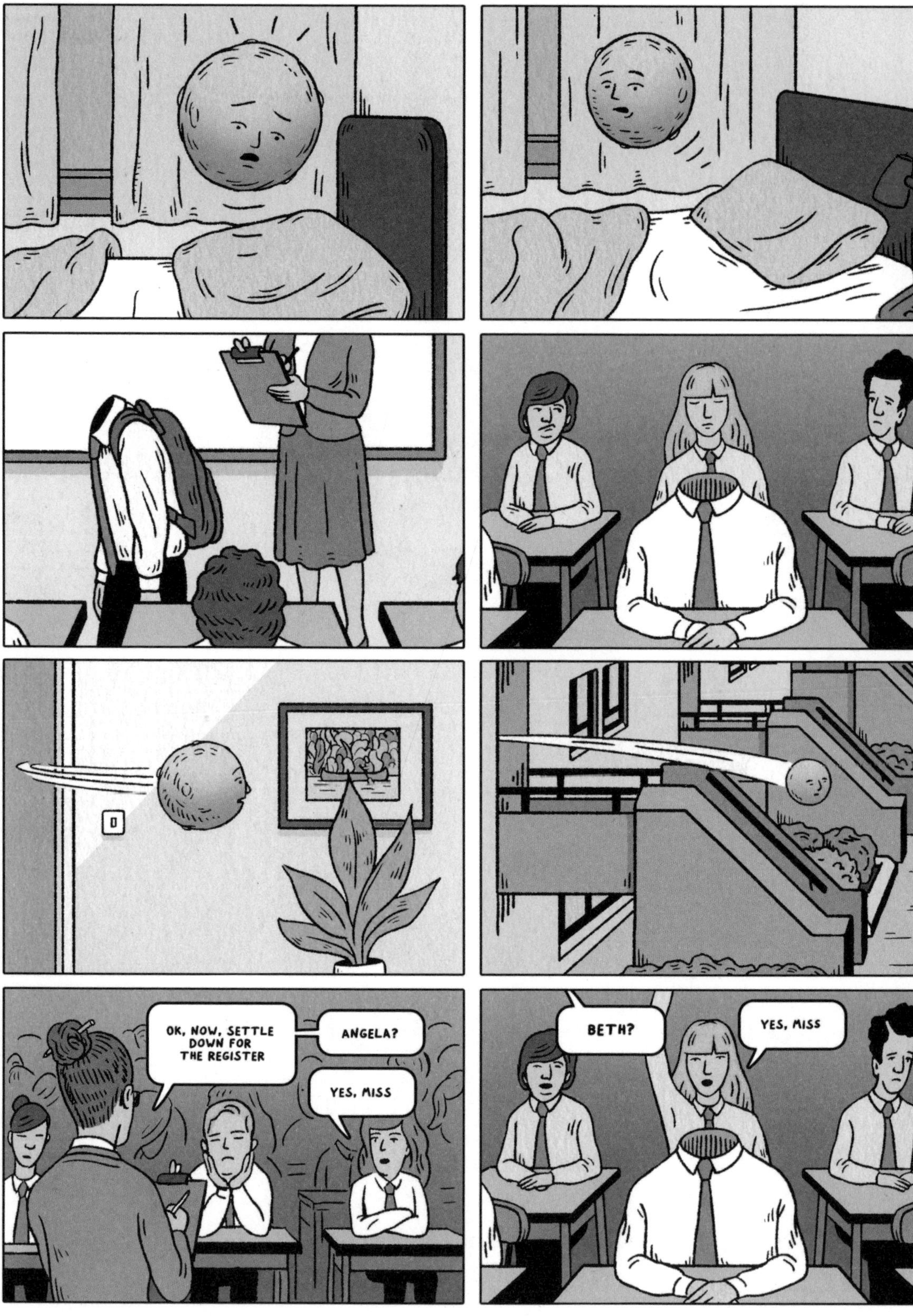
OK, NOW, SETTLE DOWN FOR THE REGISTER
ANGELA?
YES, MISS
BETH?
YES, MISS

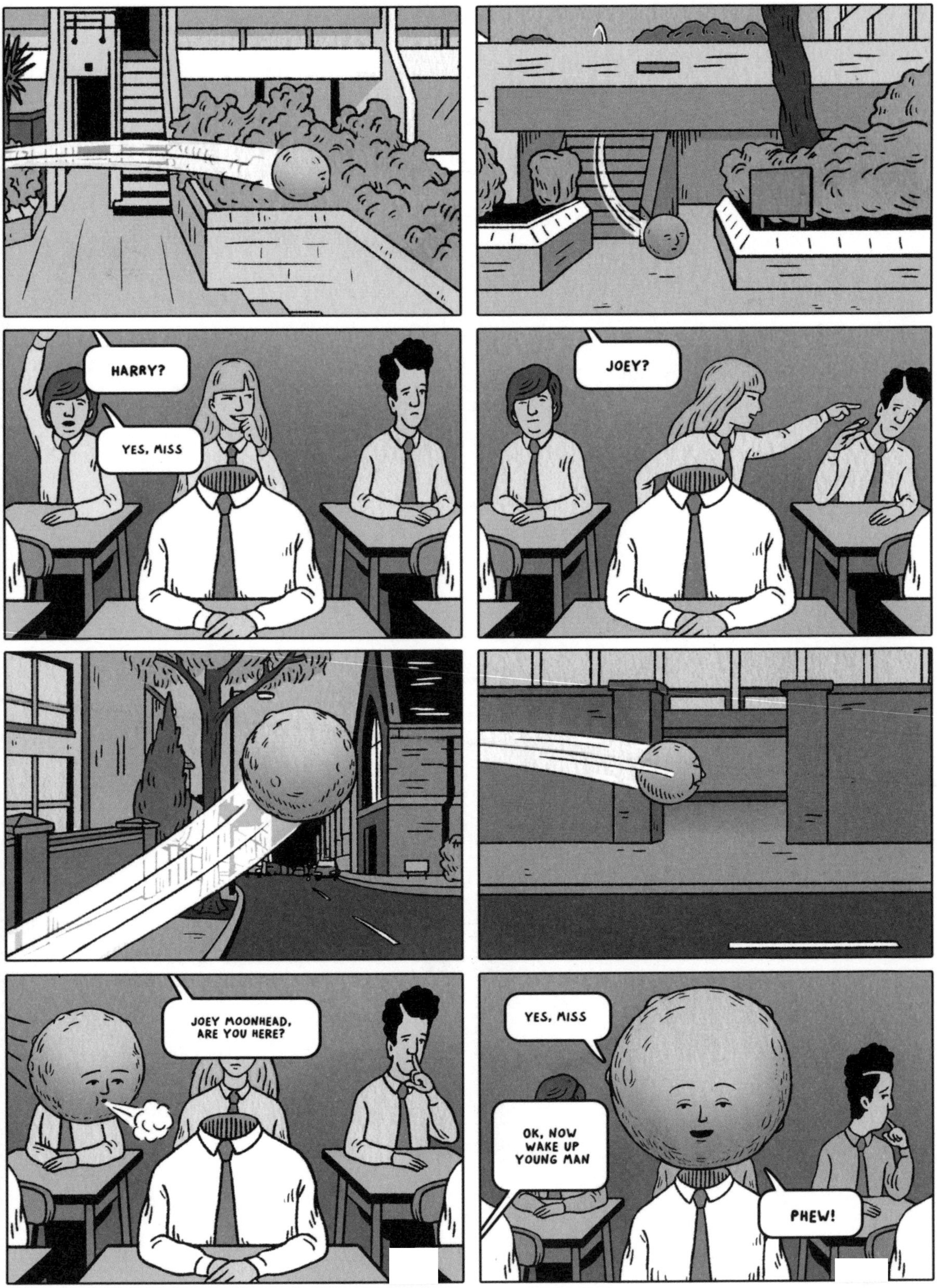
HARRY?
YES, MISS
JOEY?
JOEY MOONHEAD, ARE YOU HERE?
YES, MISS
OK, NOW WAKE UP YOUNG MAN
PHEW!

MEET
JOEY MOONHEAD

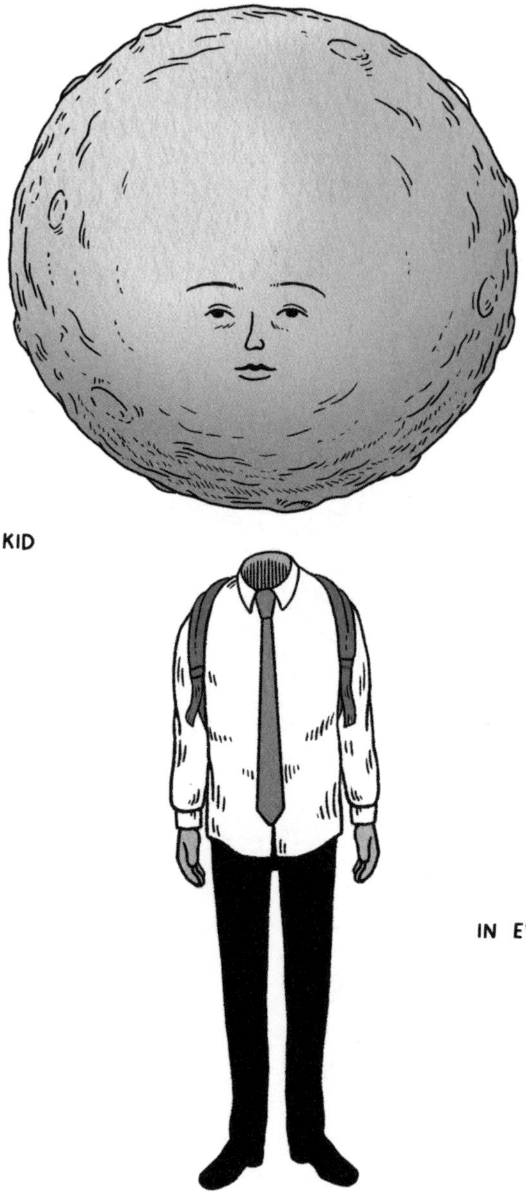

A NORMAL KID

IN EVERY WAY

EXCEPT ONE

HE HAS A MOON FOR A HEAD

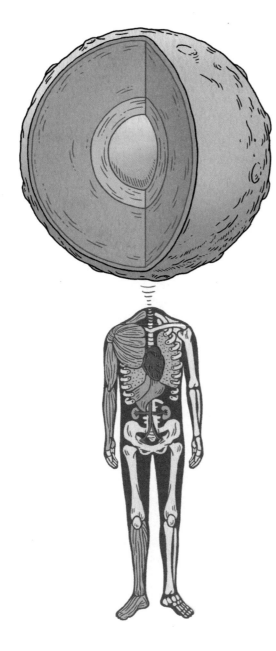

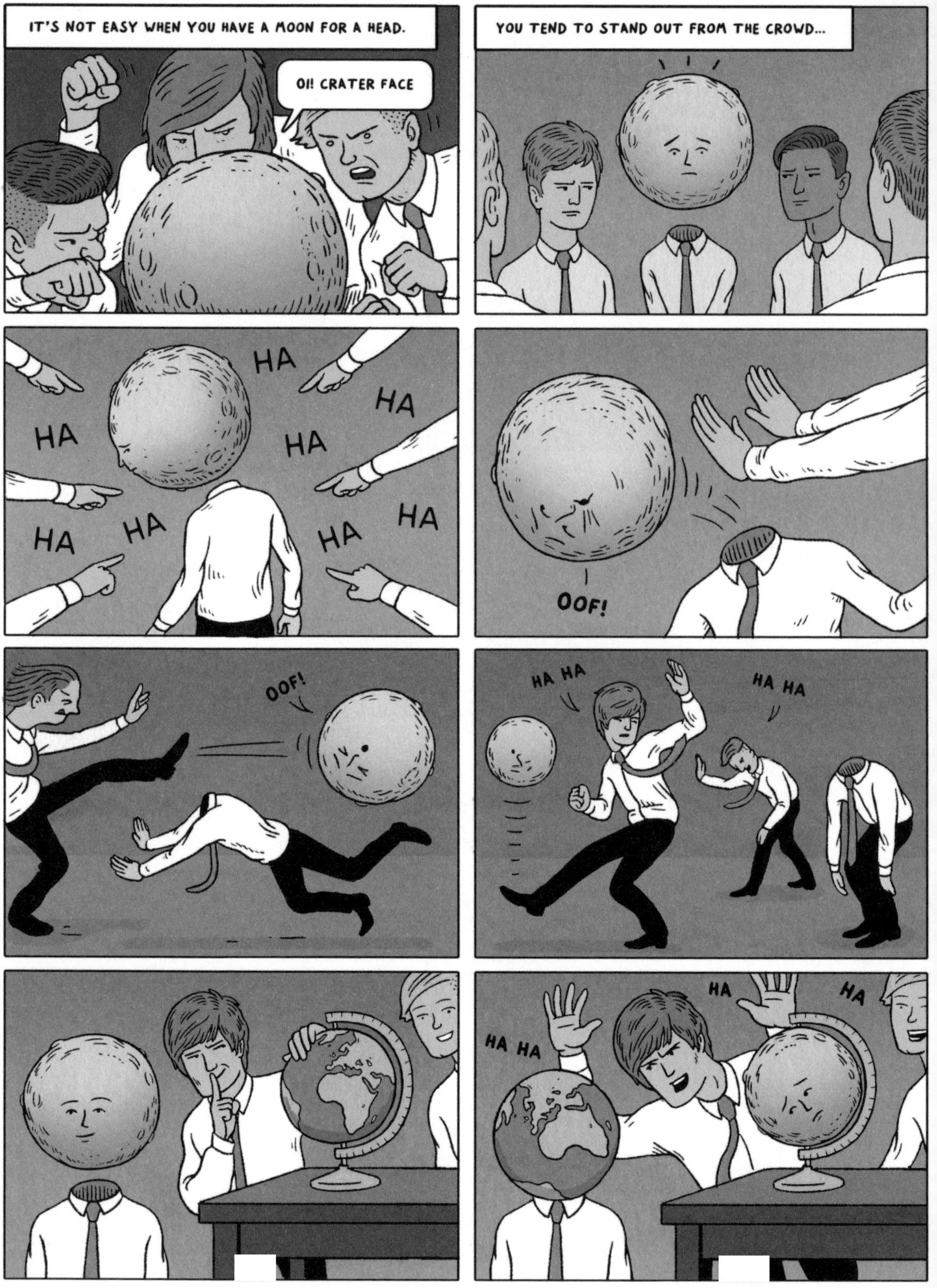
IT'S NOT EASY WHEN YOU HAVE A MOON FOR A HEAD.
OI! CRATER FACE
YOU TEND TO STAND OUT FROM THE CROWD...
HA
HA
HA
HA
HA
HA
HA
HA
OOF!
OOF!
HA HA
HA HA
HA
HA
HA HA

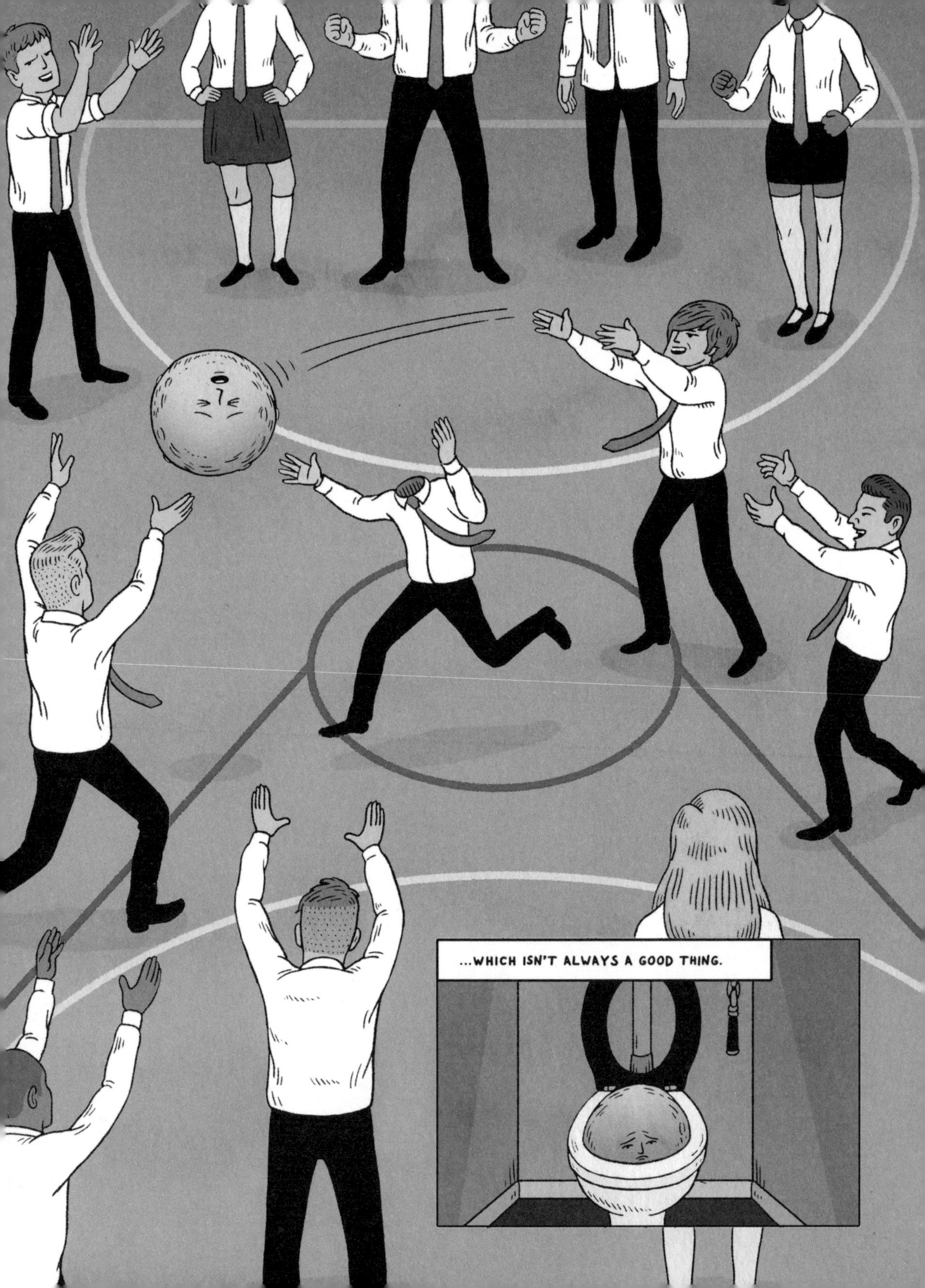
...WHICH ISN'T ALWAYS A GOOD THING.

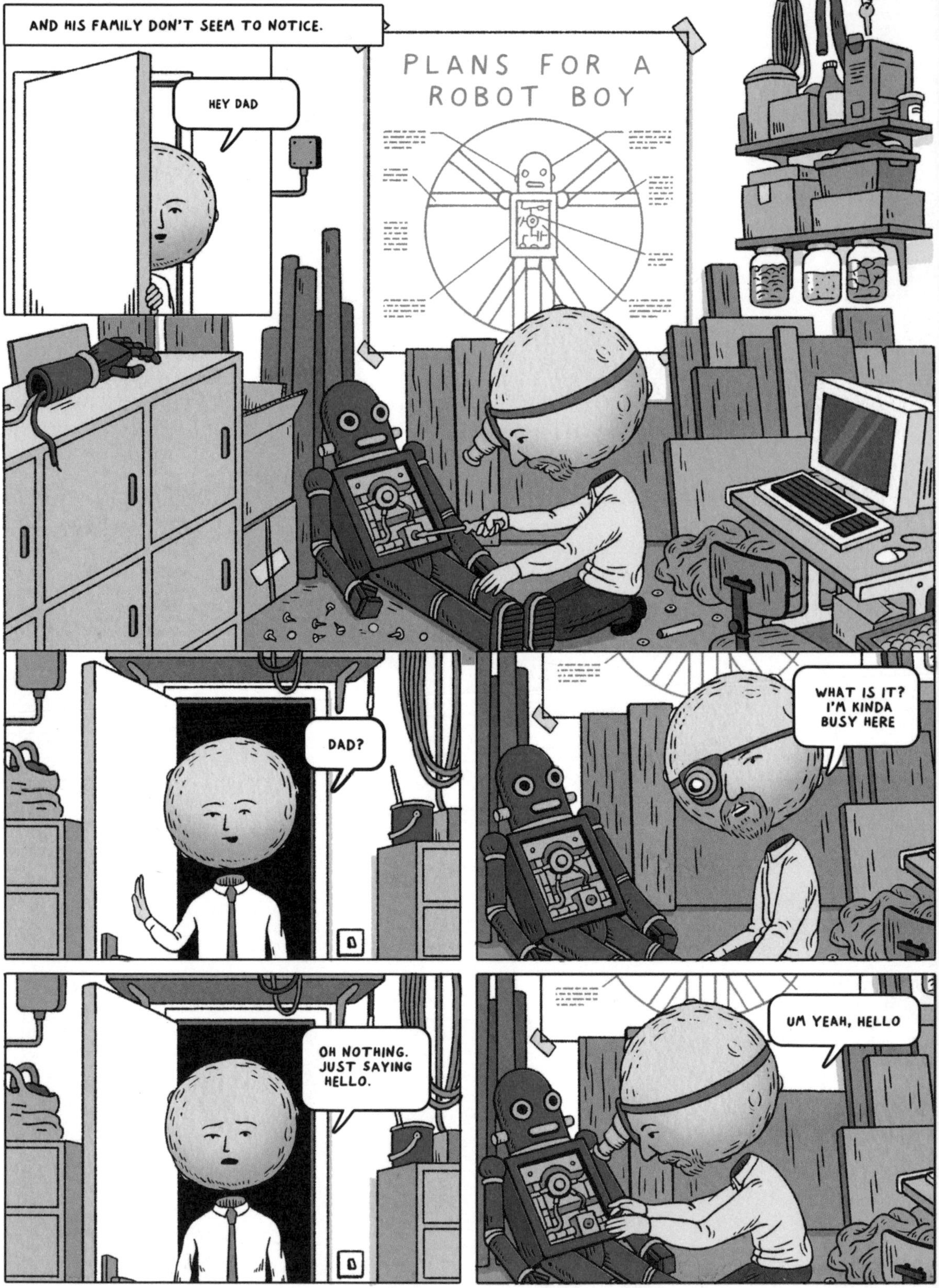
AND HIS FAMILY DON'T SEEM TO NOTICE.
HEY DAD
PLANS FOR A ROBOT BOY
DAD?
WHAT IS IT? I'M KINDA BUSY HERE
OH NOTHING. JUST SAYING HELLO.
UM YEAH, HELLO

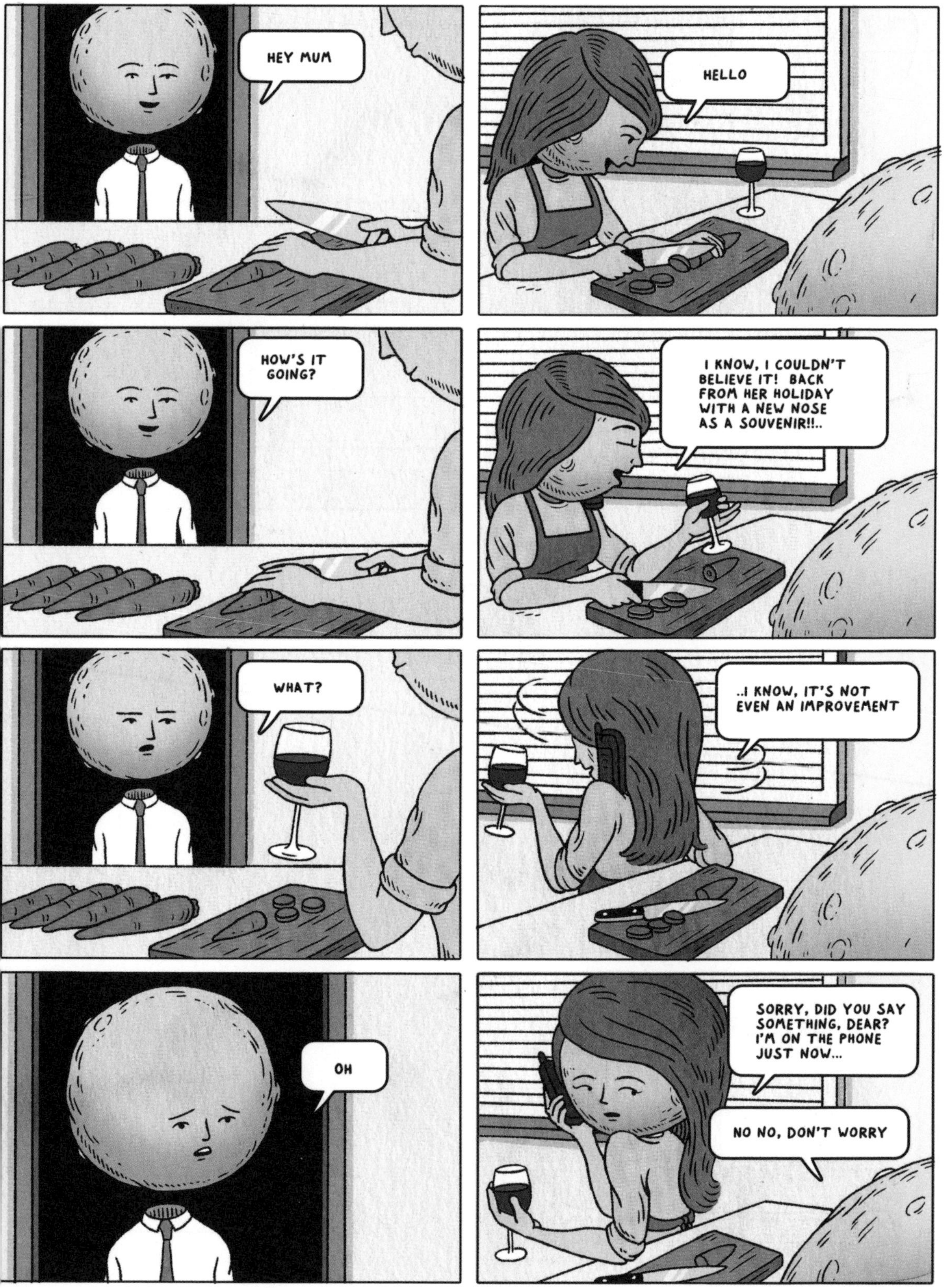
HEY MUM
HELLO
HOW'S IT GOING?
I KNOW, I COULDN'T BELIEVE IT! BACK FROM HER HOLIDAY WITH A NEW NOSE AS A SOUVENIR!!..
WHAT?
..I KNOW, IT'S NOT EVEN AN IMPROVEMENT
OH
SORRY, DID YOU SAY SOMETHING, DEAR? I'M ON THE PHONE JUST NOW...
NO NO, DON'T WORRY

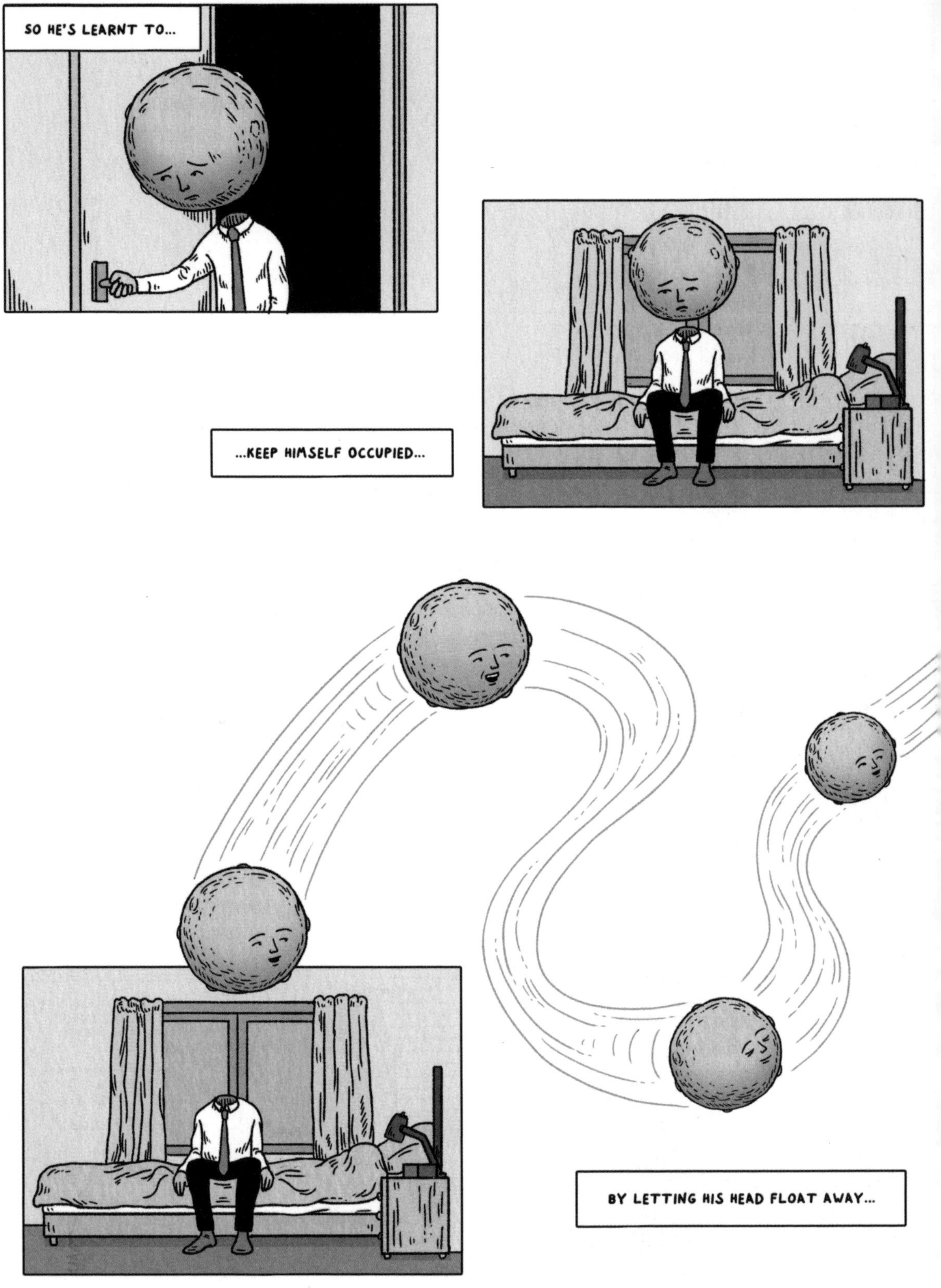
SO HE'S LEARNT TO...
...KEEP HIMSELF OCCUPIED...
BY LETTING HIS HEAD FLOAT AWAY...

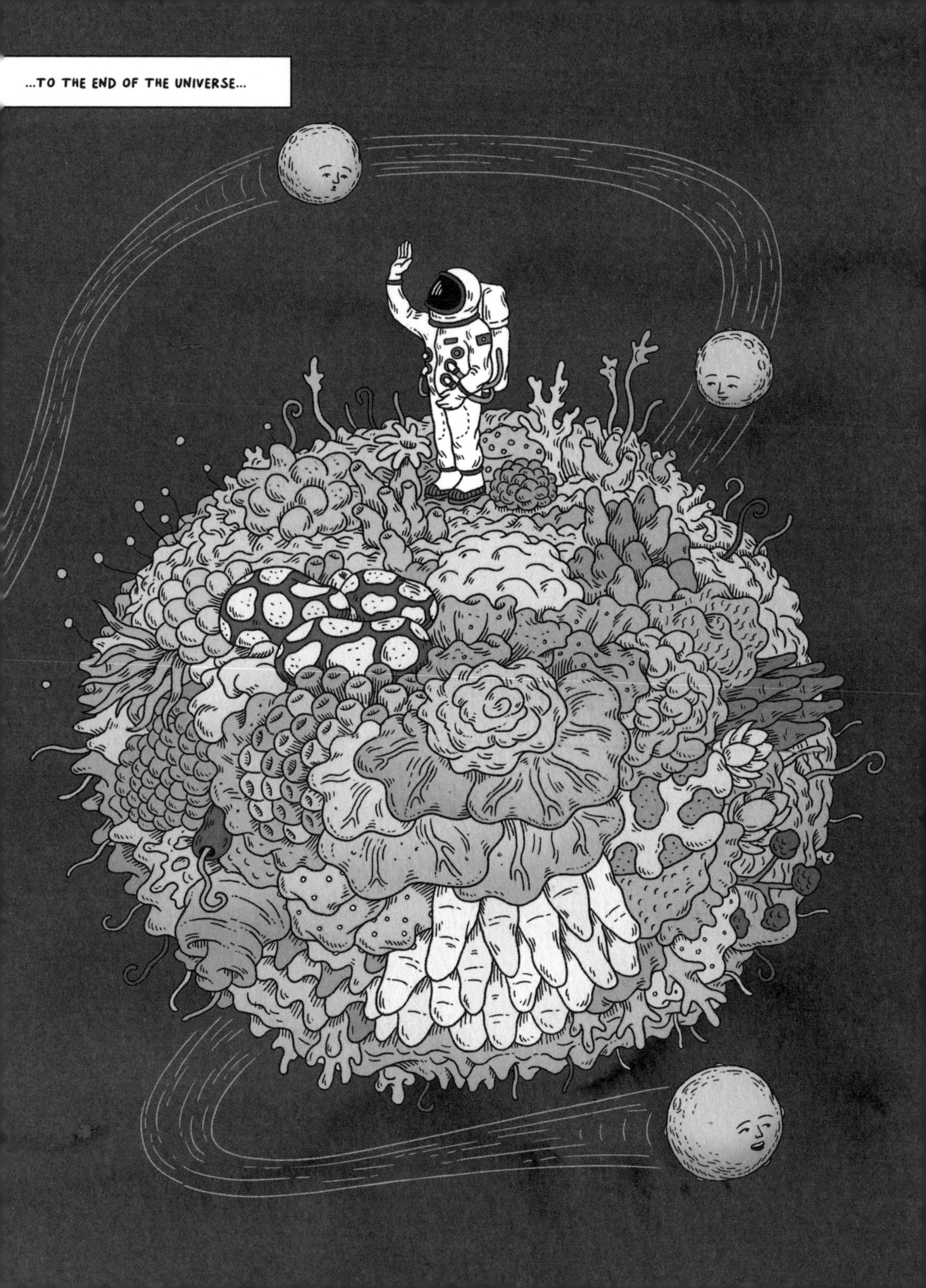
...TO THE END OF THE UNIVERSE...

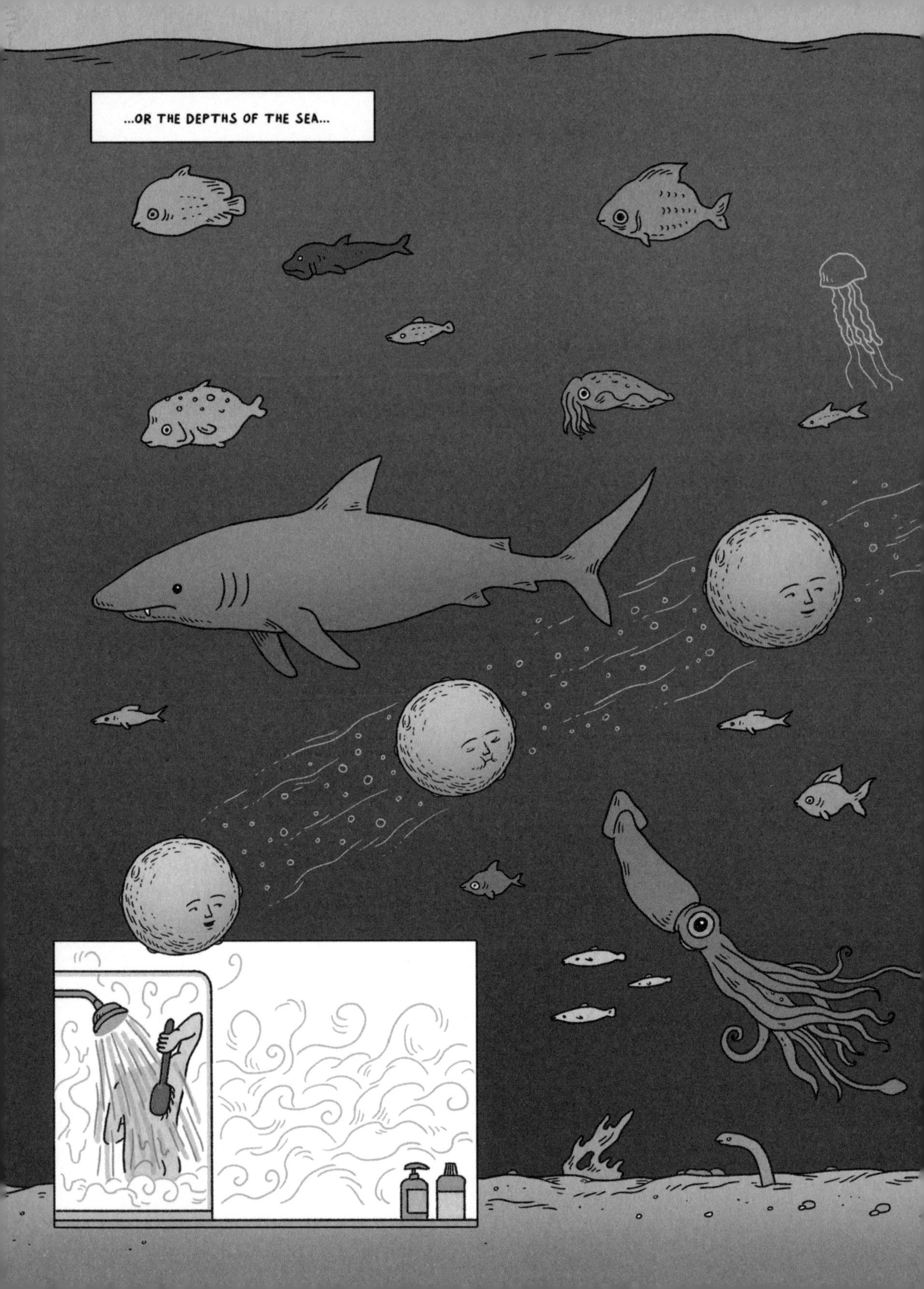
...OR THE DEPTHS OF THE SEA...

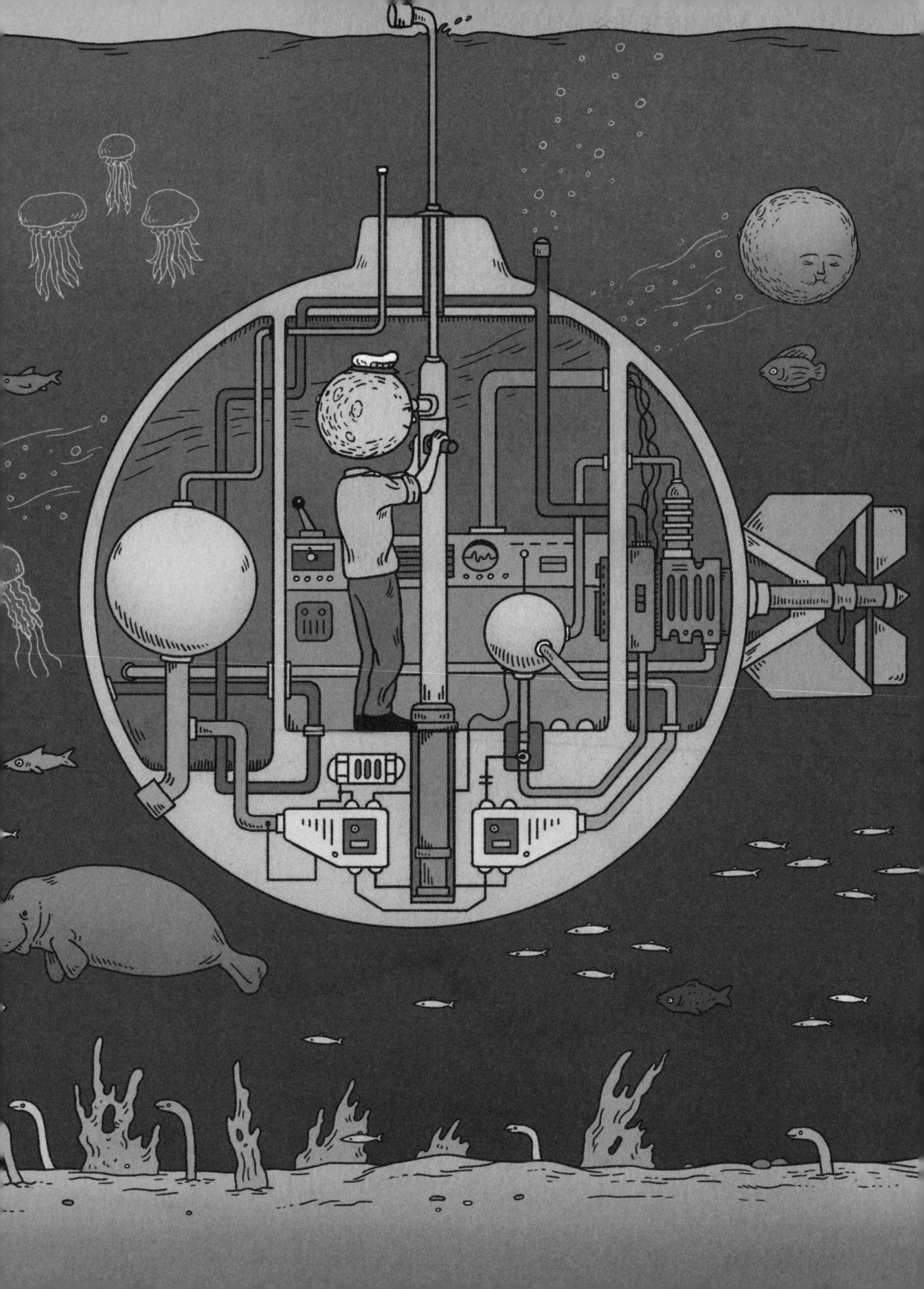

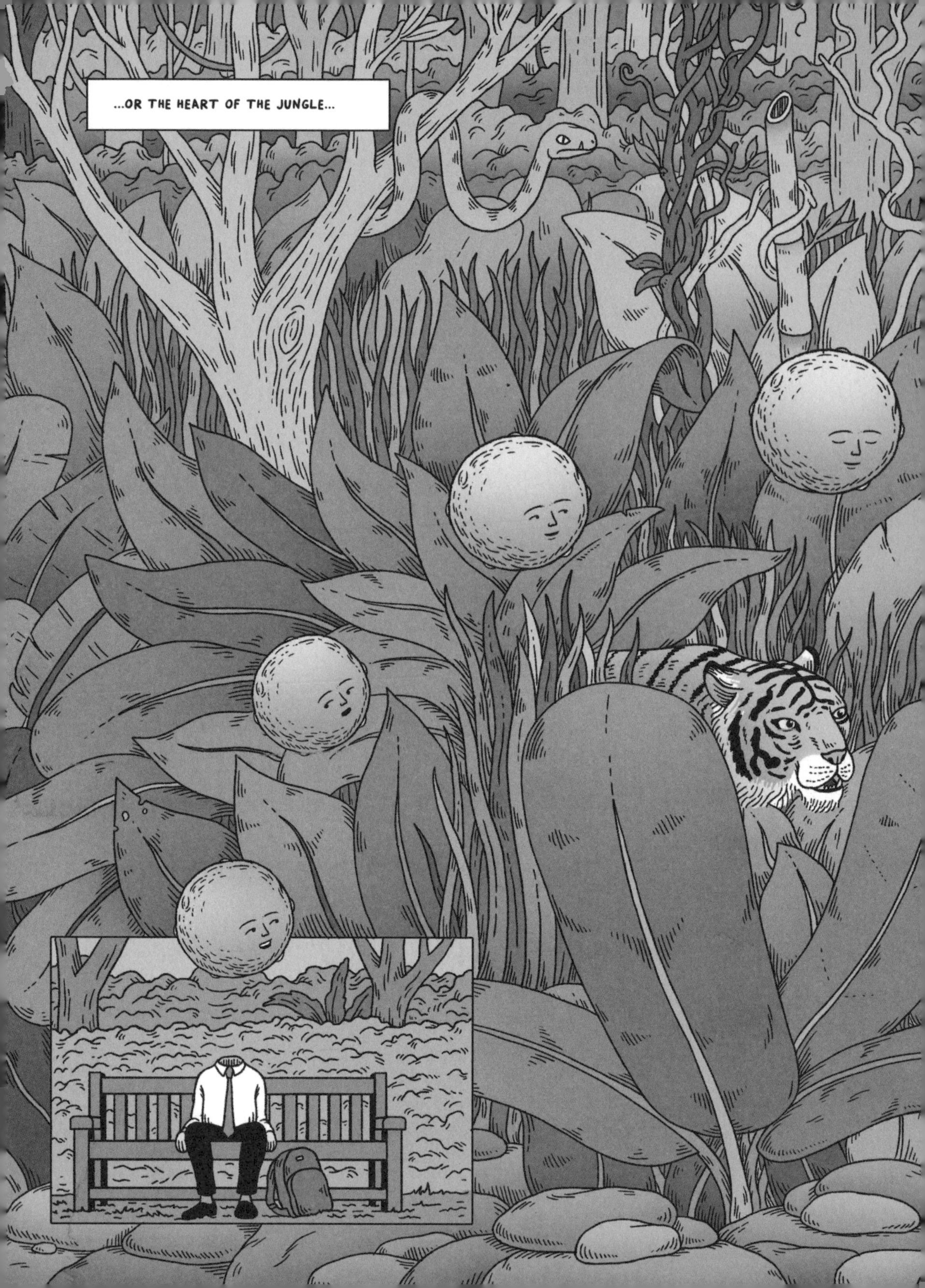
...OR THE HEART OF THE JUNGLE...

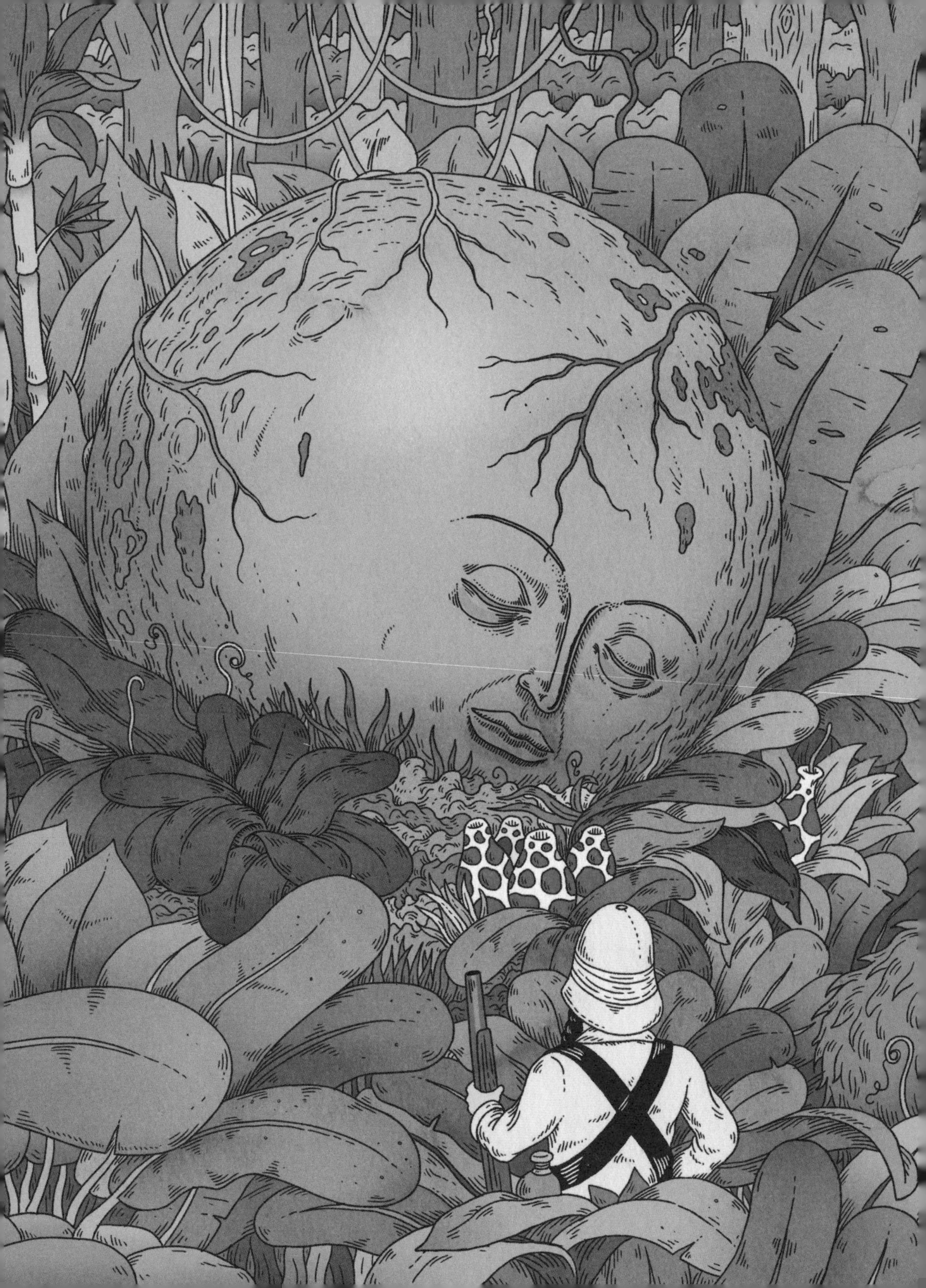

SCHOOL

RIIINNNGG!!

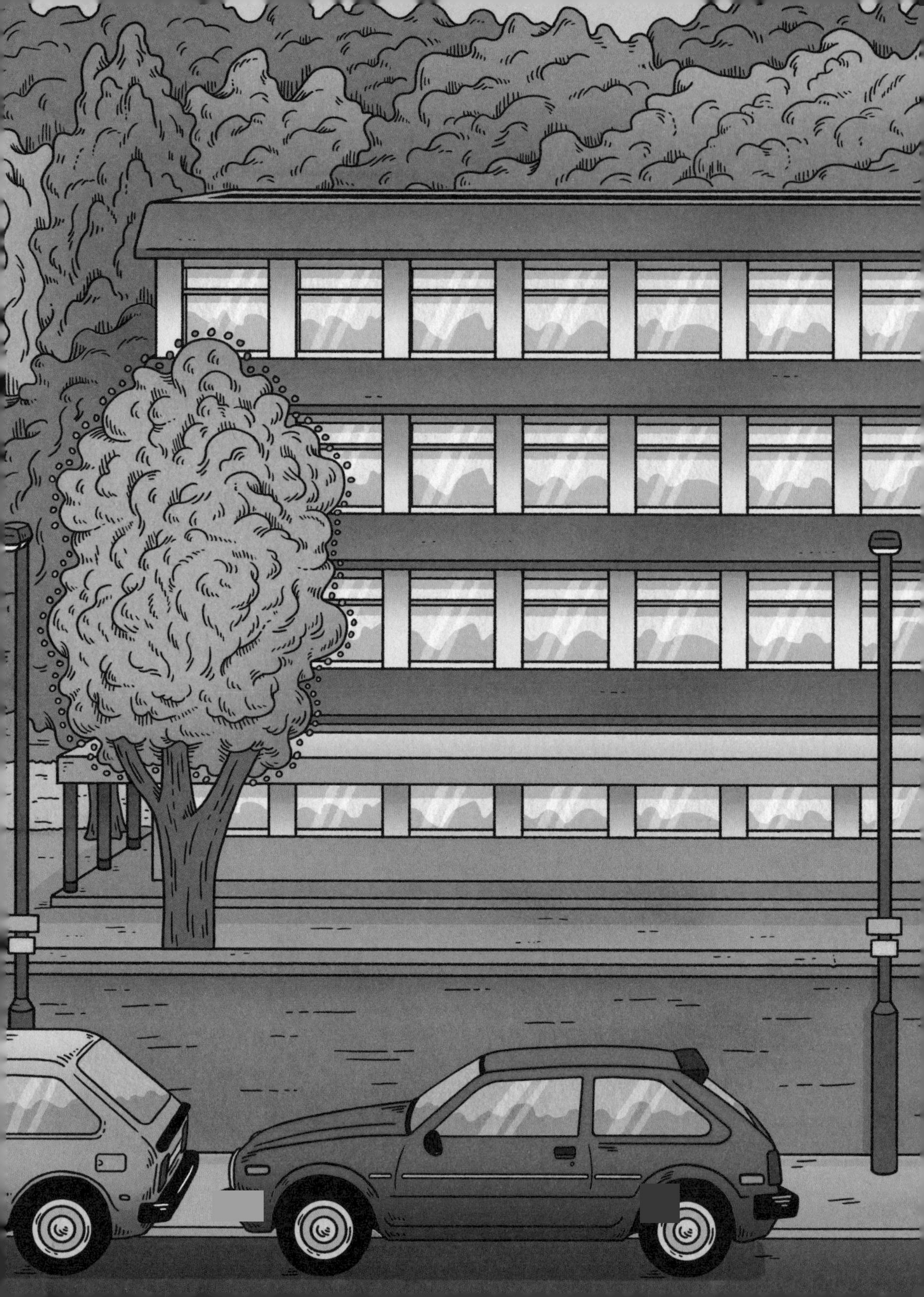

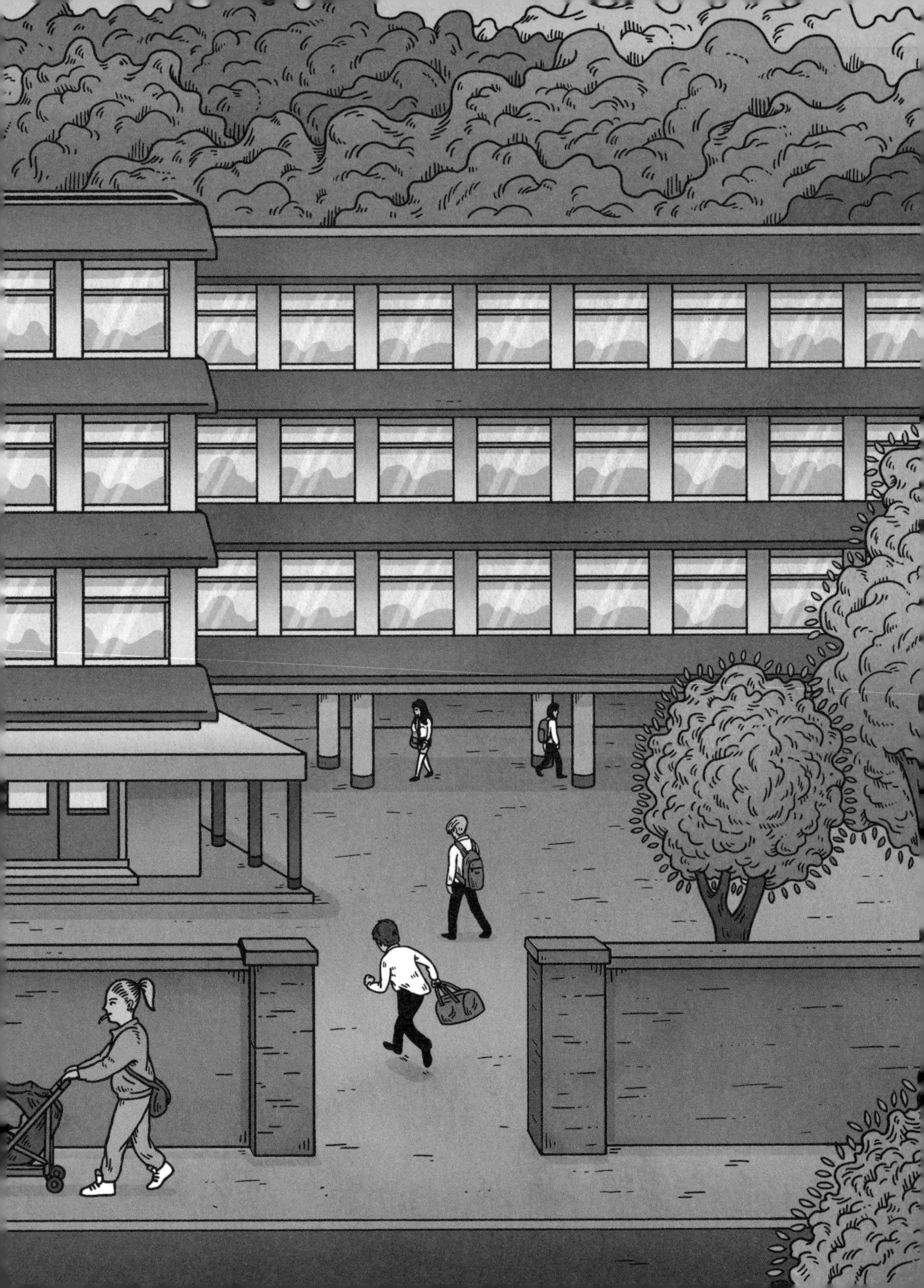

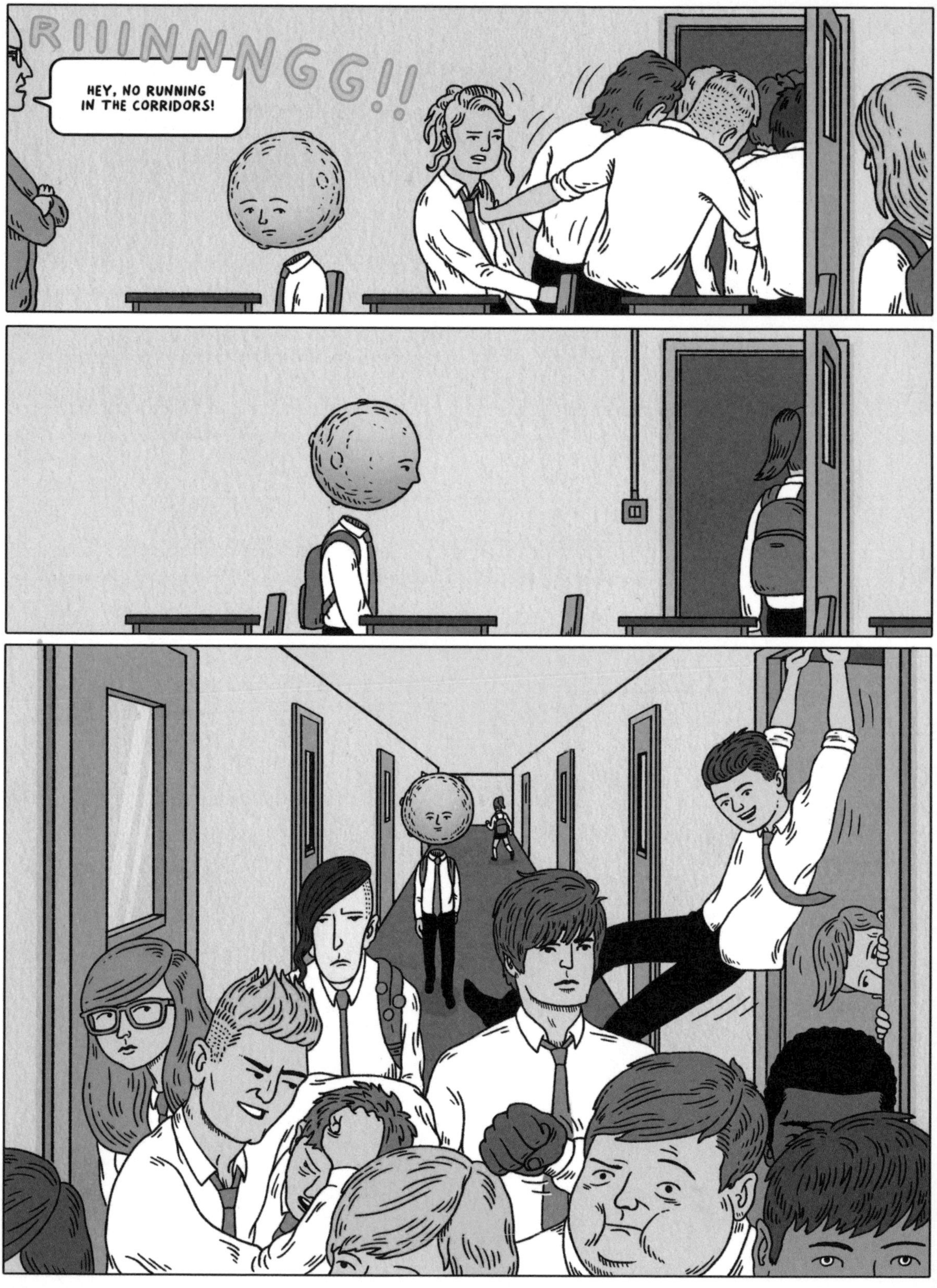
RIIINNNGG!!
HEY, NO RUNNING IN THE CORRIDORS!

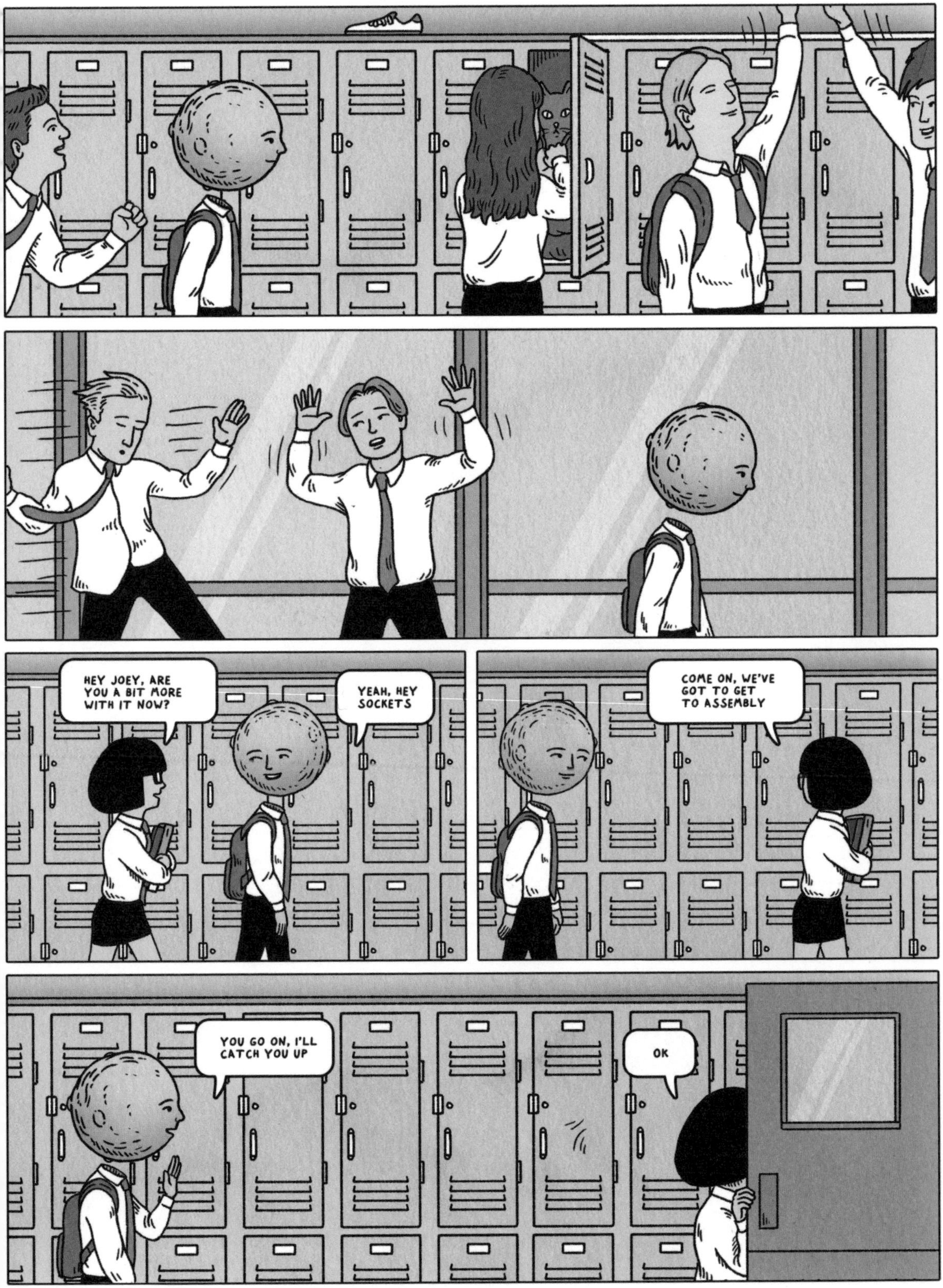
HEY JOEY, ARE YOU A BIT MORE WITH IT NOW?
YEAH, HEY SOCKETS
COME ON, WE'VE GOT TO GET TO ASSEMBLY
YOU GO ON, I'LL CATCH YOU UP
OK

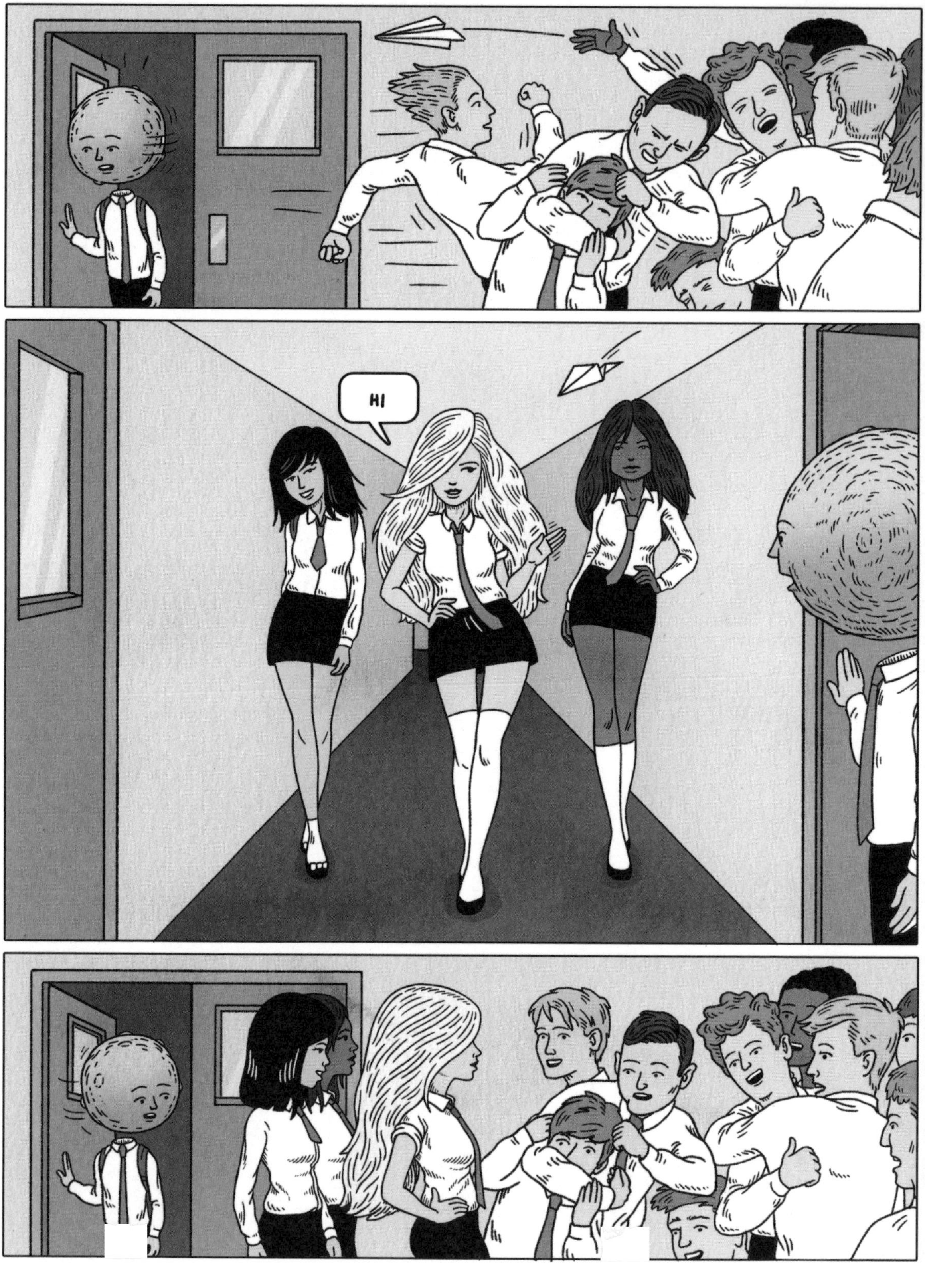
HI

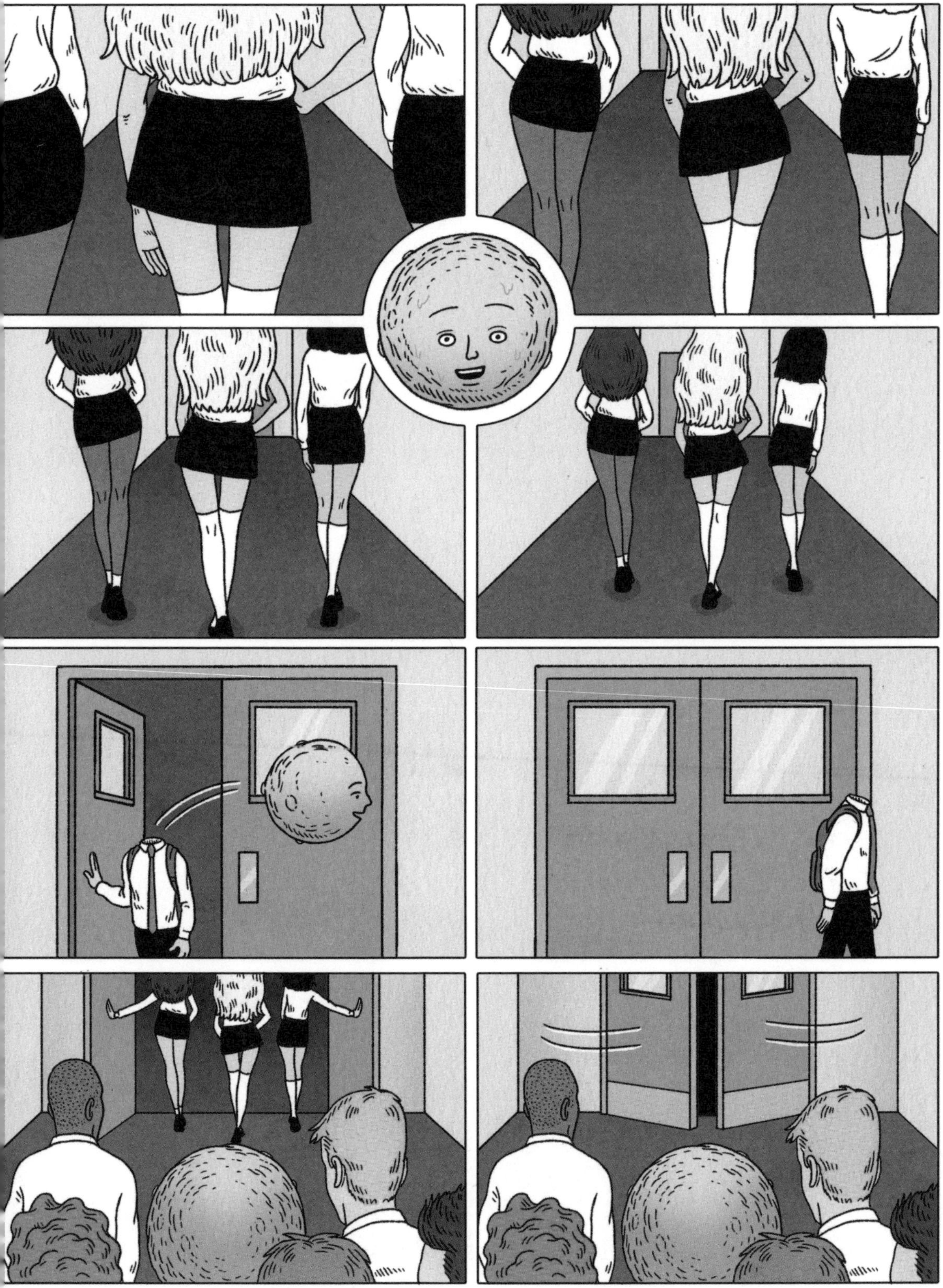

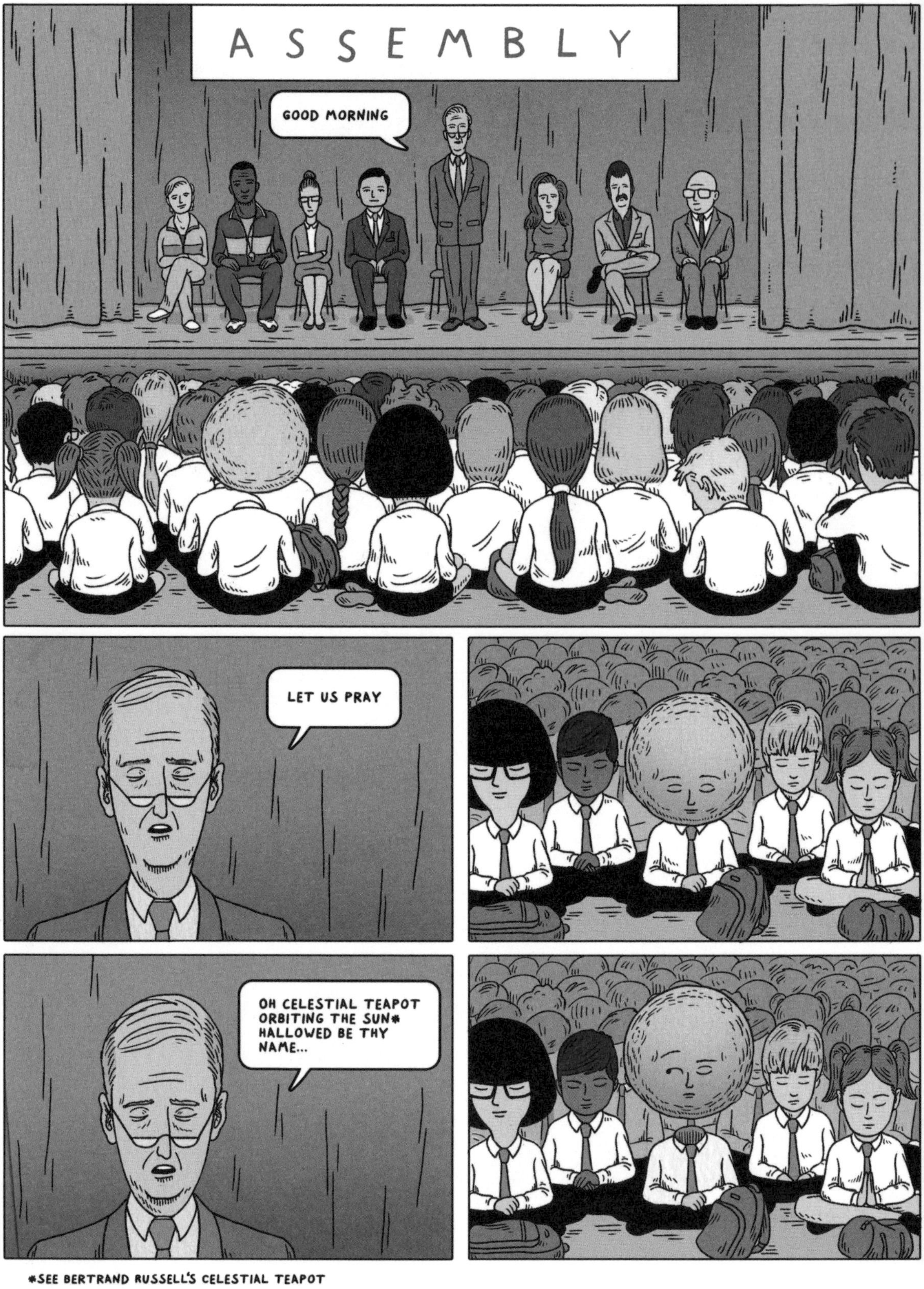
ASSEMBLY
GOOD MORNING
LET US PRAY
OH CELESTIAL TEAPOT ORBITING THE SUN* HALLOWED BE THY NAME...

*SEE BERTRAND RUSSELL'S CELESTIAL TEAPOT

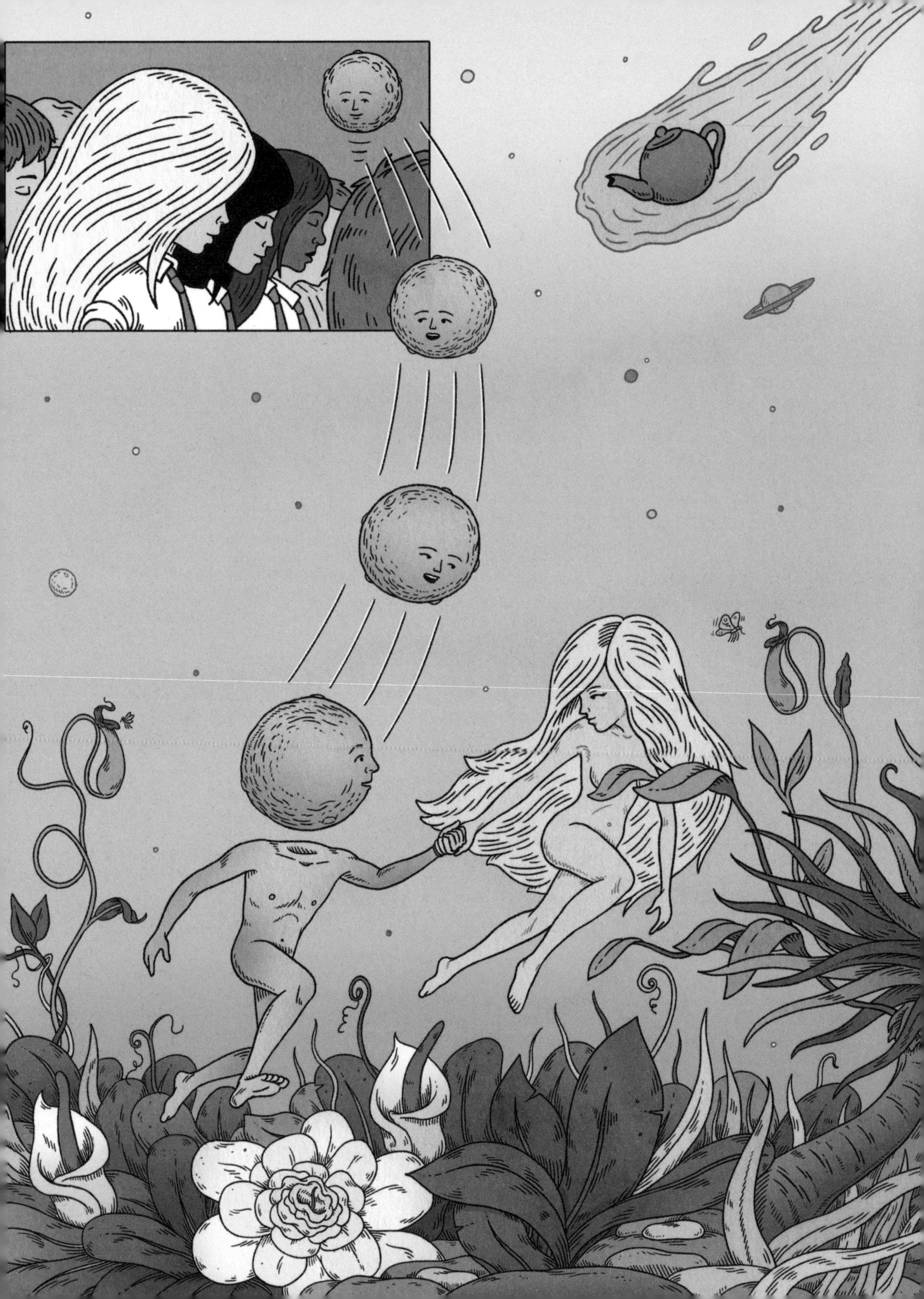

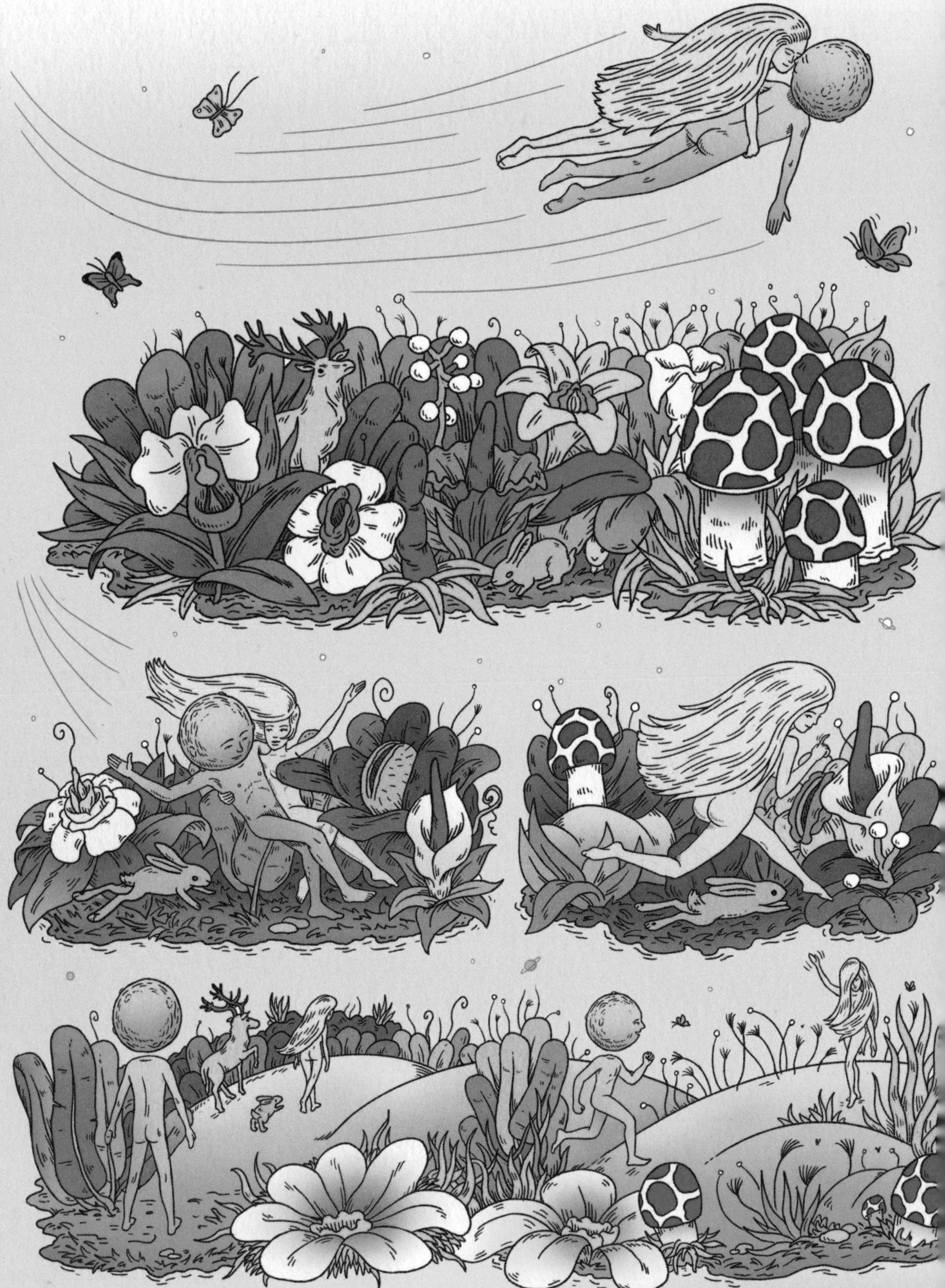

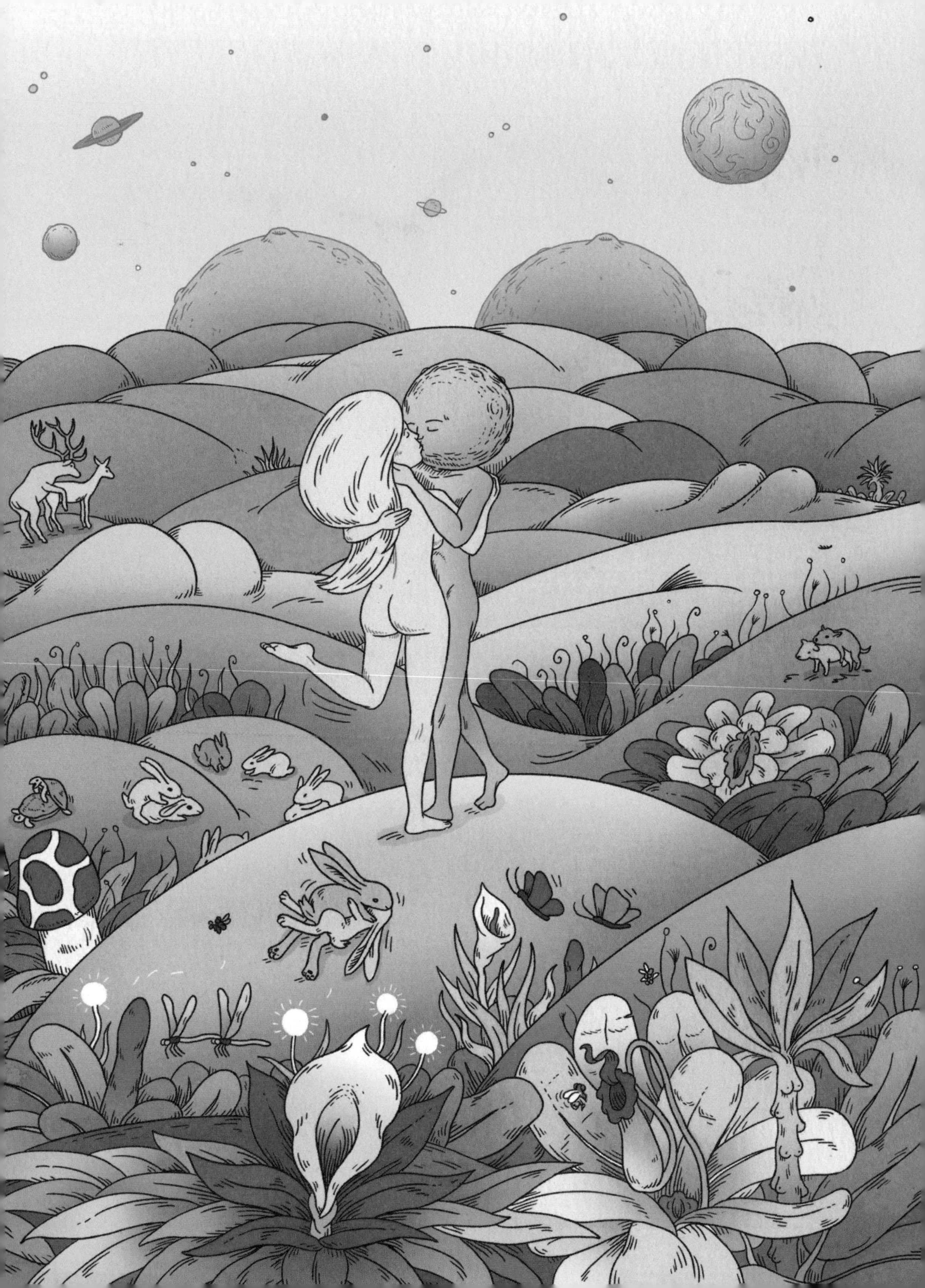

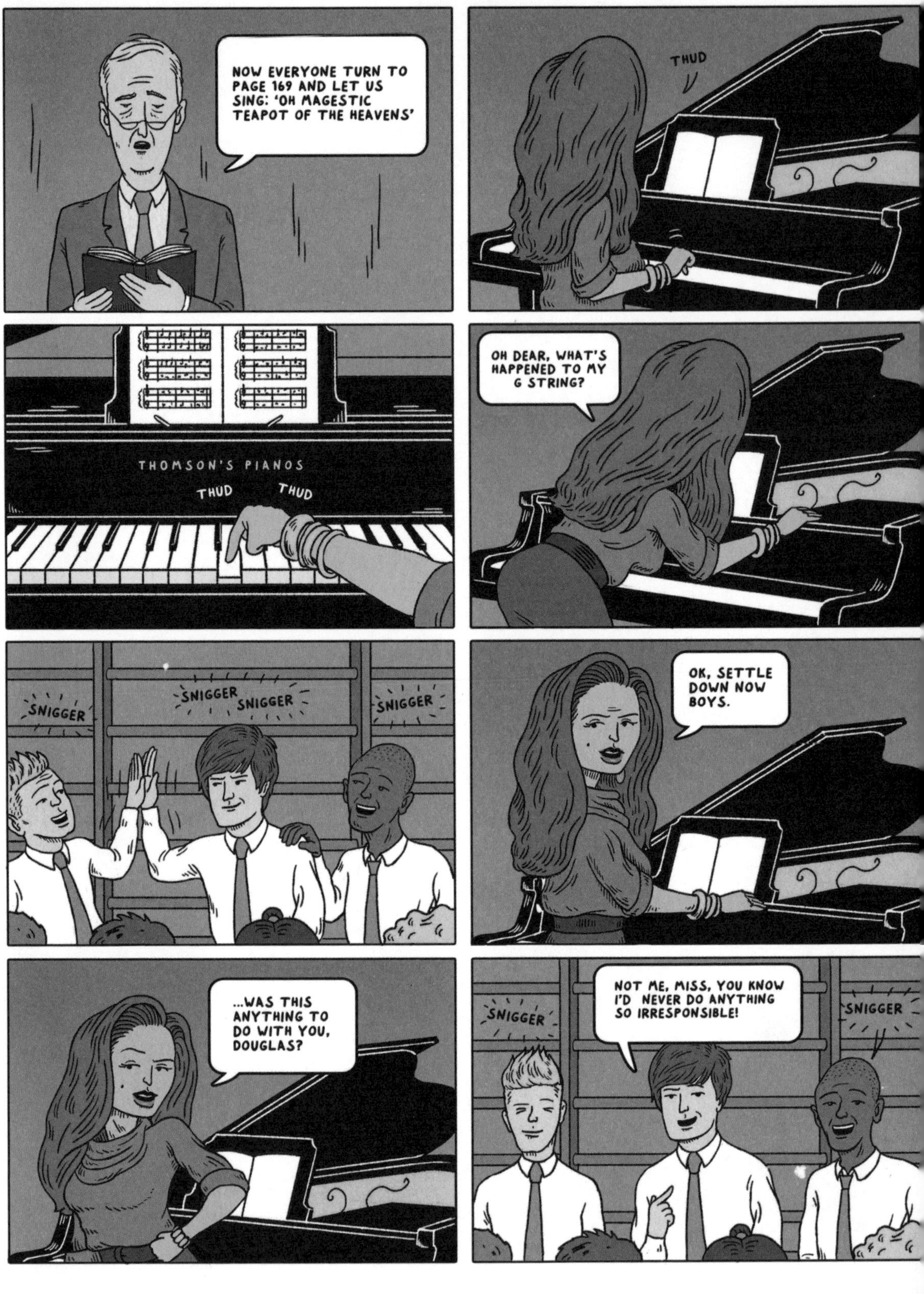
NOW EVERYONE TURN TO PAGE 169 AND LET US SING: 'OH MAGESTIC TEAPOT OF THE HEAVENS'
THUD
THOMSON'S PIANOS
THUD
THUD
OH DEAR, WHAT'S HAPPENED TO MY G STRING?
SNIGGER
SNIGGER
SNIGGER
SNIGGER
OK, SETTLE DOWN NOW BOYS.
...WAS THIS ANYTHING TO DO WITH YOU, DOUGLAS?
SNIGGER
NOT ME, MISS, YOU KNOW I'D NEVER DO ANYTHING SO IRRESPONSIBLE!
SNIGGER

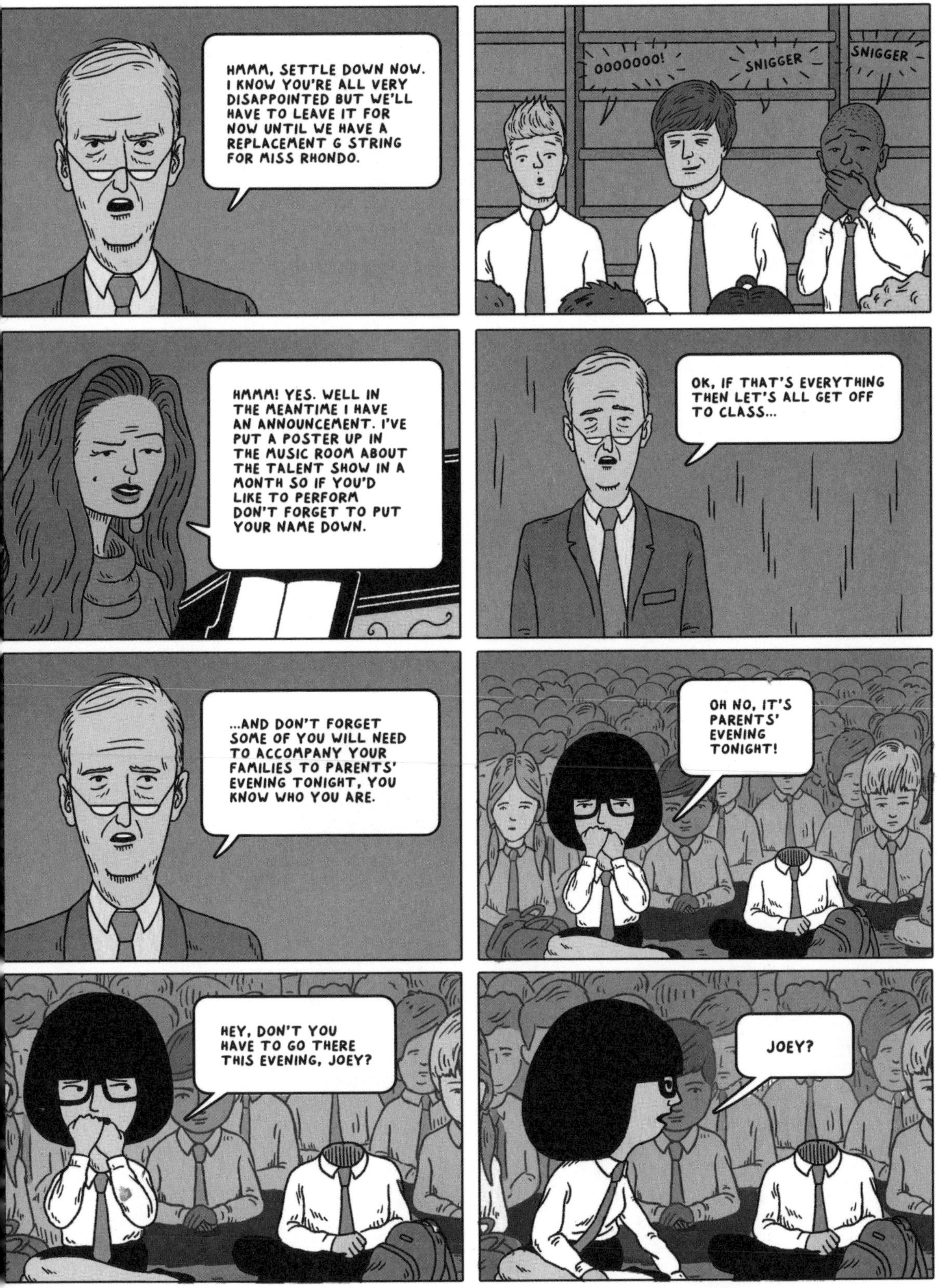
HMMM, SETTLE DOWN NOW. I KNOW YOU'RE ALL VERY DISAPPOINTED BUT WE'LL HAVE TO LEAVE IT FOR NOW UNTIL WE HAVE A REPLACEMENT G STRING FOR MISS RHONDO.
OOOOOOO!
SNIGGER
SNIGGER
HMMM! YES. WELL IN THE MEANTIME I HAVE AN ANNOUNCEMENT. I'VE PUT A POSTER UP IN THE MUSIC ROOM ABOUT THE TALENT SHOW IN A MONTH SO IF YOU'D LIKE TO PERFORM DON'T FORGET TO PUT YOUR NAME DOWN.
OK, IF THAT'S EVERYTHING THEN LET'S ALL GET OFF TO CLASS...
...AND DON'T FORGET SOME OF YOU WILL NEED TO ACCOMPANY YOUR FAMILIES TO PARENTS' EVENING TONIGHT, YOU KNOW WHO YOU ARE.
OH NO, IT'S PARENTS' EVENING TONIGHT!
HEY, DON'T YOU HAVE TO GO THERE THIS EVENING, JOEY?
JOEY?

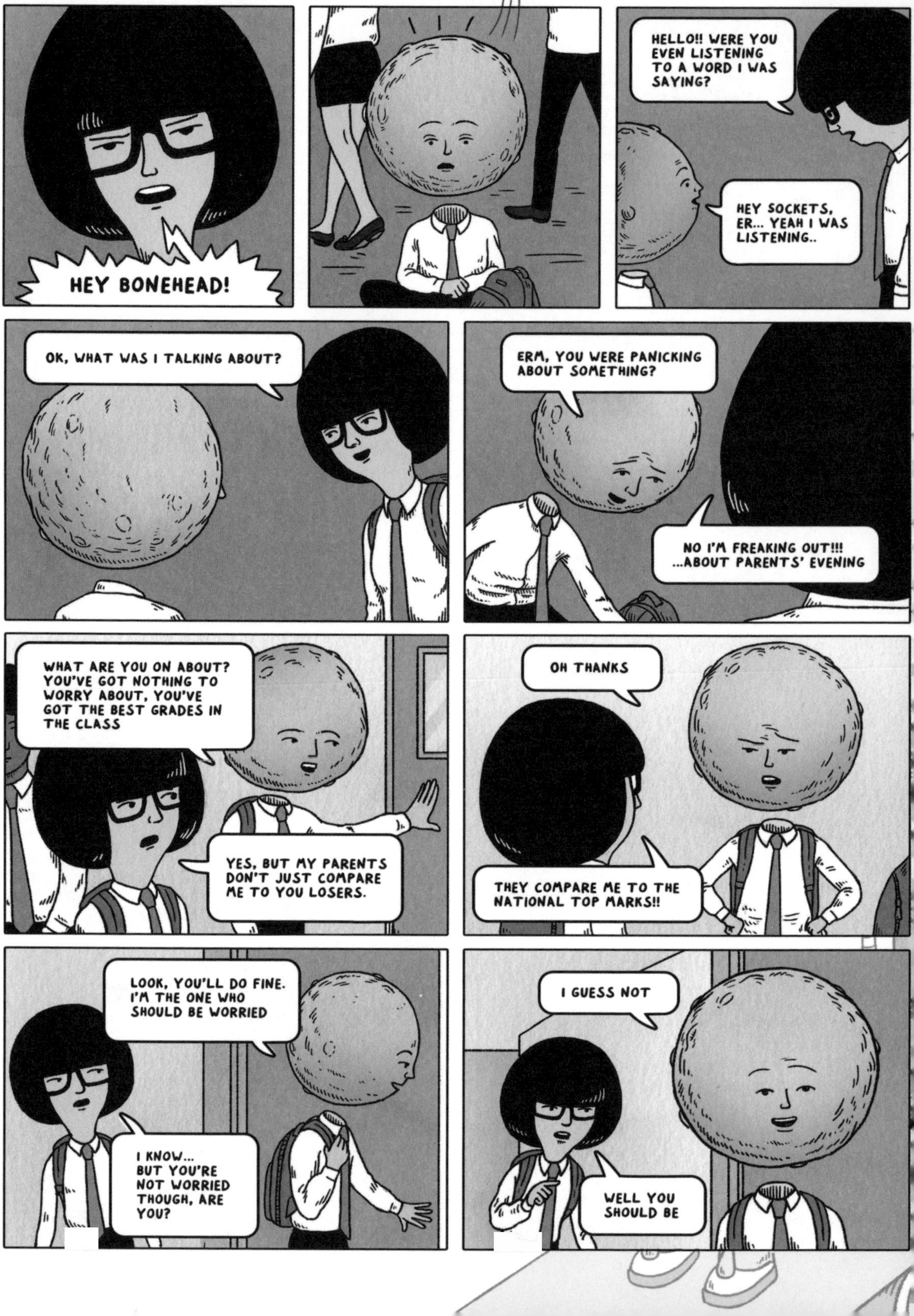
HEY BONEHEAD!
HELLO!! WERE YOU EVEN LISTENING TO A WORD I WAS SAYING?
HEY SOCKETS, ER... YEAH I WAS LISTENING..
OK, WHAT WAS I TALKING ABOUT?
ERM, YOU WERE PANICKING ABOUT SOMETHING?
NO I'M FREAKING OUT!!! ...ABOUT PARENTS' EVENING
WHAT ARE YOU ON ABOUT? YOU'VE GOT NOTHING TO WORRY ABOUT, YOU'VE GOT THE BEST GRADES IN THE CLASS
YES, BUT MY PARENTS DON'T JUST COMPARE ME TO YOU LOSERS.
OH THANKS
THEY COMPARE ME TO THE NATIONAL TOP MARKS!!
LOOK, YOU'LL DO FINE. I'M THE ONE WHO SHOULD BE WORRIED
I KNOW... BUT YOU'RE NOT WORRIED THOUGH, ARE YOU?
I GUESS NOT
WELL YOU SHOULD BE

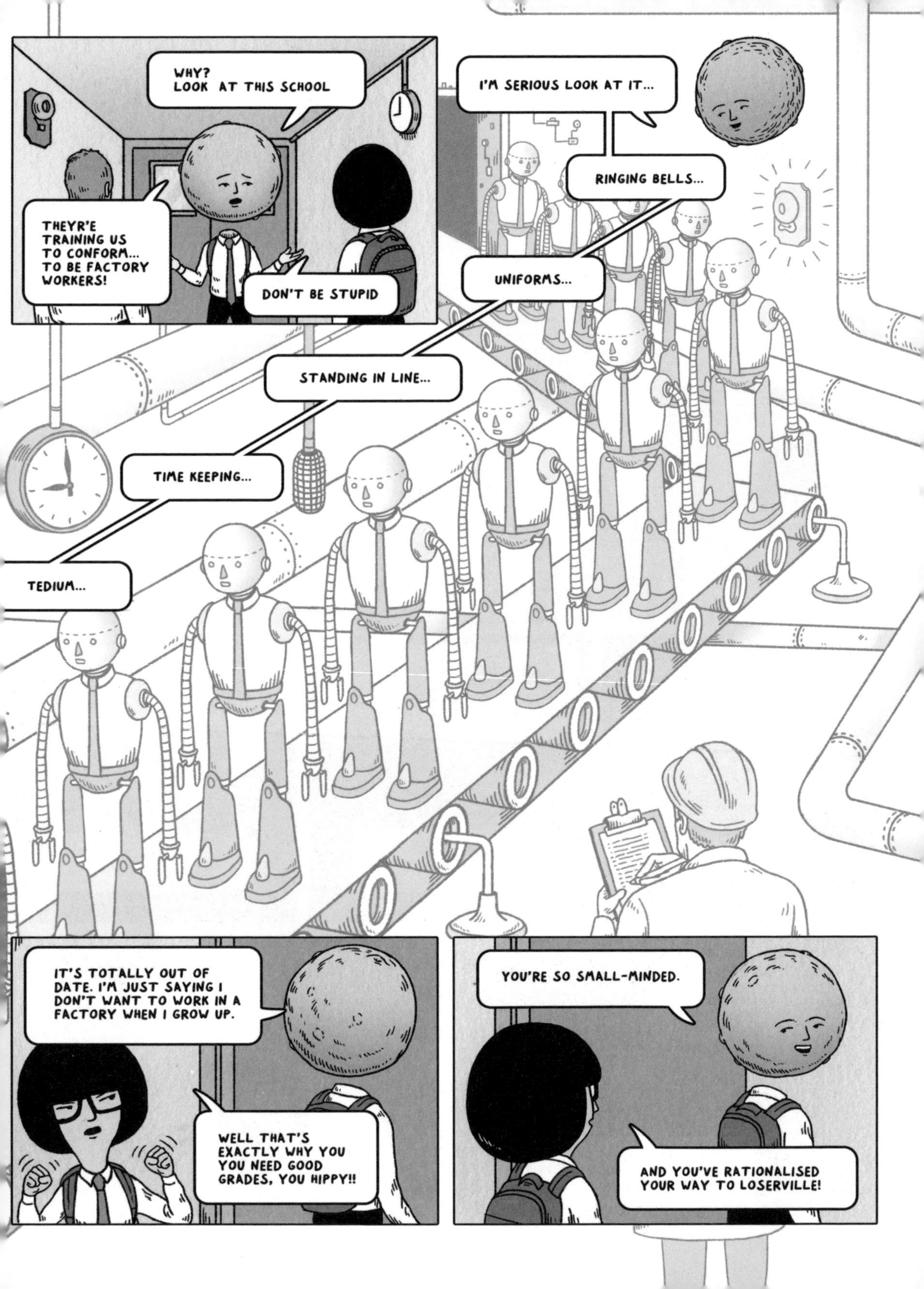
WHY?
LOOK AT THIS SCHOOL
THEYR'E TRAINING US TO CONFORM... TO BE FACTORY WORKERS!
DON'T BE STUPID
I'M SERIOUS LOOK AT IT...
RINGING BELLS...
UNIFORMS...
STANDING IN LINE...
TIME KEEPING...
TEDIUM...
IT'S TOTALLY OUT OF DATE. I'M JUST SAYING I DON'T WANT TO WORK IN A FACTORY WHEN I GROW UP.
WELL THAT'S EXACTLY WHY YOU YOU NEED GOOD GRADES, YOU HIPPY!!
YOU'RE SO SMALL-MINDED.
AND YOU'VE RATIONALISED YOUR WAY TO LOSERVILLE!

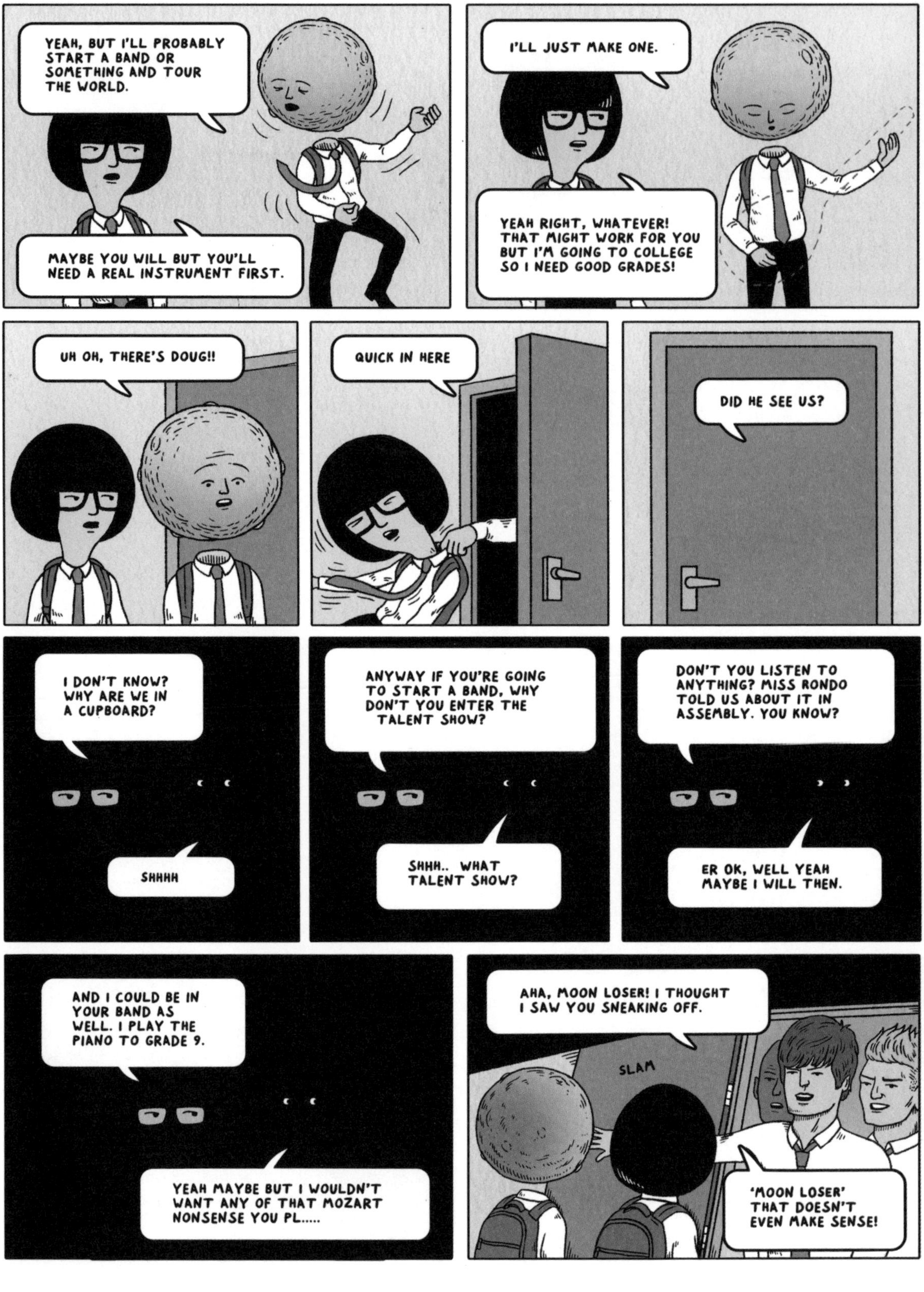
YEAH, BUT I'LL PROBABLY START A BAND OR SOMETHING AND TOUR THE WORLD.
MAYBE YOU WILL BUT YOU'LL NEED A REAL INSTRUMENT FIRST.
I'LL JUST MAKE ONE.
YEAH RIGHT, WHATEVER! THAT MIGHT WORK FOR YOU BUT I'M GOING TO COLLEGE SO I NEED GOOD GRADES!
UH OH, THERE'S DOUG!!
QUICK IN HERE
DID HE SEE US?
I DON'T KNOW? WHY ARE WE IN A CUPBOARD?
SHHHH
ANYWAY IF YOU'RE GOING TO START A BAND, WHY DON'T YOU ENTER THE TALENT SHOW?
SHHH.. WHAT TALENT SHOW?
DON'T YOU LISTEN TO ANYTHING? MISS RONDO TOLD US ABOUT IT IN ASSEMBLY. YOU KNOW?
ER OK, WELL YEAH MAYBE I WILL THEN.
AND I COULD BE IN YOUR BAND AS WELL. I PLAY THE PIANO TO GRADE 9.
YEAH MAYBE BUT I WOULDN'T WANT ANY OF THAT MOZART NONSENSE YOU PL.....
AHA, MOON LOSER! I THOUGHT I SAW YOU SNEAKING OFF.
SLAM
'MOON LOSER' THAT DOESN'T EVEN MAKE SENSE!

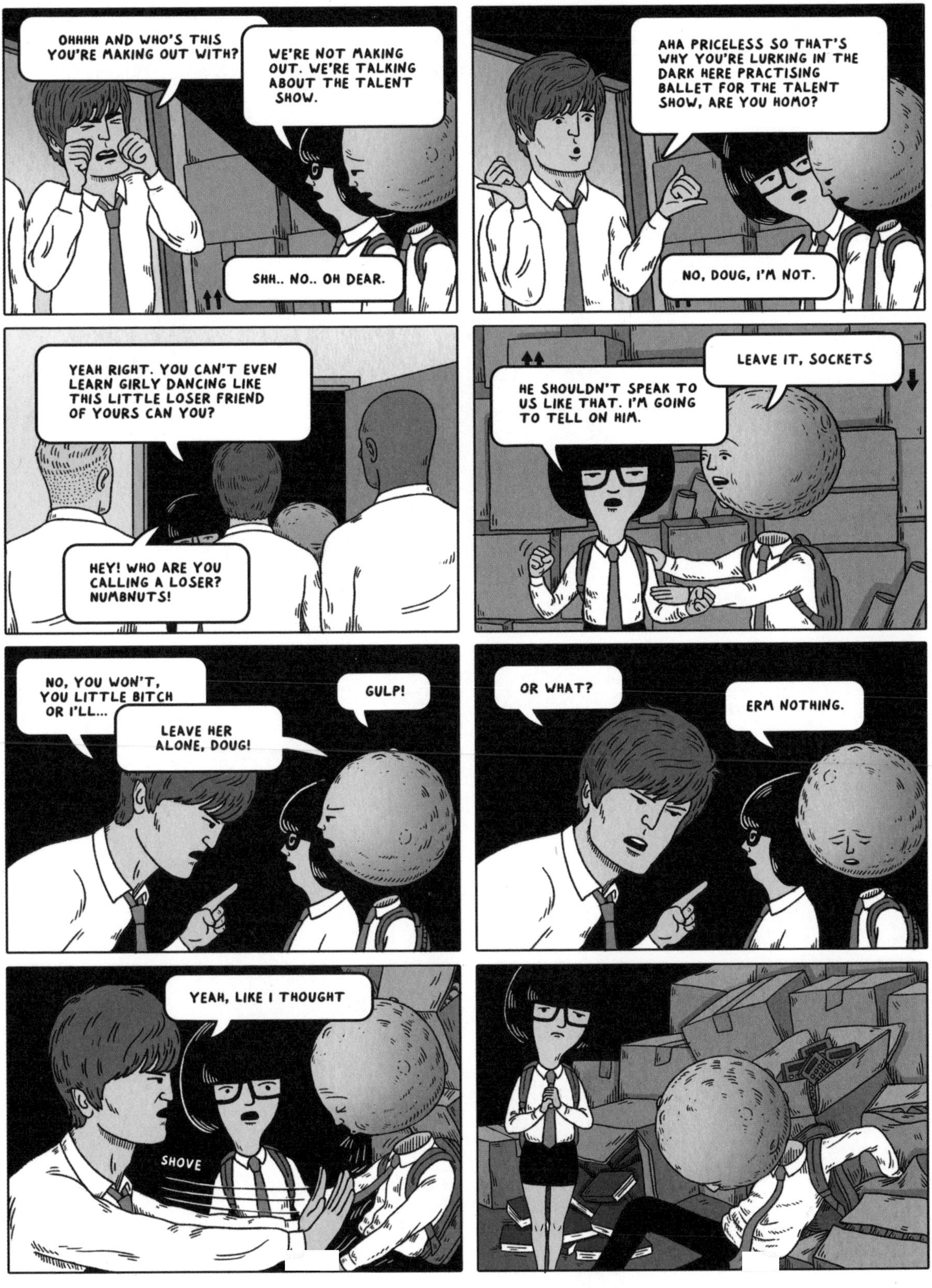
OHHHH AND WHO'S THIS YOU'RE MAKING OUT WITH?
WE'RE NOT MAKING OUT. WE'RE TALKING ABOUT THE TALENT SHOW.
SHH.. NO.. OH DEAR.
AHA PRICELESS SO THAT'S WHY YOU'RE LURKING IN THE DARK HERE PRACTISING BALLET FOR THE TALENT SHOW, ARE YOU HOMO?
NO, DOUG, I'M NOT.
YEAH RIGHT. YOU CAN'T EVEN LEARN GIRLY DANCING LIKE THIS LITTLE LOSER FRIEND OF YOURS CAN YOU?
HEY! WHO ARE YOU CALLING A LOSER? NUMBNUTS!
HE SHOULDN'T SPEAK TO US LIKE THAT. I'M GOING TO TELL ON HIM.
LEAVE IT, SOCKETS
NO, YOU WON'T, YOU LITTLE BITCH OR I'LL...
LEAVE HER ALONE, DOUG!
GULP!
OR WHAT?
ERM NOTHING.
YEAH, LIKE I THOUGHT
SHOVE

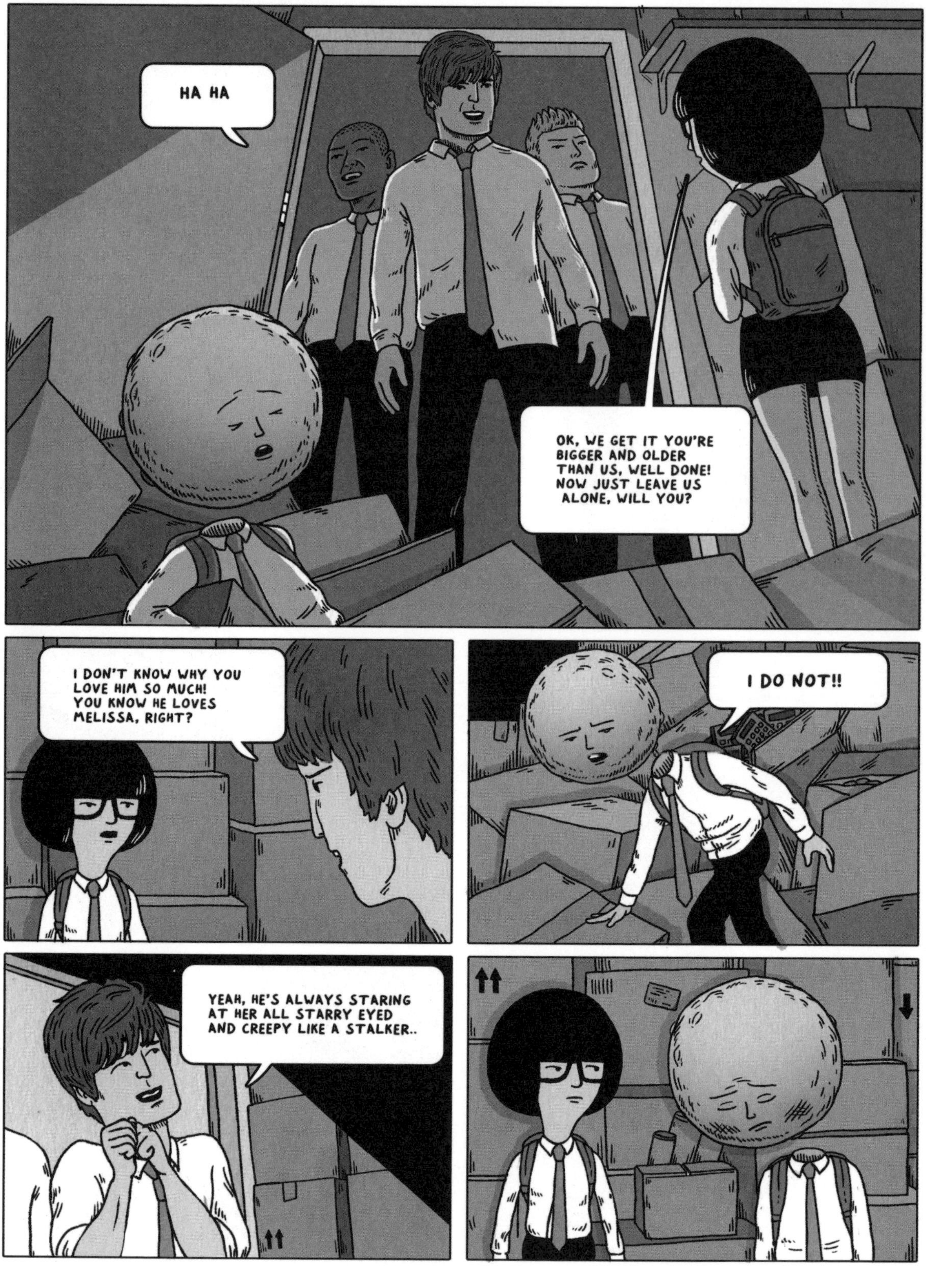
HA HA
OK, WE GET IT YOU'RE BIGGER AND OLDER THAN US, WELL DONE! NOW JUST LEAVE US ALONE, WILL YOU?
I DON'T KNOW WHY YOU LOVE HIM SO MUCH! YOU KNOW HE LOVES MELISSA, RIGHT?
I DO NOT!!
YEAH, HE'S ALWAYS STARING AT HER ALL STARRY EYED AND CREEPY LIKE A STALKER..

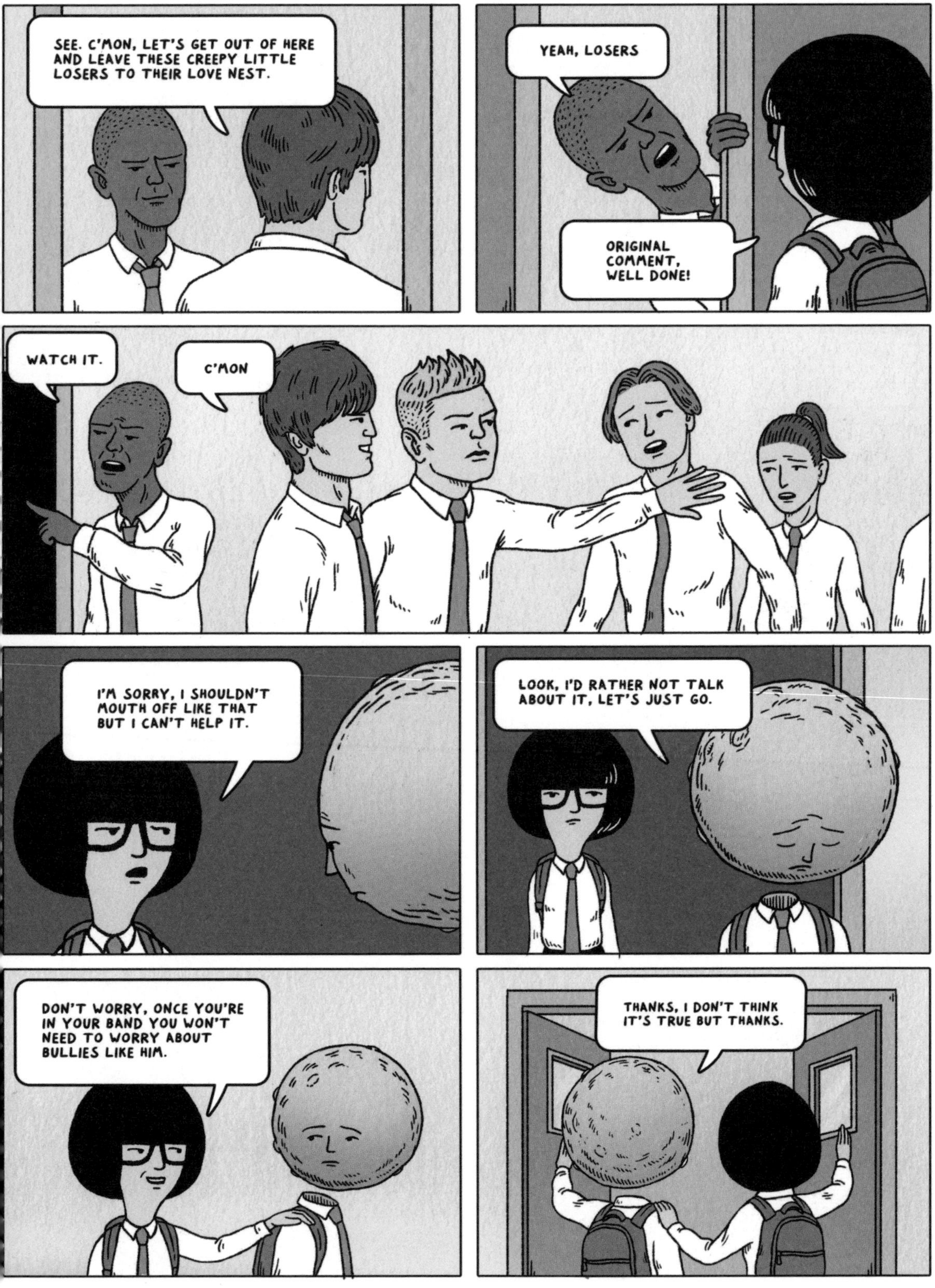

SEE. C'MON, LET'S GET OUT OF HERE AND LEAVE THESE CREEPY LITTLE LOSERS TO THEIR LOVE NEST.
YEAH, LOSERS
ORIGINAL COMMENT, WELL DONE!
WATCH IT.
C'MON
I'M SORRY, I SHOULDN'T MOUTH OFF LIKE THAT BUT I CAN'T HELP IT.
LOOK, I'D RATHER NOT TALK ABOUT IT, LET'S JUST GO.
DON'T WORRY, ONCE YOU'RE IN YOUR BAND YOU WON'T NEED TO WORRY ABOUT BULLIES LIKE HIM.
THANKS, I DON'T THINK IT'S TRUE BUT THANKS.

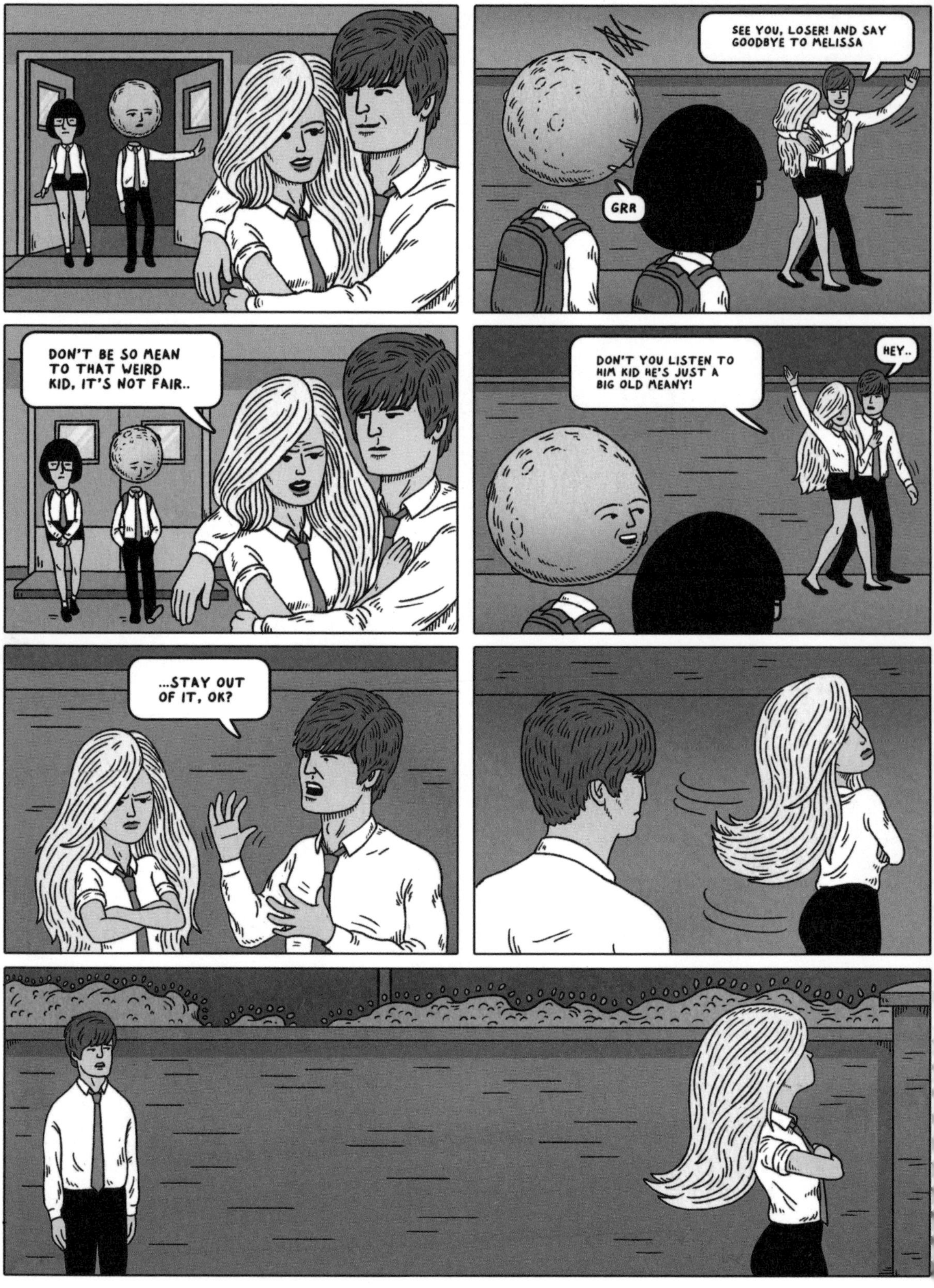
SEE YOU, LOSER! AND SAY GOODBYE TO MELISSA
GRR
DON'T BE SO MEAN TO THAT WEIRD KID, IT'S NOT FAIR..
DON'T YOU LISTEN TO HIM KID HE'S JUST A BIG OLD MEANY!
HEY..
...STAY OUT OF IT, OK?

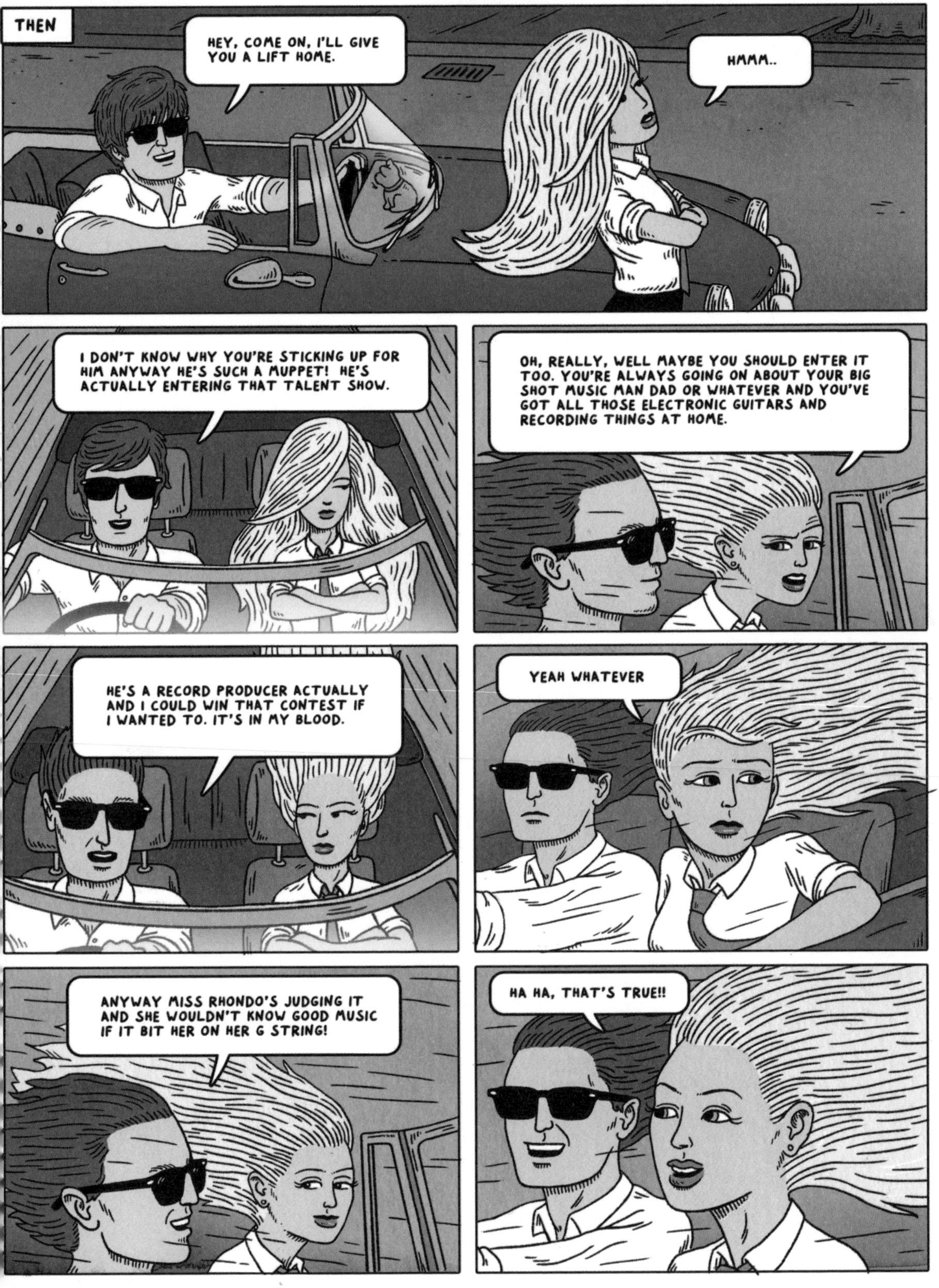
THEN
HEY, COME ON, I'LL GIVE YOU A LIFT HOME.
HMMM..
I DON'T KNOW WHY YOU'RE STICKING UP FOR HIM ANYWAY HE'S SUCH A MUPPET! HE'S ACTUALLY ENTERING THAT TALENT SHOW.
OH, REALLY, WELL MAYBE YOU SHOULD ENTER IT TOO. YOU'RE ALWAYS GOING ON ABOUT YOUR BIG SHOT MUSIC MAN DAD OR WHATEVER AND YOU'VE GOT ALL THOSE ELECTRONIC GUITARS AND RECORDING THINGS AT HOME.
HE'S A RECORD PRODUCER ACTUALLY AND I COULD WIN THAT CONTEST IF I WANTED TO. IT'S IN MY BLOOD.
YEAH WHATEVER
ANYWAY MISS RHONDO'S JUDGING IT AND SHE WOULDN'T KNOW GOOD MUSIC IF IT BIT HER ON HER G STRING!
HA HA, THAT'S TRUE!!

PARENTS'
EVENING

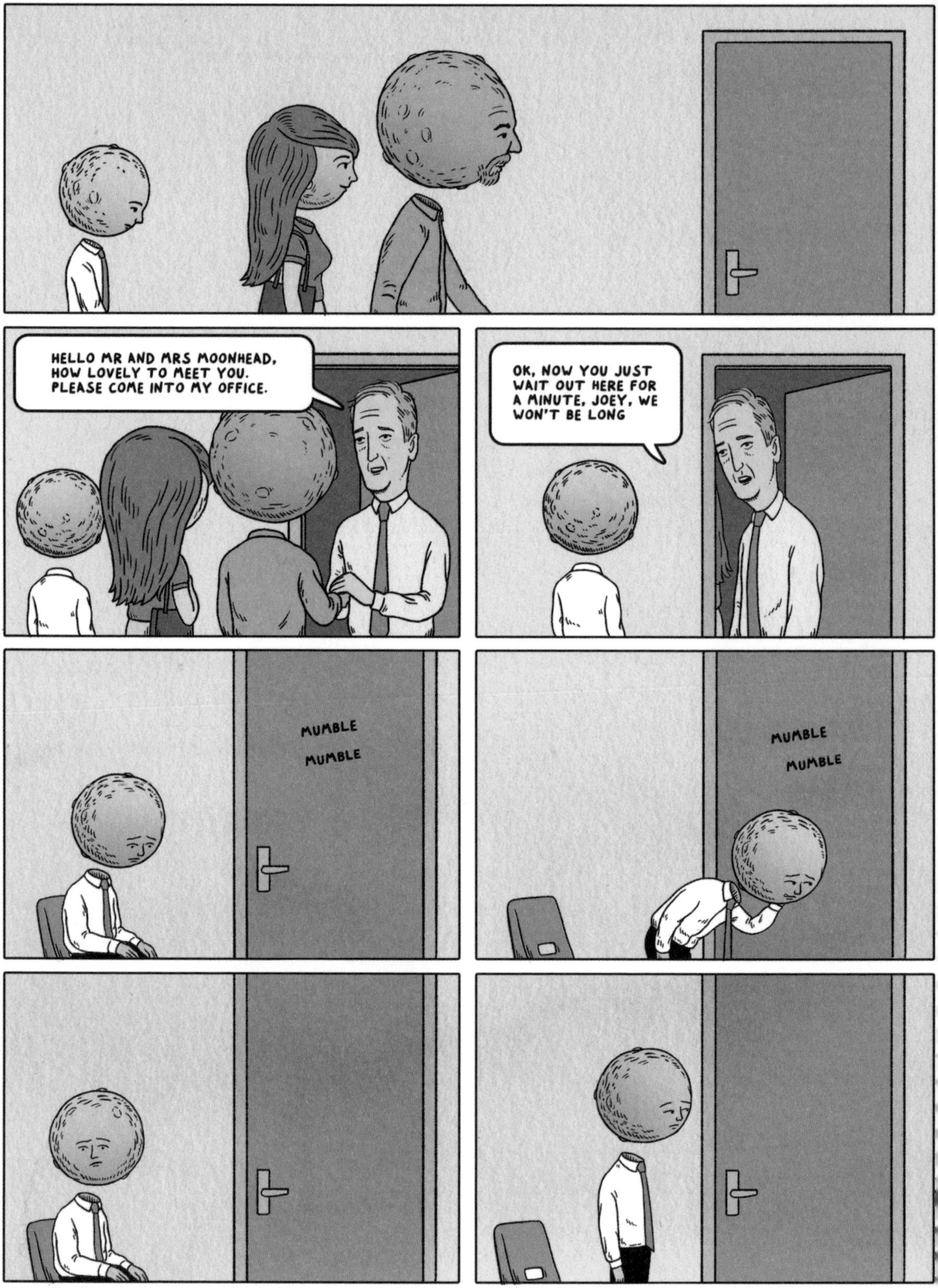
HELLO MR AND MRS MOONHEAD, HOW LOVELY TO MEET YOU. PLEASE COME INTO MY OFFICE.
OK, NOW YOU JUST WAIT OUT HERE FOR A MINUTE, JOEY, WE WON'T BE LONG
MUMBLE
MUMBLE
MUMBLE
MUMBLE

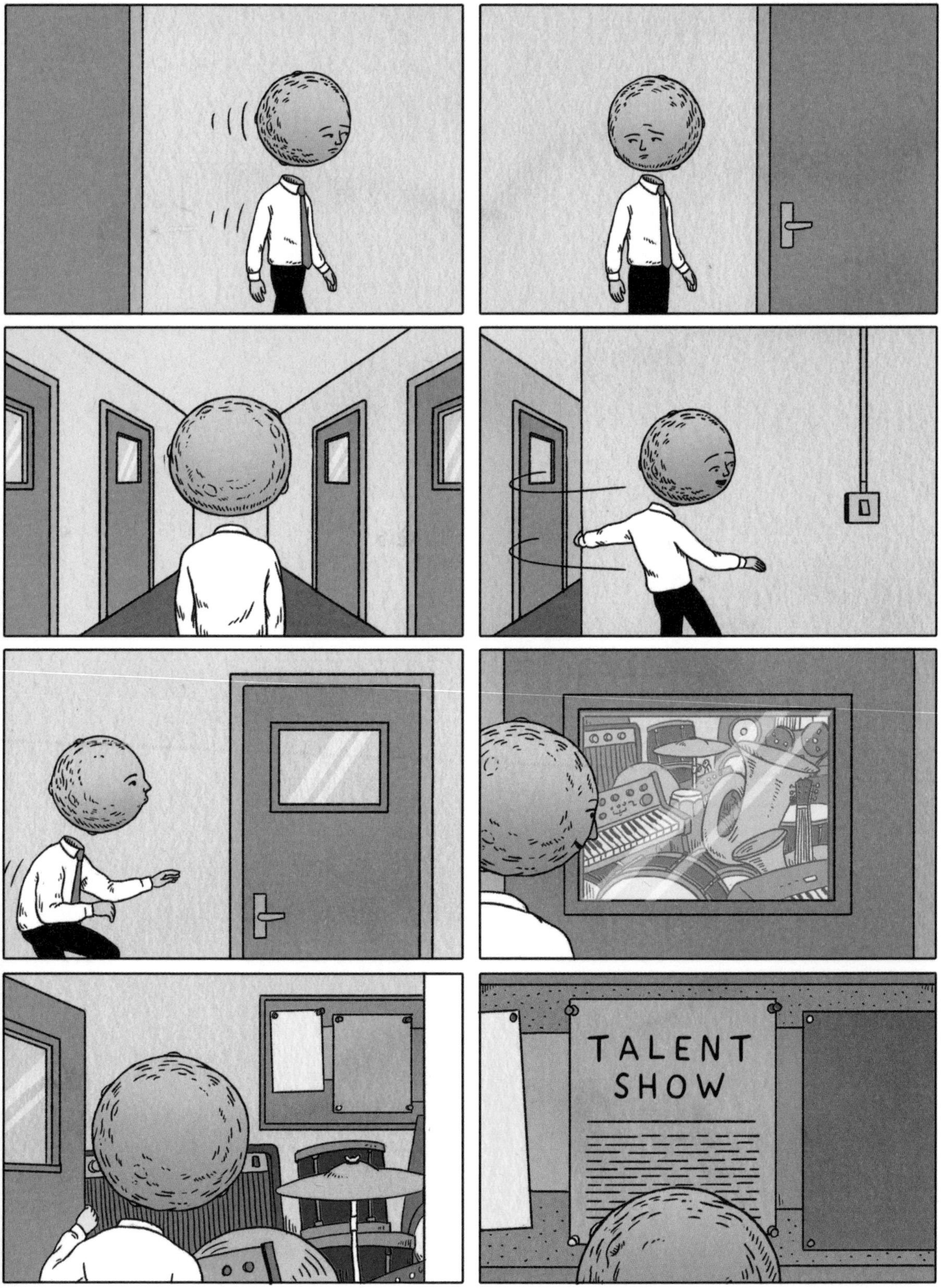
TALENT
SHOW

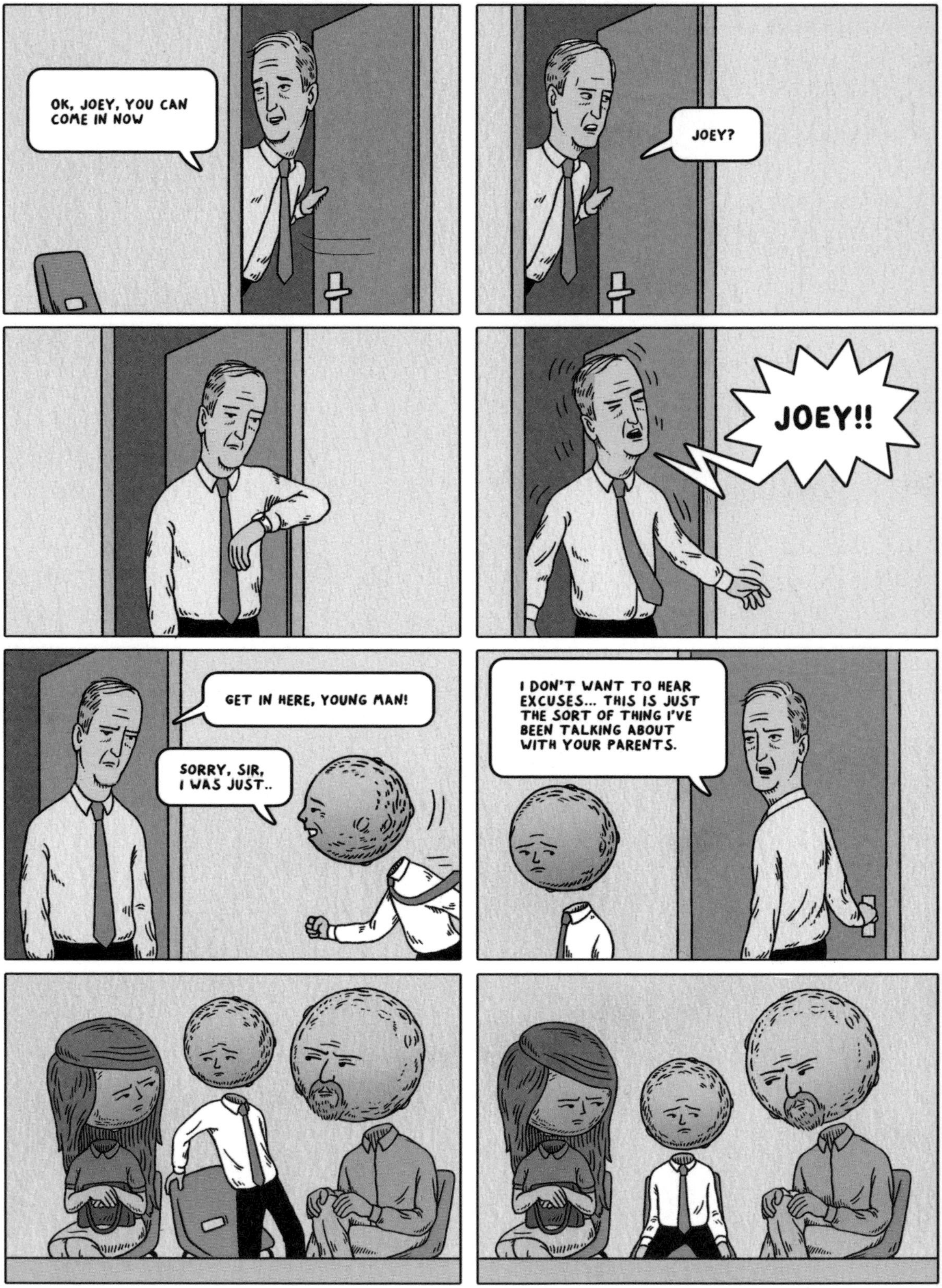
OK, JOEY, YOU CAN COME IN NOW
JOEY?
JOEY!!
GET IN HERE, YOUNG MAN!
SORRY, SIR, I WAS JUST..
I DON'T WANT TO HEAR EXCUSES... THIS IS JUST THE SORT OF THING I'VE BEEN TALKING ABOUT WITH YOUR PARENTS.

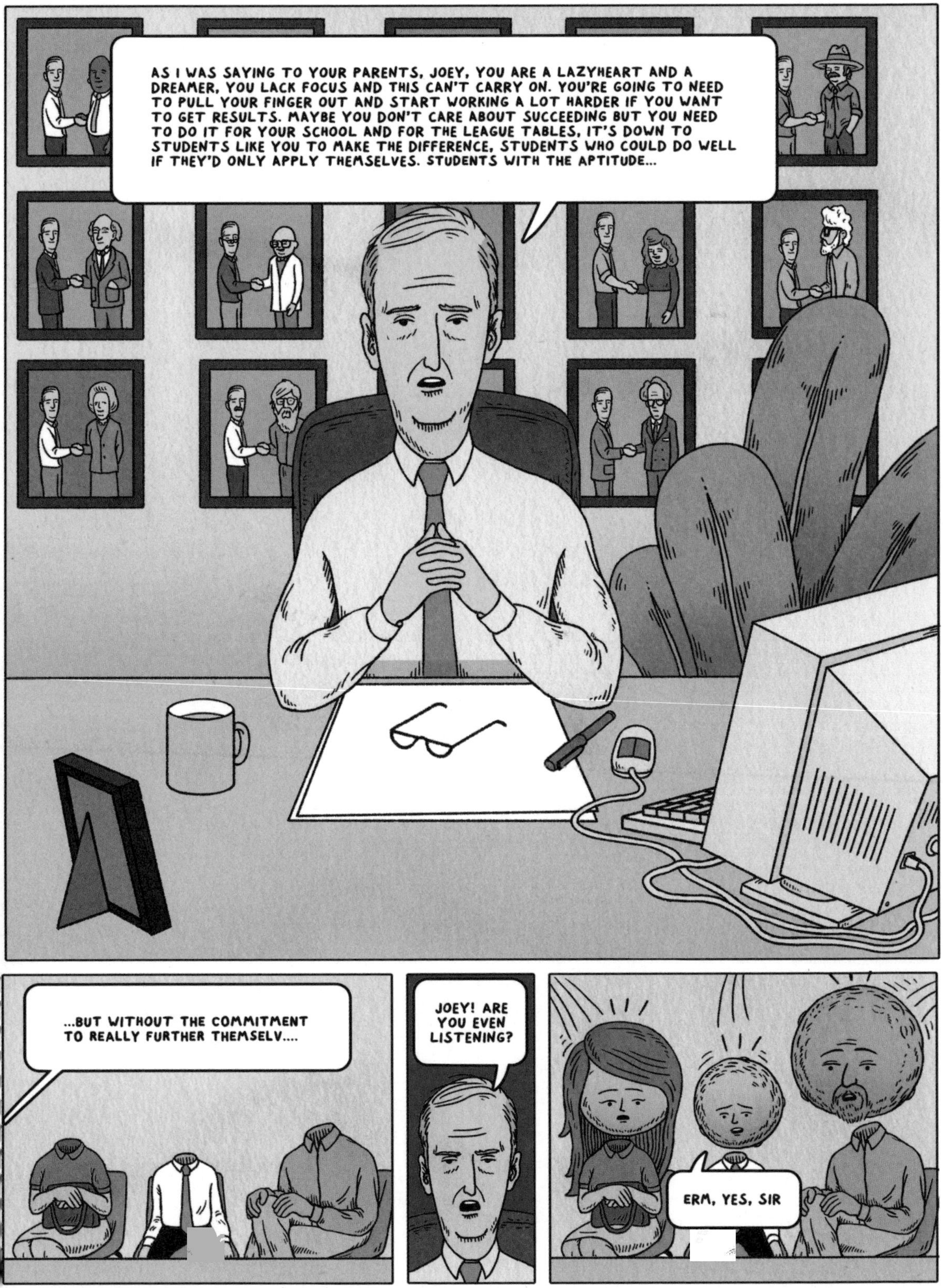
AS I WAS SAYING TO YOUR PARENTS, JOEY, YOU ARE A LAZYHEART AND A DREAMER, YOU LACK FOCUS AND THIS CAN'T CARRY ON. YOU'RE GOING TO NEED TO PULL YOUR FINGER OUT AND START WORKING A LOT HARDER IF YOU WANT TO GET RESULTS. MAYBE YOU DON'T CARE ABOUT SUCCEEDING BUT YOU NEED TO DO IT FOR YOUR SCHOOL AND FOR THE LEAGUE TABLES, IT'S DOWN TO STUDENTS LIKE YOU TO MAKE THE DIFFERENCE, STUDENTS WHO COULD DO WELL IF THEY'D ONLY APPLY THEMSELVES. STUDENTS WITH THE APTITUDE...
...BUT WITHOUT THE COMMITMENT TO REALLY FURTHER THEMSELV....
JOEY! ARE YOU EVEN LISTENING?
ERM, YES, SIR

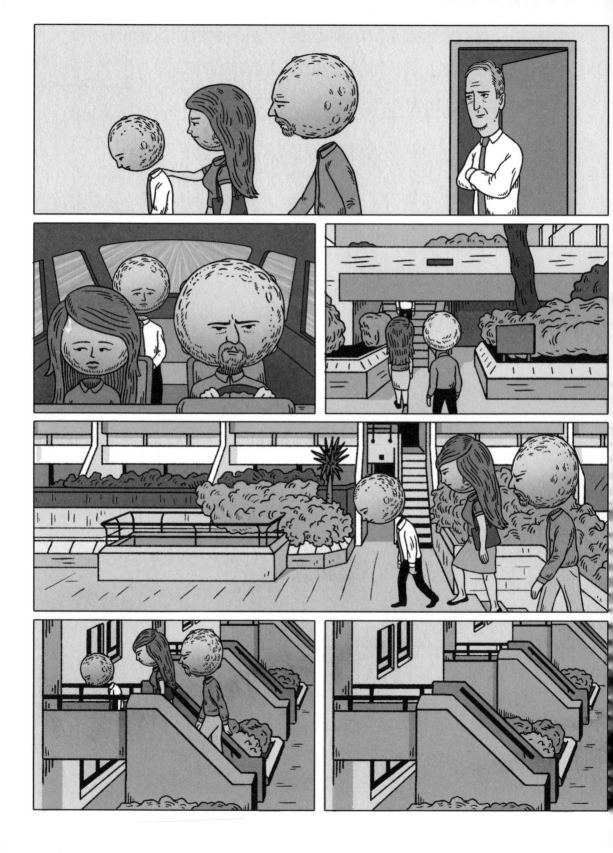

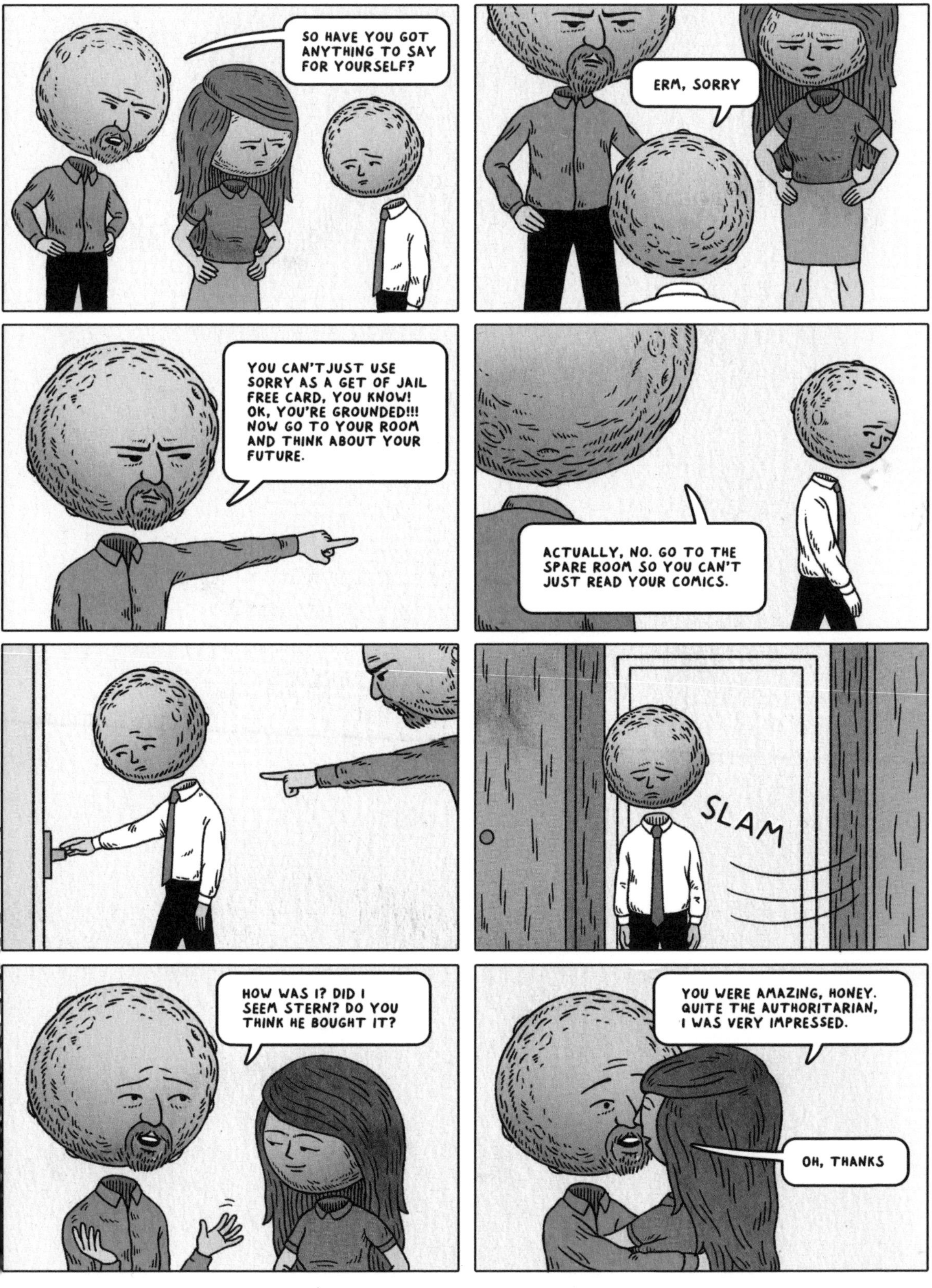
SO HAVE YOU GOT ANYTHING TO SAY FOR YOURSELF?
ERM, SORRY
YOU CAN'TJUST USE SORRY AS A GET OF JAIL FREE CARD, YOU KNOW! OK, YOU'RE GROUNDED!!! NOW GO TO YOUR ROOM AND THINK ABOUT YOUR FUTURE.
ACTUALLY, NO. GO TO THE SPARE ROOM SO YOU CAN'T JUST READ YOUR COMICS.
SLAM
HOW WAS I? DID I SEEM STERN? DO YOU THINK HE BOUGHT IT?
YOU WERE AMAZING, HONEY. QUITE THE AUTHORITARIAN, I WAS VERY IMPRESSED.
OH, THANKS

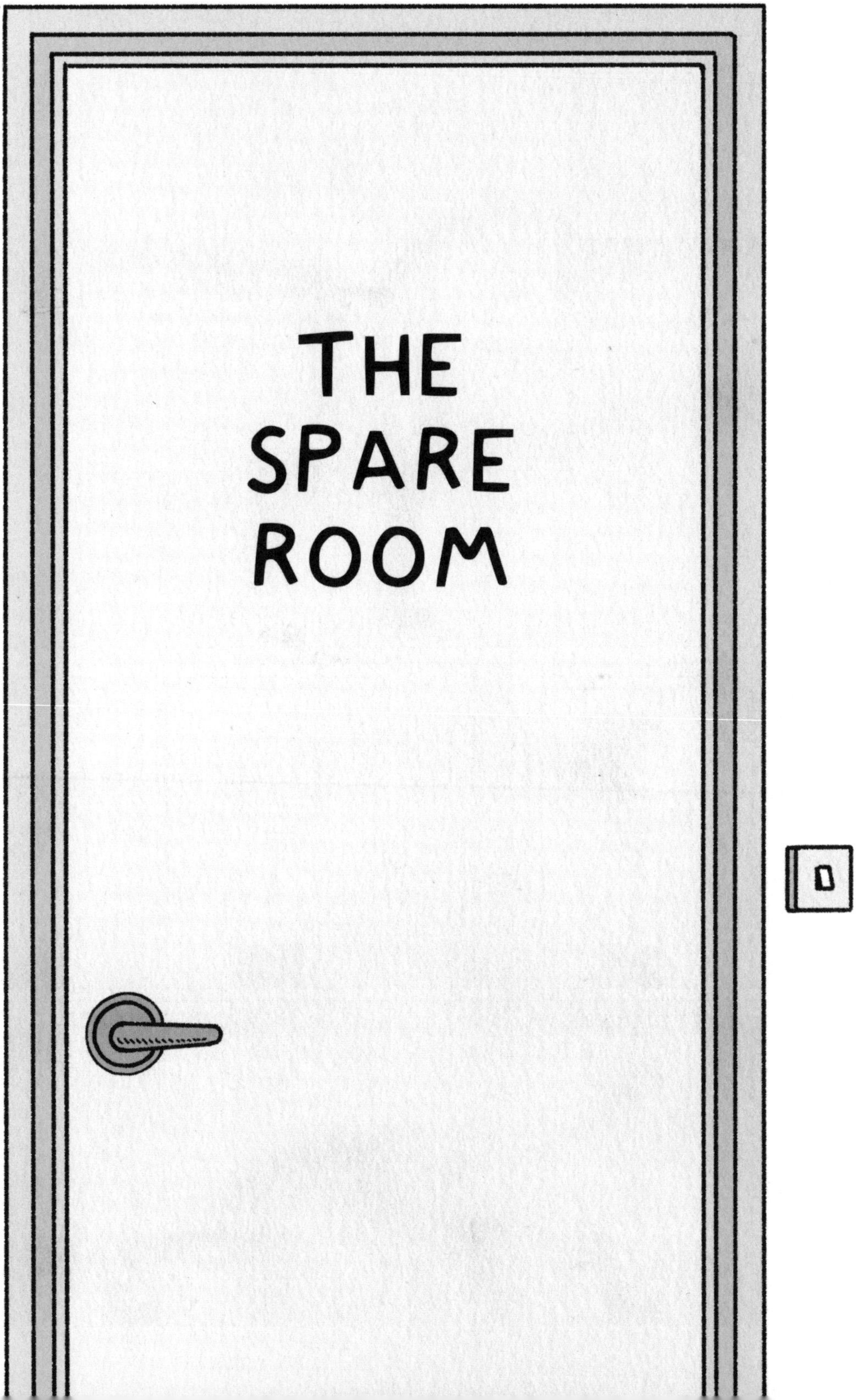
THE SPARE ROOM

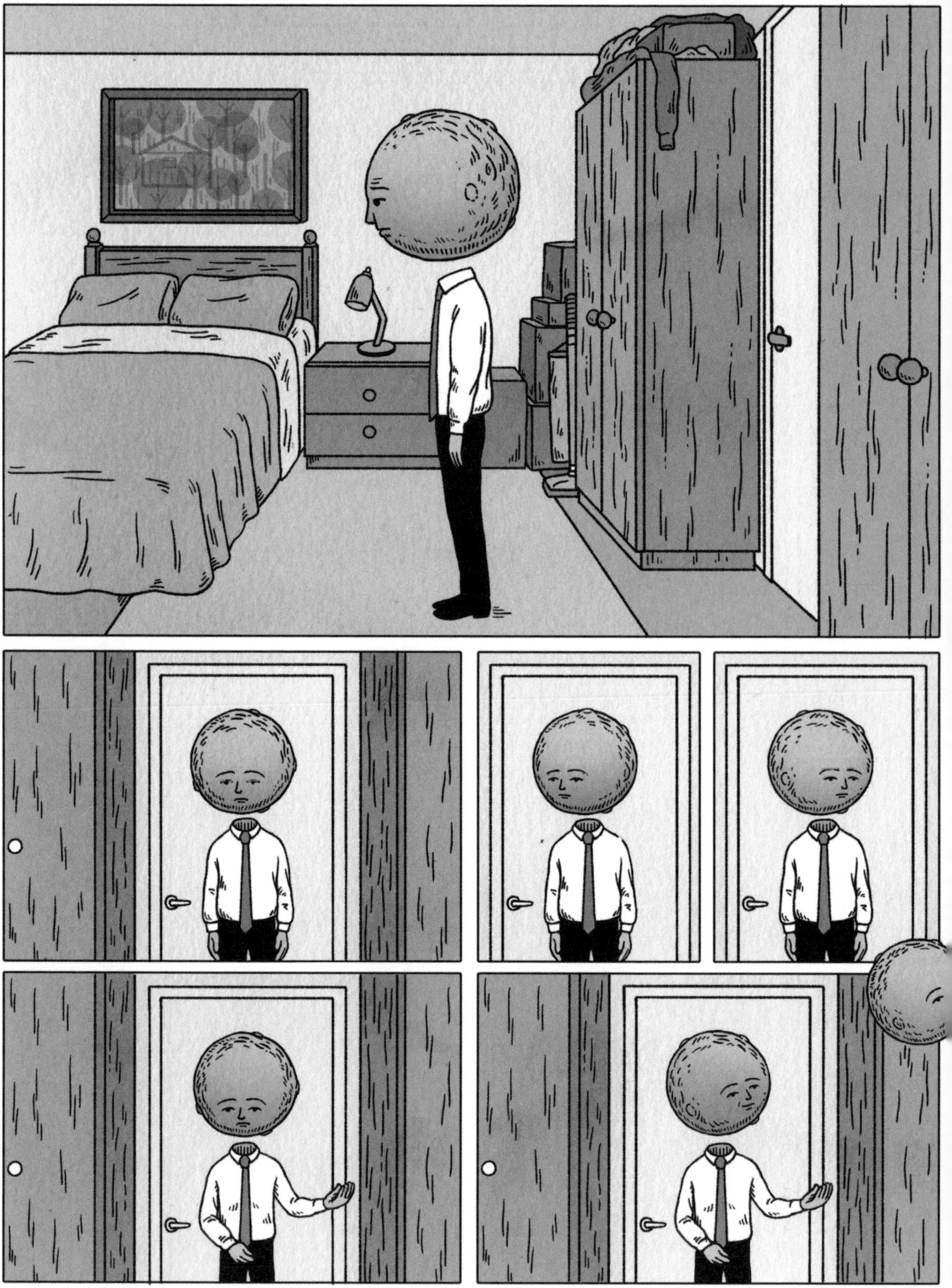

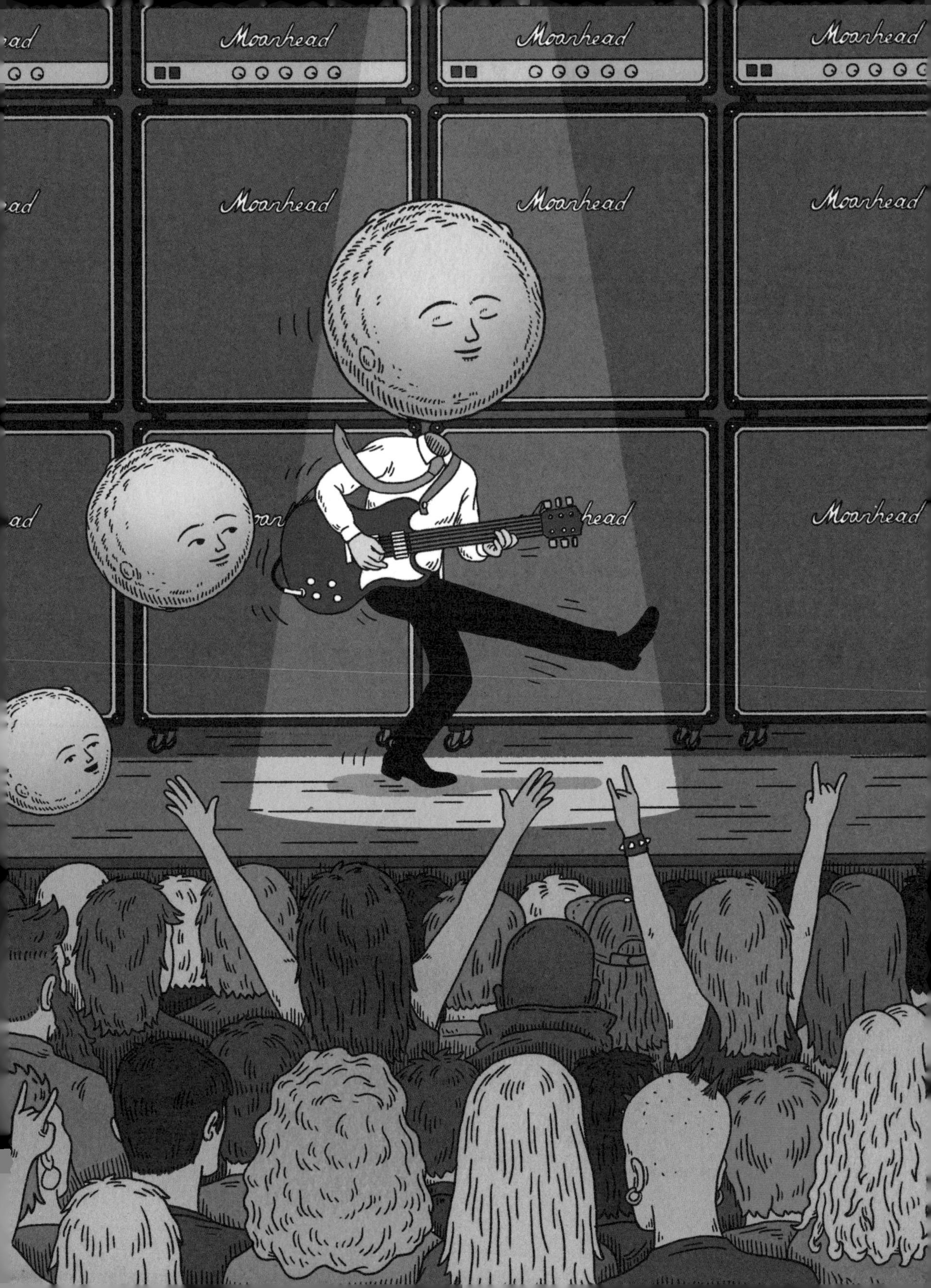
Moonhead
Moonhead
Moonhead
Moonhead
Moonhead
Moonhead
Moonhead

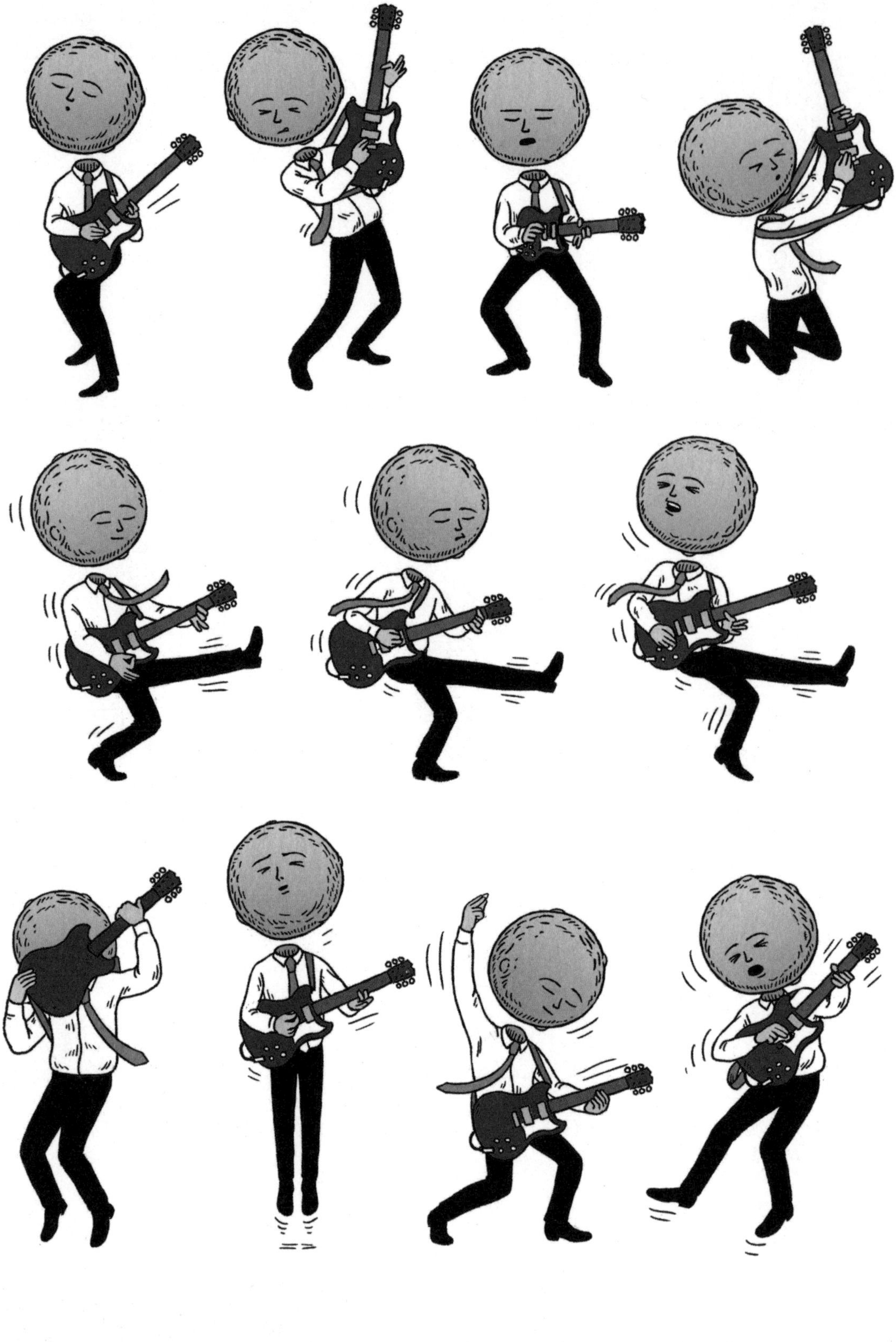

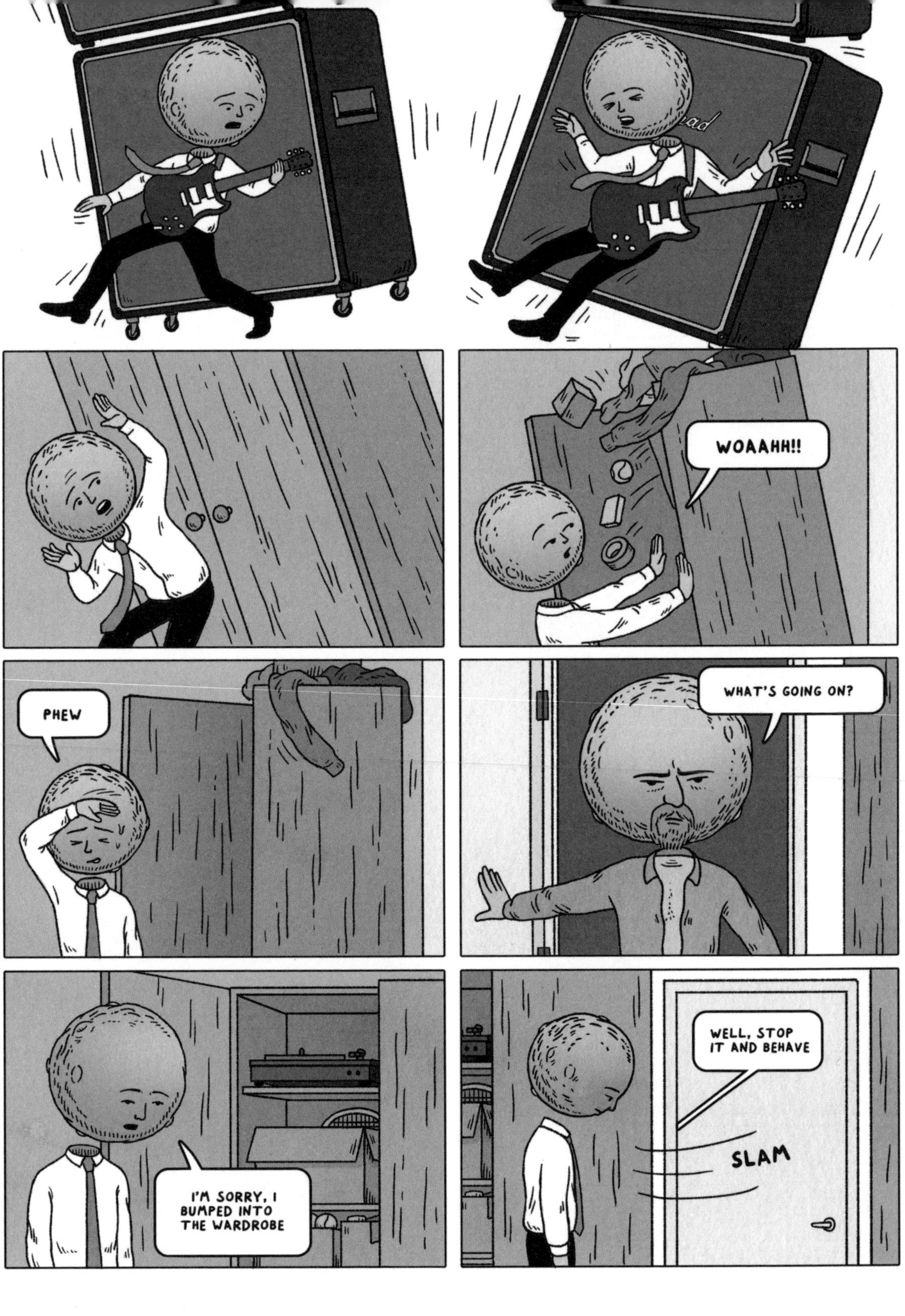
WOAAHH!!
PHEW
WHAT'S GOING ON?
I'M SORRY, I BUMPED INTO THE WARDROBE
WELL, STOP IT AND BEHAVE
SLAM

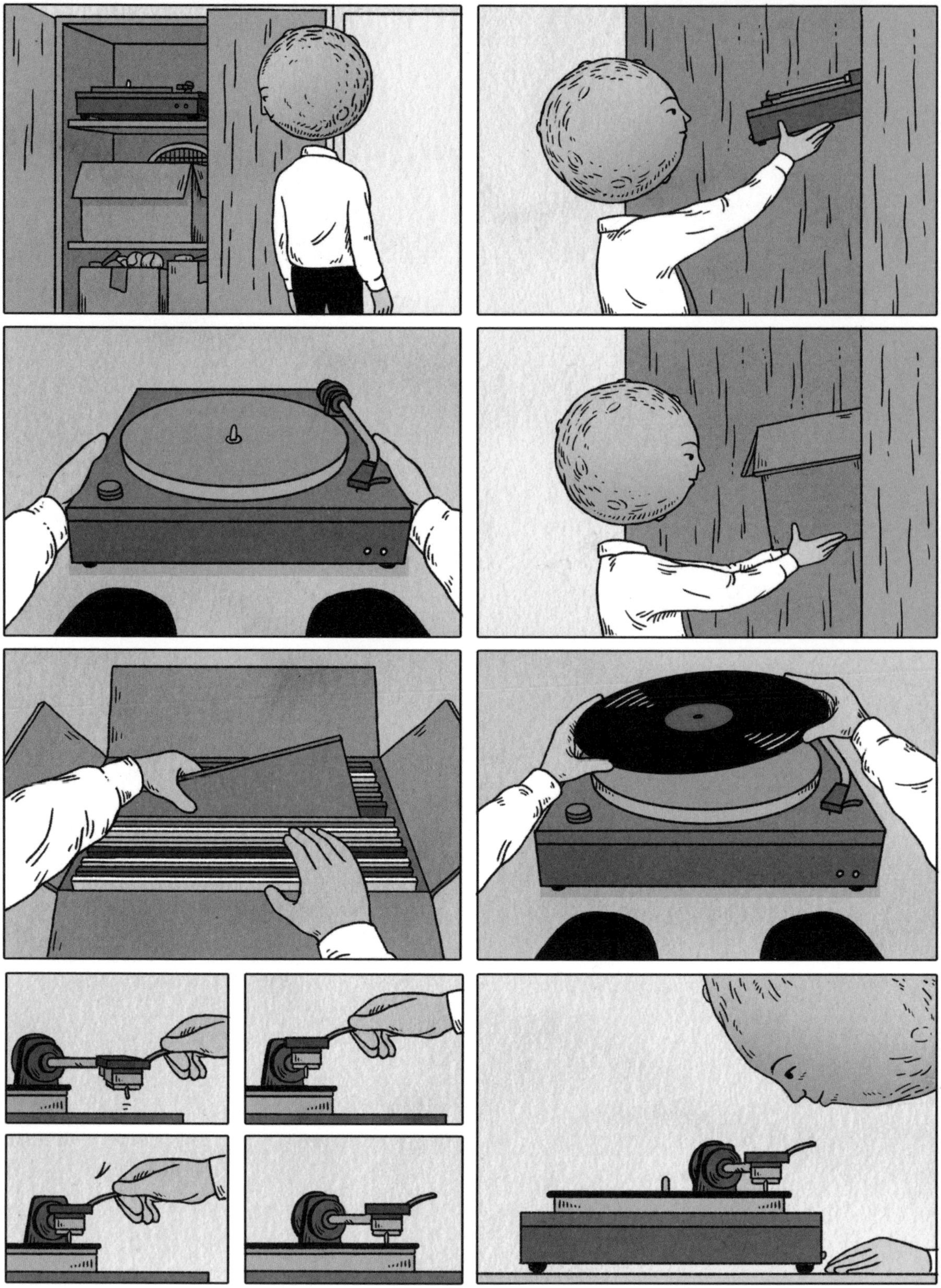

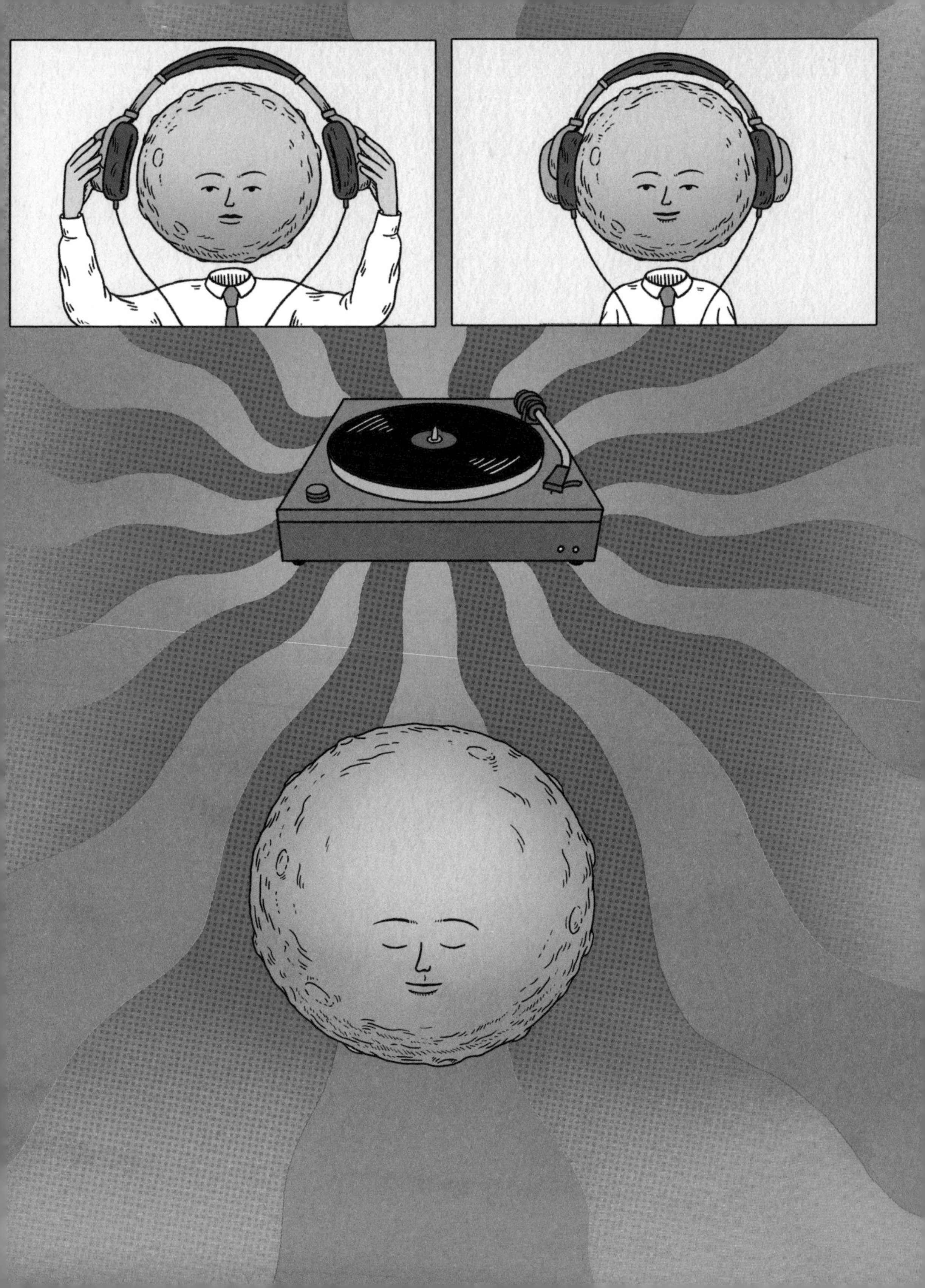

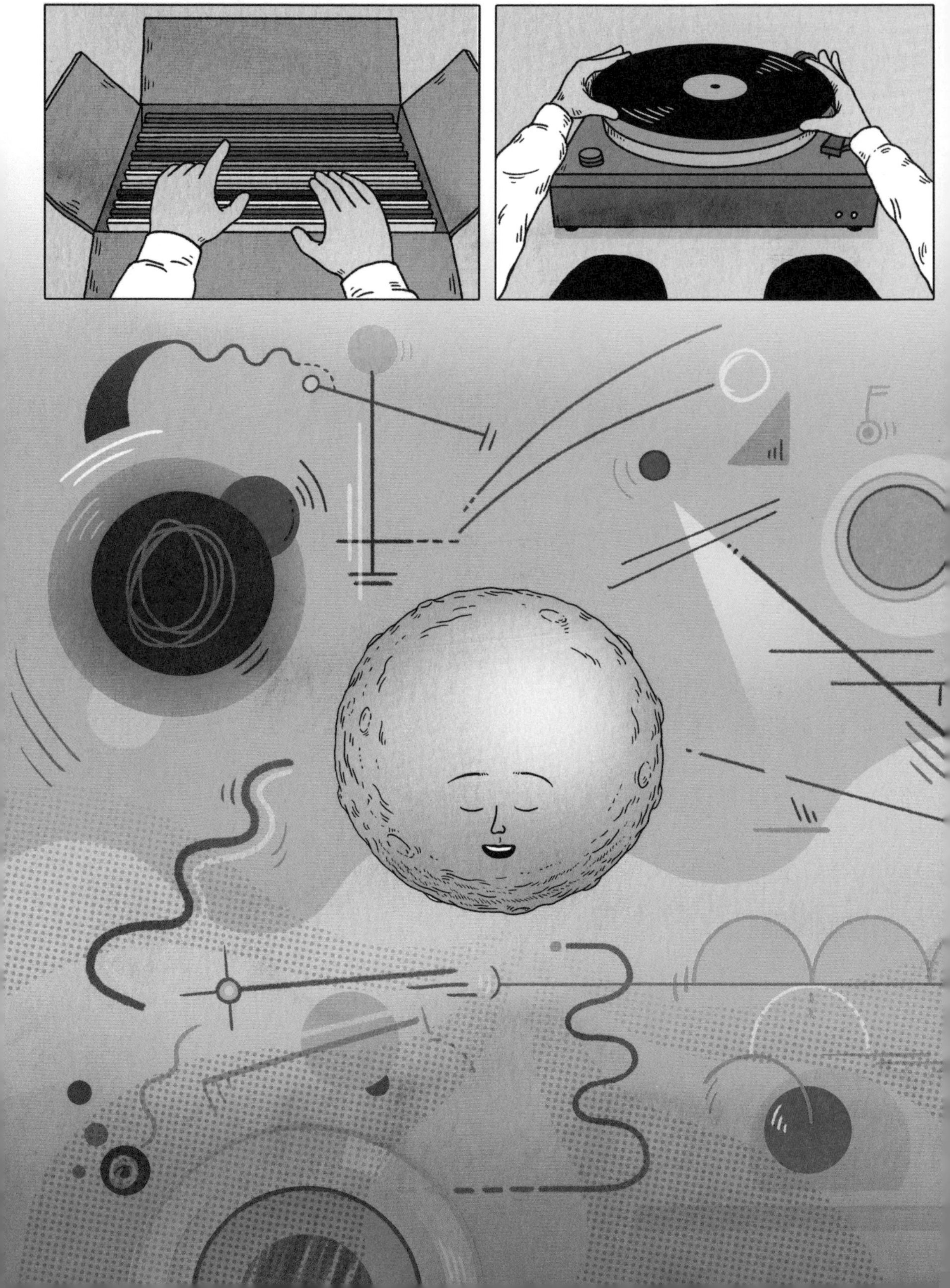

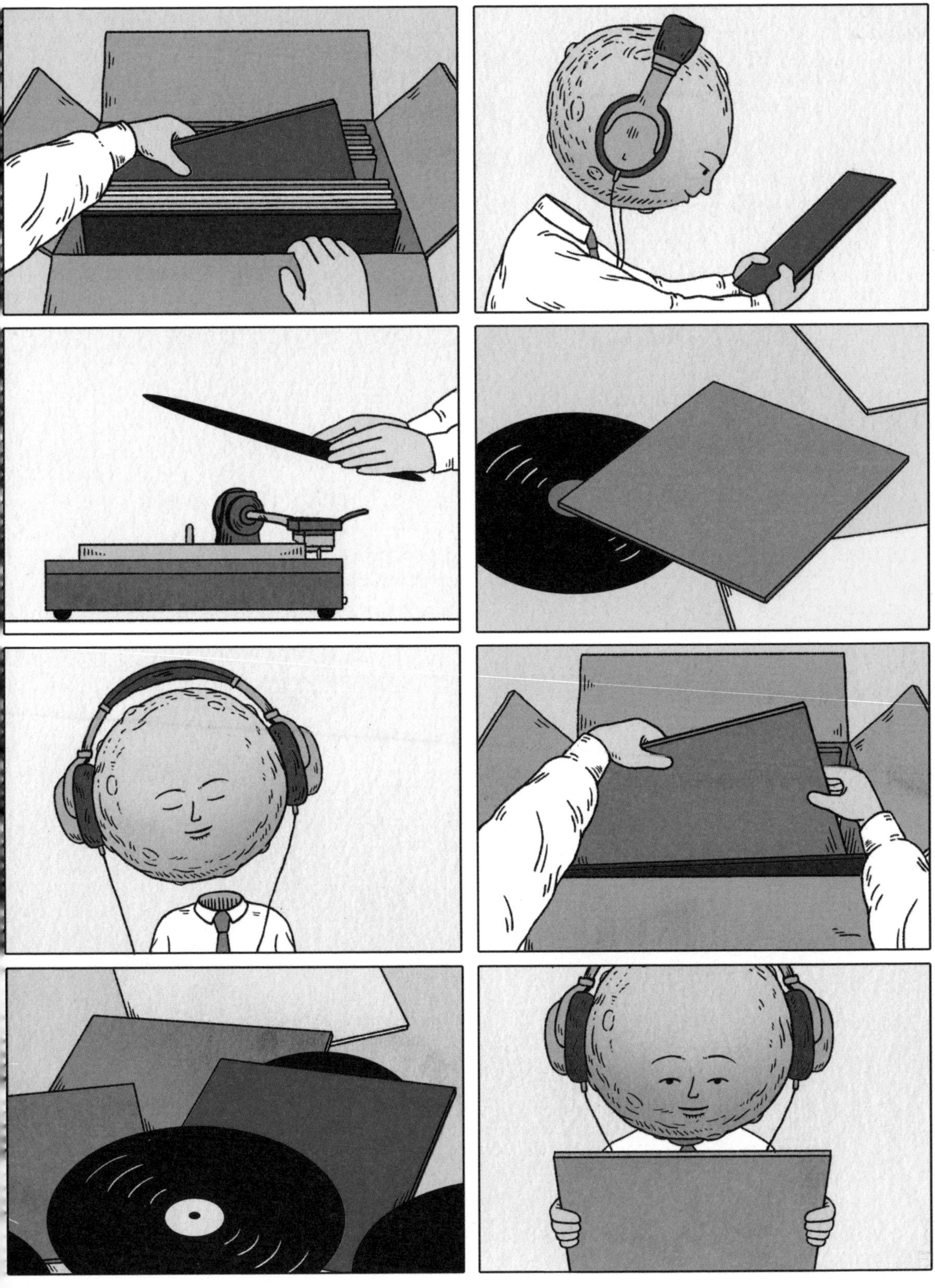

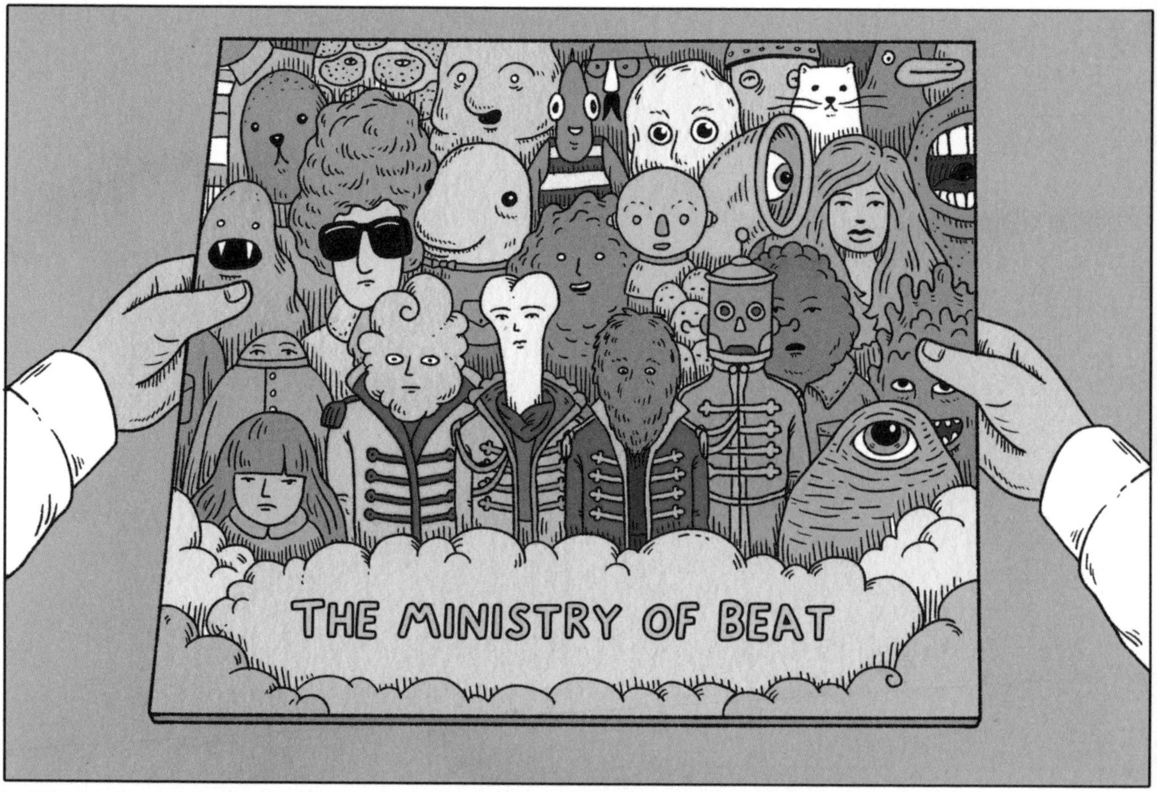
THE MINISTRY OF BEAT

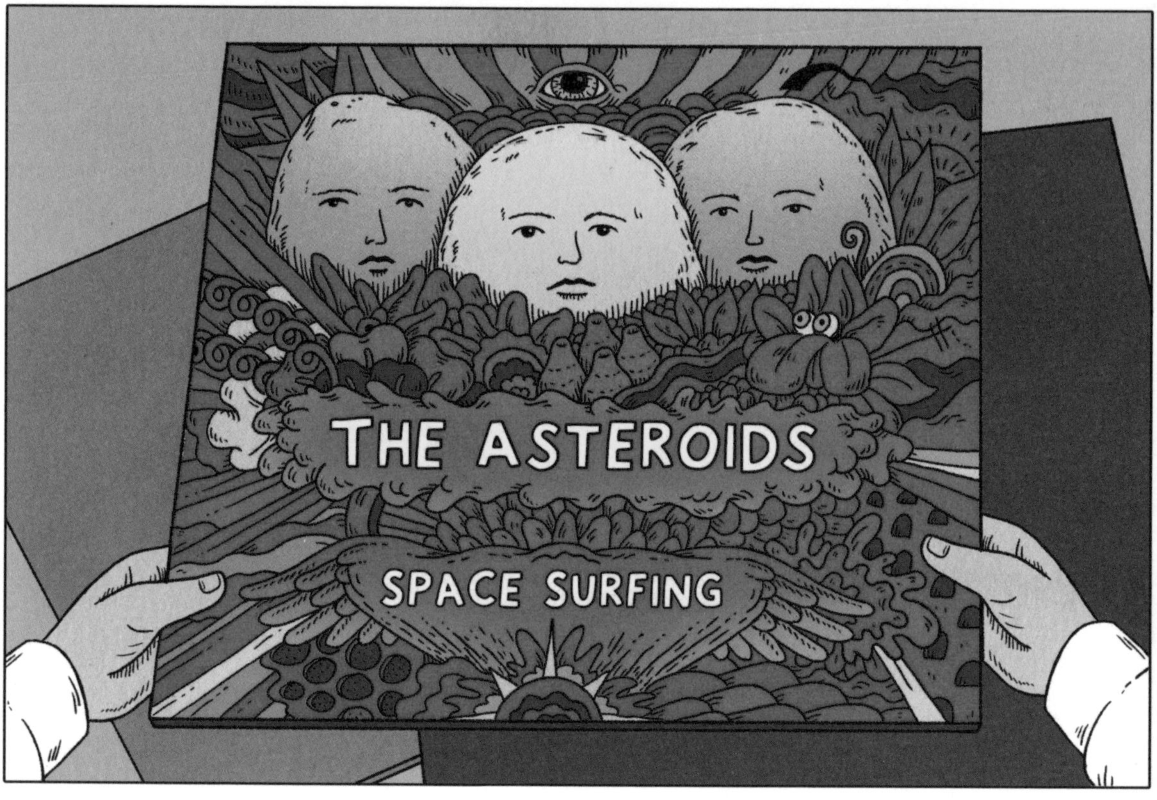
THE ASTEROIDS
SPACE SURFING

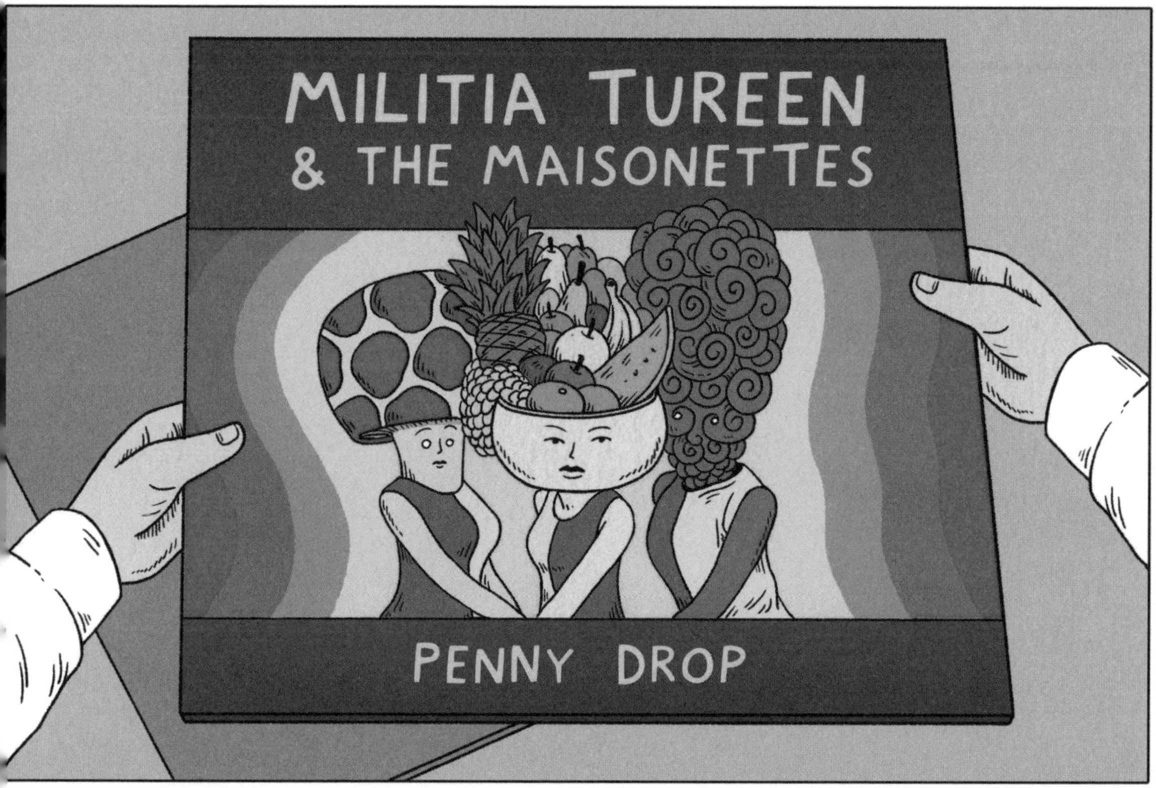
MILITIA TUREEN
& THE MAISONETTES
PENNY DROP

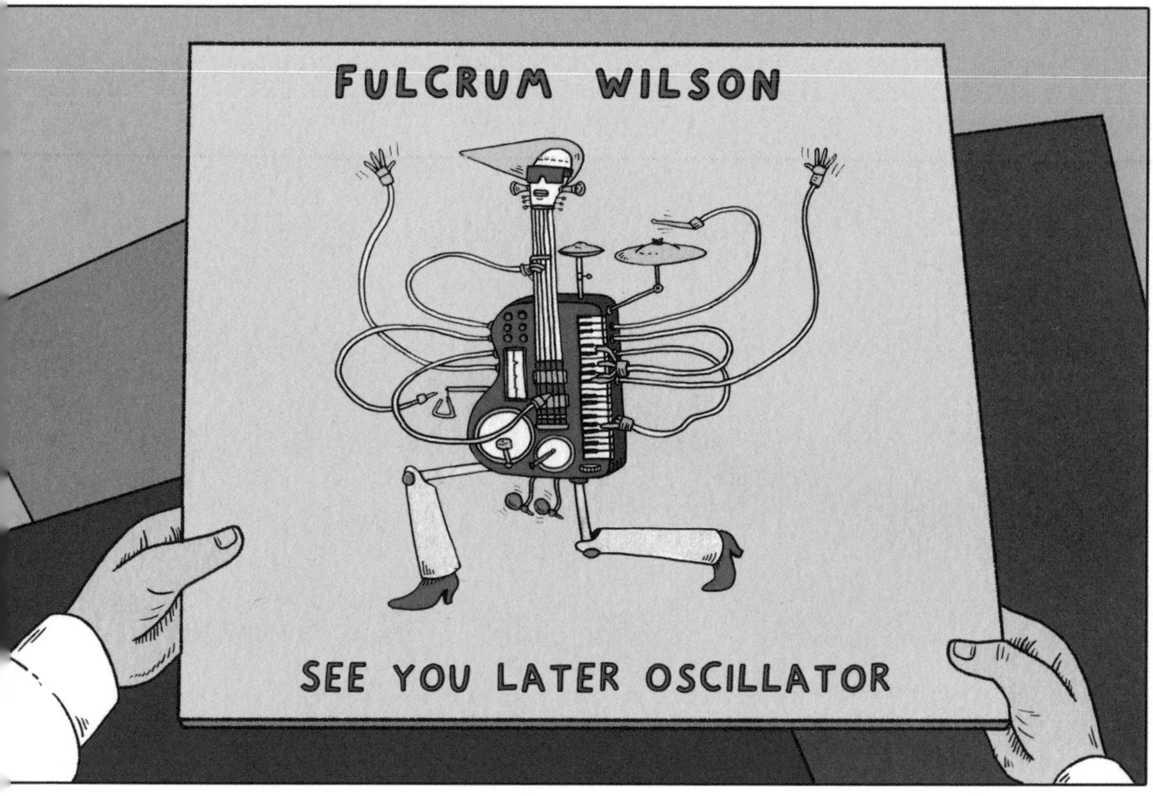
FULCRUM WILSON
SEE YOU LATER OSCILLATOR

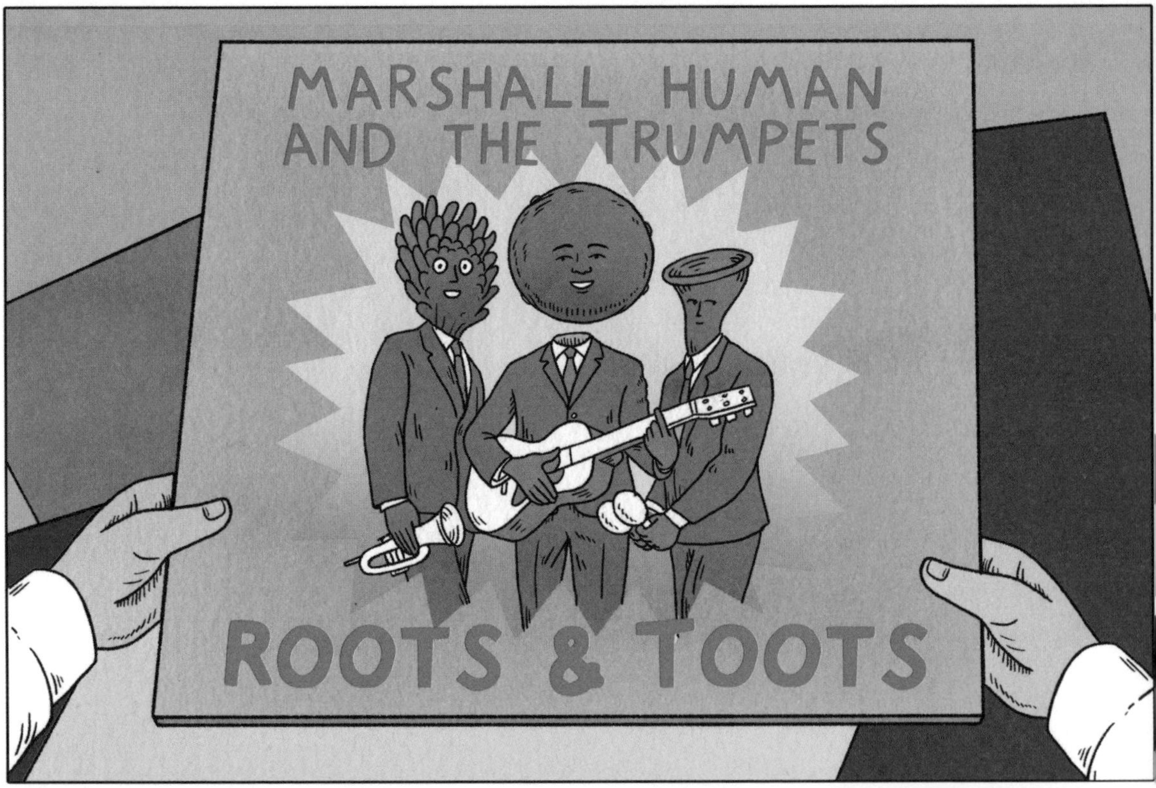
MARSHALL HUMAN
AND THE TRUMPETS
ROOTS & TOOTS

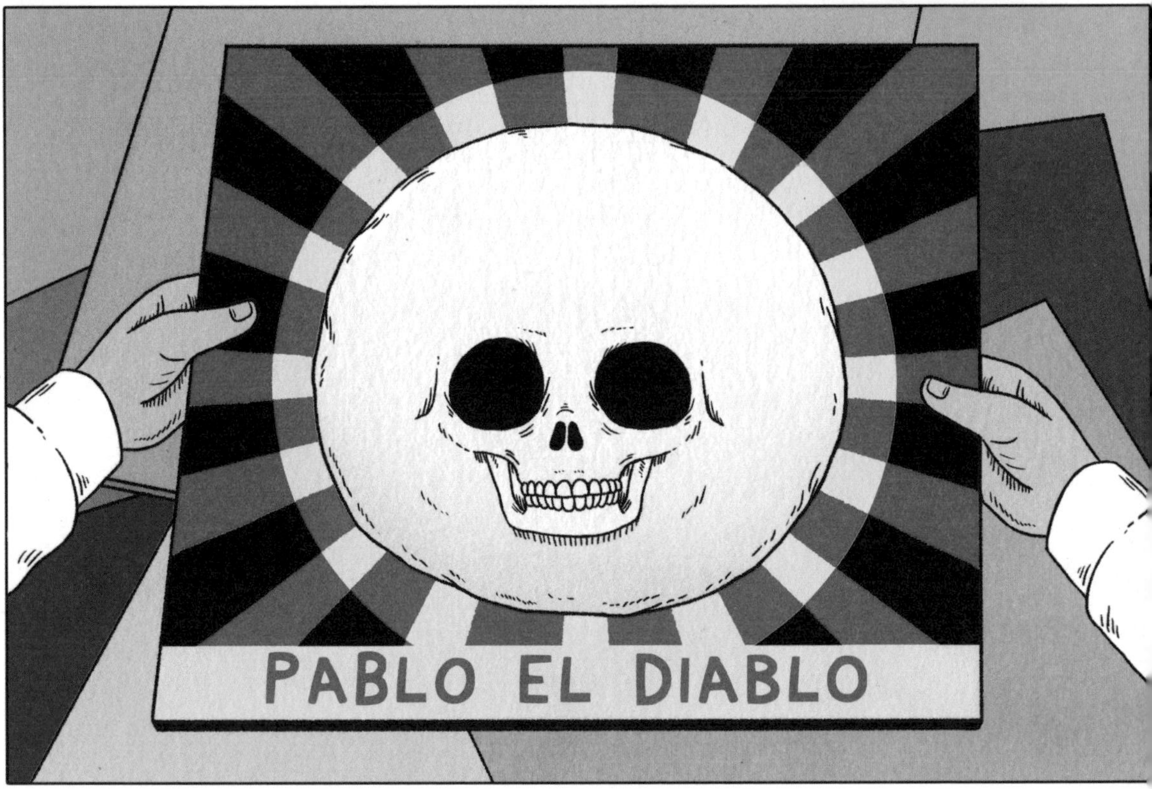
PABLO EL DIABLO

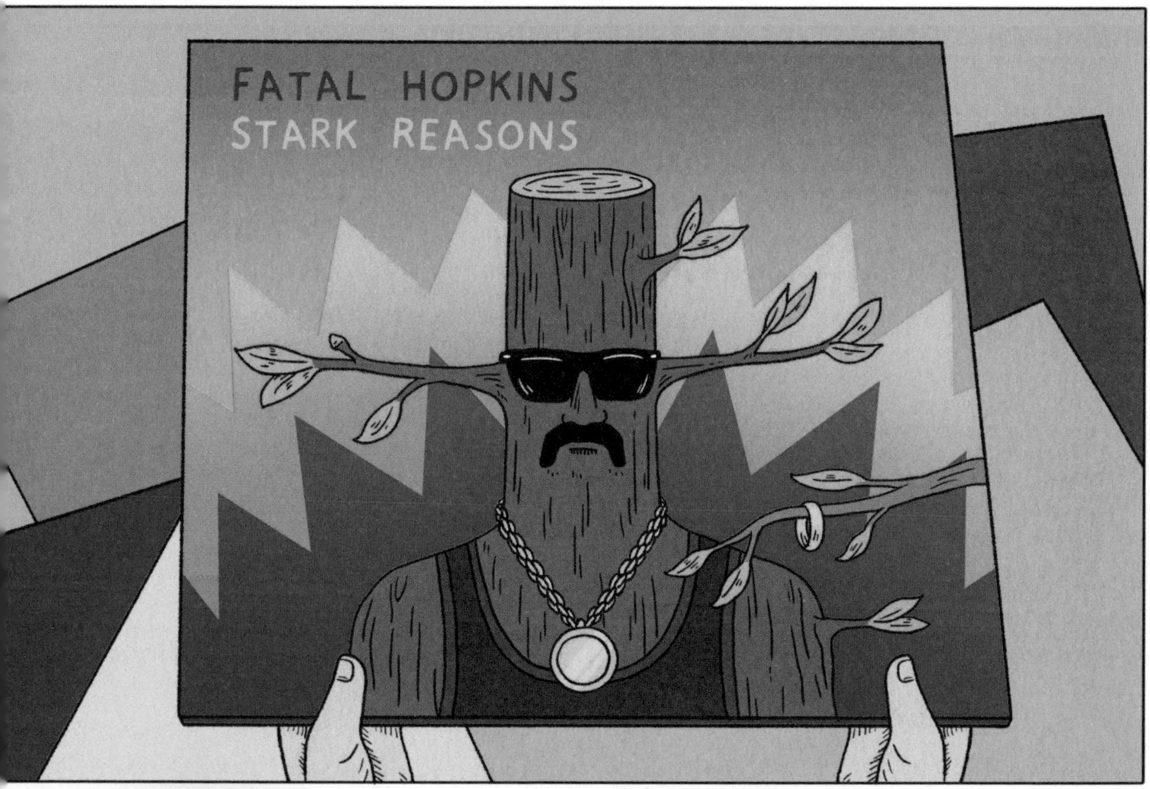
FATAL HOPKINS
STARK REASONS

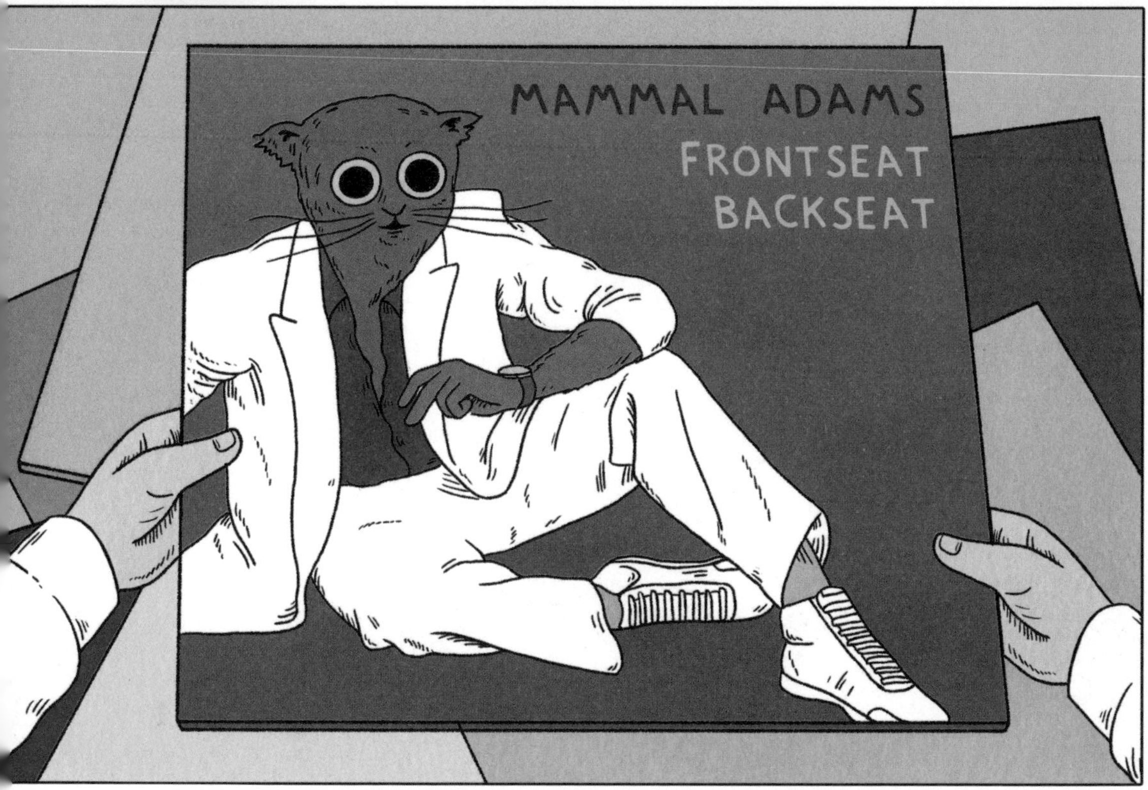
MAMMAL ADAMS
FRONTSEAT
BACKSEAT

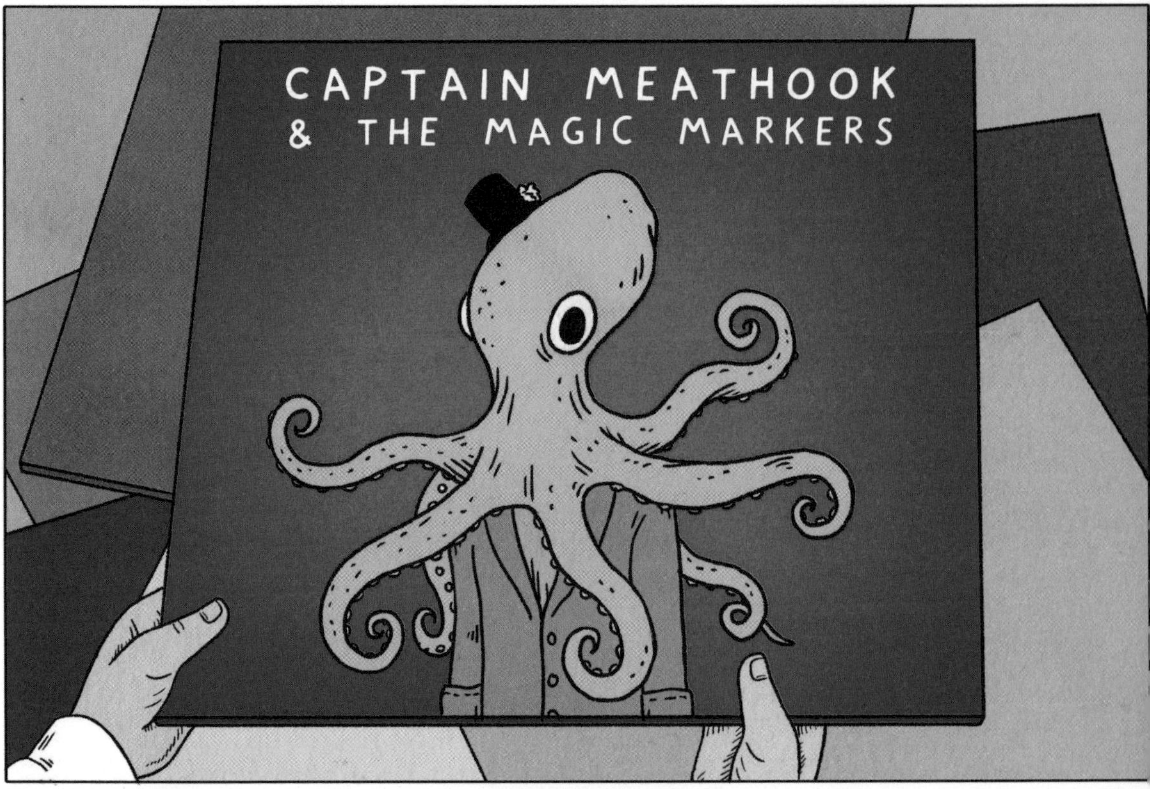
CAPTAIN MEATHOOK
& THE MAGIC MARKERS

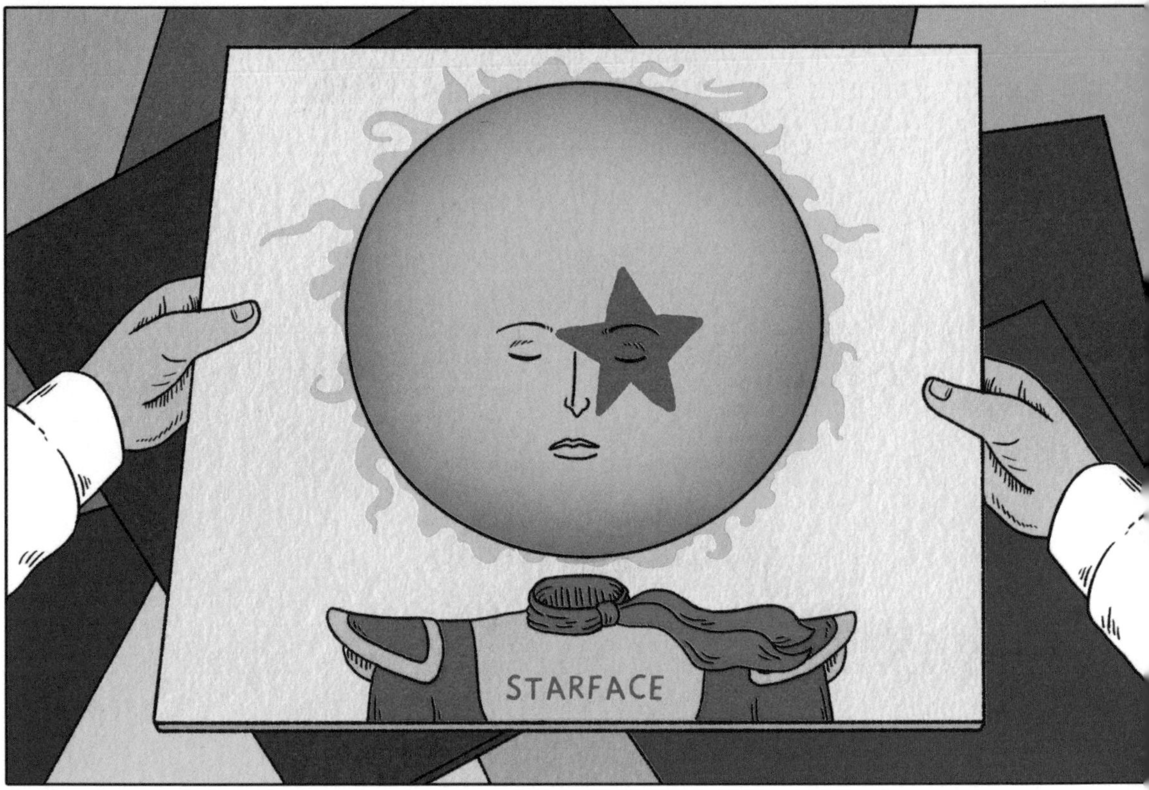
STARFACE

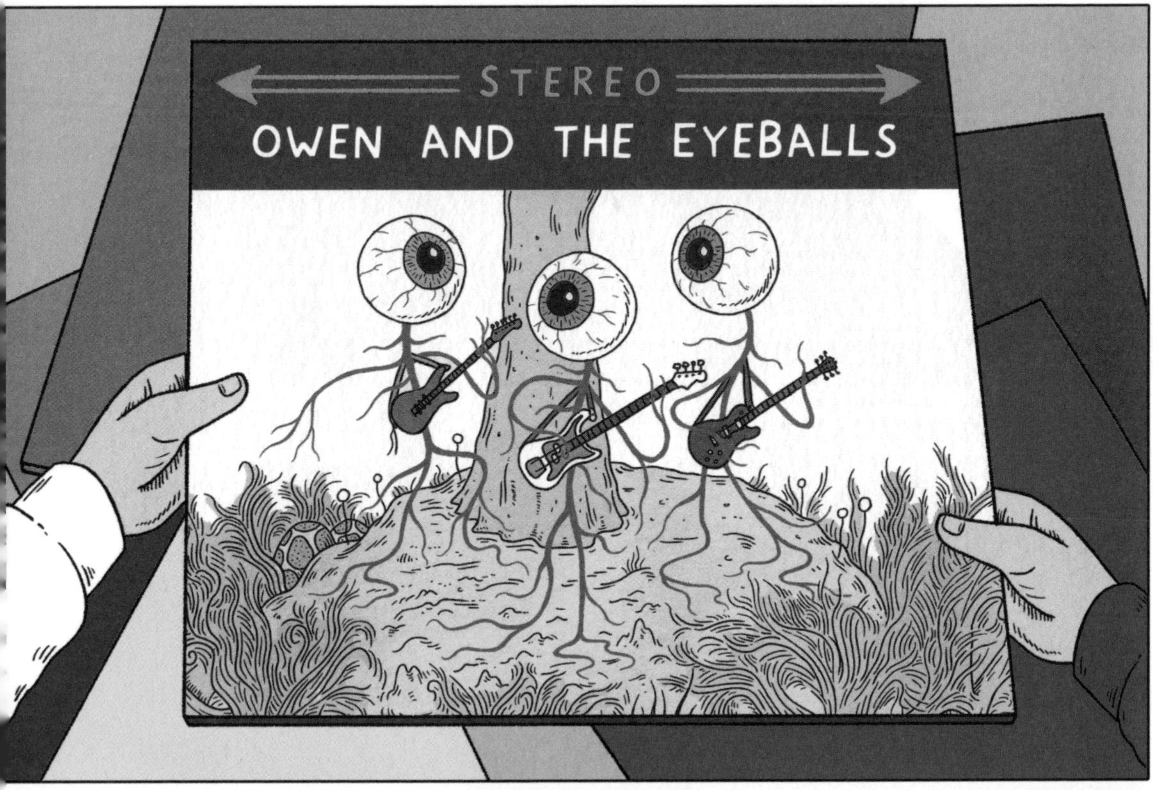
STEREO
OWEN AND THE EYEBALLS

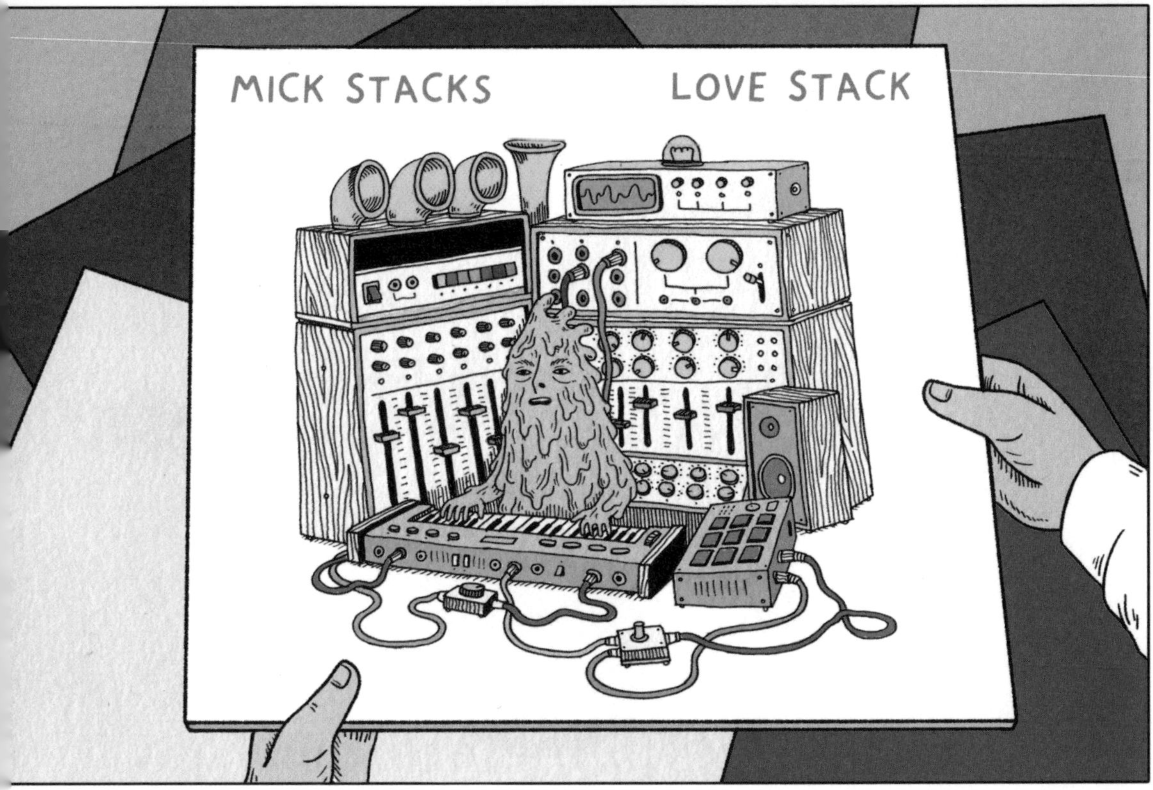
MICK STACKS
LOVE STACK

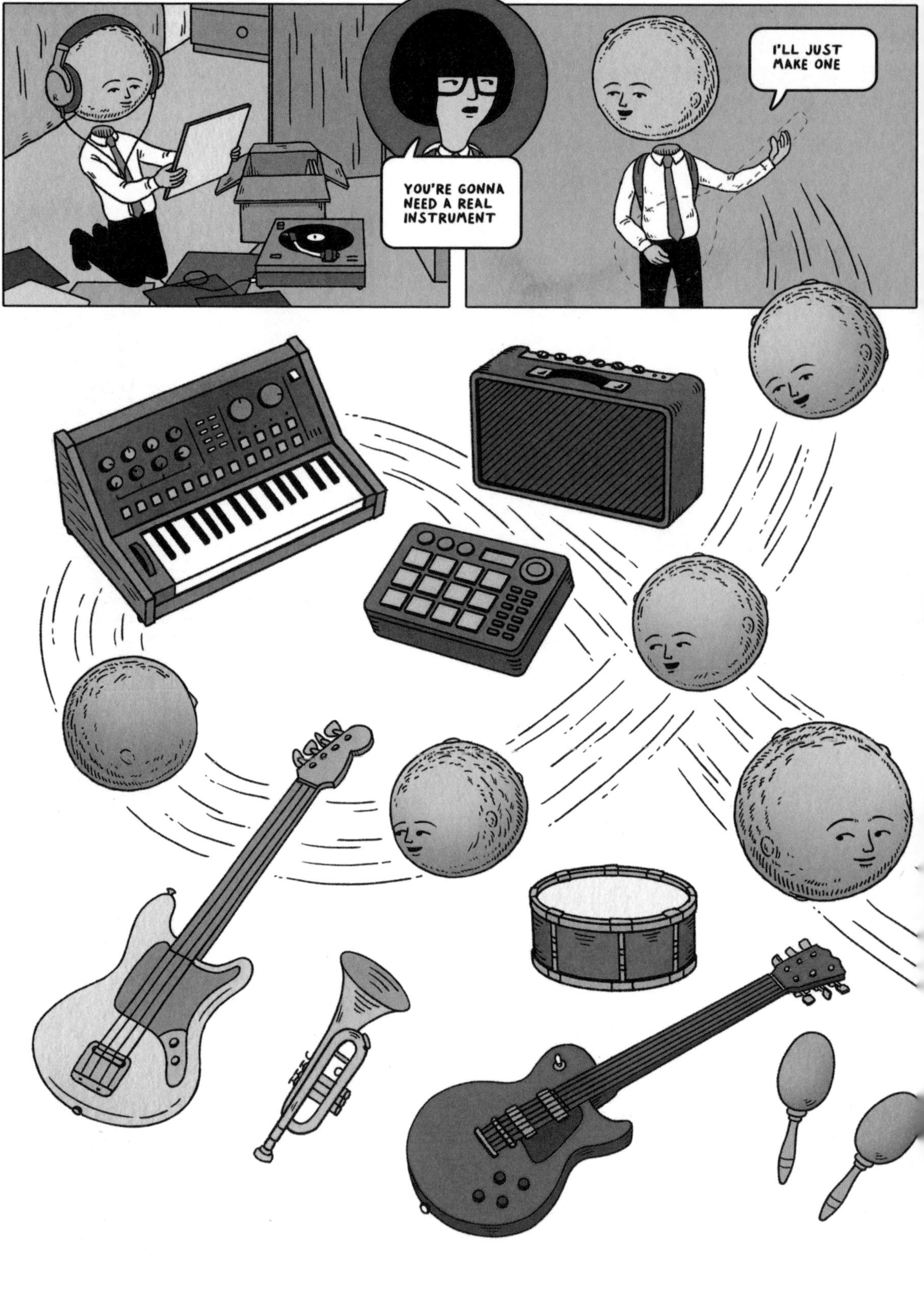
YOU'RE GONNA NEED A REAL INSTRUMENT
I'LL JUST MAKE ONE

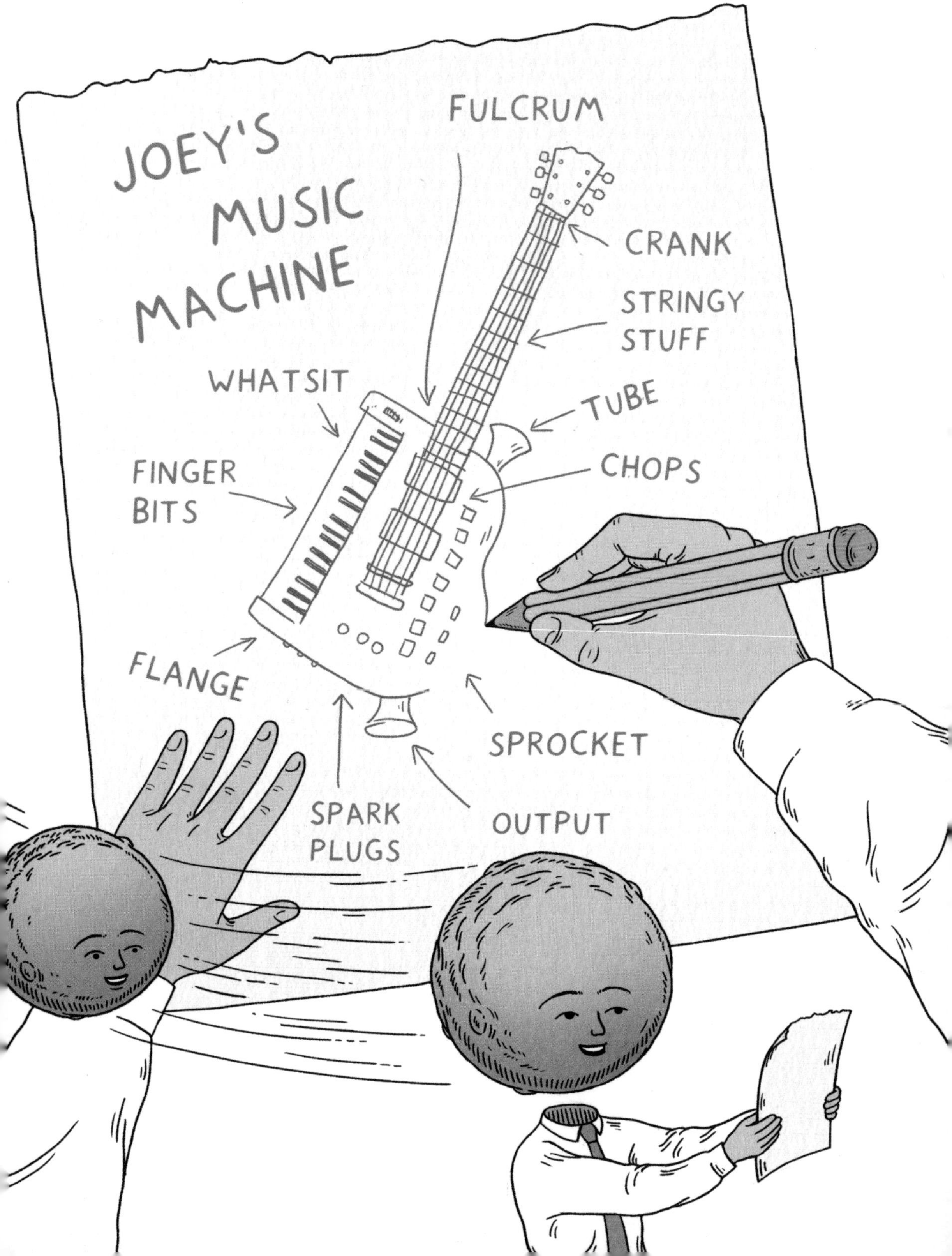
JOEY'S MUSIC MACHINE
FULCRUM
CRANK
STRINGY STUFF
WHATSIT
TUBE
FINGER BITS
CHOPS
FLANGE
SPROCKET
SPARK PLUGS
OUTPUT

THE
WORKSHOP

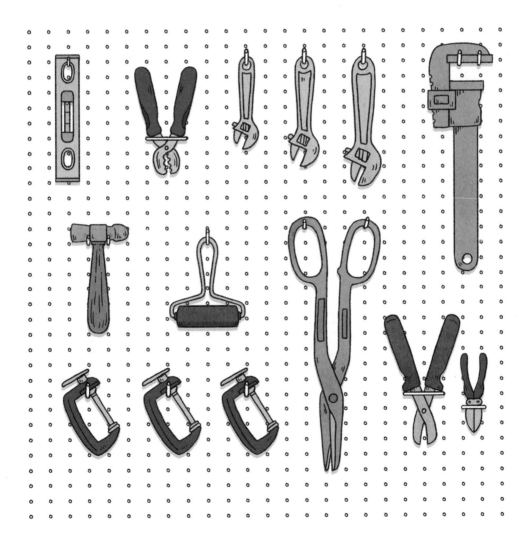

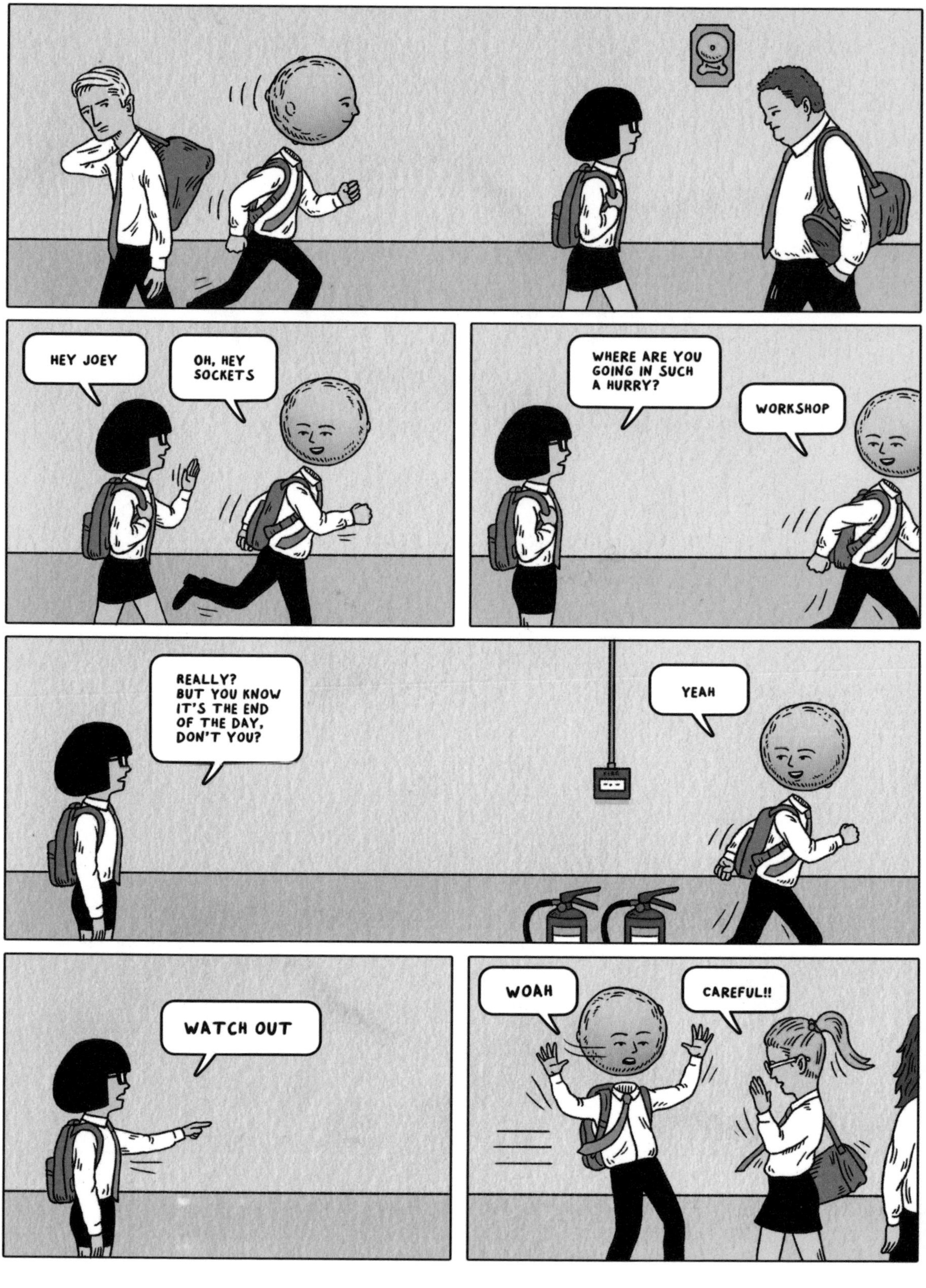
HEY JOEY
OH, HEY SOCKETS
WHERE ARE YOU GOING IN SUCH A HURRY?
WORKSHOP
REALLY? BUT YOU KNOW IT'S THE END OF THE DAY, DON'T YOU?
YEAH
WATCH OUT
WOAH
CAREFUL!!

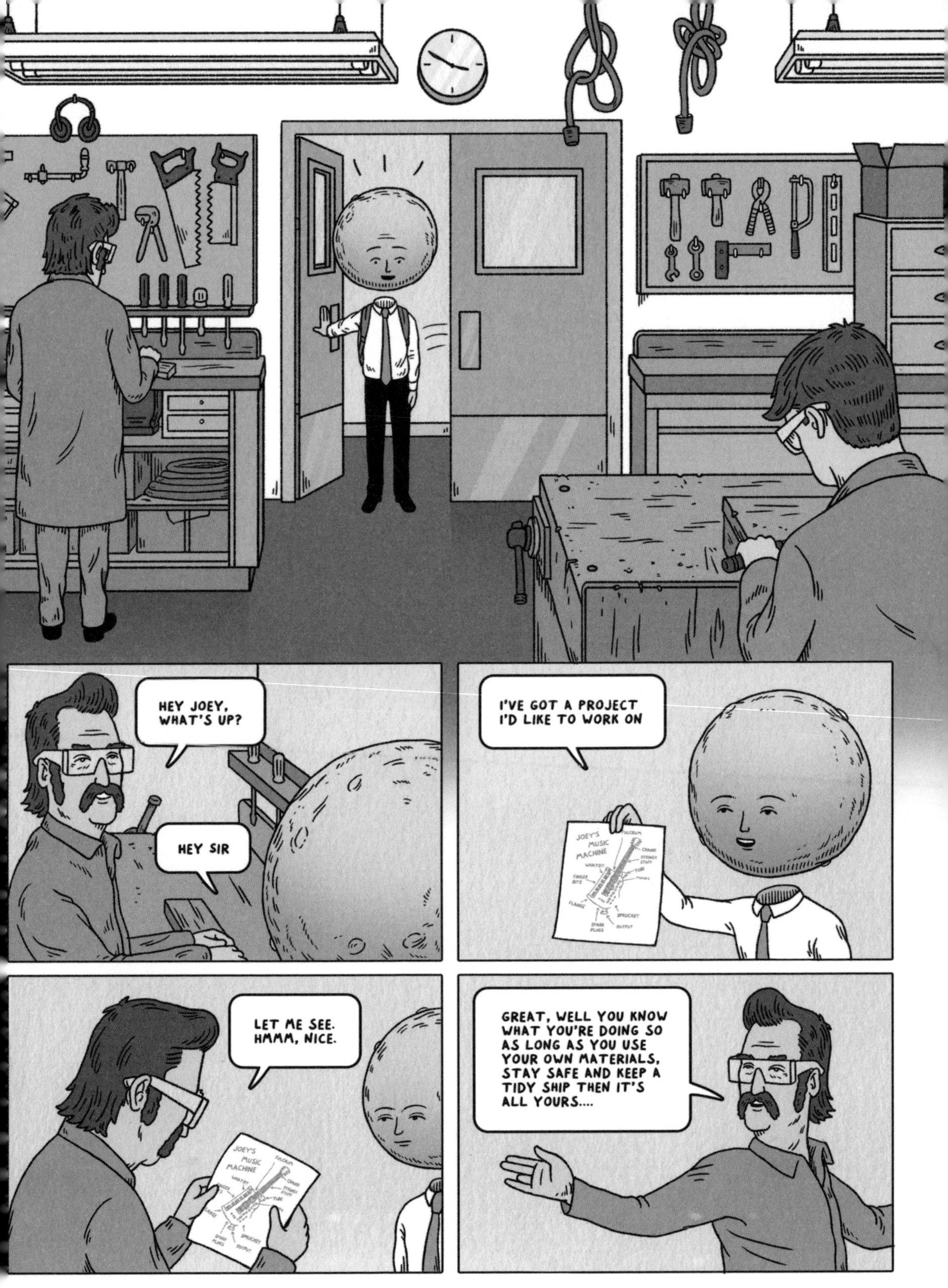
HEY JOEY,
WHAT'S UP?
HEY SIR
I'VE GOT A PROJECT
I'D LIKE TO WORK ON
JOEY'S MUSIC MACHINE
FULCRUM
CRANK
STRINGY STUFF
WHATSIT
TUBE
FINGER BITS
FLANGE
SPROCKET
SPARK PLUGS
OUTPUT
LET ME SEE.
HMMM, NICE.
GREAT, WELL YOU KNOW WHAT YOU'RE DOING SO AS LONG AS YOU USE YOUR OWN MATERIALS, STAY SAFE AND KEEP A TIDY SHIP THEN IT'S ALL YOURS....

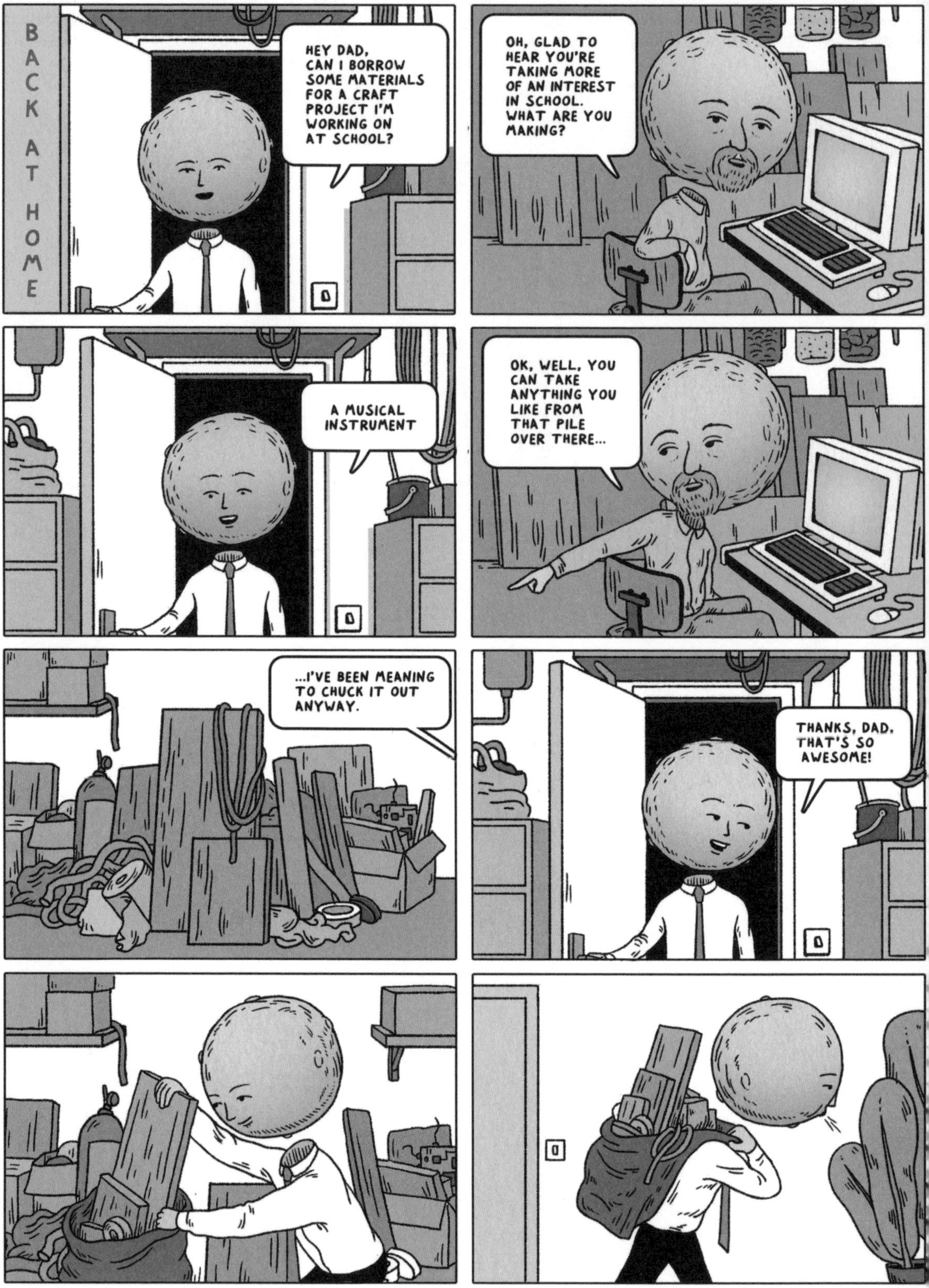
BACK AT HOME
HEY DAD, CAN I BORROW SOME MATERIALS FOR A CRAFT PROJECT I'M WORKING ON AT SCHOOL?
OH, GLAD TO HEAR YOU'RE TAKING MORE OF AN INTEREST IN SCHOOL. WHAT ARE YOU MAKING?
A MUSICAL INSTRUMENT
OK, WELL, YOU CAN TAKE ANYTHING YOU LIKE FROM THAT PILE OVER THERE...
...I'VE BEEN MEANING TO CHUCK IT OUT ANYWAY.
THANKS, DAD. THAT'S SO AWESOME!

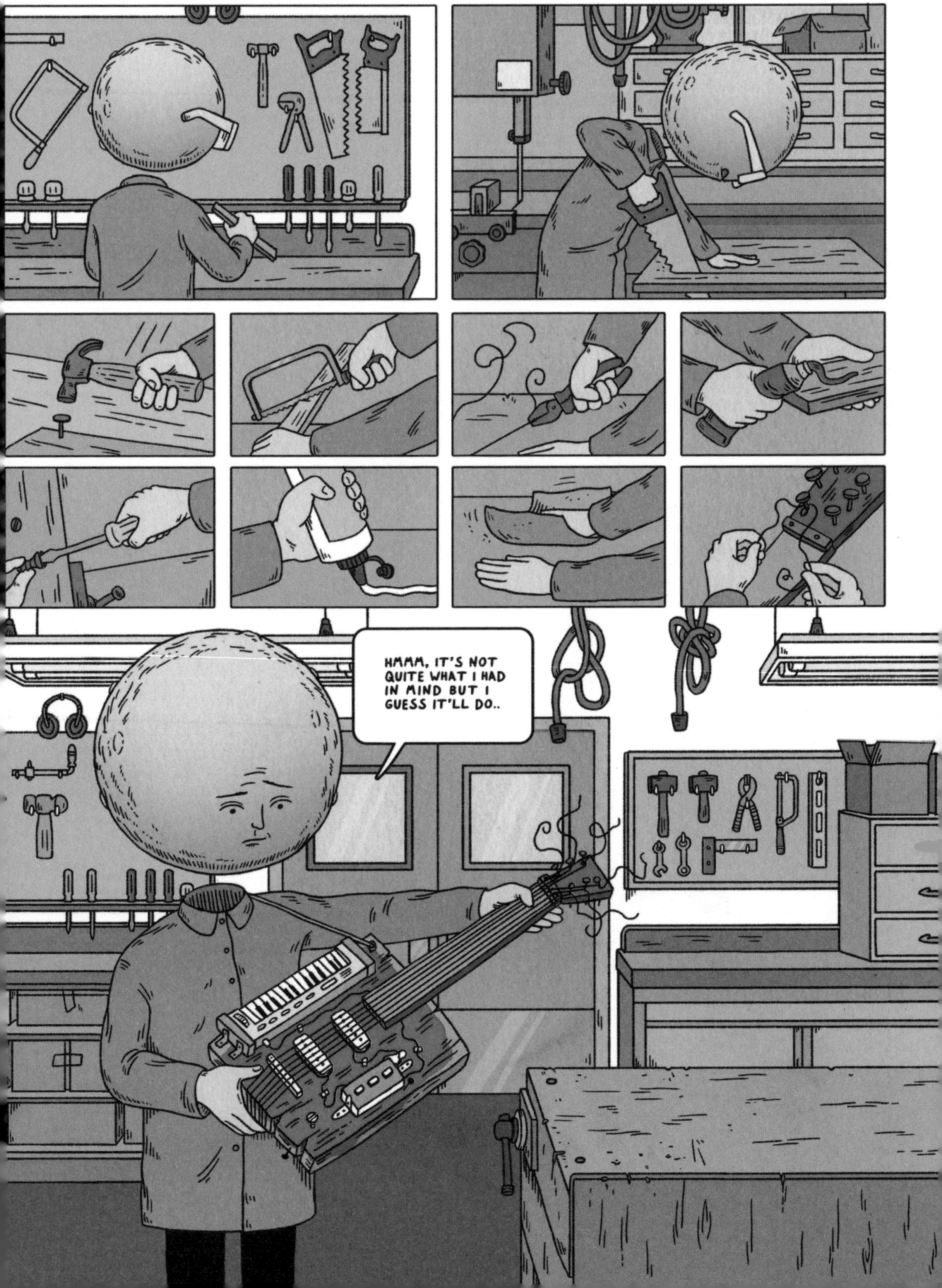
HMMM, IT'S NOT QUITE WHAT I HAD IN MIND BUT I GUESS IT'LL DO..

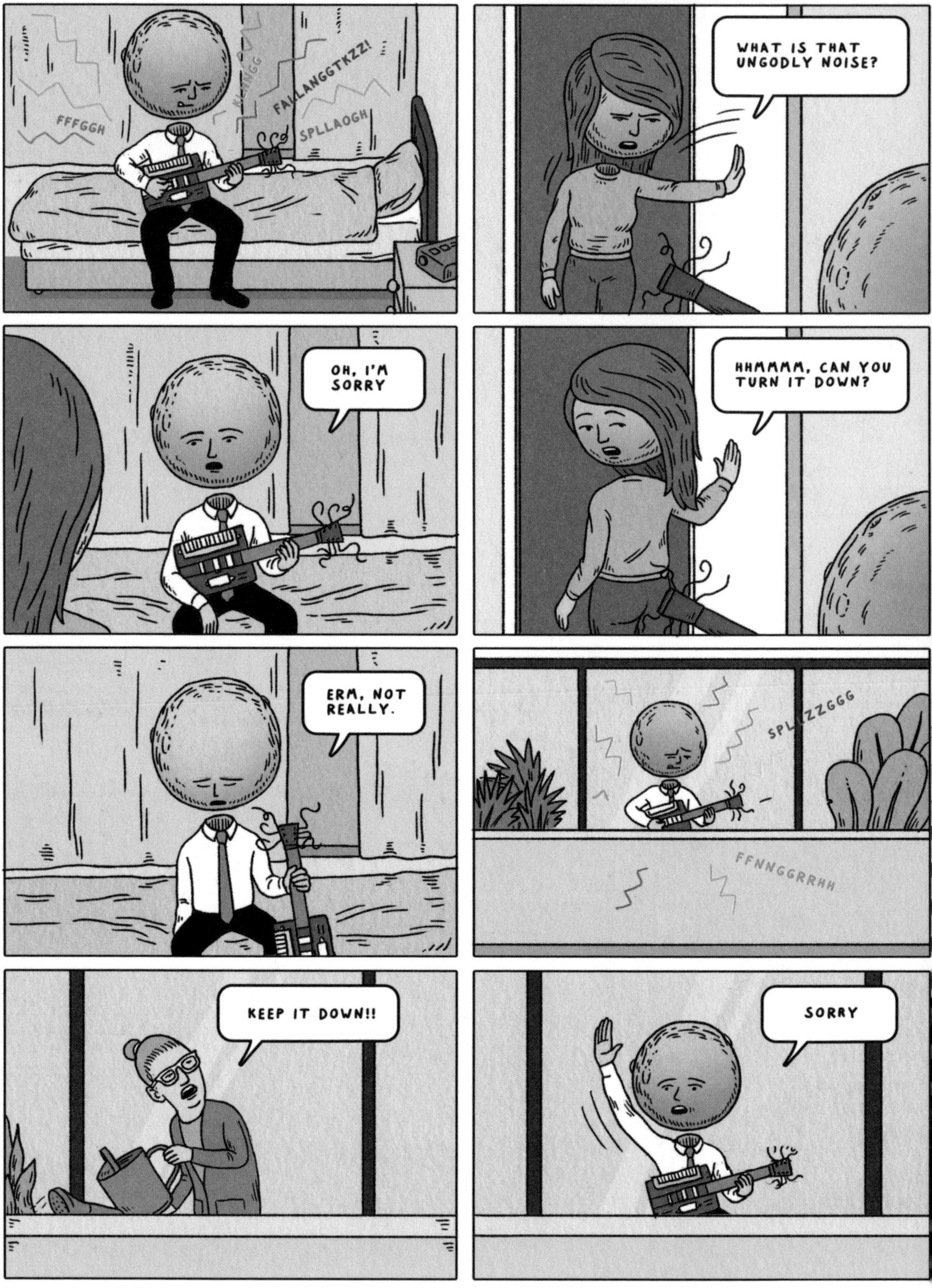
FFFGGH
FALLANGGTKZZ!
SPLLAOGH
WHAT IS THAT UNGODLY NOISE?
OH, I'M SORRY
HHMMMM, CAN YOU TURN IT DOWN?
ERM, NOT REALLY.
FFNNGGRRHH
KEEP IT DOWN!!
SORRY

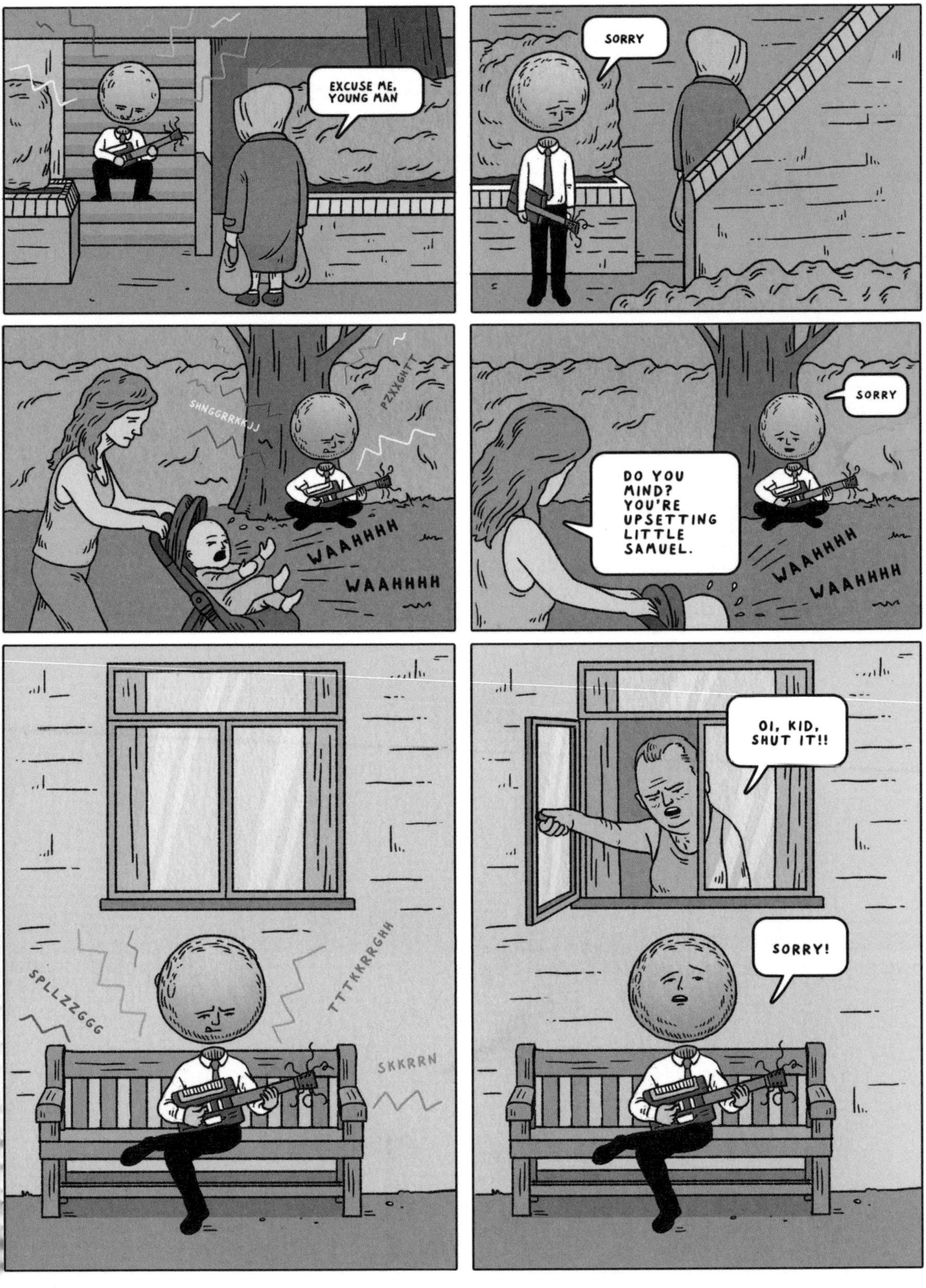

EXCUSE ME, YOUNG MAN
SORRY
SHNGGRRRKKJJ
PZXXGHTT
WAAHHHH
WAAHHHH
SORRY
DO YOU MIND? YOU'RE UPSETTING LITTLE SAMUEL.
WAAHHHH
WAAHHHH
SPLLZZGGG
TTTKKRRGHH
SKKRRN
OI, KID, SHUT IT!!
SORRY!

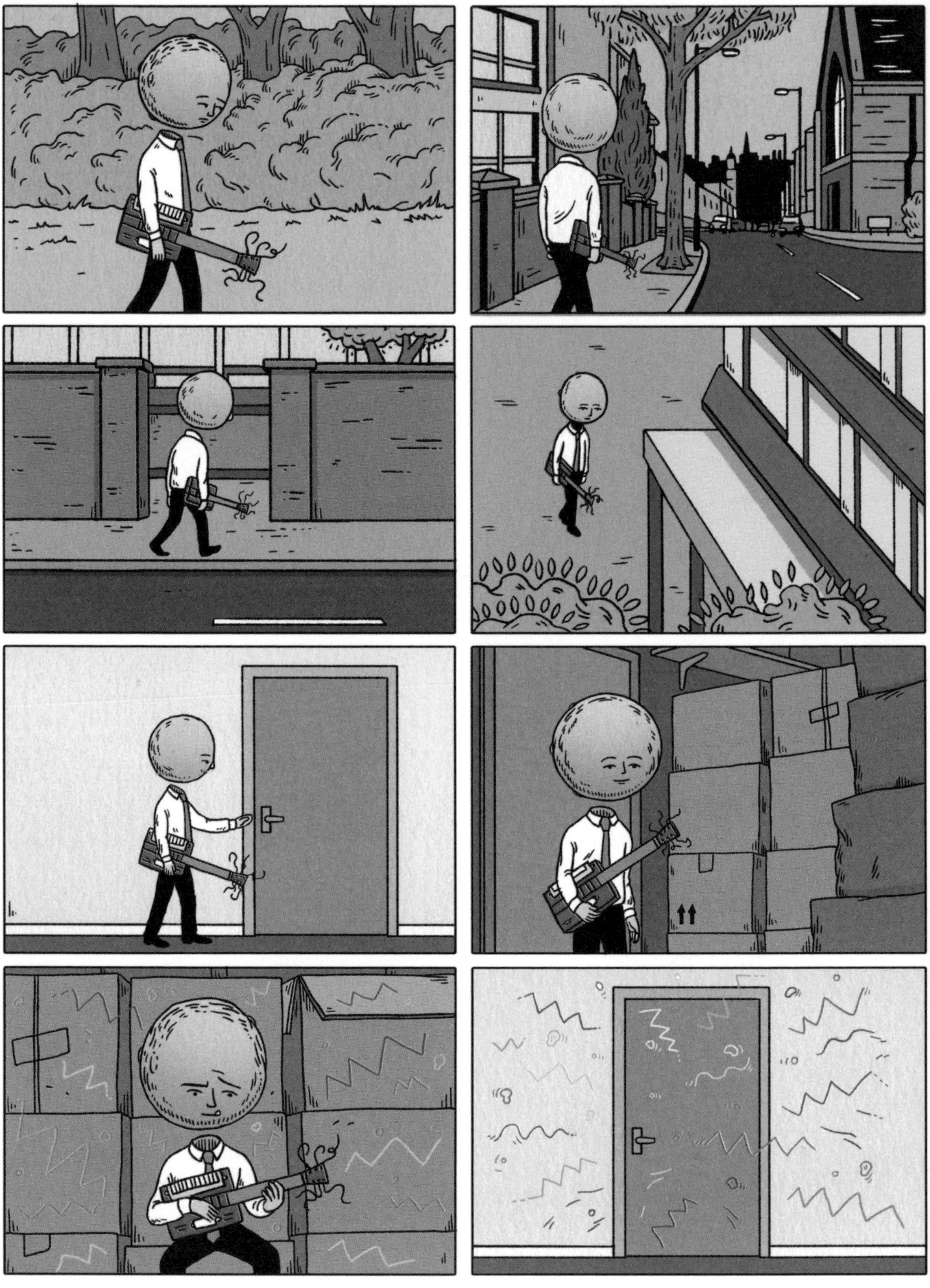

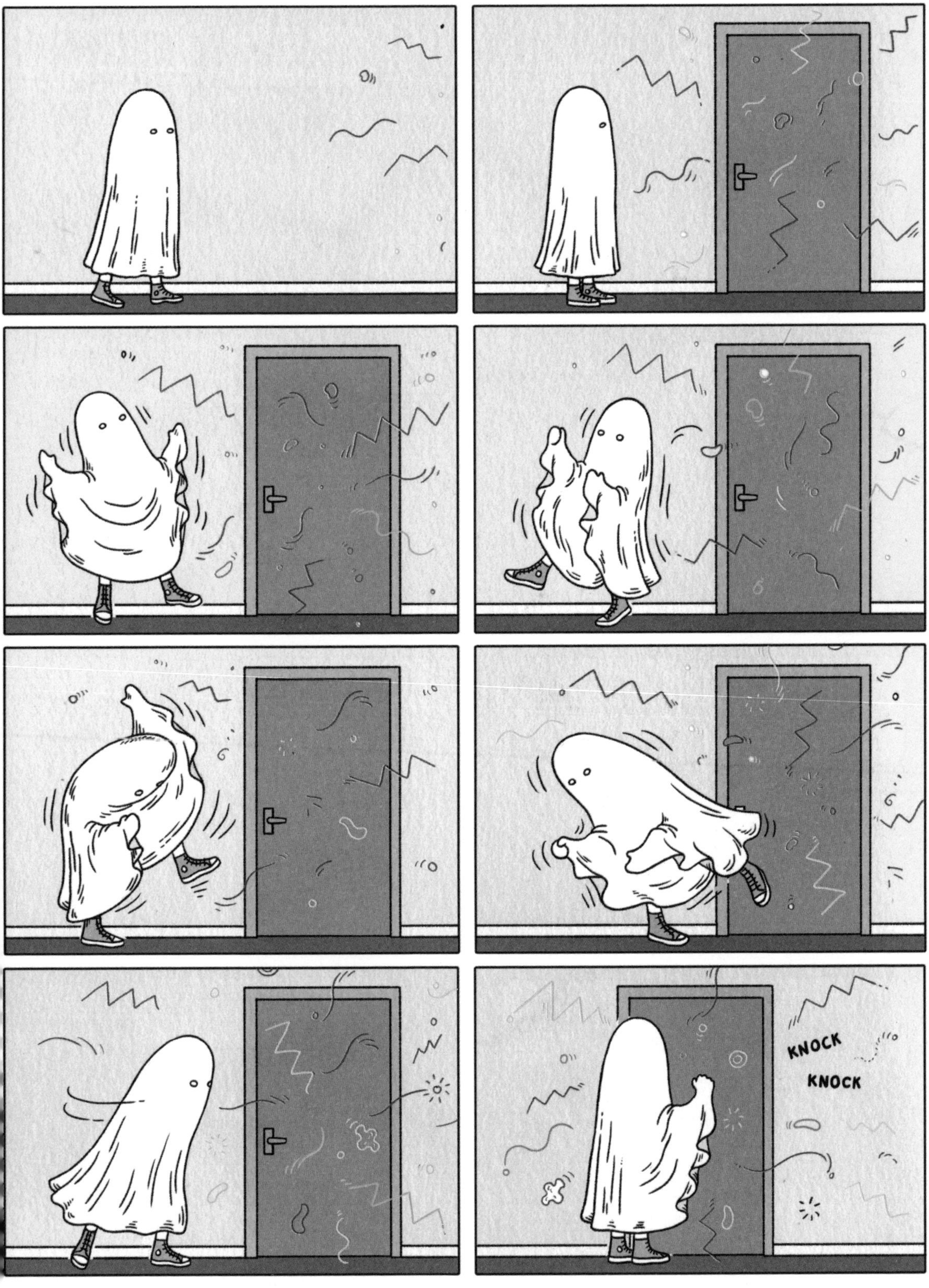
KNOCK
KNOCK

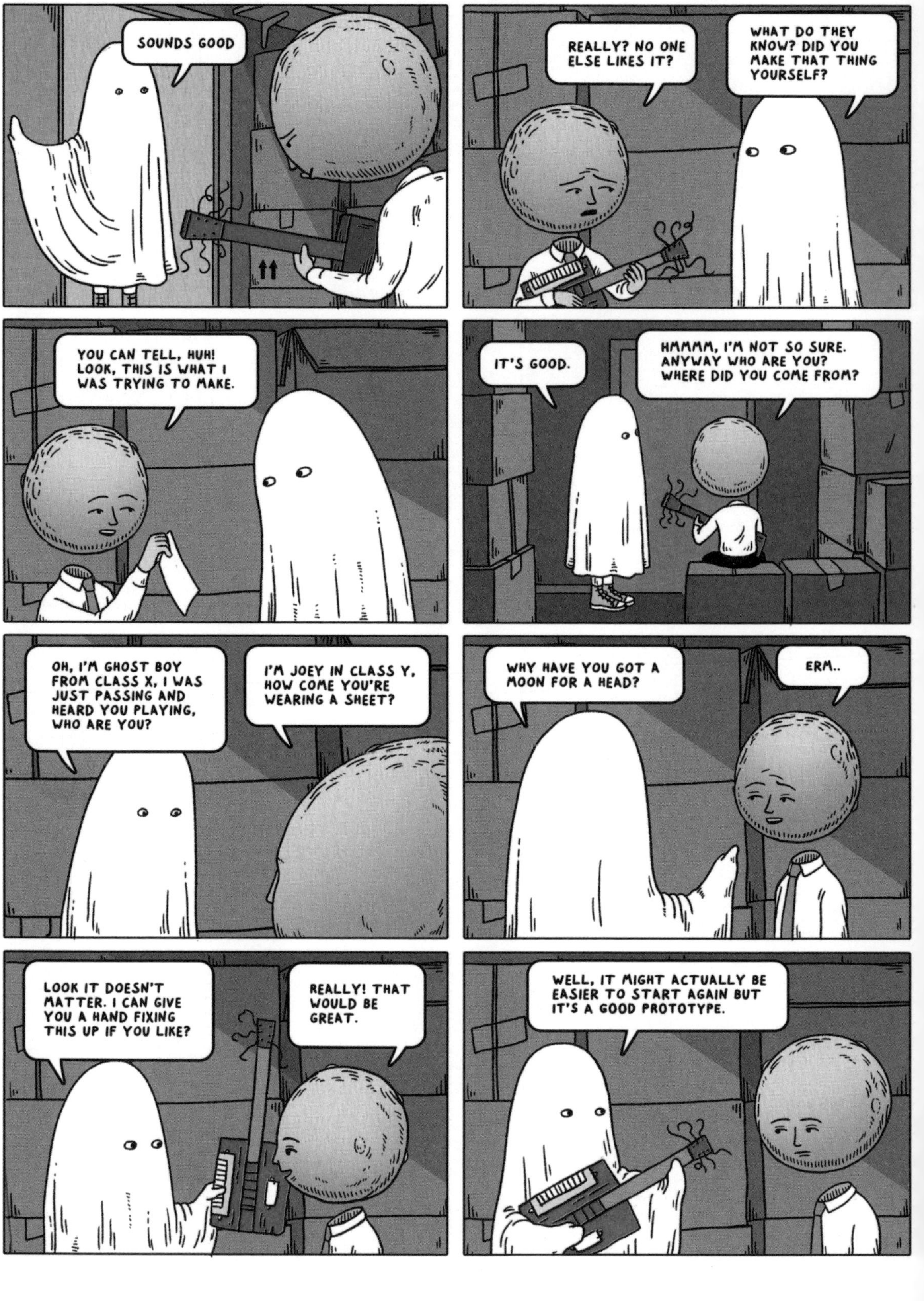
SOUNDS GOOD
REALLY? NO ONE ELSE LIKES IT?
WHAT DO THEY KNOW? DID YOU MAKE THAT THING YOURSELF?
YOU CAN TELL, HUH! LOOK, THIS IS WHAT I WAS TRYING TO MAKE.
IT'S GOOD.
HMMMM, I'M NOT SO SURE. ANYWAY WHO ARE YOU? WHERE DID YOU COME FROM?
OH, I'M GHOST BOY FROM CLASS X, I WAS JUST PASSING AND HEARD YOU PLAYING, WHO ARE YOU?
I'M JOEY IN CLASS Y, HOW COME YOU'RE WEARING A SHEET?
WHY HAVE YOU GOT A MOON FOR A HEAD?
ERM..
LOOK IT DOESN'T MATTER. I CAN GIVE YOU A HAND FIXING THIS UP IF YOU LIKE?
REALLY! THAT WOULD BE GREAT.
WELL, IT MIGHT ACTUALLY BE EASIER TO START AGAIN BUT IT'S A GOOD PROTOTYPE.

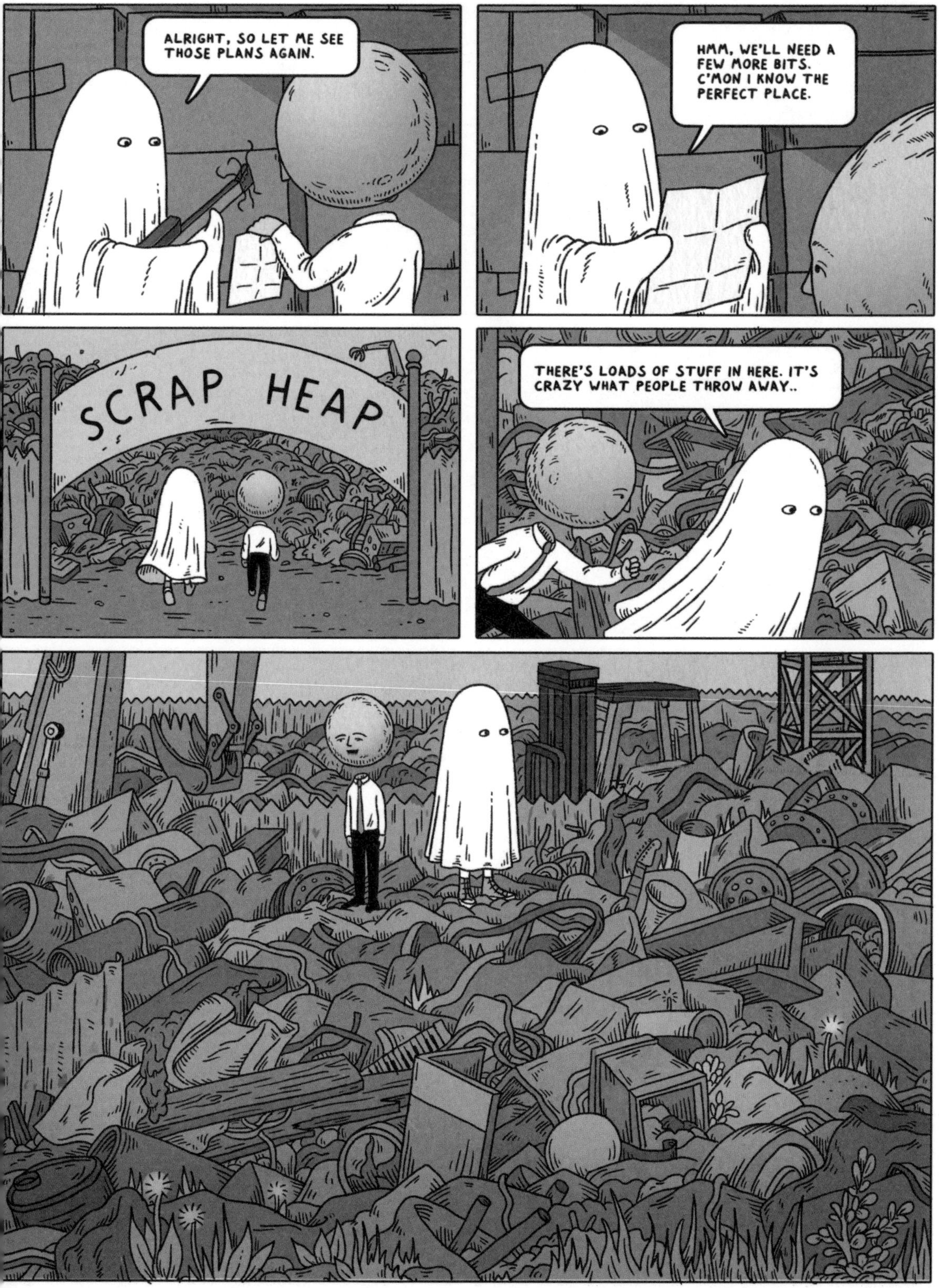
ALRIGHT, SO LET ME SEE THOSE PLANS AGAIN.
HMM, WE'LL NEED A FEW MORE BITS. C'MON I KNOW THE PERFECT PLACE.
SCRAP HEAP
THERE'S LOADS OF STUFF IN HERE. IT'S CRAZY WHAT PEOPLE THROW AWAY..

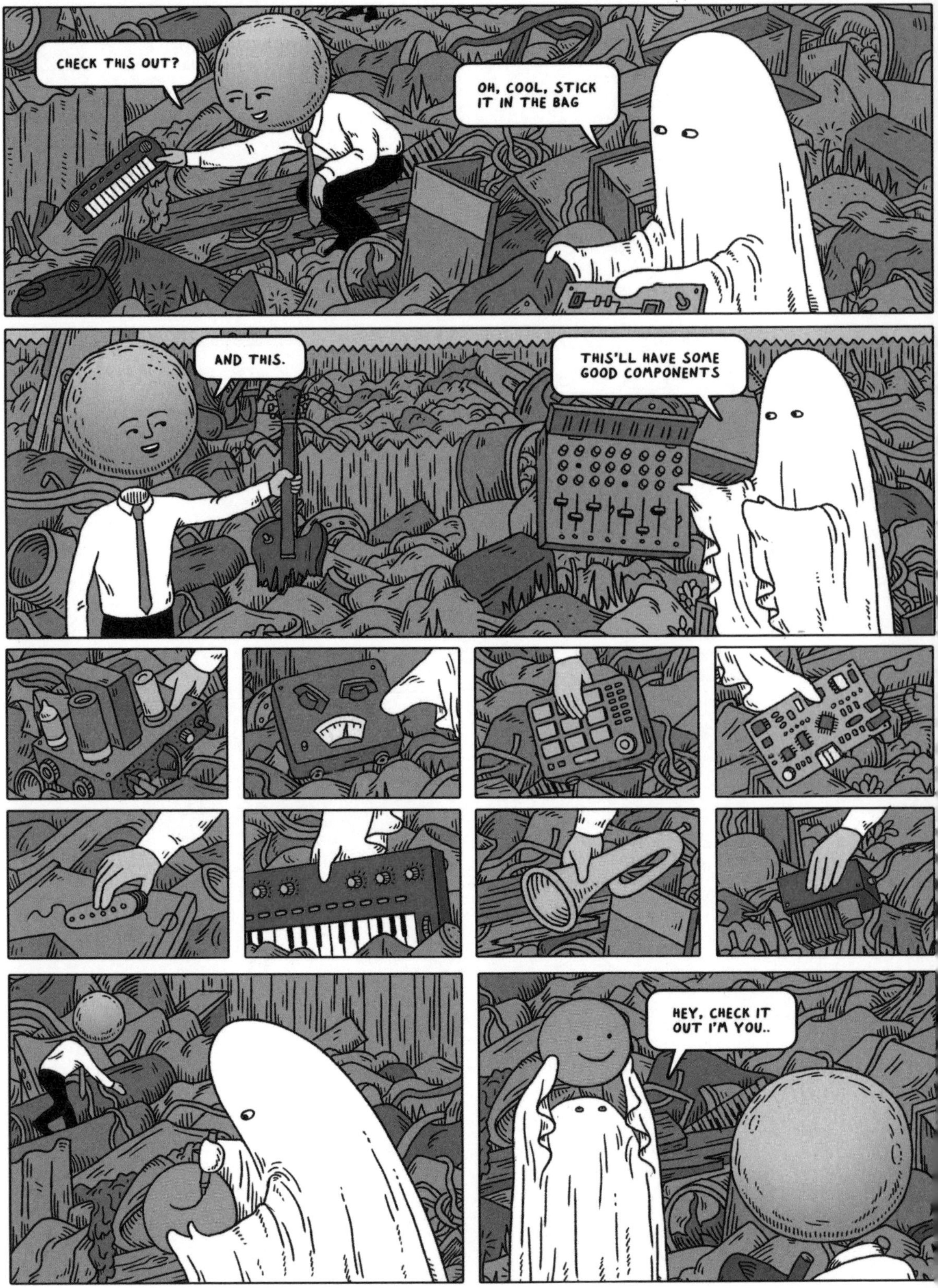
CHECK THIS OUT?
OH, COOL, STICK IT IN THE BAG
AND THIS.
THIS'LL HAVE SOME GOOD COMPONENTS
HEY, CHECK IT OUT I'M YOU..

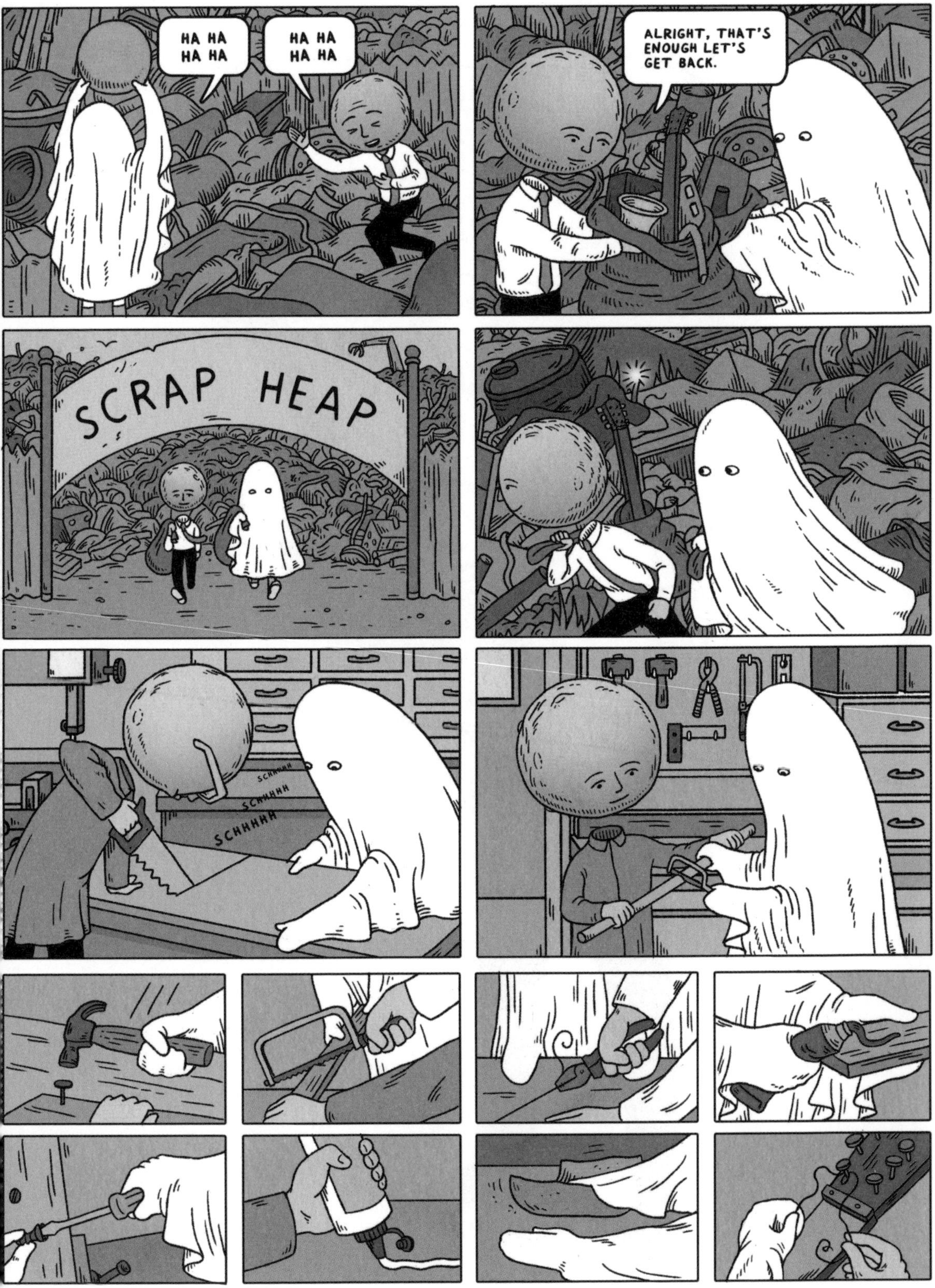
HA HA
HA HA
HA HA
HA HA
ALRIGHT, THAT'S ENOUGH LET'S GET BACK.
SCRAP HEAP
SCHHHHH
SCHHHHH
SCHHHHH

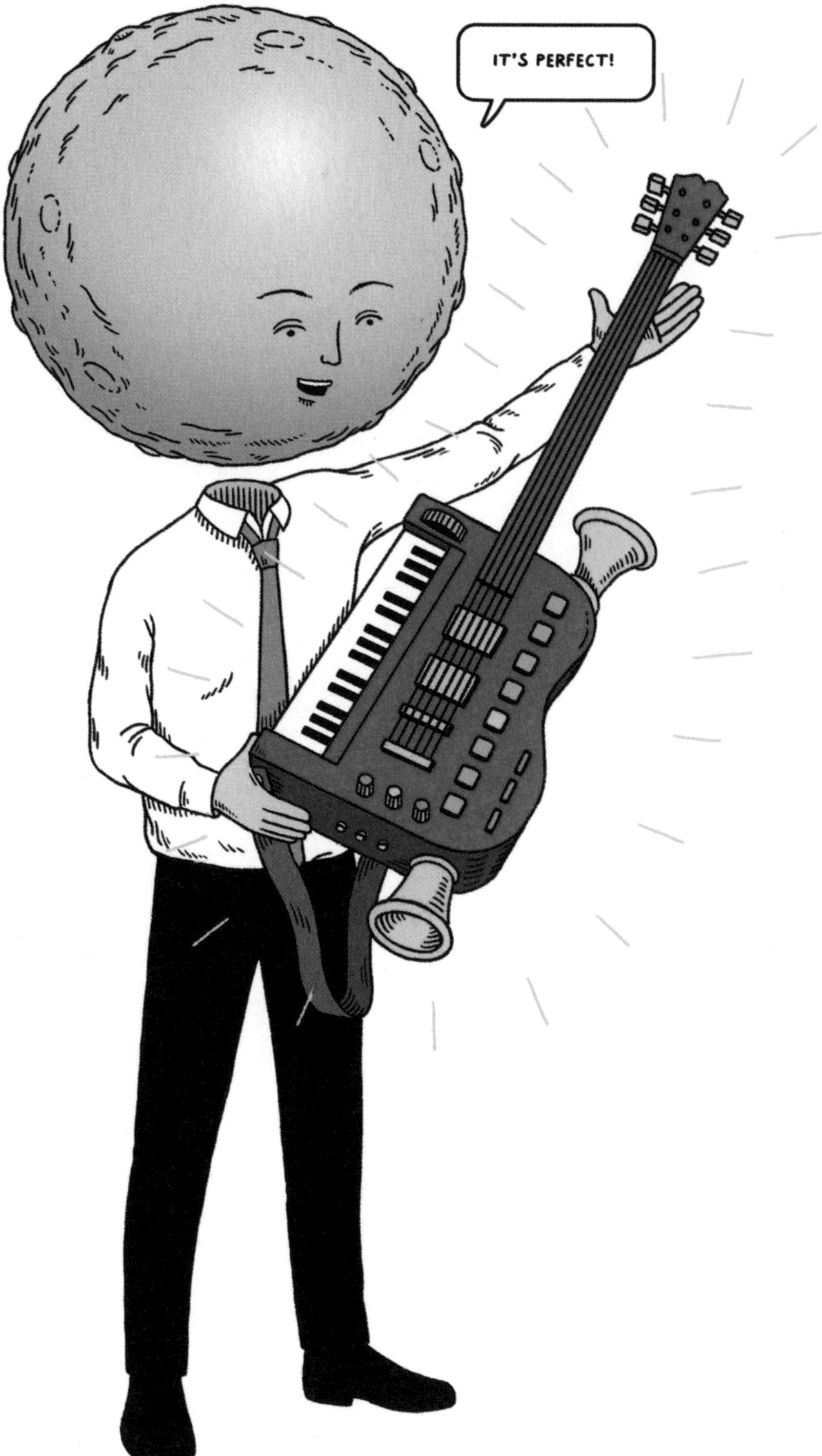
IT'S PERFECT!

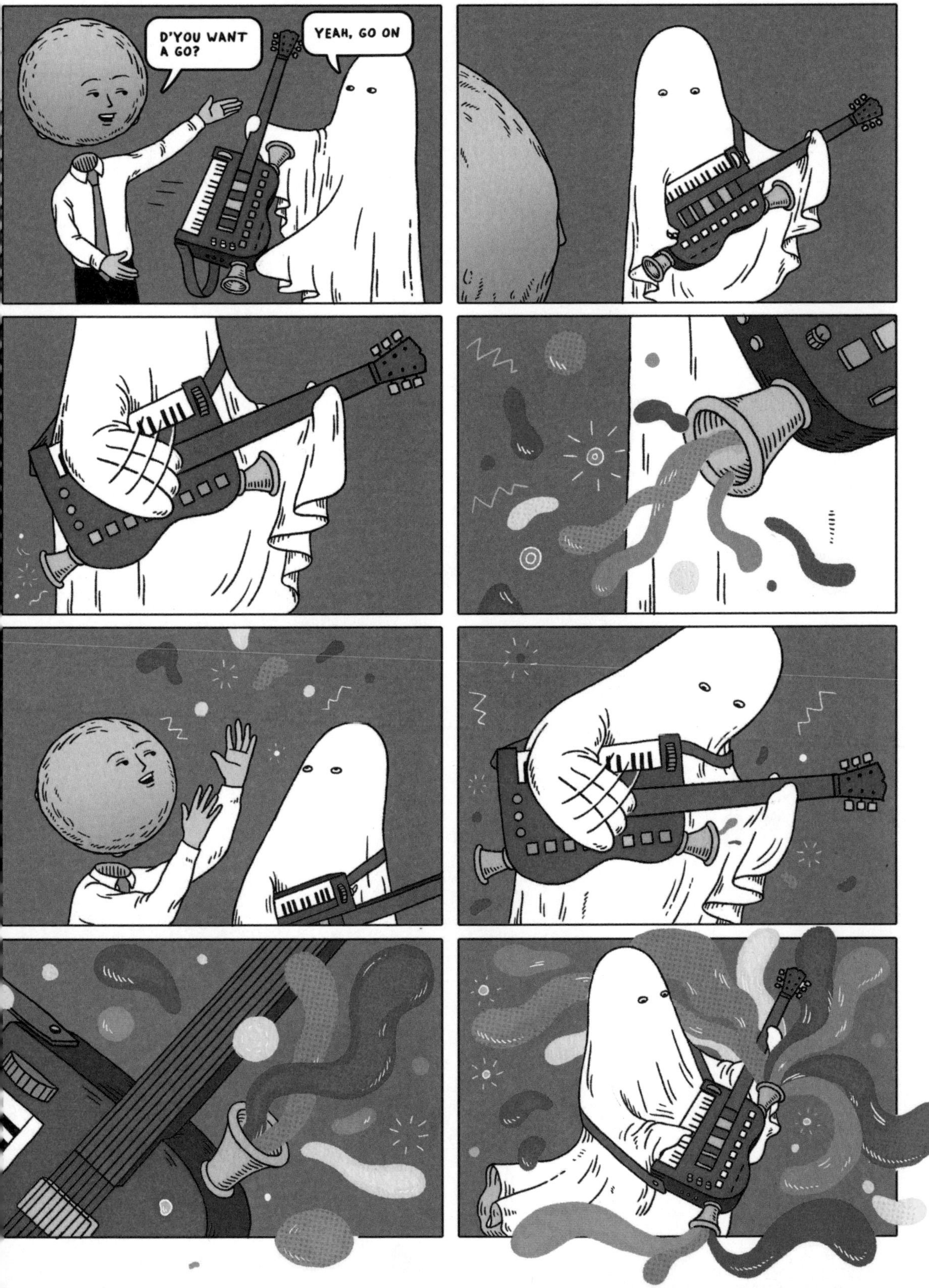
D'YOU WANT A GO?
YEAH, GO ON

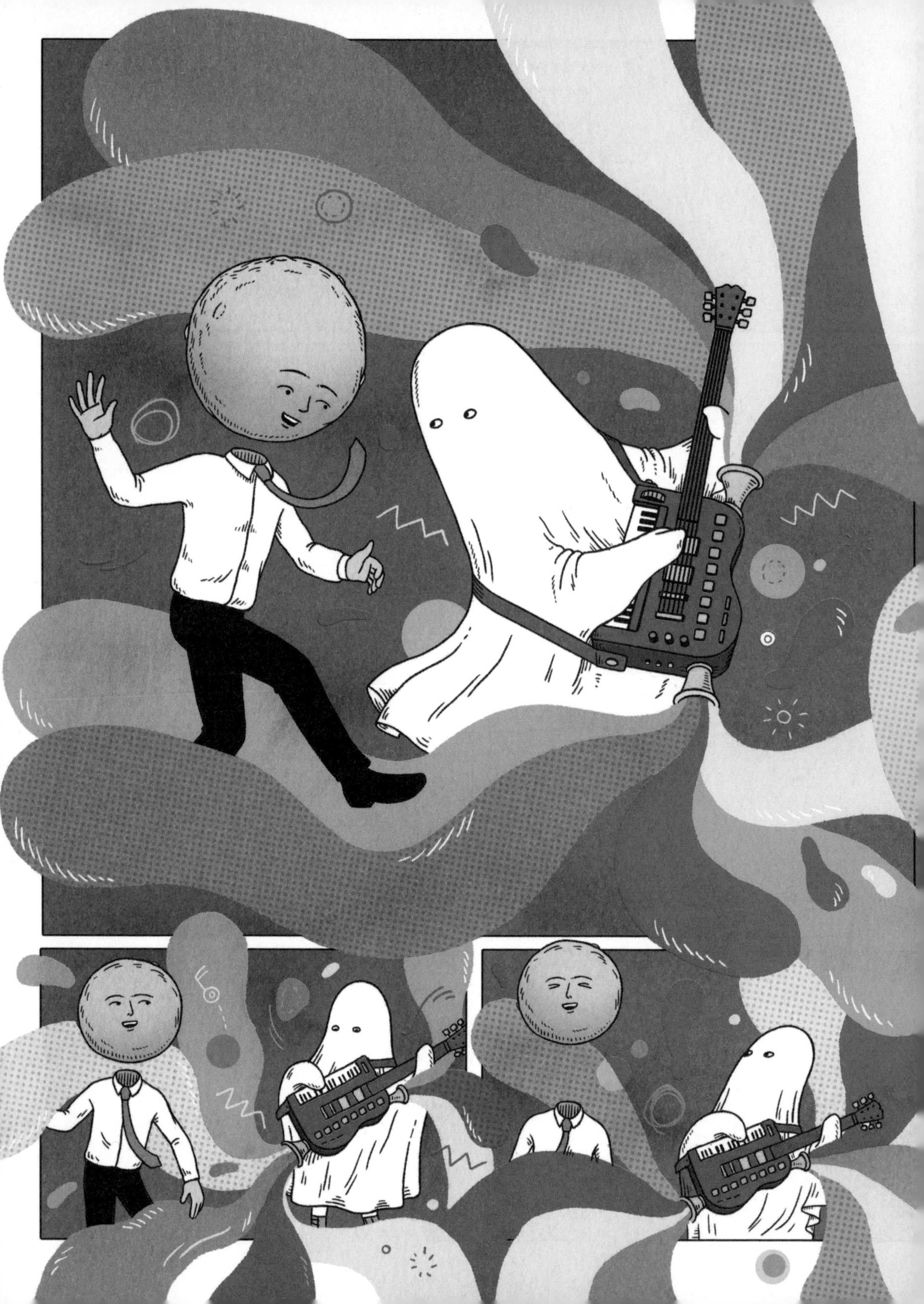

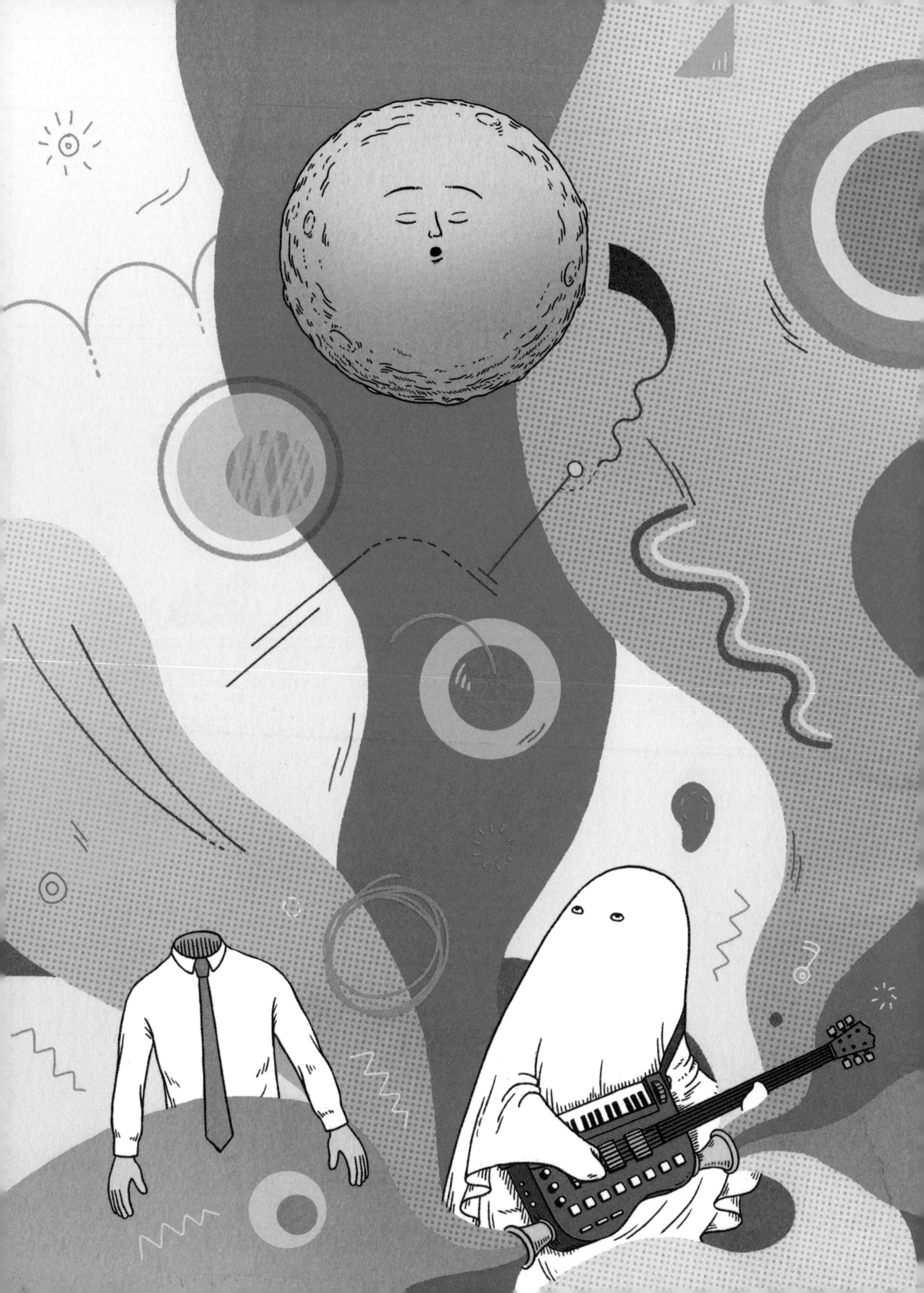

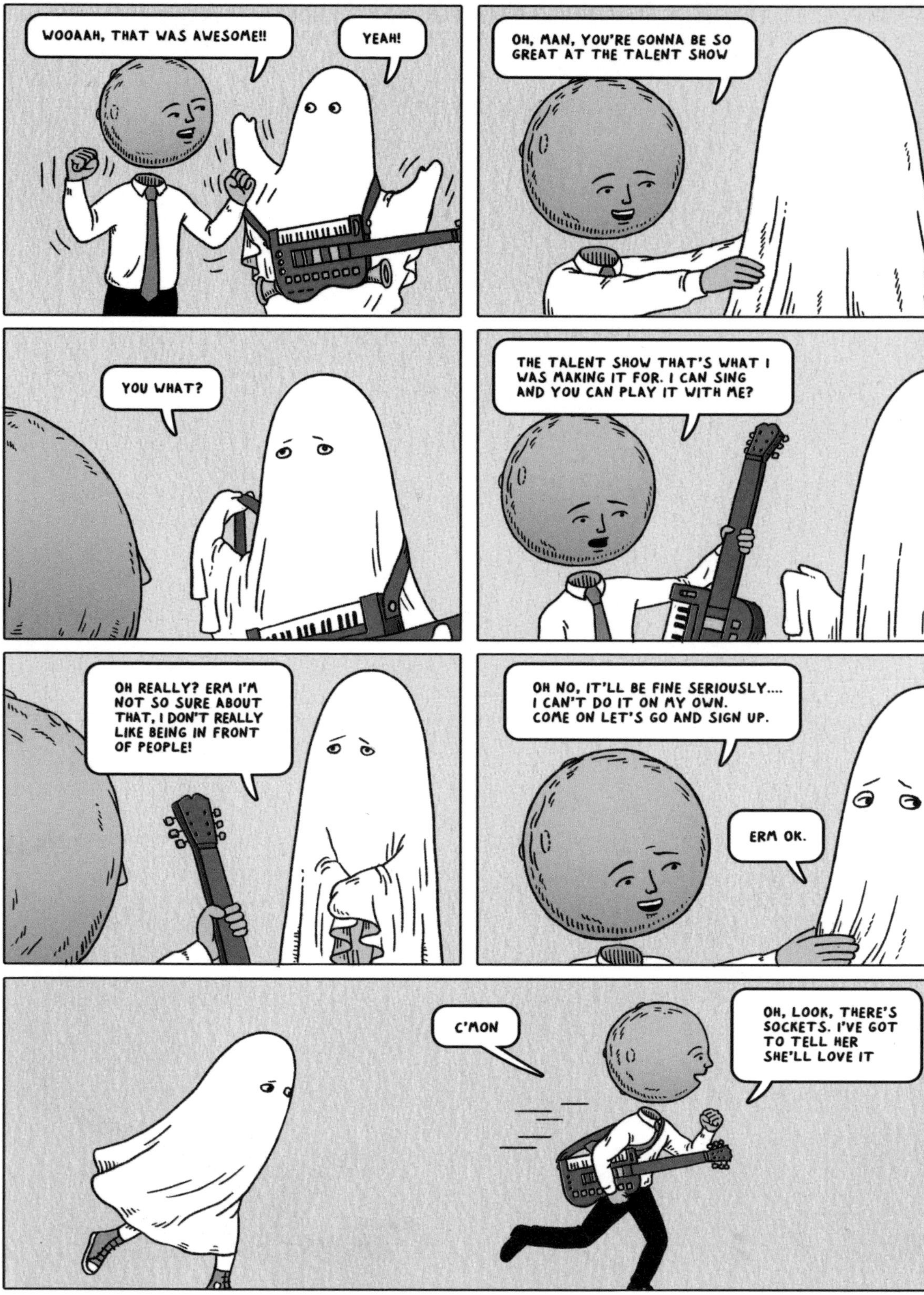
WOOAAH, THAT WAS AWESOME!!
YEAH!
OH, MAN, YOU'RE GONNA BE SO GREAT AT THE TALENT SHOW
YOU WHAT?
THE TALENT SHOW THAT'S WHAT I WAS MAKING IT FOR. I CAN SING AND YOU CAN PLAY IT WITH ME?
OH REALLY? ERM I'M NOT SO SURE ABOUT THAT, I DON'T REALLY LIKE BEING IN FRONT OF PEOPLE!
OH NO, IT'LL BE FINE SERIOUSLY.... I CAN'T DO IT ON MY OWN. COME ON LET'S GO AND SIGN UP.
ERM OK.
C'MON
OH, LOOK, THERE'S SOCKETS. I'VE GOT TO TELL HER SHE'LL LOVE IT

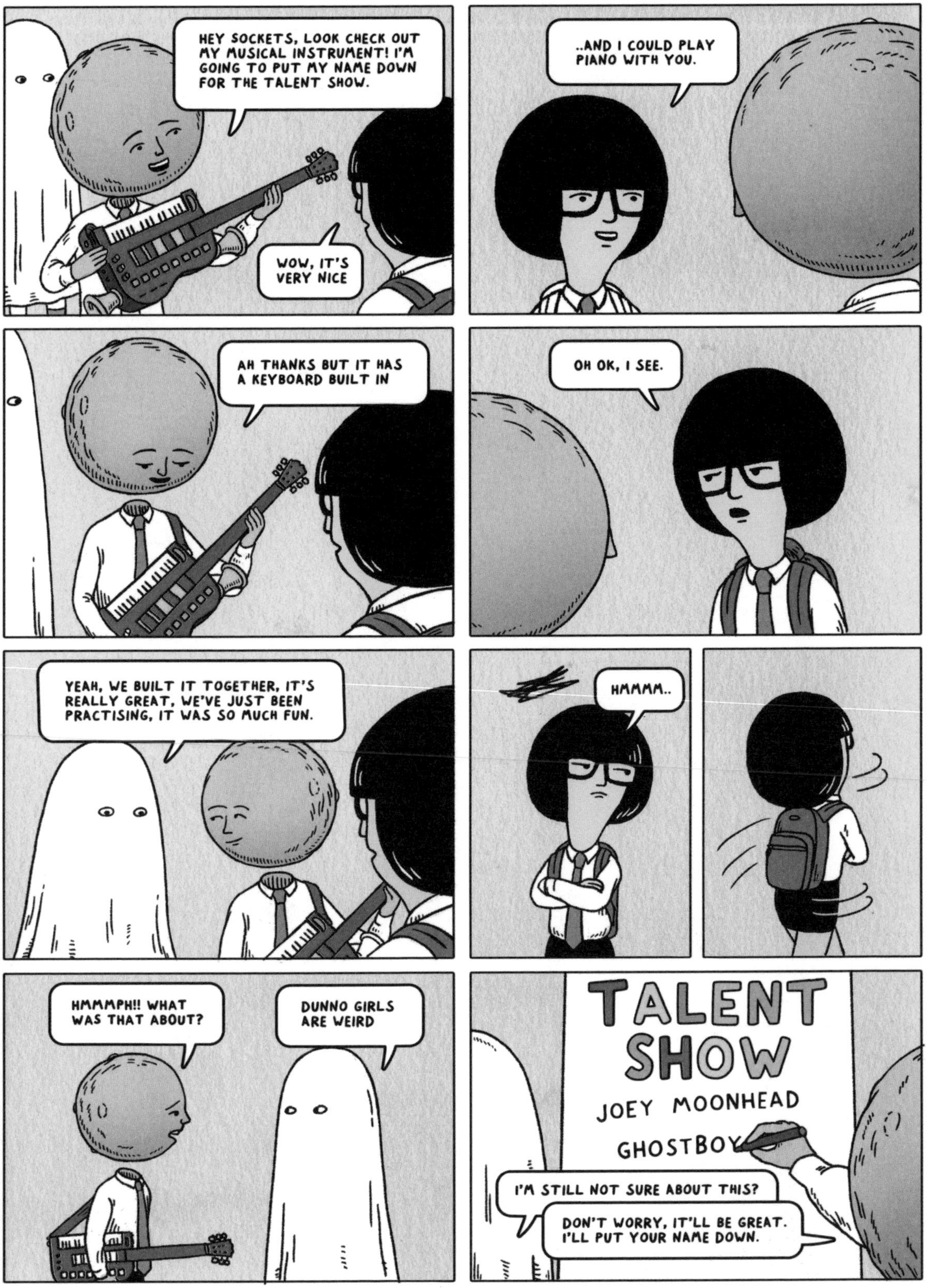
HEY SOCKETS, LOOK CHECK OUT MY MUSICAL INSTRUMENT! I'M GOING TO PUT MY NAME DOWN FOR THE TALENT SHOW.
WOW, IT'S VERY NICE
..AND I COULD PLAY PIANO WITH YOU.
AH THANKS BUT IT HAS A KEYBOARD BUILT IN
OH OK, I SEE.
YEAH, WE BUILT IT TOGETHER, IT'S REALLY GREAT, WE'VE JUST BEEN PRACTISING, IT WAS SO MUCH FUN.
HMMMM..
HMMMPH!! WHAT WAS THAT ABOUT?
DUNNO GIRLS ARE WEIRD
TALENT SHOW
JOEY MOONHEAD
GHOSTBOY
I'M STILL NOT SURE ABOUT THIS?
DON'T WORRY, IT'LL BE GREAT. I'LL PUT YOUR NAME DOWN.

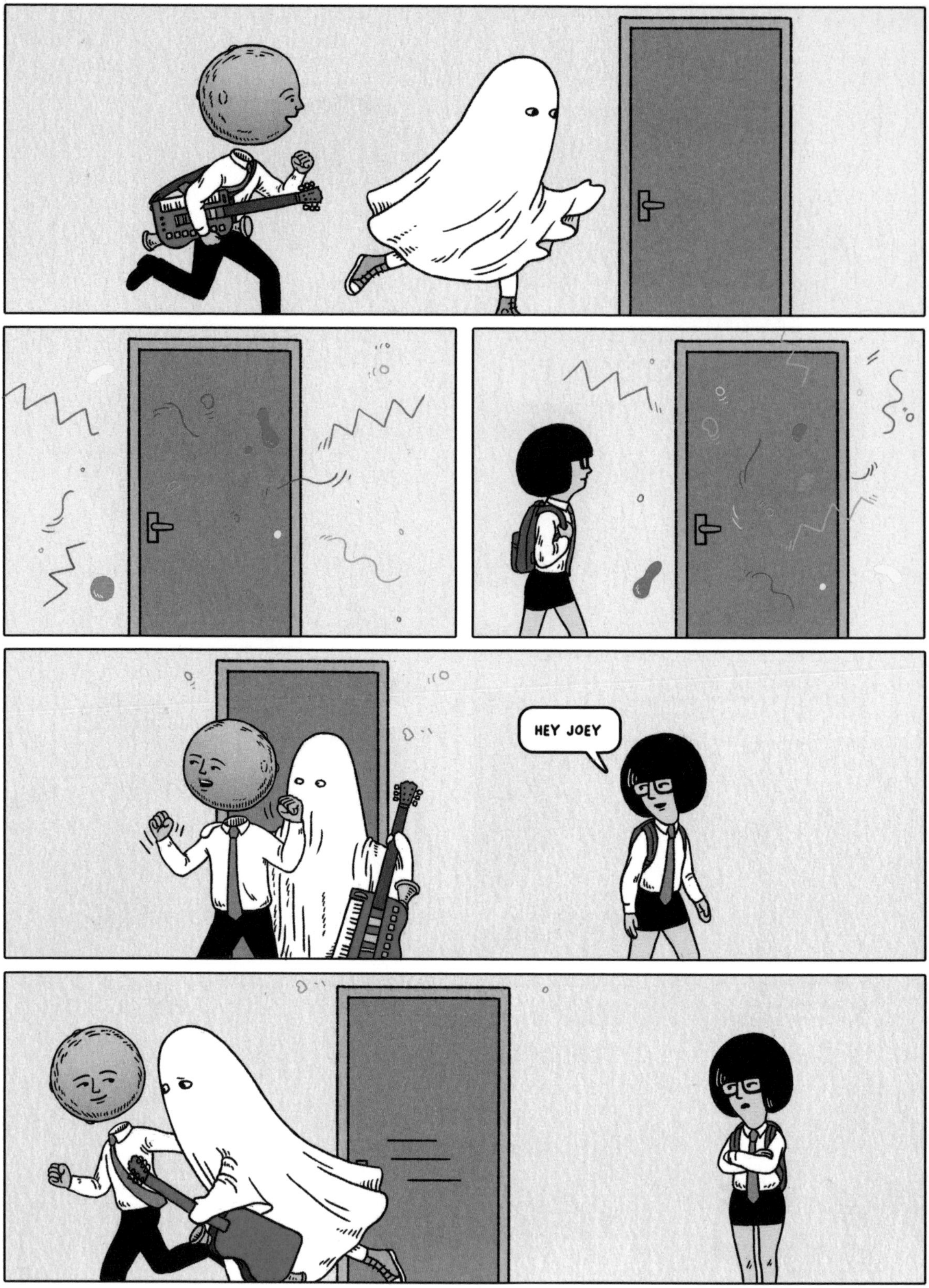
HEY JOEY

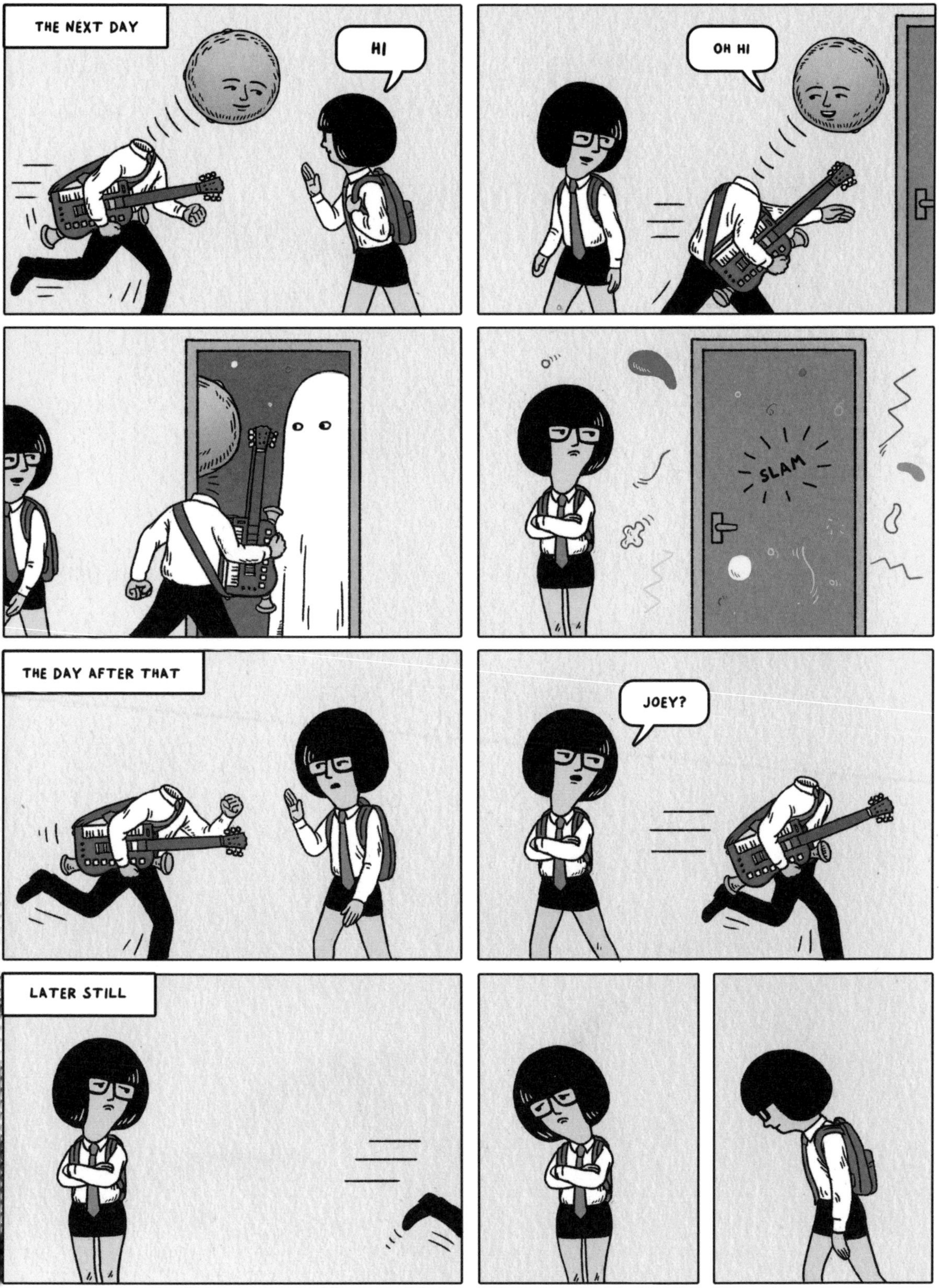
THE NEXT DAY
HI
OH HI
SLAM
THE DAY AFTER THAT
JOEY?
LATER STILL

THE
TALENT
SHOW

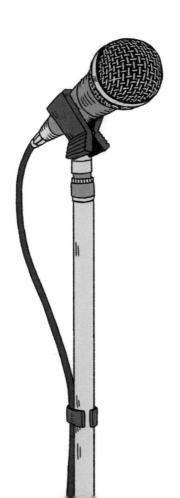

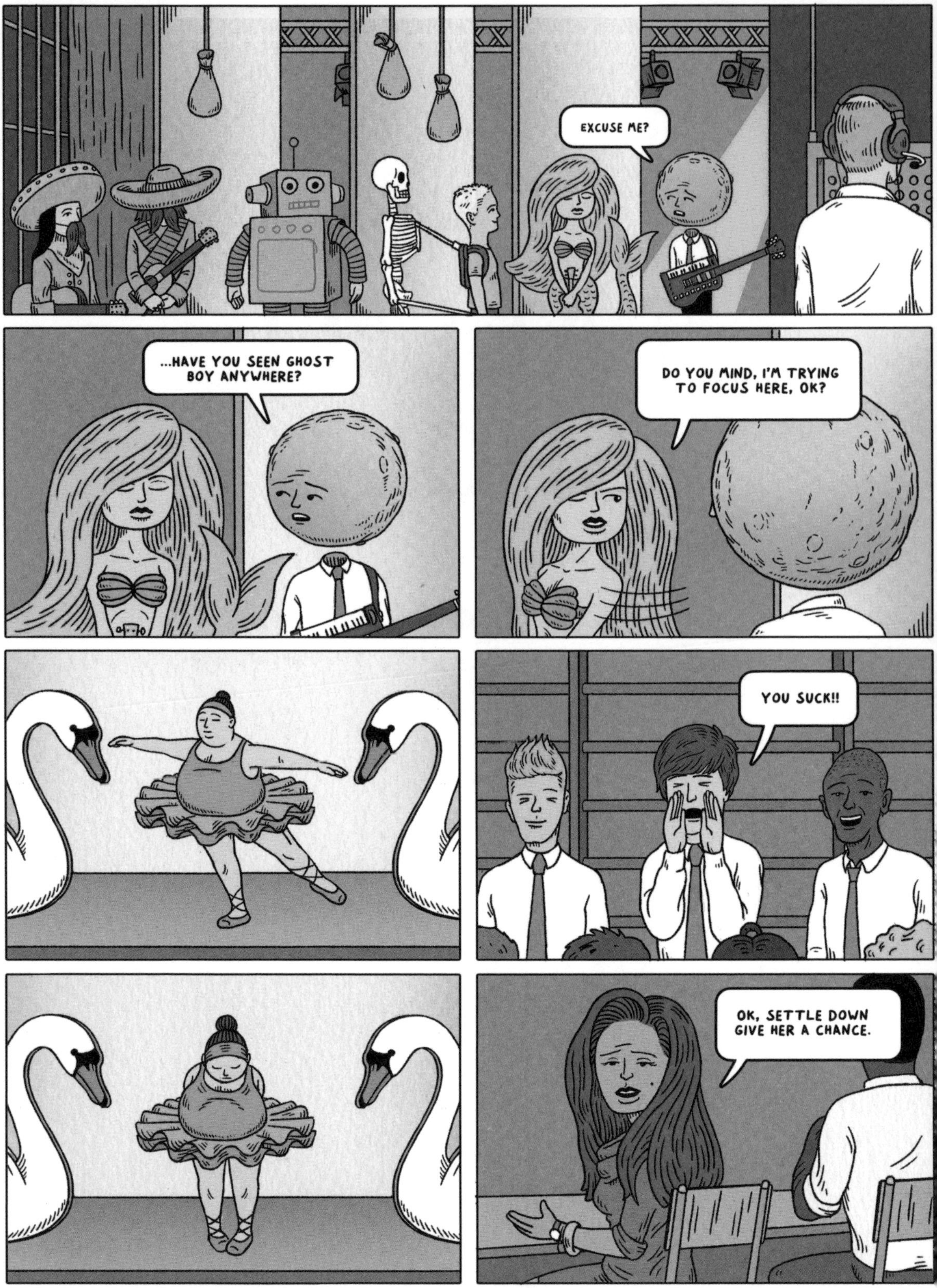
EXCUSE ME?
...HAVE YOU SEEN GHOST BOY ANYWHERE?
DO YOU MIND, I'M TRYING TO FOCUS HERE, OK?
YOU SUCK!!
OK, SETTLE DOWN GIVE HER A CHANCE.

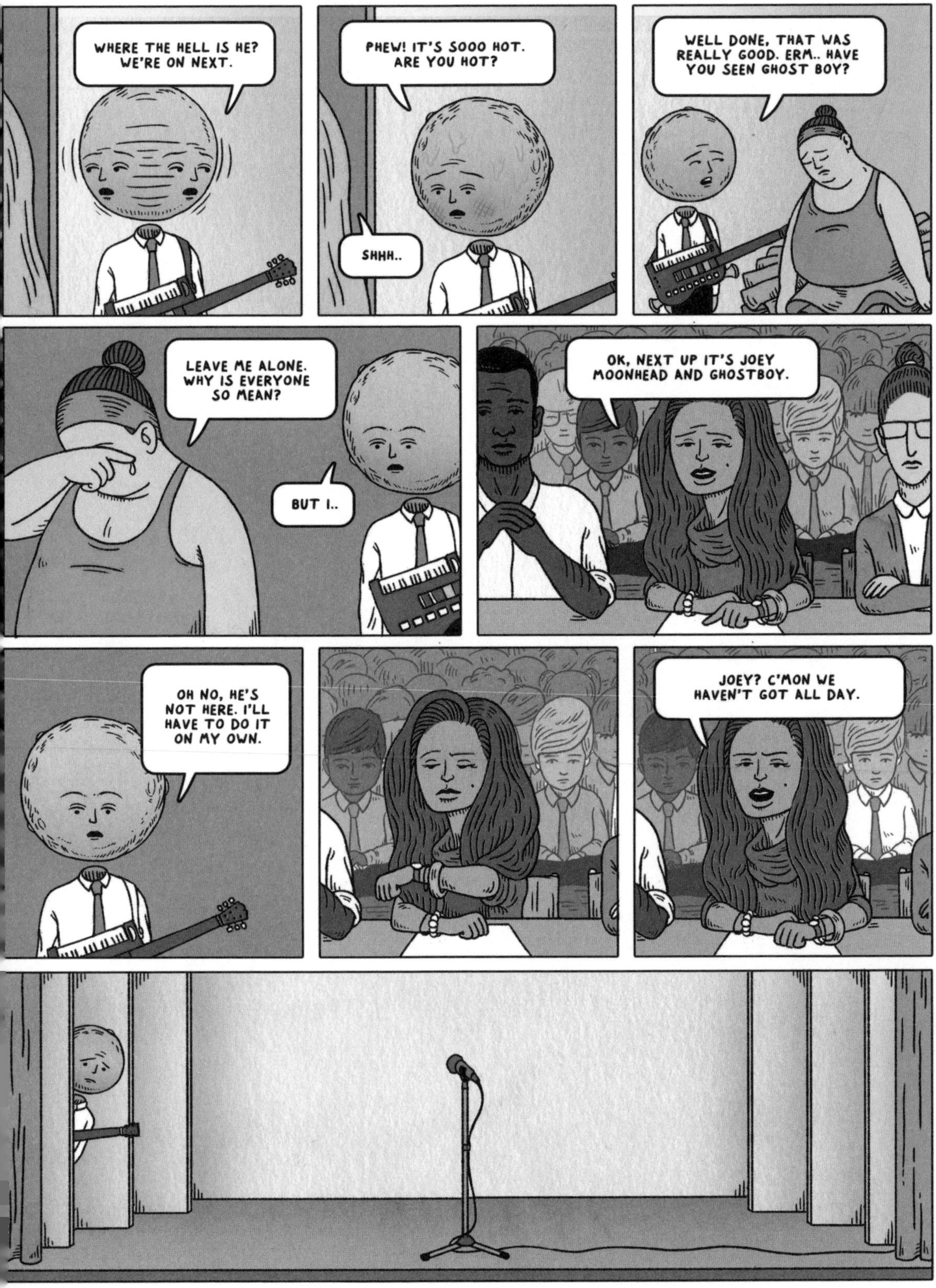
WHERE THE HELL IS HE? WE'RE ON NEXT.
PHEW! IT'S SOOO HOT. ARE YOU HOT?
SHHH..
WELL DONE, THAT WAS REALLY GOOD. ERM.. HAVE YOU SEEN GHOST BOY?
LEAVE ME ALONE. WHY IS EVERYONE SO MEAN?
BUT I..
OK, NEXT UP IT'S JOEY MOONHEAD AND GHOSTBOY.
OH NO, HE'S NOT HERE. I'LL HAVE TO DO IT ON MY OWN.
JOEY? C'MON WE HAVEN'T GOT ALL DAY.

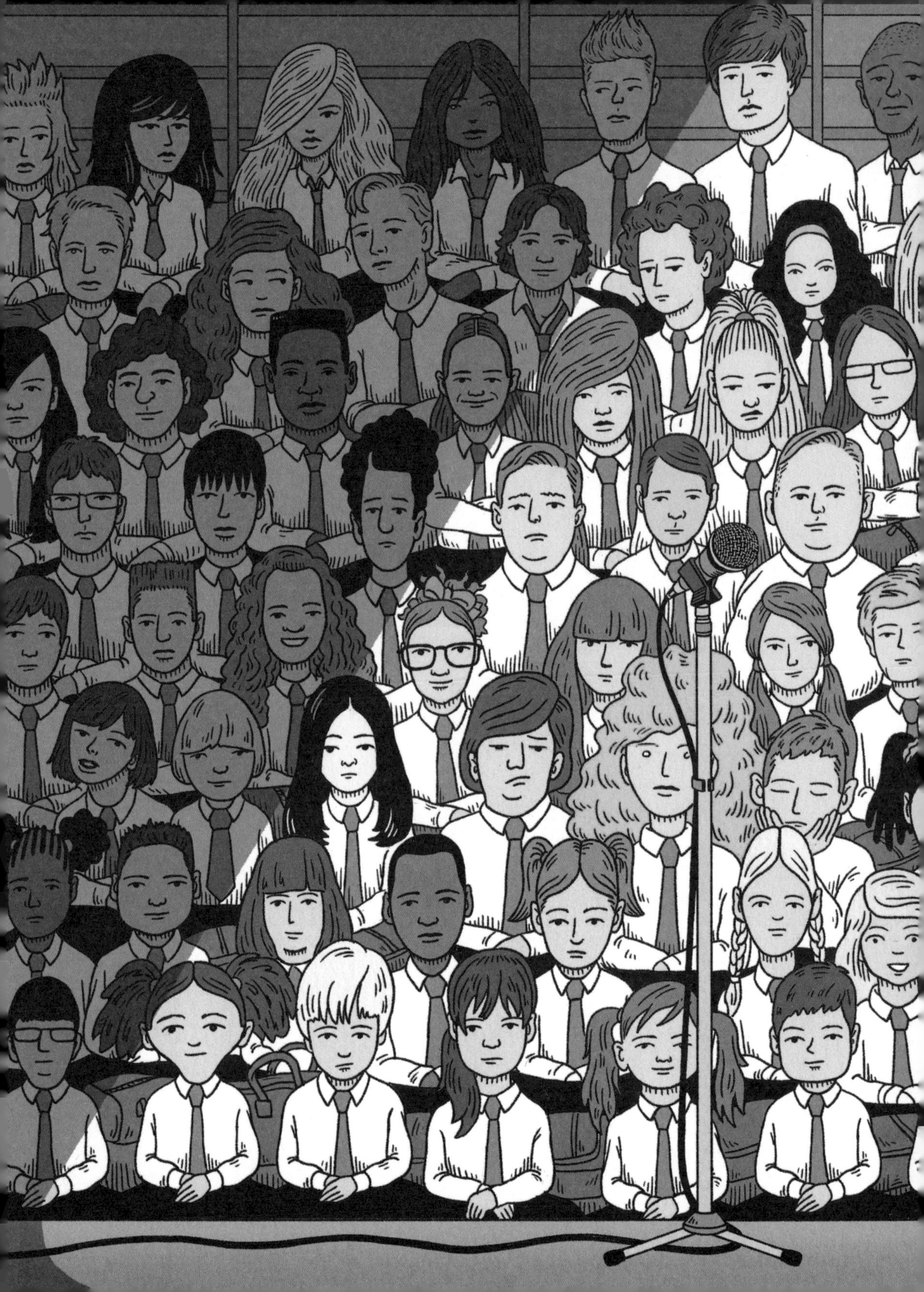

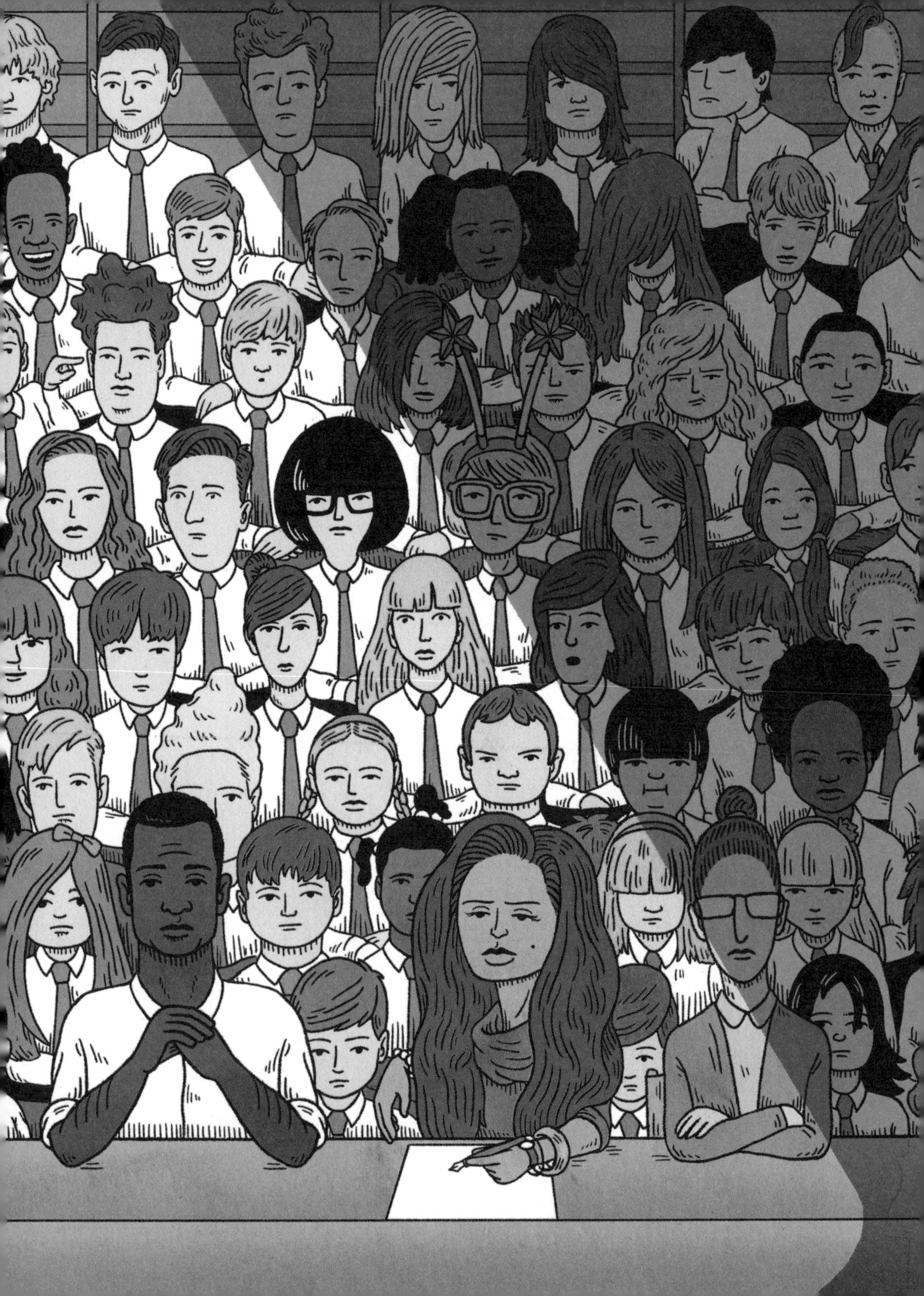

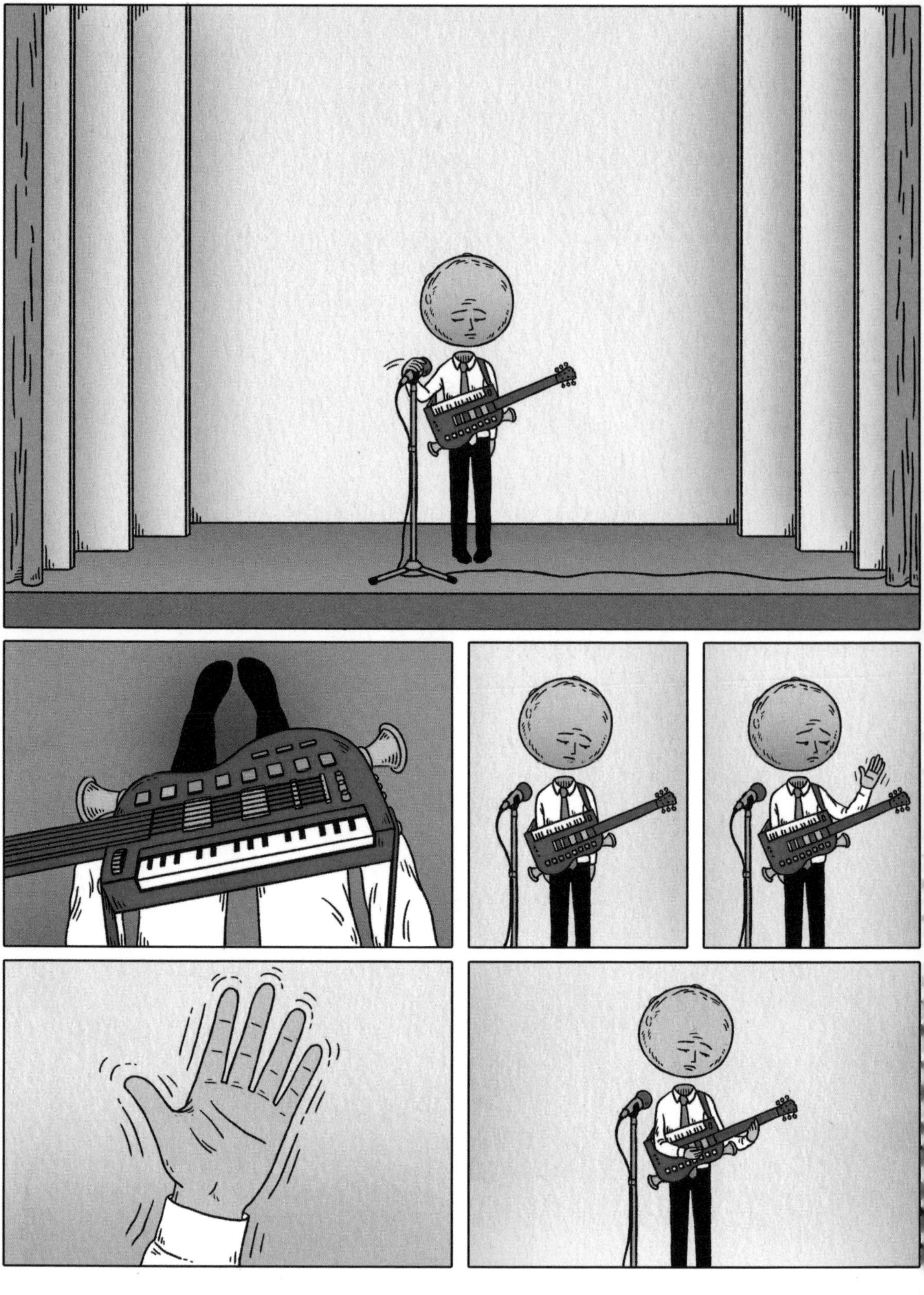

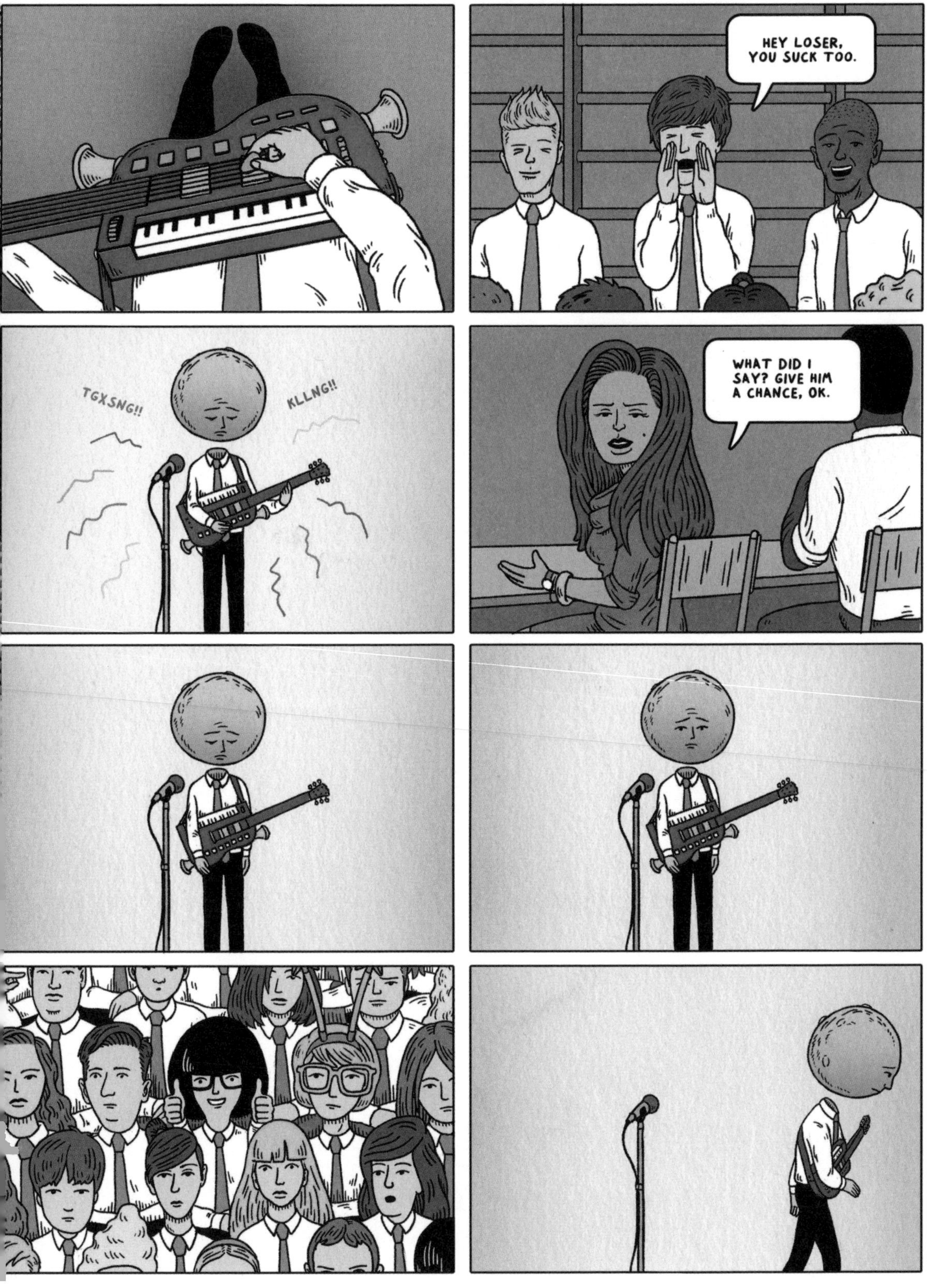
HEY LOSER, YOU SUCK TOO.
TGXSNG!!
KLLNG!!
WHAT DID I SAY? GIVE HIM A CHANCE, OK.

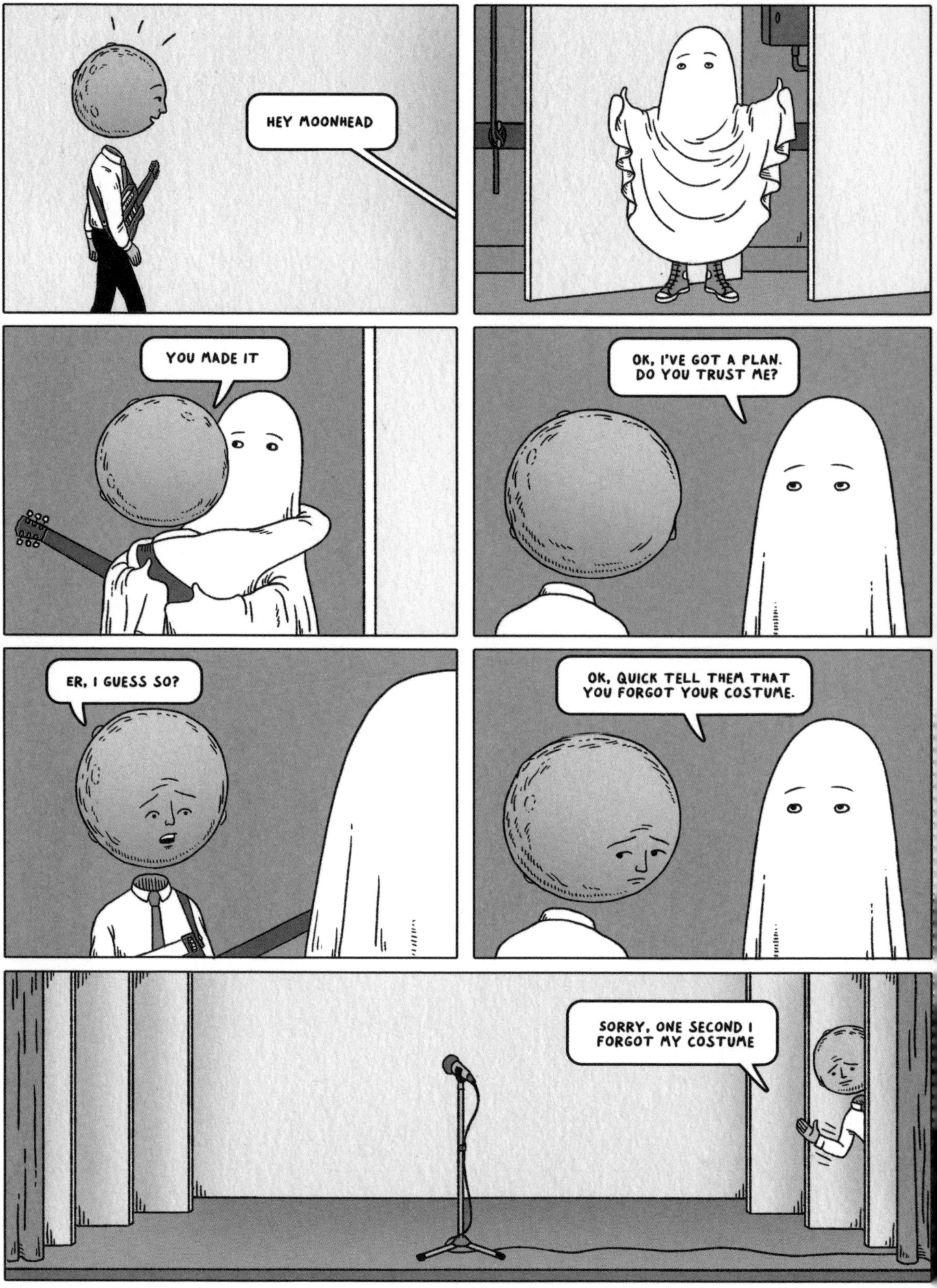
HEY MOONHEAD
YOU MADE IT
OK, I'VE GOT A PLAN. DO YOU TRUST ME?
ER, I GUESS SO?
OK, QUICK TELL THEM THAT YOU FORGOT YOUR COSTUME.
SORRY, ONE SECOND I FORGOT MY COSTUME

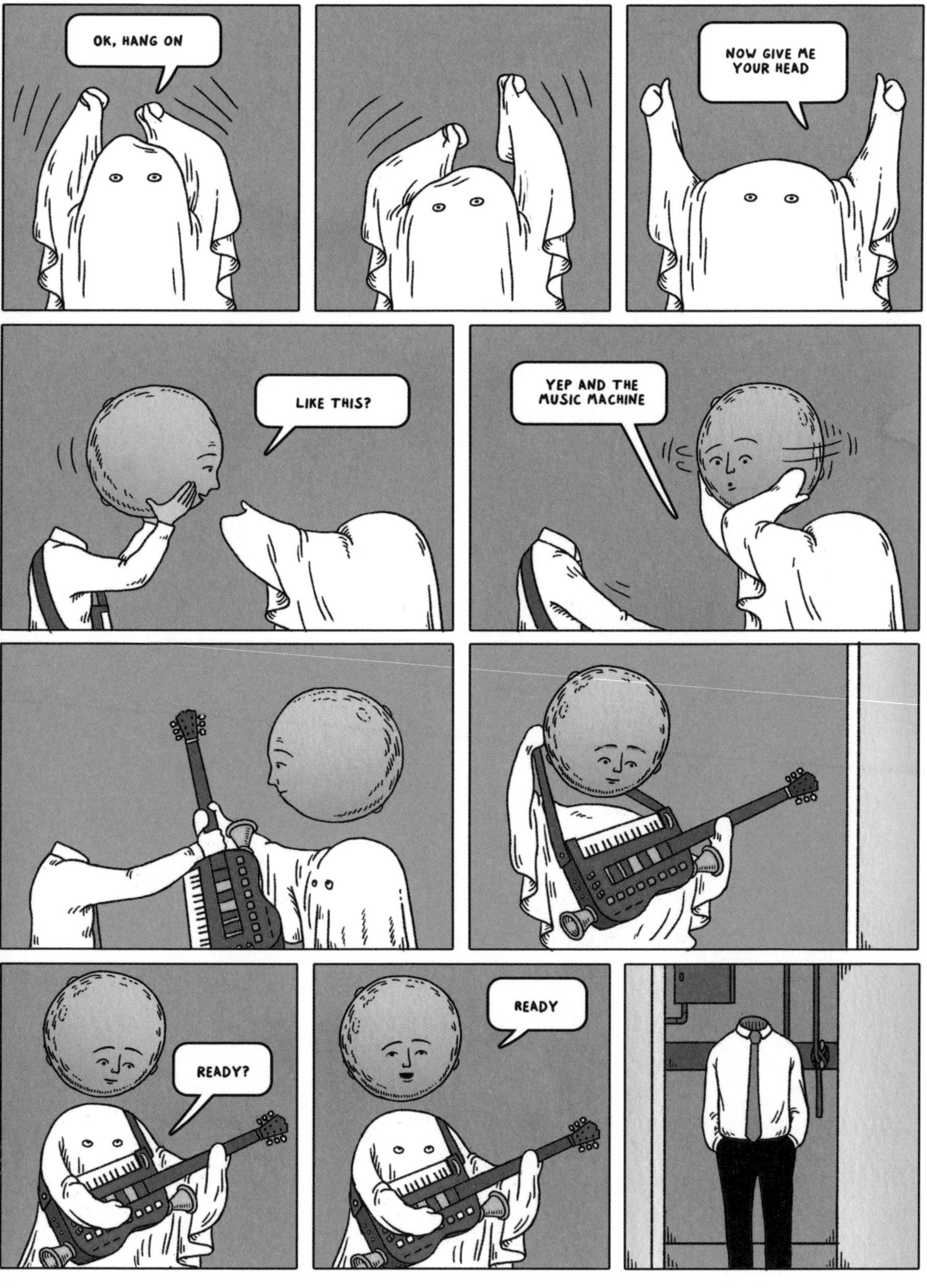
OK, HANG ON
NOW GIVE ME YOUR HEAD
LIKE THIS?
YEP AND THE MUSIC MACHINE
READY?
READY

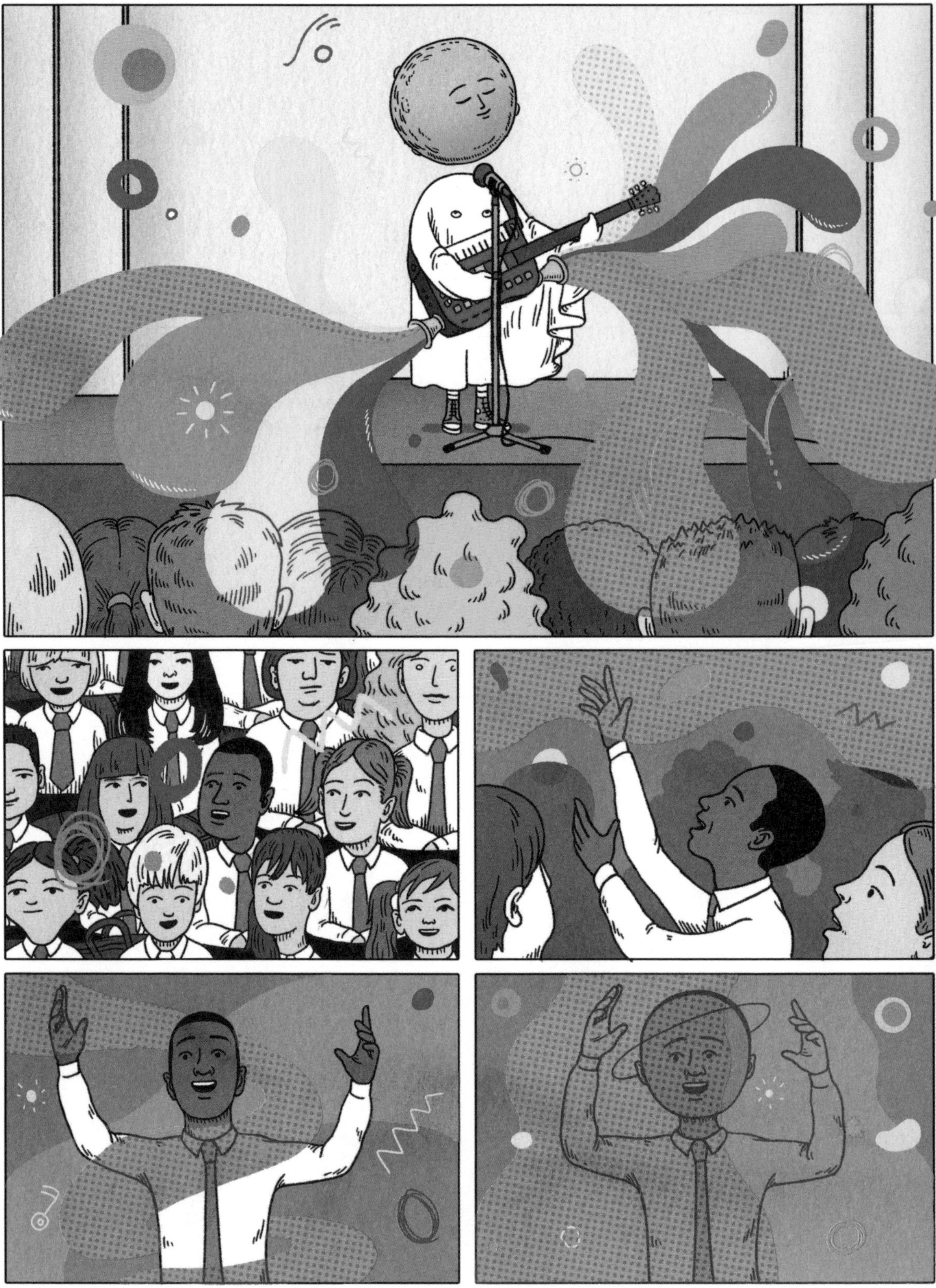

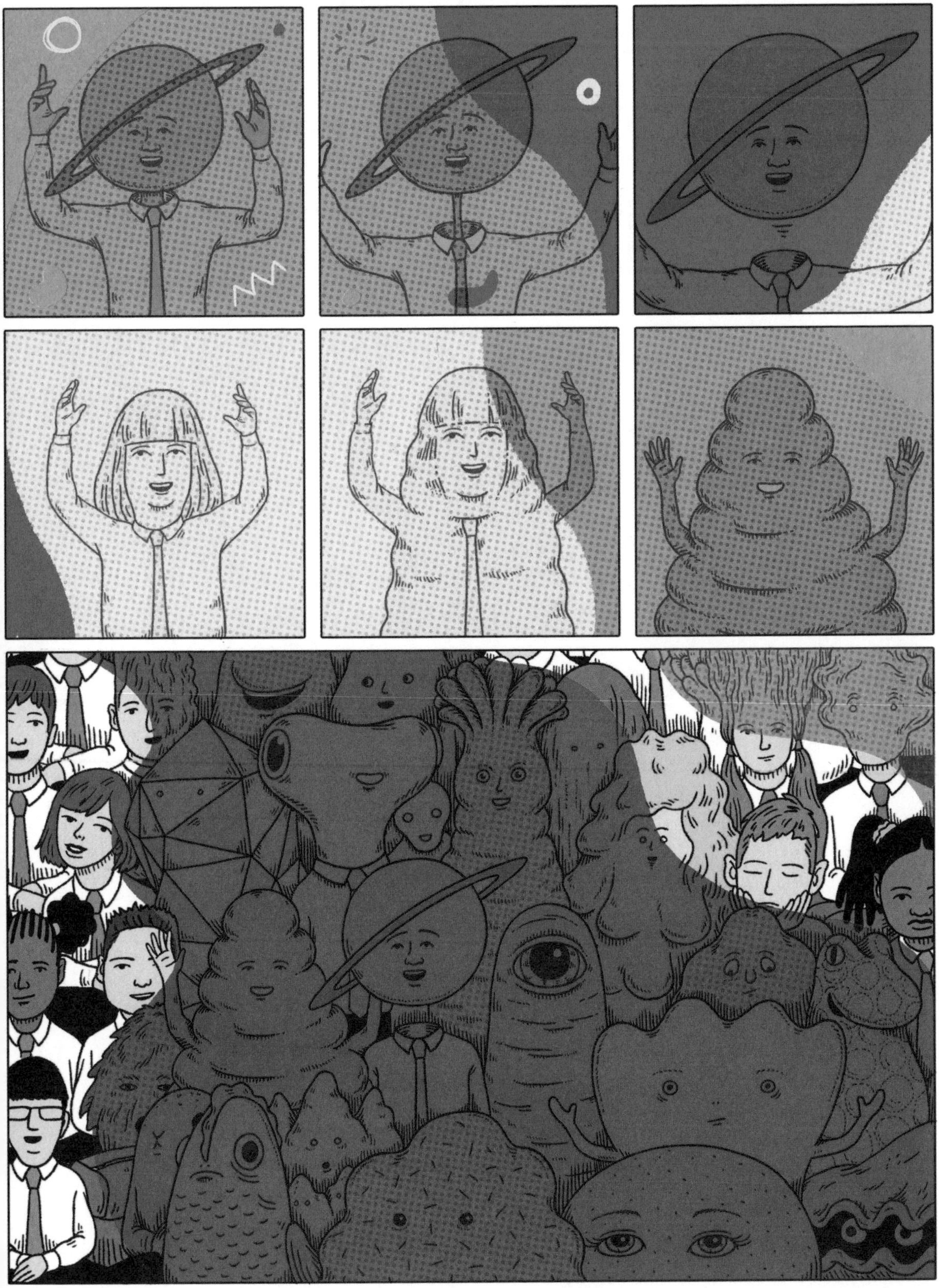

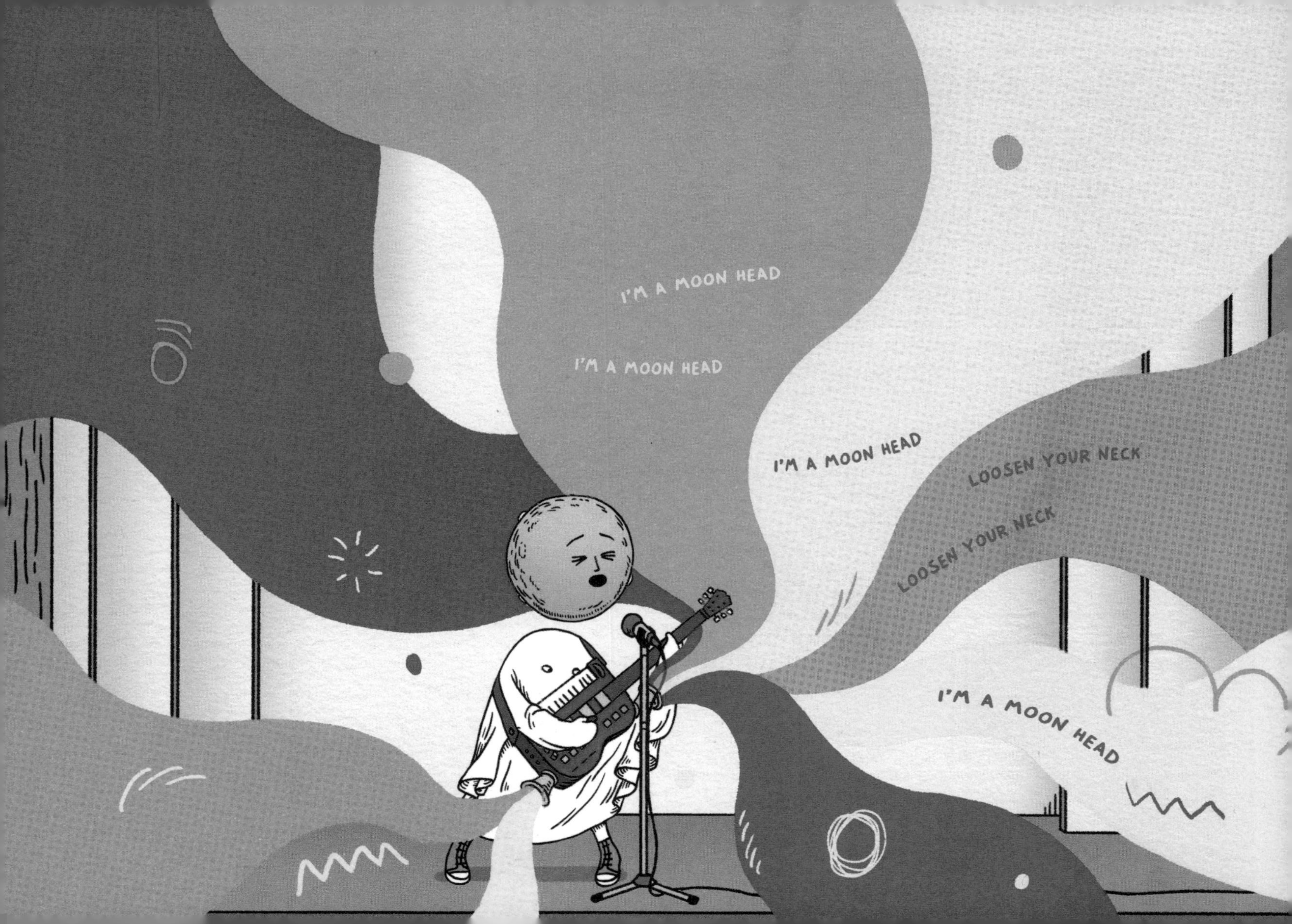
I'M A MOON HEAD
I'M A MOON HEAD
I'M A MOON HEAD
LOOSEN YOUR NECK
LOOSEN YOUR NECK
I'M A MOON HEAD

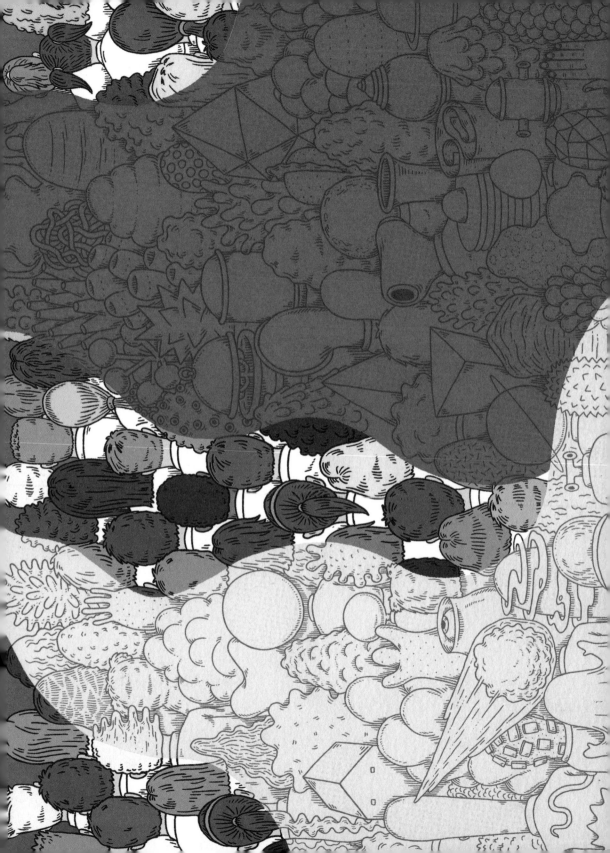

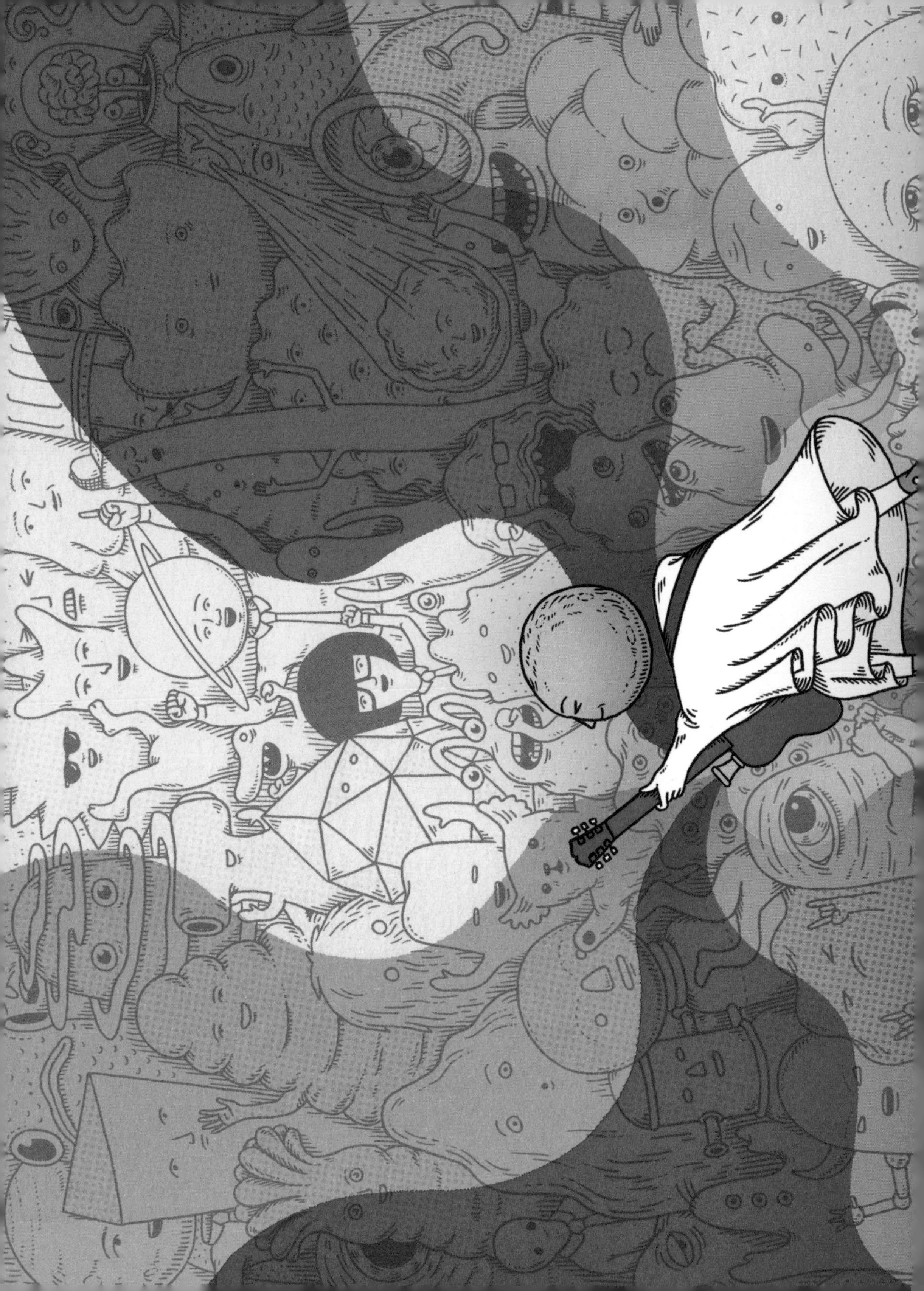

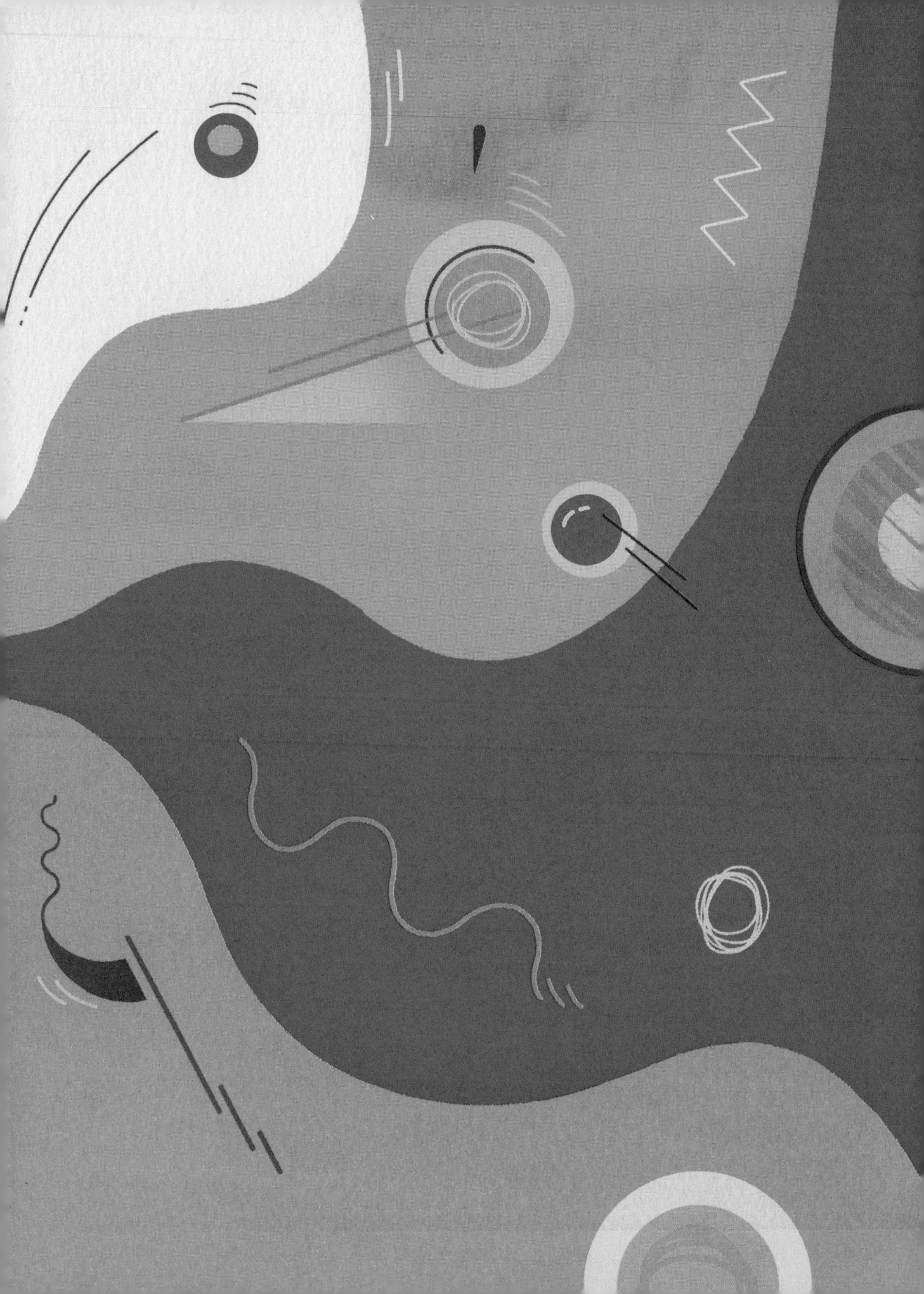

THE NEXT DAY

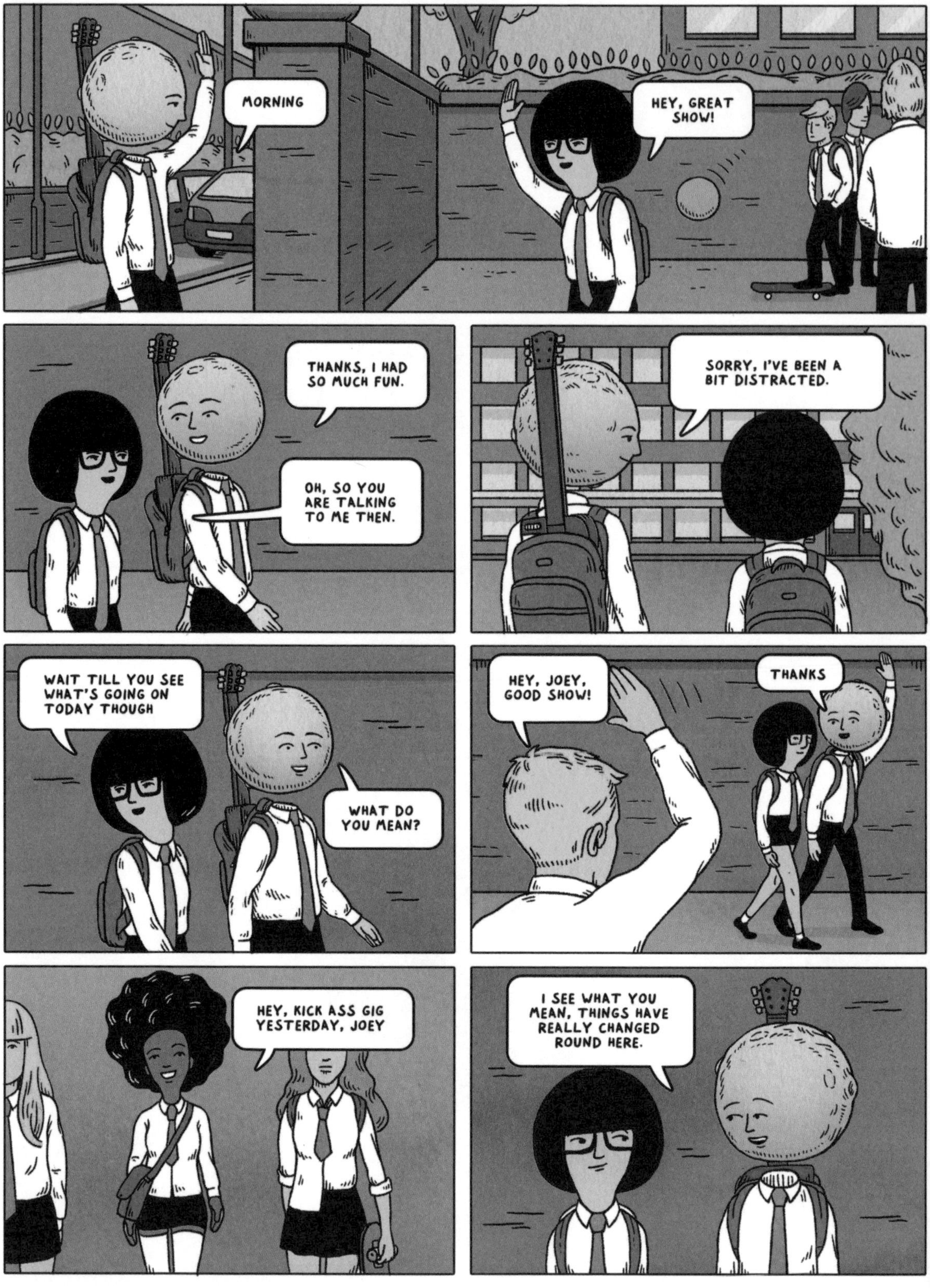
MORNING
HEY, GREAT SHOW!
THANKS, I HAD SO MUCH FUN.
OH, SO YOU ARE TALKING TO ME THEN.
SORRY, I'VE BEEN A BIT DISTRACTED.
WAIT TILL YOU SEE WHAT'S GOING ON TODAY THOUGH
WHAT DO YOU MEAN?
HEY, JOEY, GOOD SHOW!
THANKS
HEY, KICK ASS GIG YESTERDAY, JOEY
I SEE WHAT YOU MEAN, THINGS HAVE REALLY CHANGED ROUND HERE.

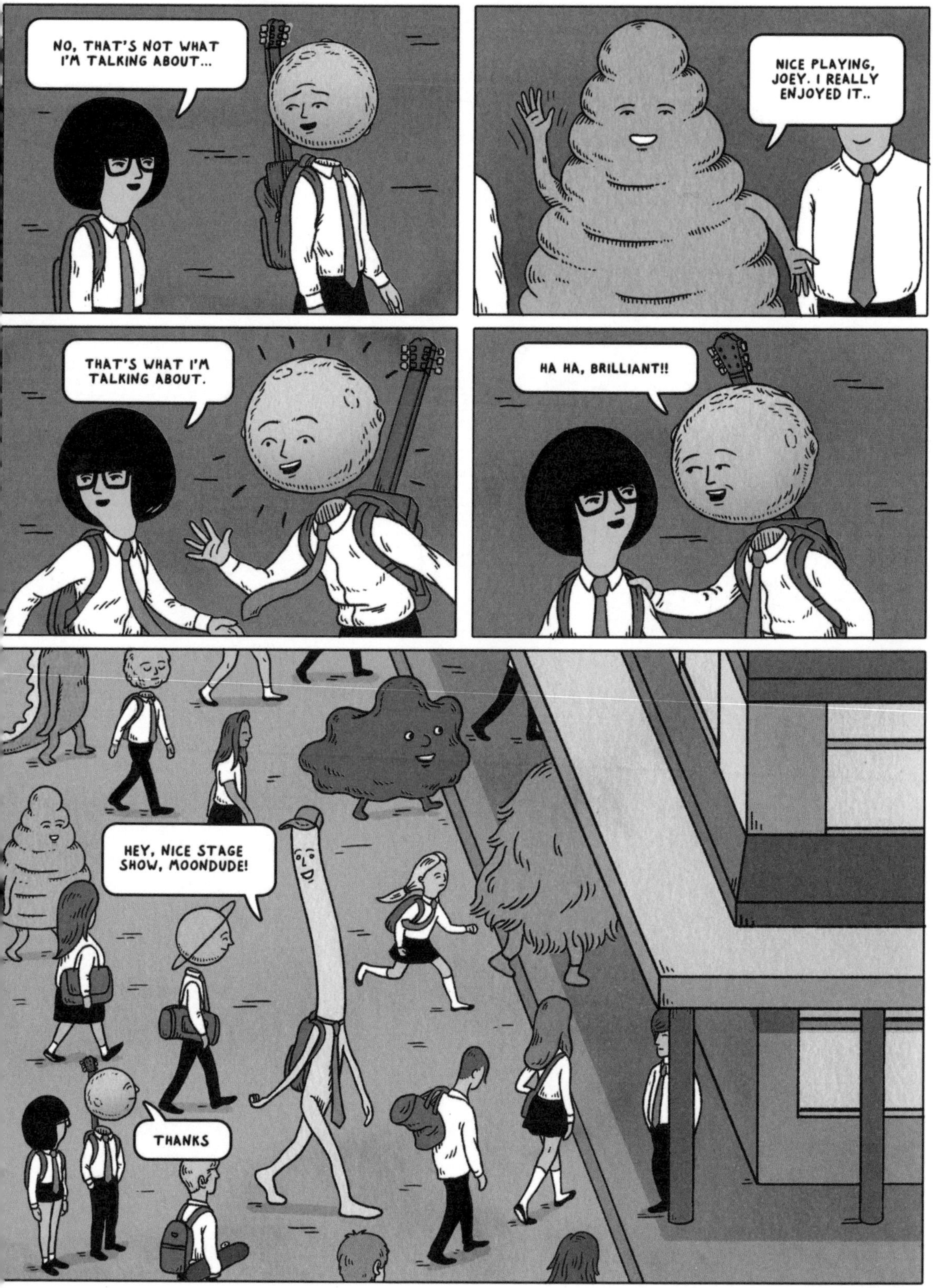
NO, THAT'S NOT WHAT I'M TALKING ABOUT...
NICE PLAYING, JOEY. I REALLY ENJOYED IT..
THAT'S WHAT I'M TALKING ABOUT.
HA HA, BRILLIANT!!
HEY, NICE STAGE SHOW, MOONDUDE!
THANKS

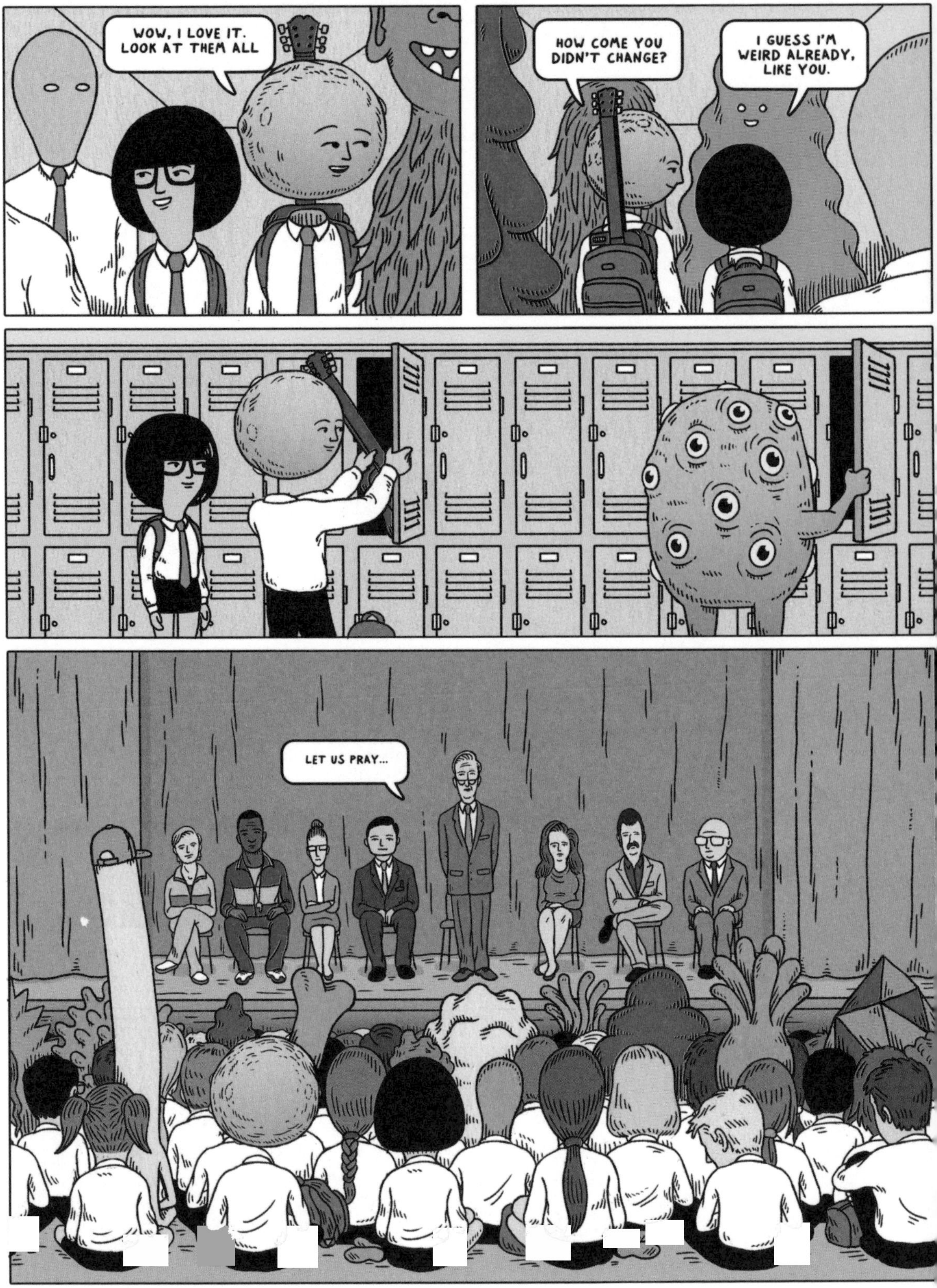
WOW, I LOVE IT. LOOK AT THEM ALL
HOW COME YOU DIDN'T CHANGE?
I GUESS I'M WEIRD ALREADY, LIKE YOU.
LET US PRAY...

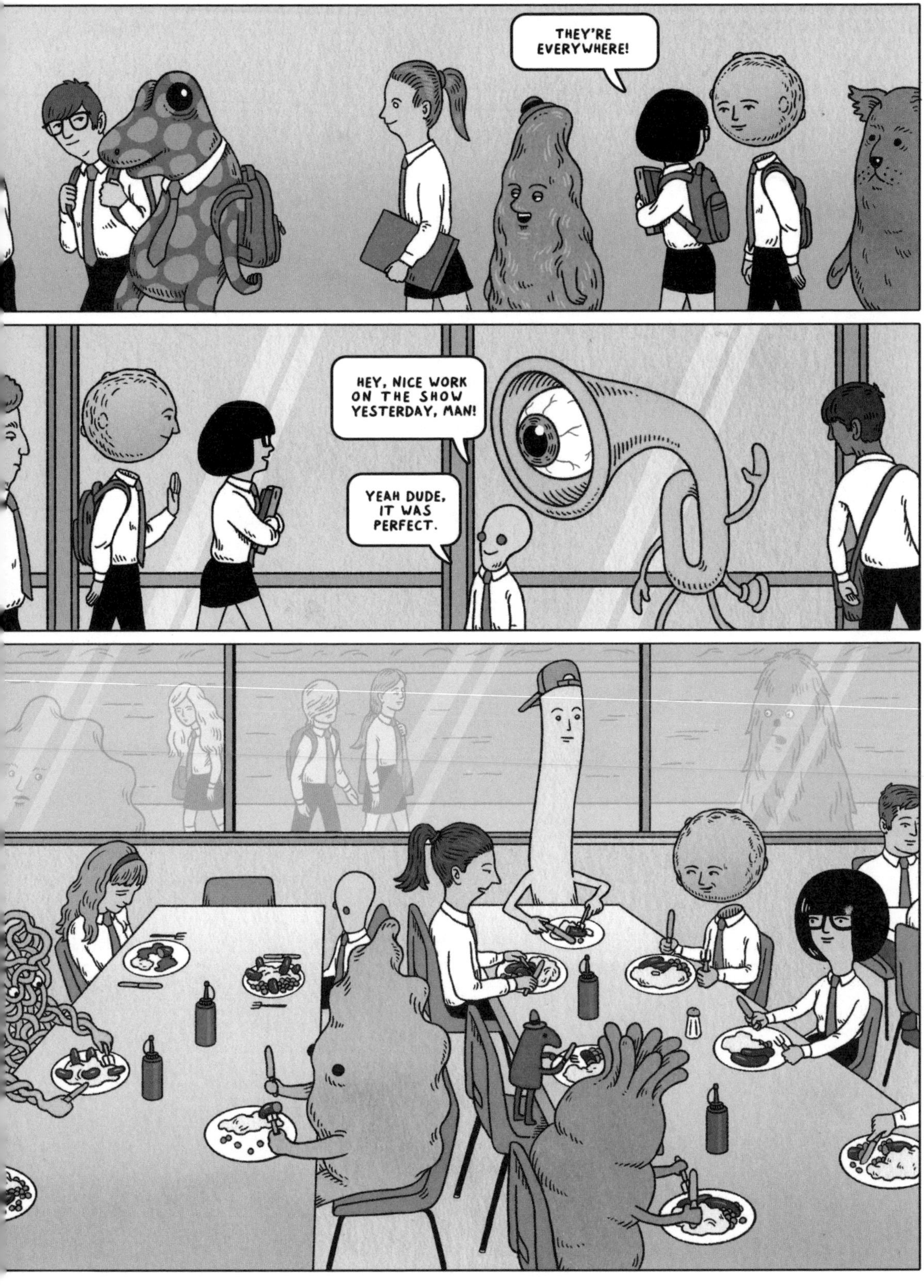
THEY'RE EVERYWHERE!
HEY, NICE WORK ON THE SHOW YESTERDAY, MAN!
YEAH DUDE, IT WAS PERFECT.

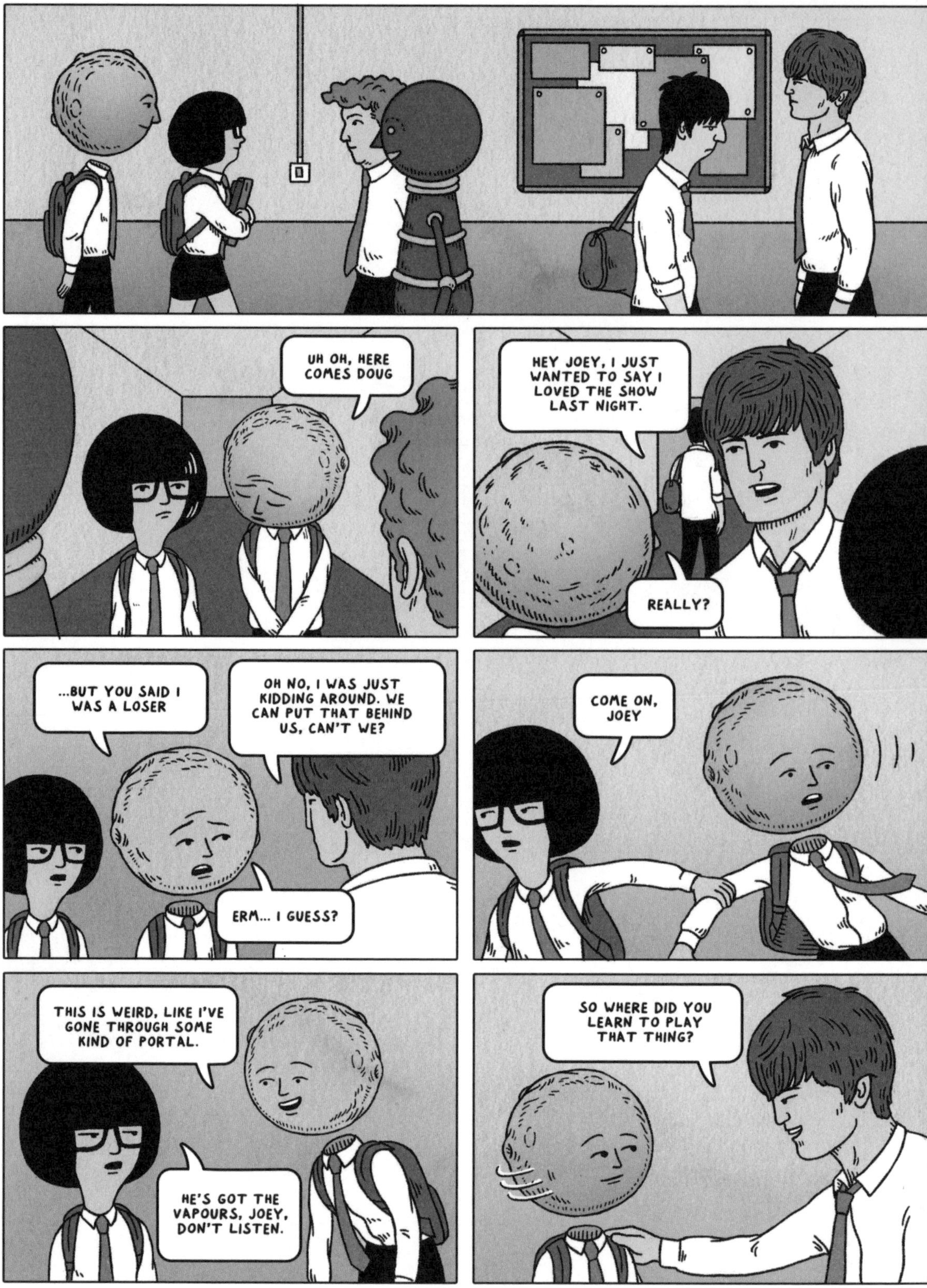
UH OH, HERE COMES DOUG
HEY JOEY, I JUST WANTED TO SAY I LOVED THE SHOW LAST NIGHT.
REALLY?
...BUT YOU SAID I WAS A LOSER
OH NO, I WAS JUST KIDDING AROUND. WE CAN PUT THAT BEHIND US, CAN'T WE?
ERM... I GUESS?
COME ON, JOEY
THIS IS WEIRD, LIKE I'VE GONE THROUGH SOME KIND OF PORTAL.
HE'S GOT THE VAPOURS, JOEY, DON'T LISTEN.
SO WHERE DID YOU LEARN TO PLAY THAT THING?

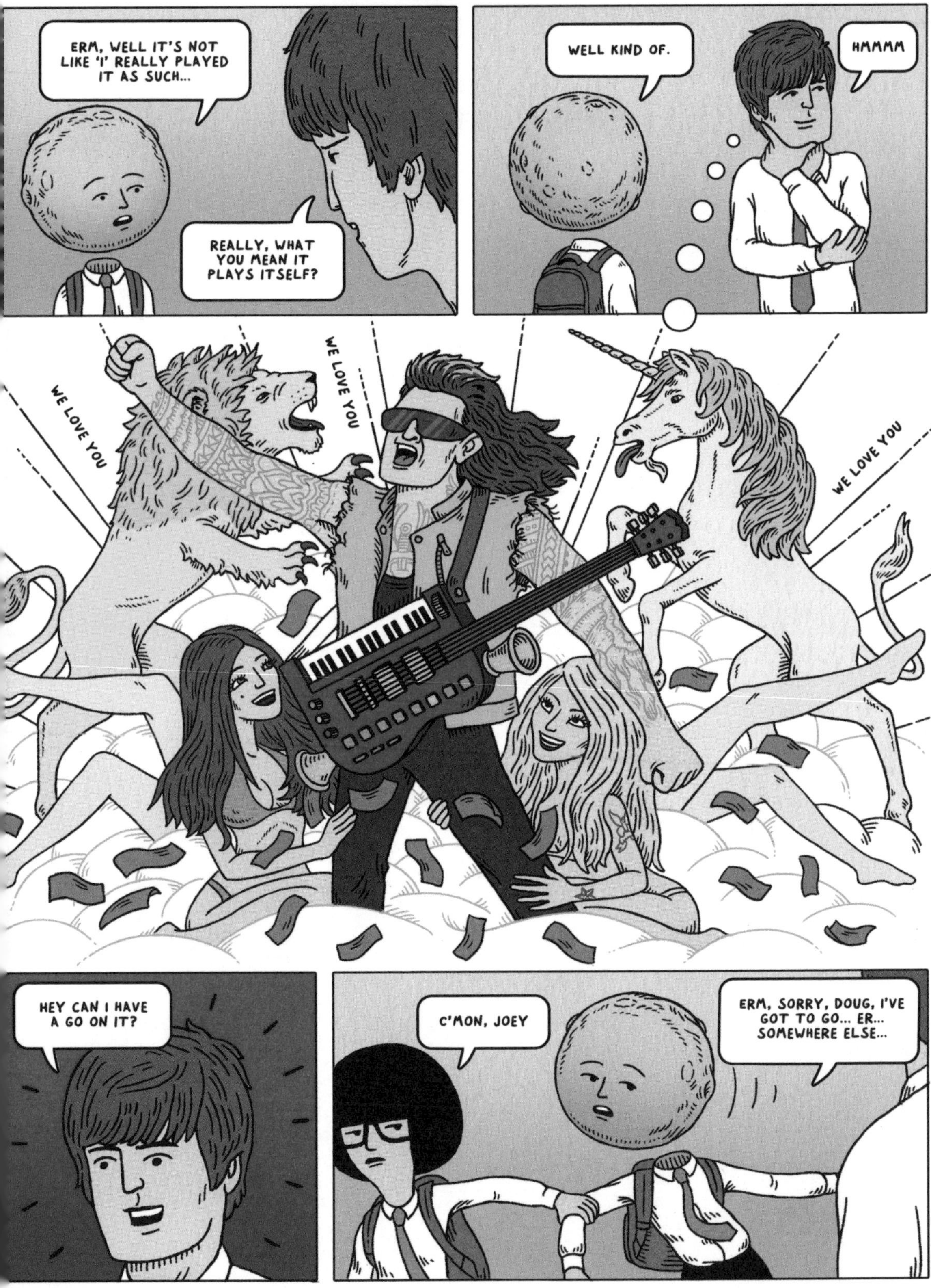

ERM, WELL IT'S NOT LIKE 'I' REALLY PLAYED IT AS SUCH...
REALLY, WHAT YOU MEAN IT PLAYS ITSELF?
WELL KIND OF.
HMMMM
WE LOVE YOU
WE LOVE YOU
WE LOVE YOU
HEY CAN I HAVE A GO ON IT?
C'MON, JOEY
ERM, SORRY, DOUG, I'VE GOT TO GO... ER... SOMEWHERE ELSE...

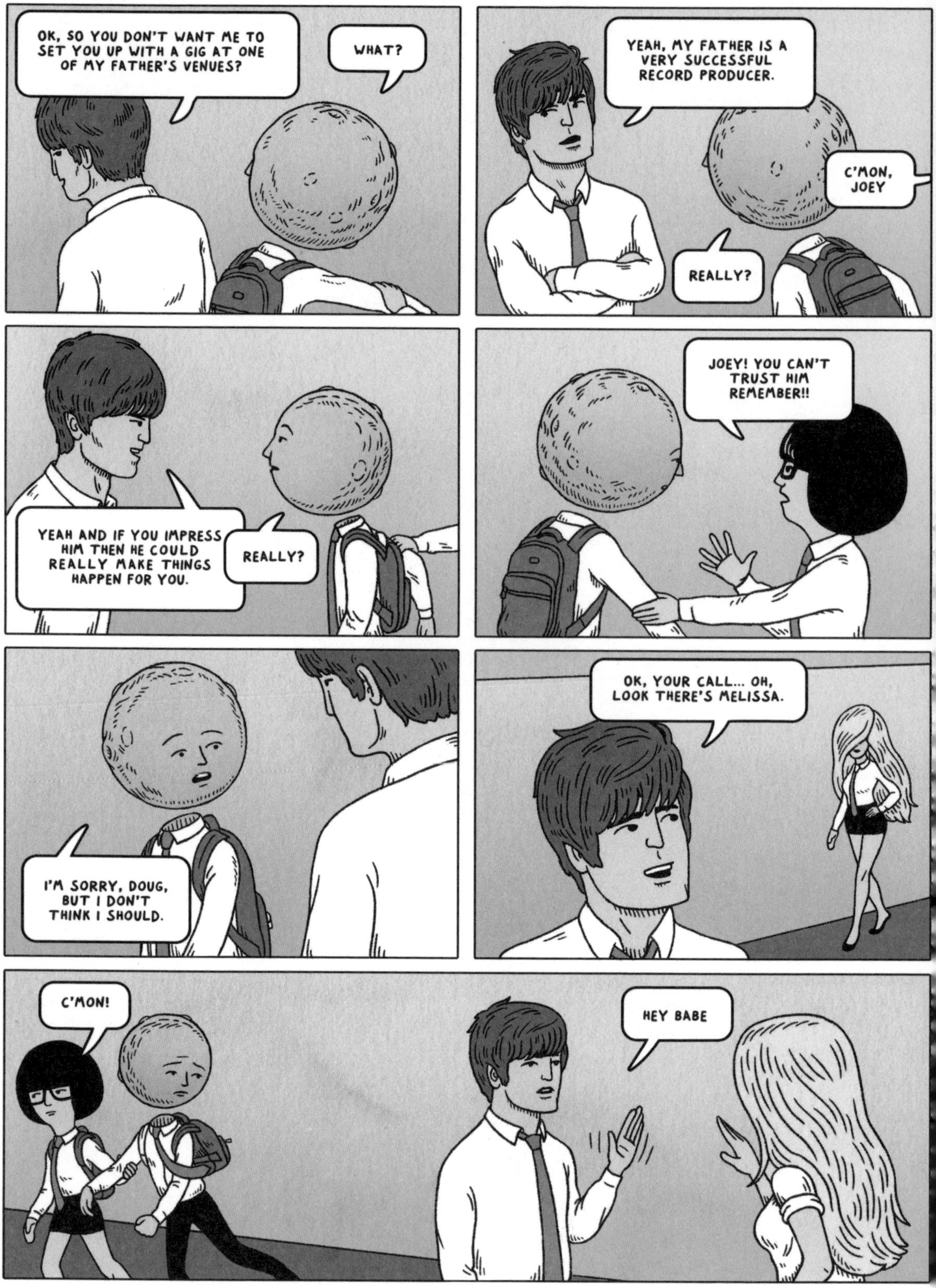
OK, SO YOU DON'T WANT ME TO SET YOU UP WITH A GIG AT ONE OF MY FATHER'S VENUES?
WHAT?
YEAH, MY FATHER IS A VERY SUCCESSFUL RECORD PRODUCER.
C'MON, JOEY
REALLY?
YEAH AND IF YOU IMPRESS HIM THEN HE COULD REALLY MAKE THINGS HAPPEN FOR YOU.
REALLY?
JOEY! YOU CAN'T TRUST HIM REMEMBER!!
I'M SORRY, DOUG, BUT I DON'T THINK I SHOULD.
OK, YOUR CALL... OH, LOOK THERE'S MELISSA.
C'MON!
HEY BABE

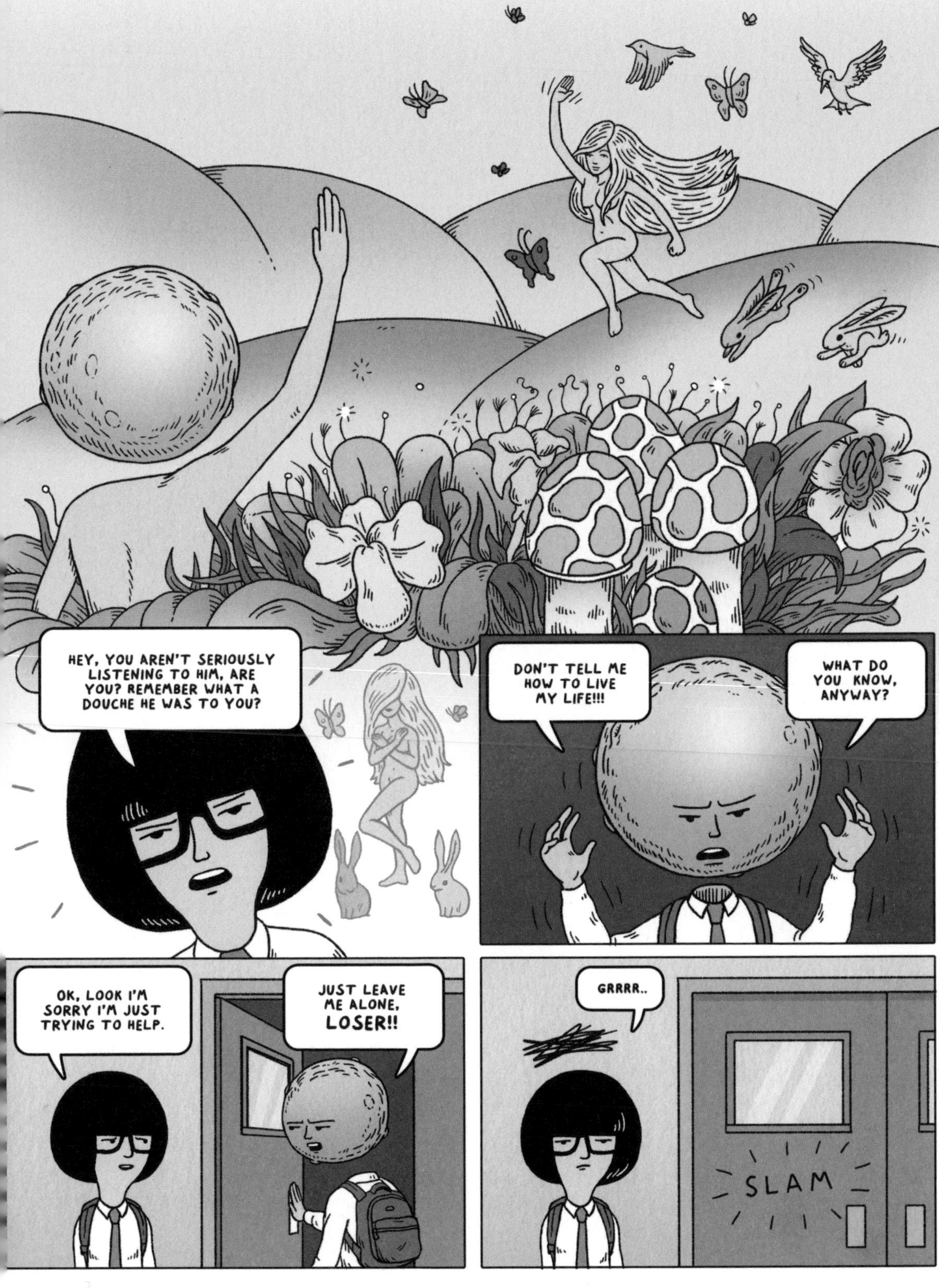
HEY, YOU AREN'T SERIOUSLY LISTENING TO HIM, ARE YOU? REMEMBER WHAT A DOUCHE HE WAS TO YOU?
DON'T TELL ME HOW TO LIVE MY LIFE!!!
WHAT DO YOU KNOW, ANYWAY?
OK, LOOK I'M SORRY I'M JUST TRYING TO HELP.
JUST LEAVE ME ALONE, LOSER!!
GRRRR..
SLAM

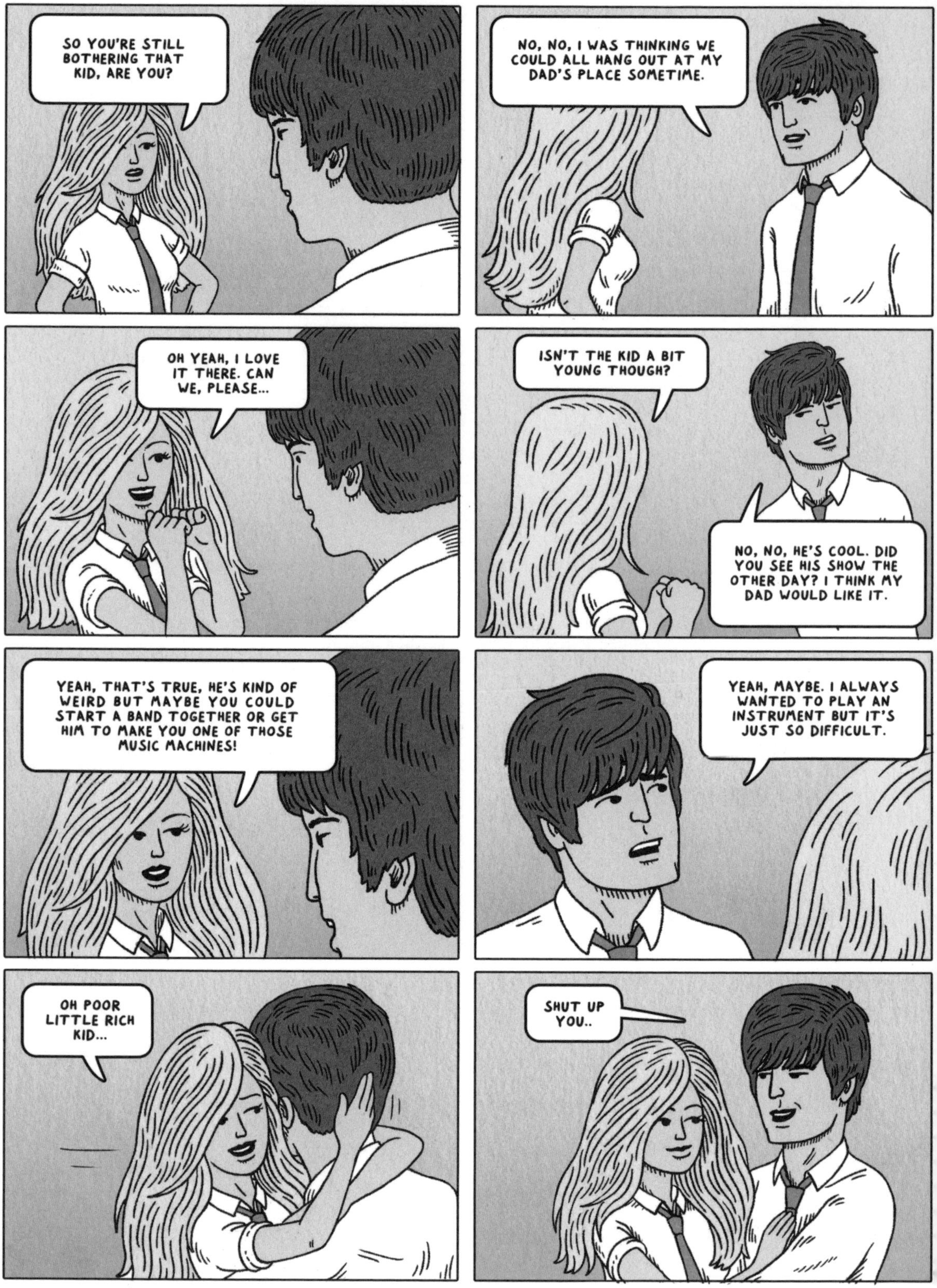
SO YOU'RE STILL BOTHERING THAT KID, ARE YOU?
NO, NO, I WAS THINKING WE COULD ALL HANG OUT AT MY DAD'S PLACE SOMETIME.
OH YEAH, I LOVE IT THERE. CAN WE, PLEASE...
ISN'T THE KID A BIT YOUNG THOUGH?
NO, NO, HE'S COOL. DID YOU SEE HIS SHOW THE OTHER DAY? I THINK MY DAD WOULD LIKE IT.
YEAH, THAT'S TRUE, HE'S KIND OF WEIRD BUT MAYBE YOU COULD START A BAND TOGETHER OR GET HIM TO MAKE YOU ONE OF THOSE MUSIC MACHINES!
YEAH, MAYBE. I ALWAYS WANTED TO PLAY AN INSTRUMENT BUT IT'S JUST SO DIFFICULT.
OH POOR LITTLE RICH KID...
SHUT UP YOU..

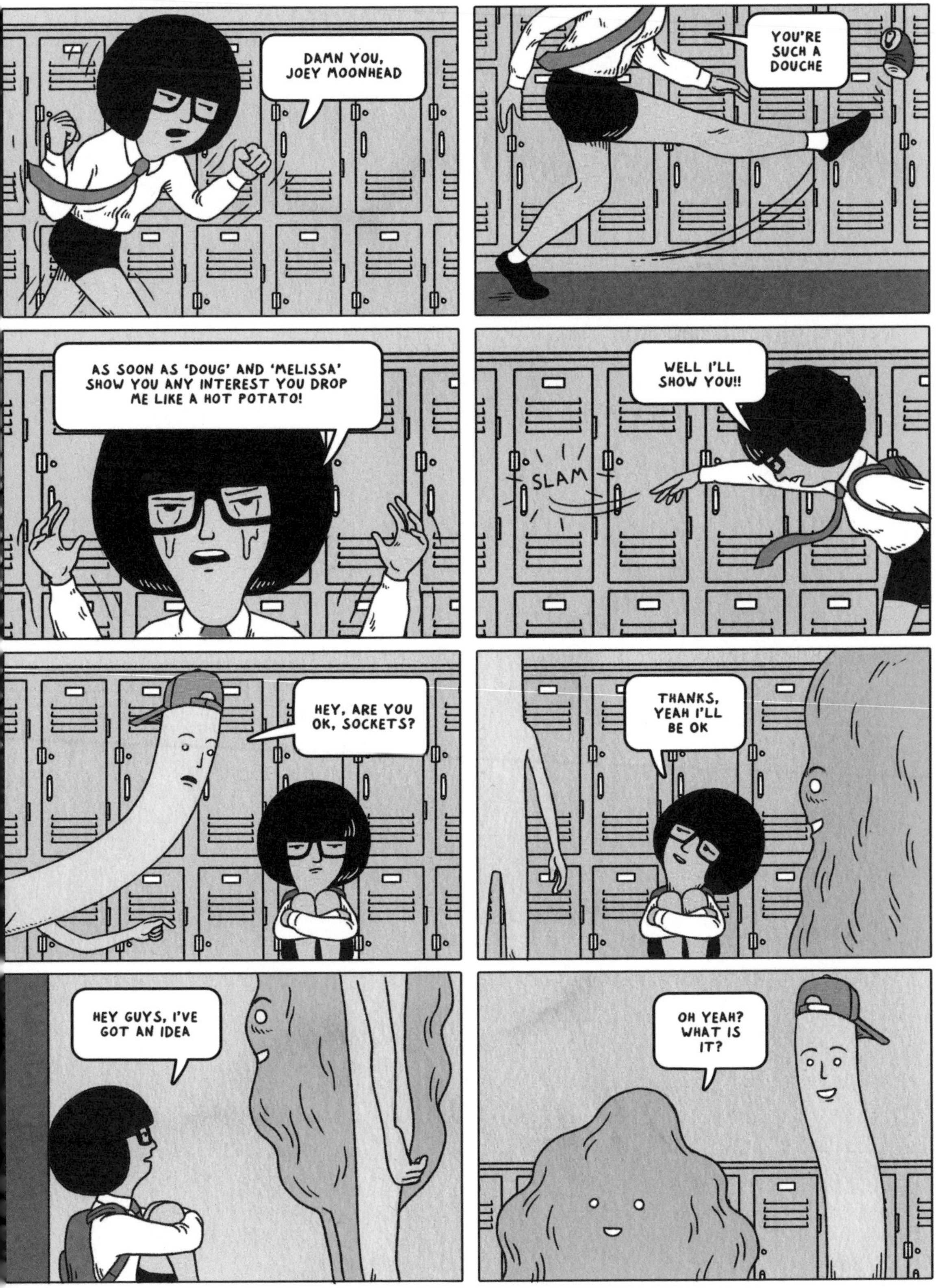
DAMN YOU, JOEY MOONHEAD
YOU'RE SUCH A DOUCHE
AS SOON AS 'DOUG' AND 'MELISSA' SHOW YOU ANY INTEREST YOU DROP ME LIKE A HOT POTATO!
WELL I'LL SHOW YOU!!
SLAM
HEY, ARE YOU OK, SOCKETS?
THANKS, YEAH I'LL BE OK
HEY GUYS, I'VE GOT AN IDEA
OH YEAH? WHAT IS IT?

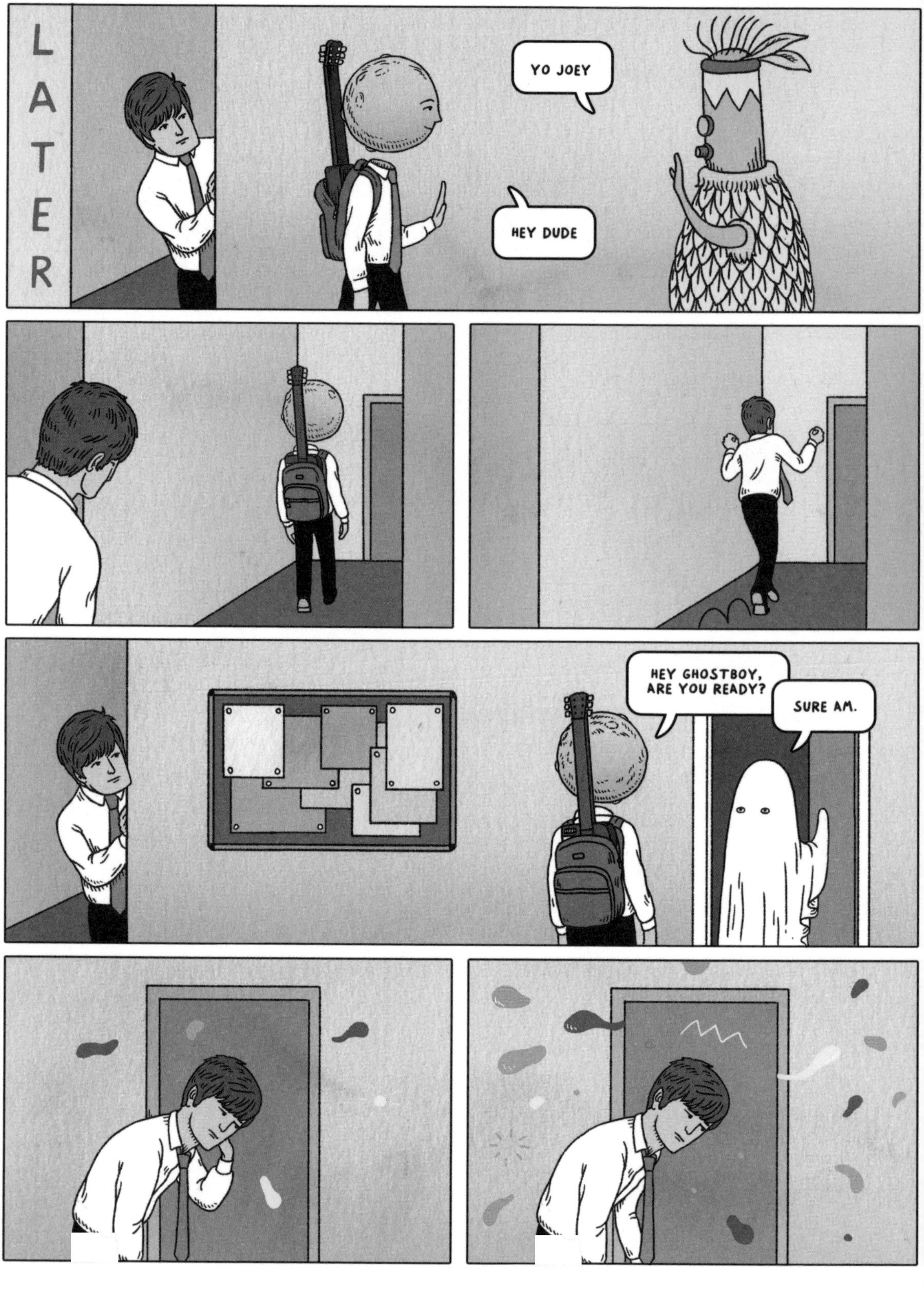
LATER
YO JOEY
HEY DUDE
HEY GHOSTBOY, ARE YOU READY?
SURE AM.

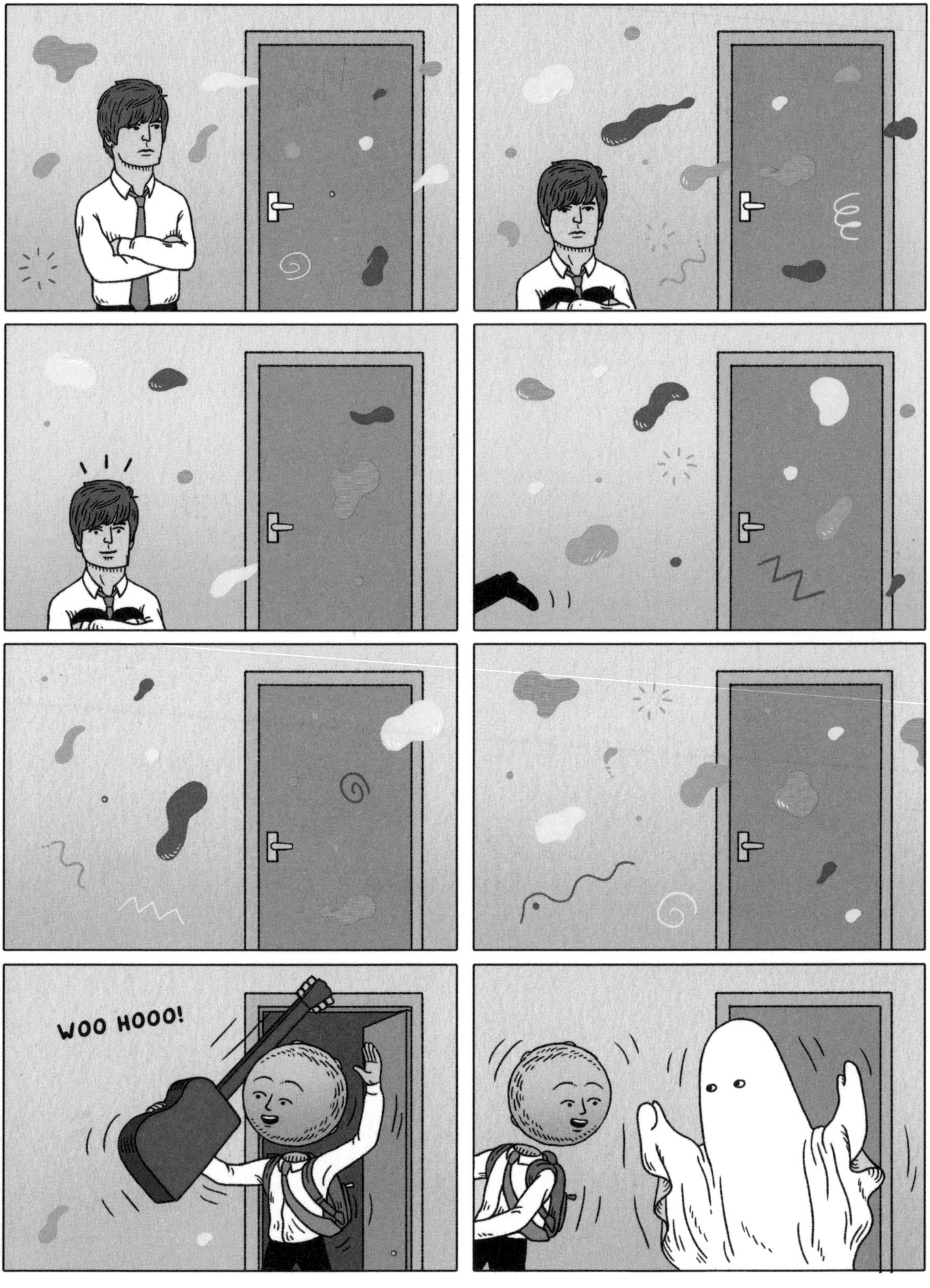
WOO HOOO!

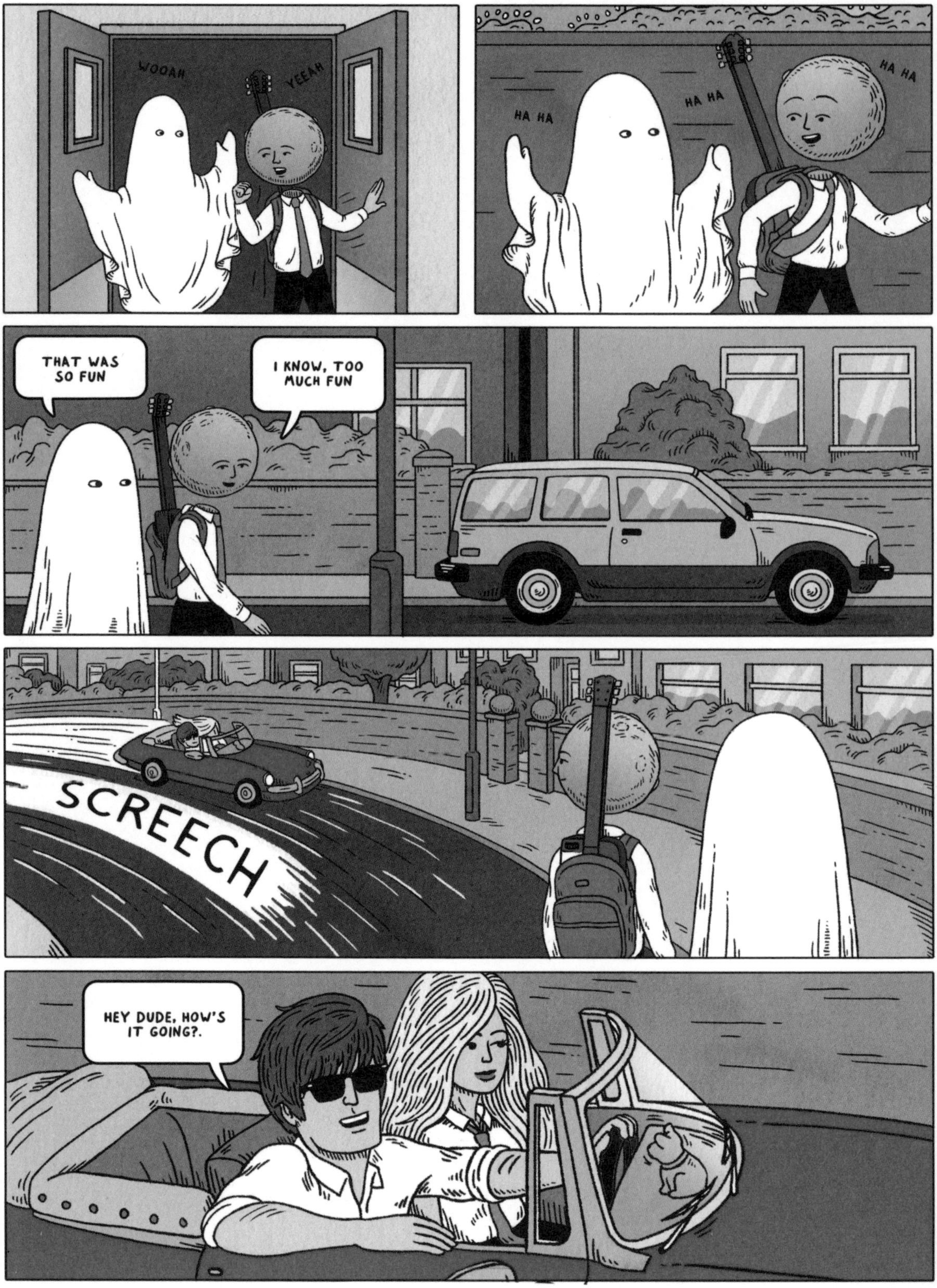
WOOAH
YEEAH
HA HA
HA HA
HA HA
THAT WAS SO FUN
I KNOW, TOO MUCH FUN
SCREECH
HEY DUDE, HOW'S IT GOING?.

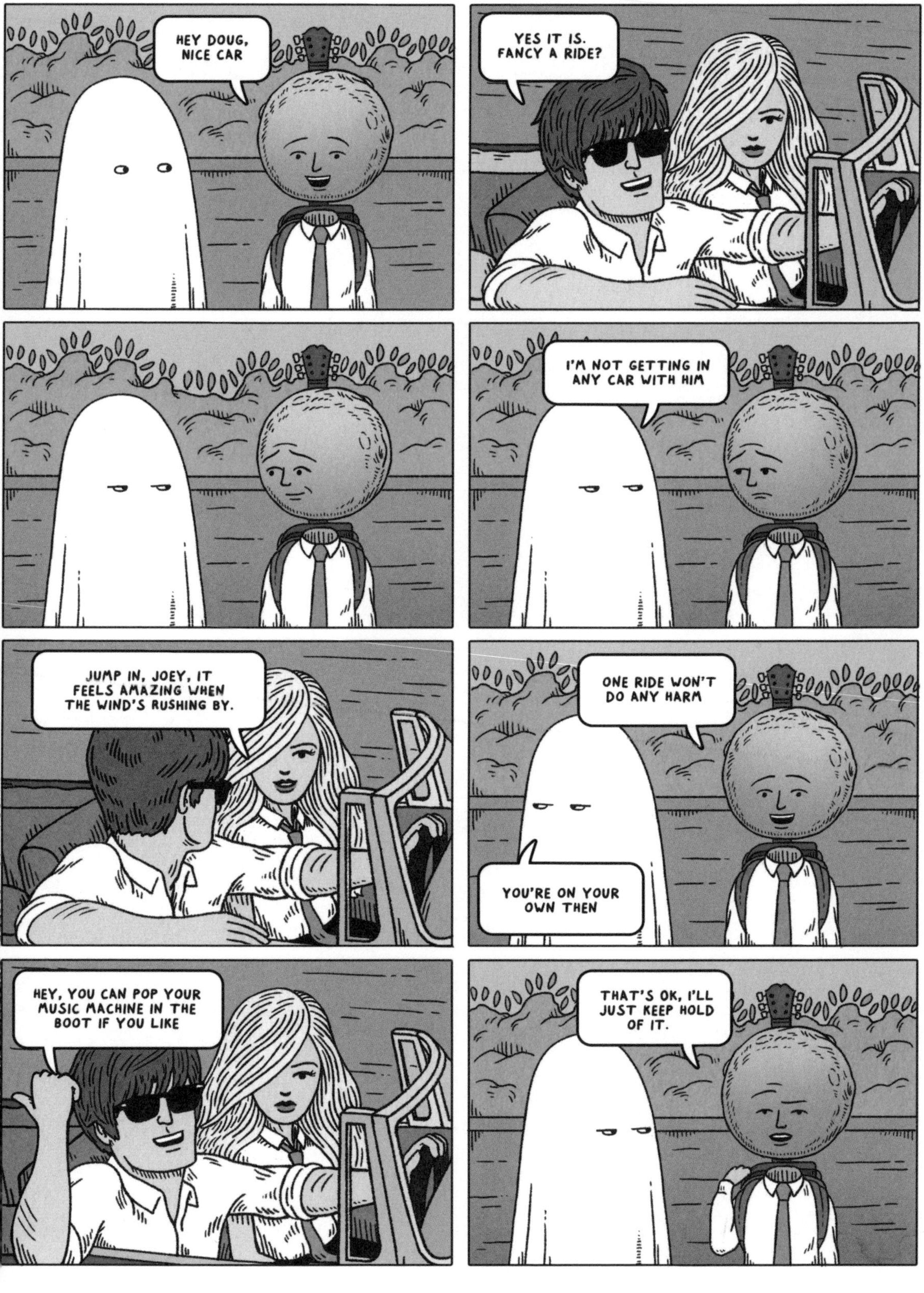
HEY DOUG, NICE CAR
YES IT IS. FANCY A RIDE?
I'M NOT GETTING IN ANY CAR WITH HIM
JUMP IN, JOEY, IT FEELS AMAZING WHEN THE WIND'S RUSHING BY.
ONE RIDE WON'T DO ANY HARM
YOU'RE ON YOUR OWN THEN
HEY, YOU CAN POP YOUR MUSIC MACHINE IN THE BOOT IF YOU LIKE
THAT'S OK, I'LL JUST KEEP HOLD OF IT.

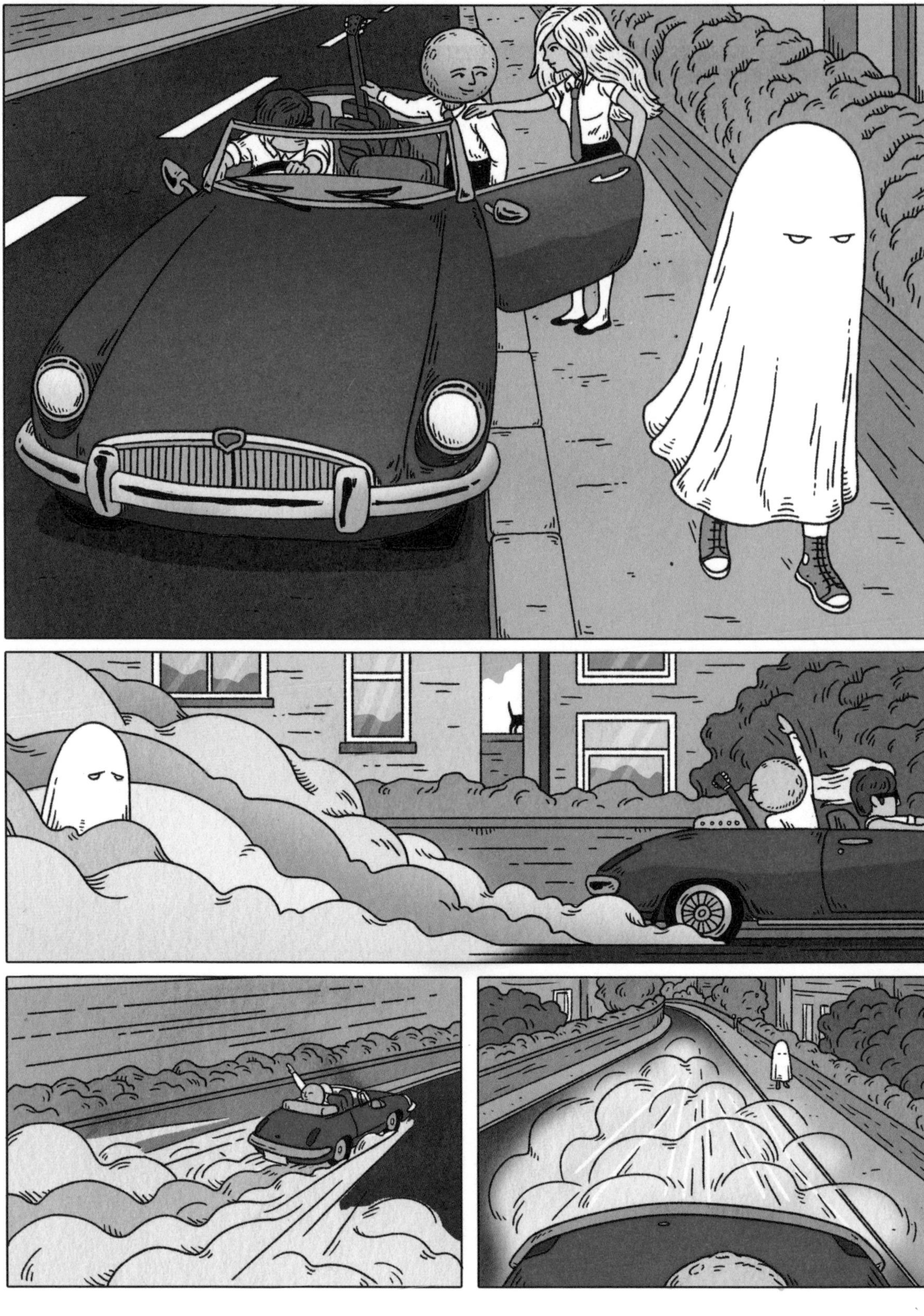

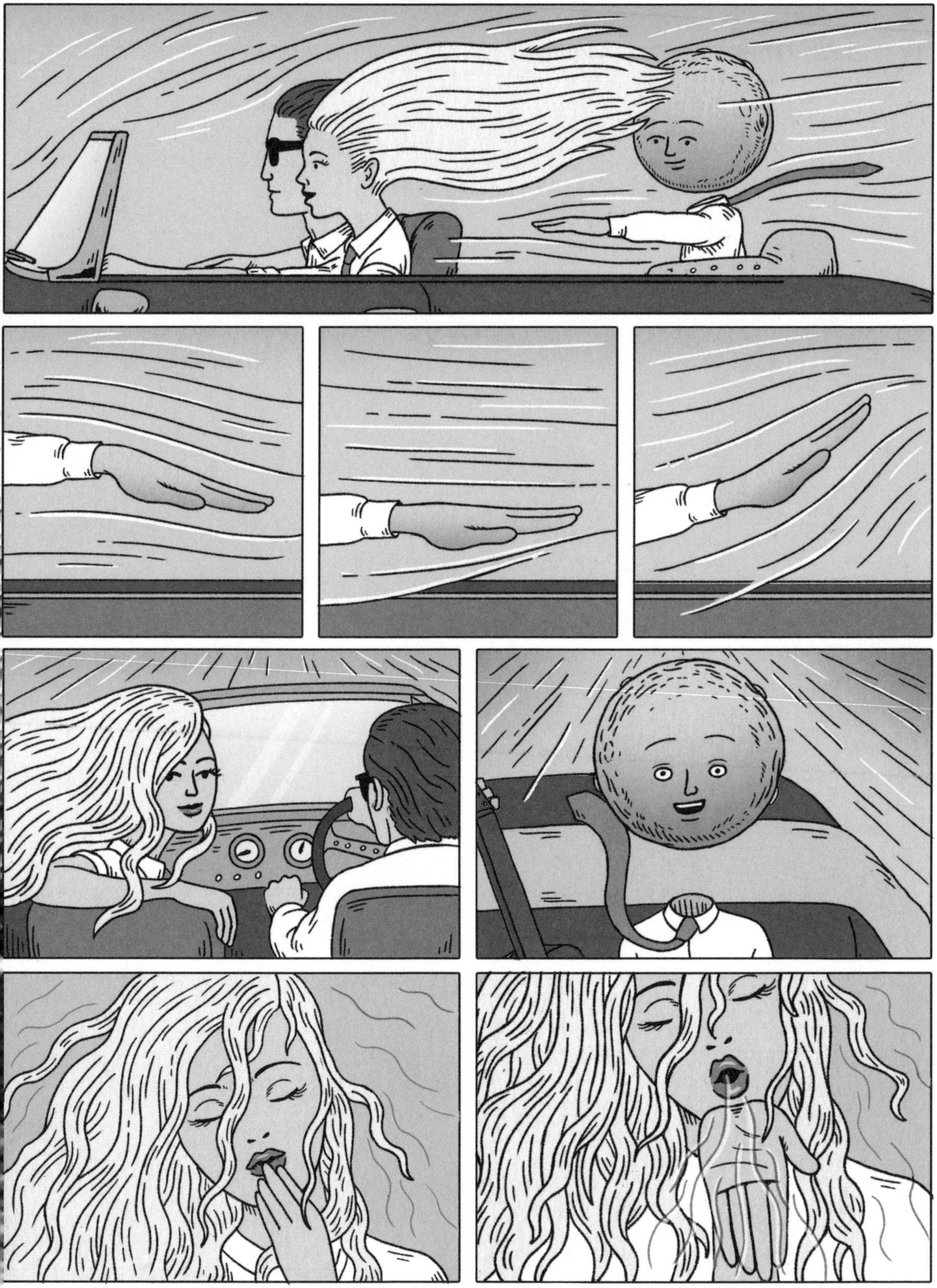

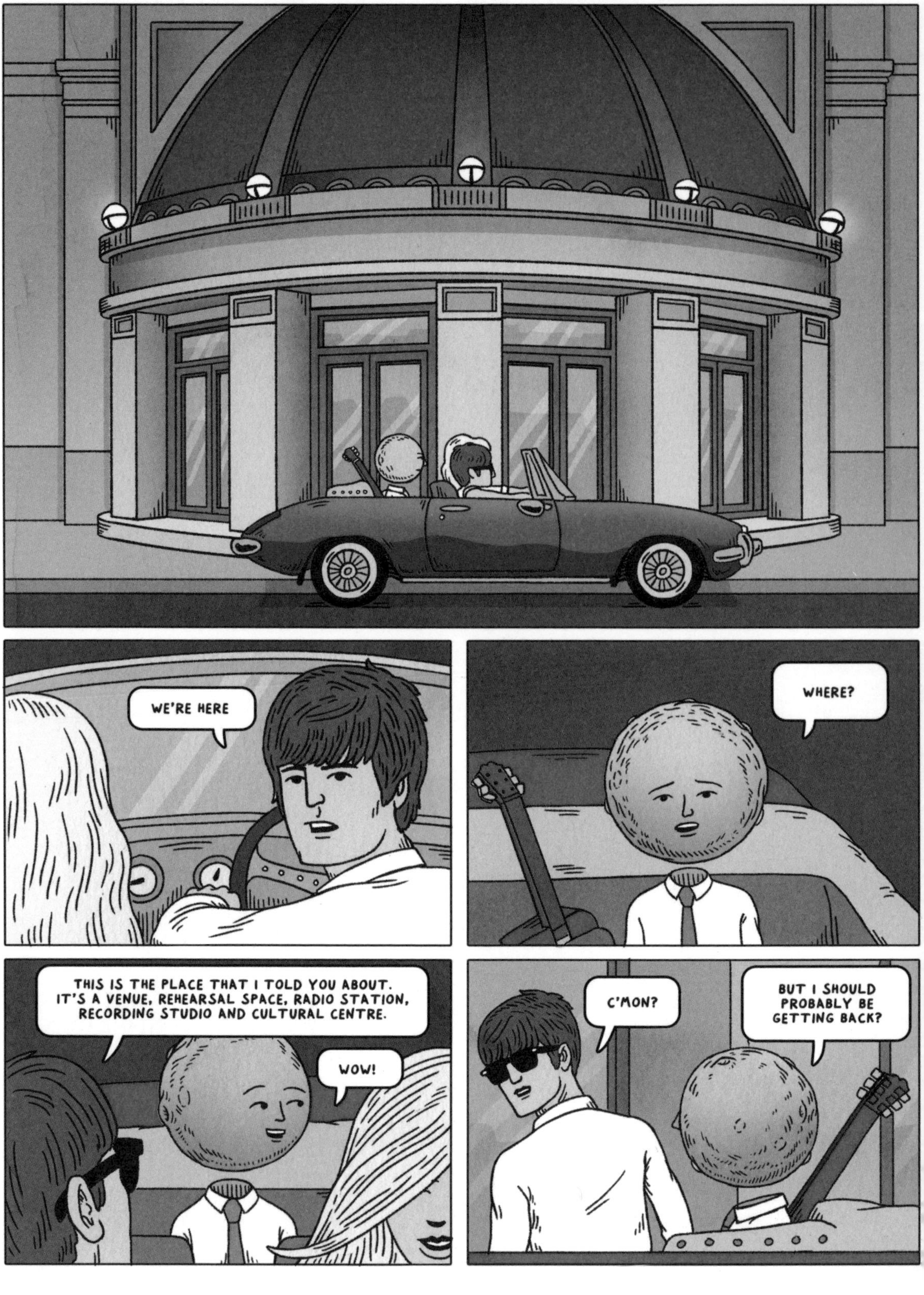
WE'RE HERE
WHERE?
THIS IS THE PLACE THAT I TOLD YOU ABOUT. IT'S A VENUE, REHEARSAL SPACE, RADIO STATION, RECORDING STUDIO AND CULTURAL CENTRE.
WOW!
C'MON?
BUT I SHOULD PROBABLY BE GETTING BACK?

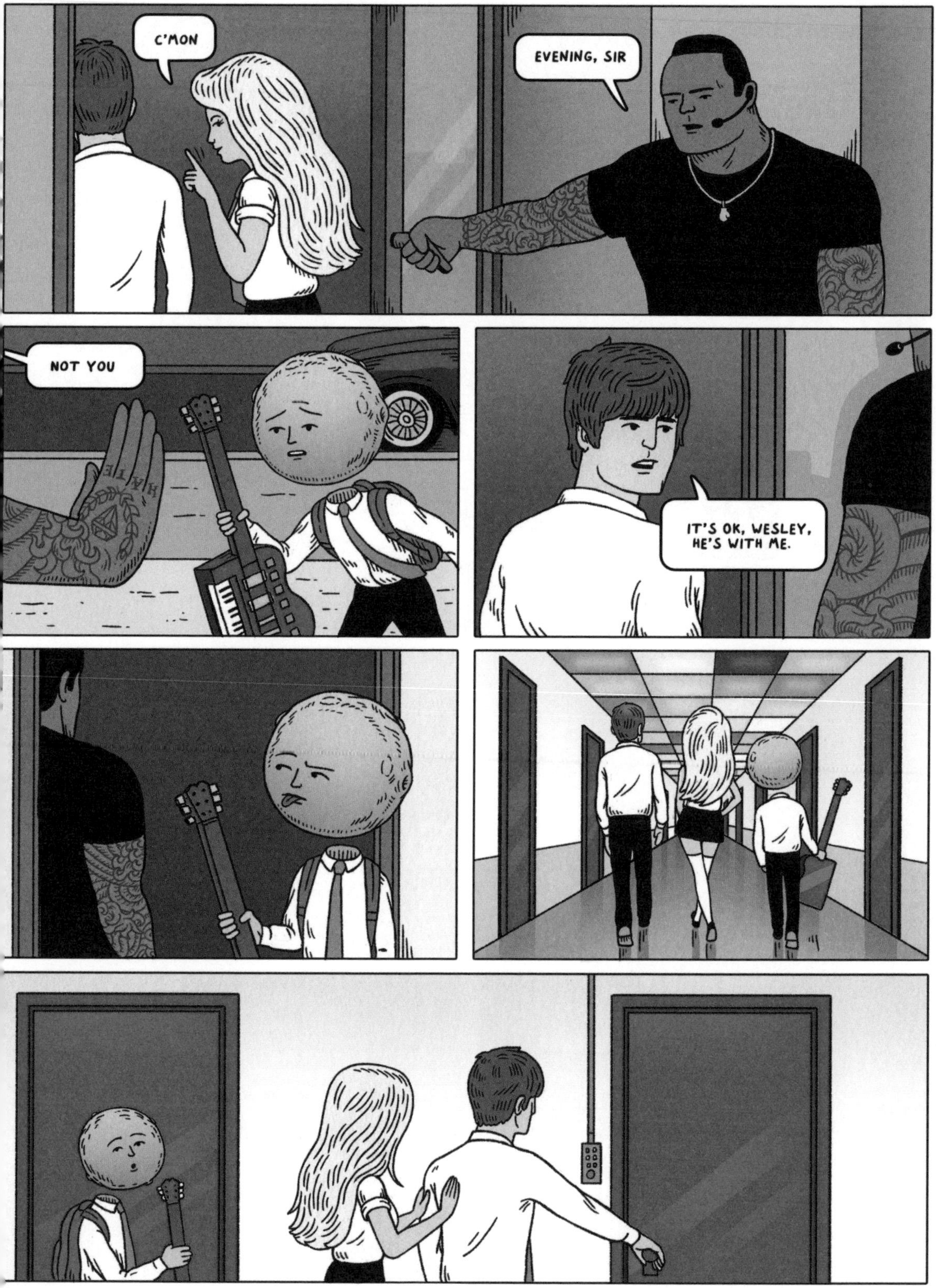
C'MON
EVENING, SIR
NOT YOU
HATE
IT'S OK, WESLEY, HE'S WITH ME.

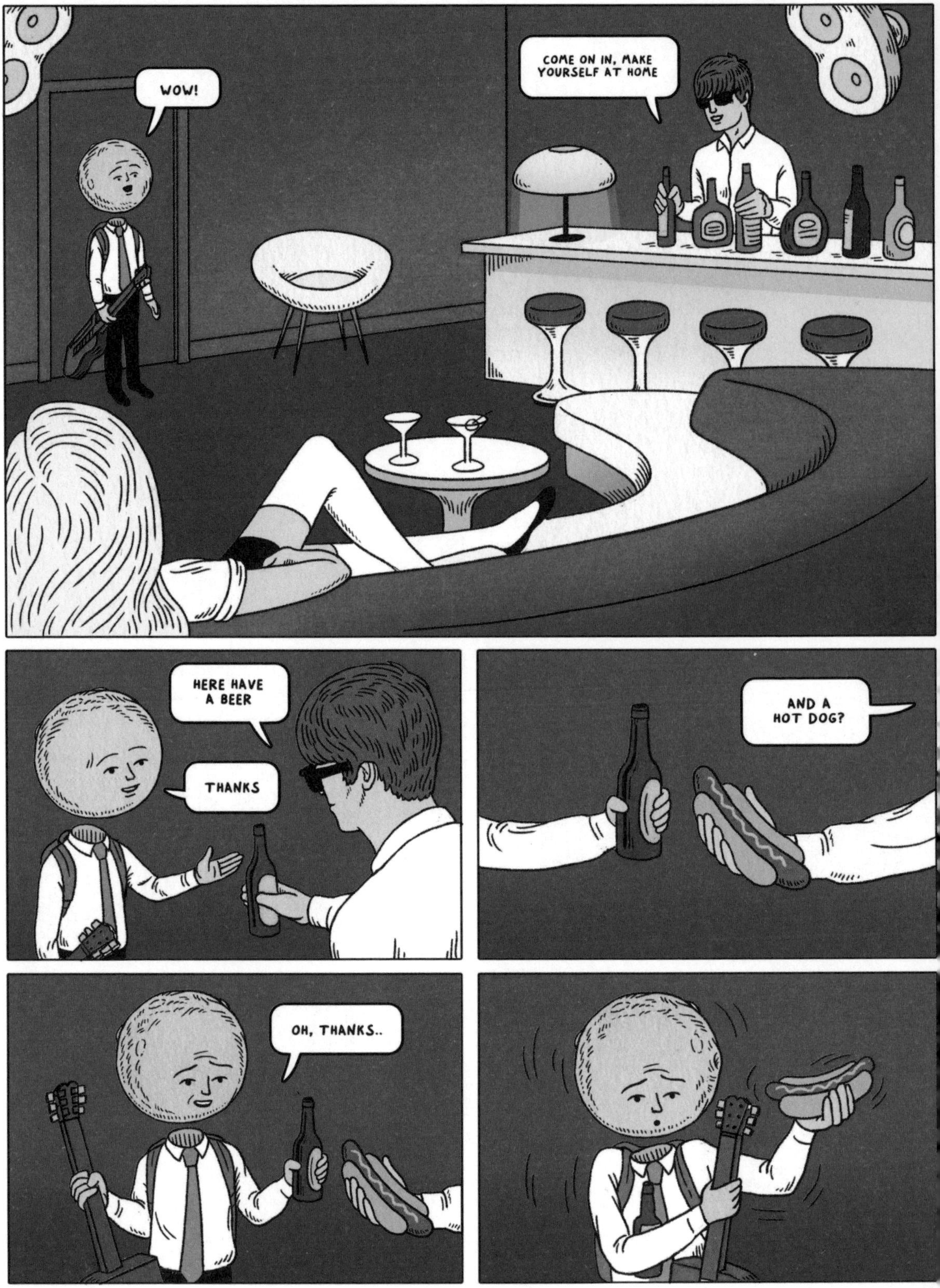
WOW!
COME ON IN, MAKE YOURSELF AT HOME
HERE HAVE A BEER
THANKS
AND A HOT DOG?
OH, THANKS..

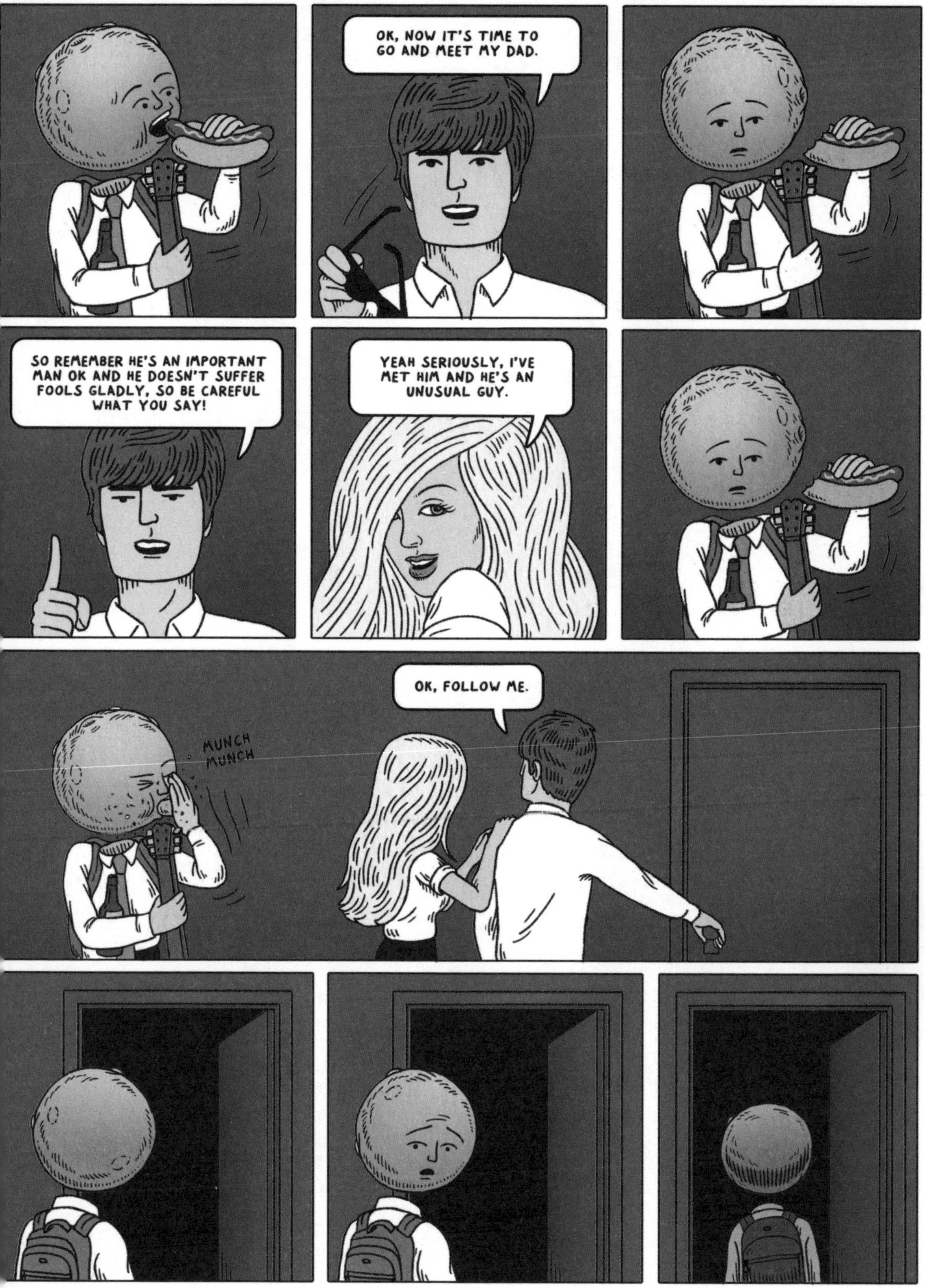
OK, NOW IT'S TIME TO GO AND MEET MY DAD.
SO REMEMBER HE'S AN IMPORTANT MAN OK AND HE DOESN'T SUFFER FOOLS GLADLY, SO BE CAREFUL WHAT YOU SAY!
YEAH SERIOUSLY, I'VE MET HIM AND HE'S AN UNUSUAL GUY.
MUNCH MUNCH
OK, FOLLOW ME.

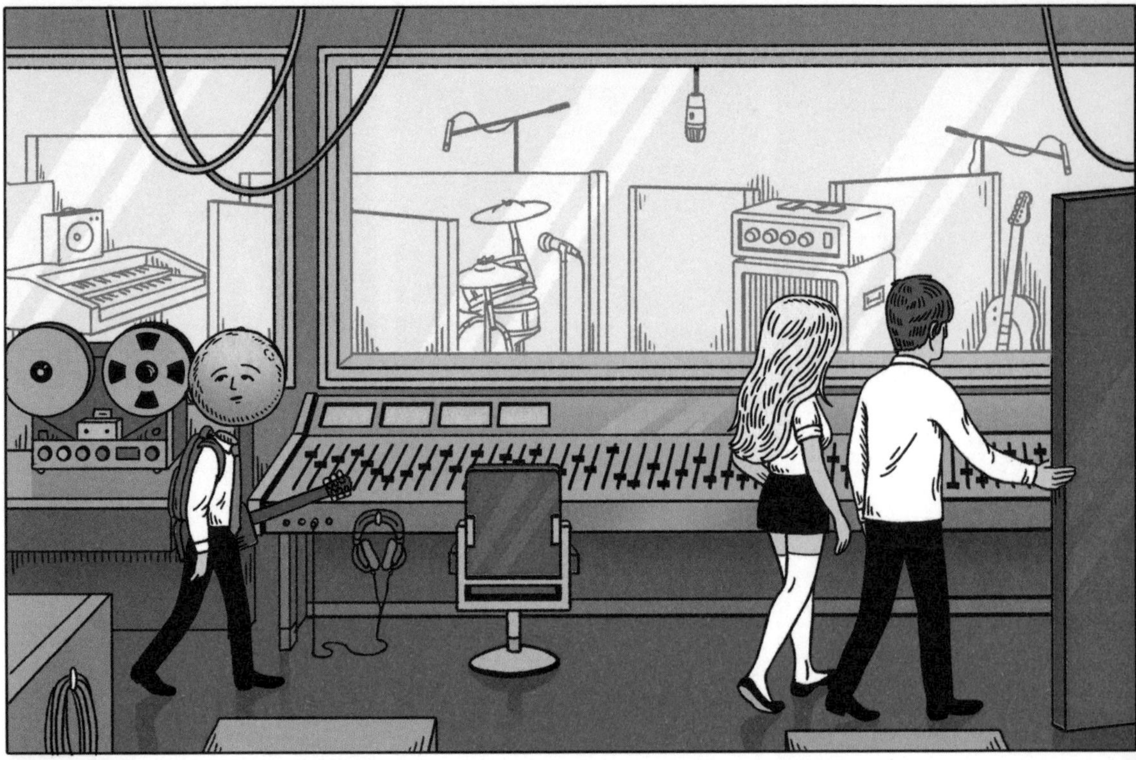

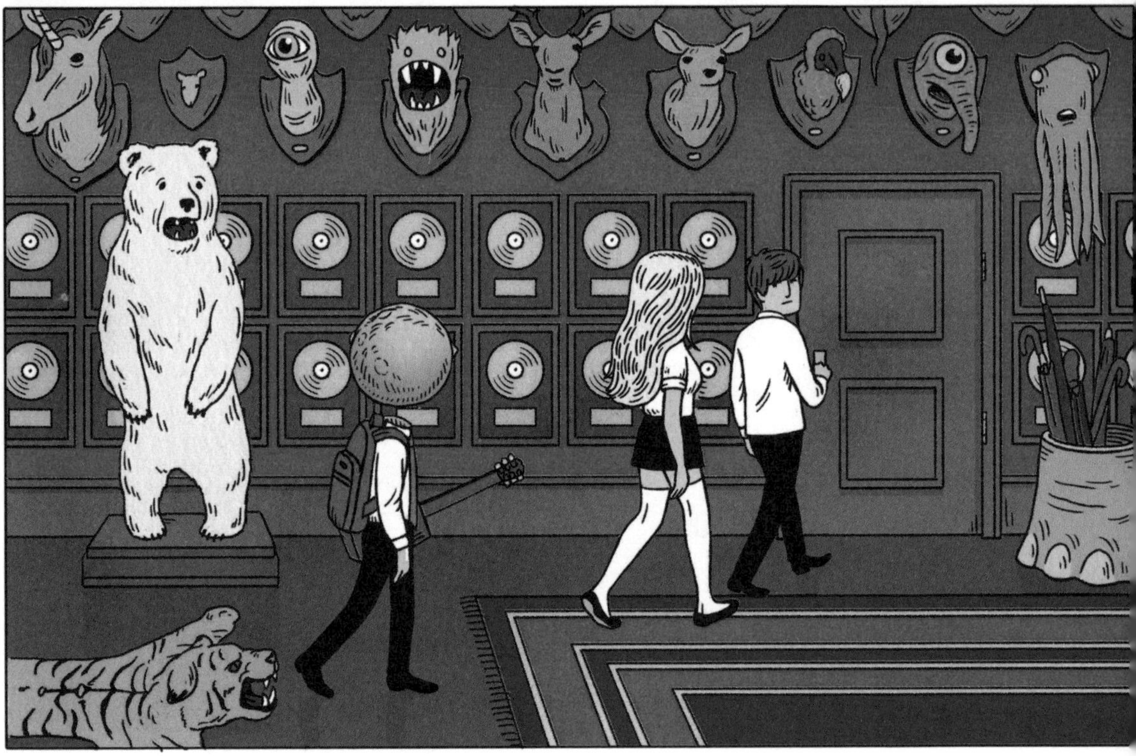

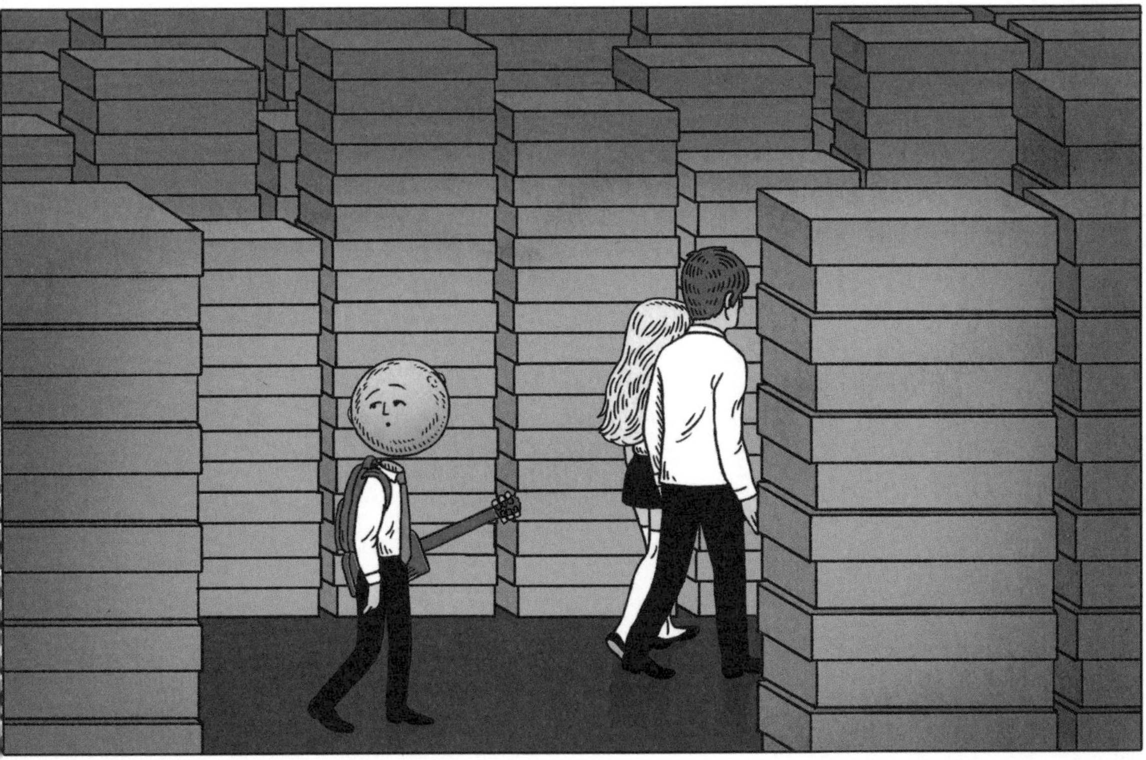

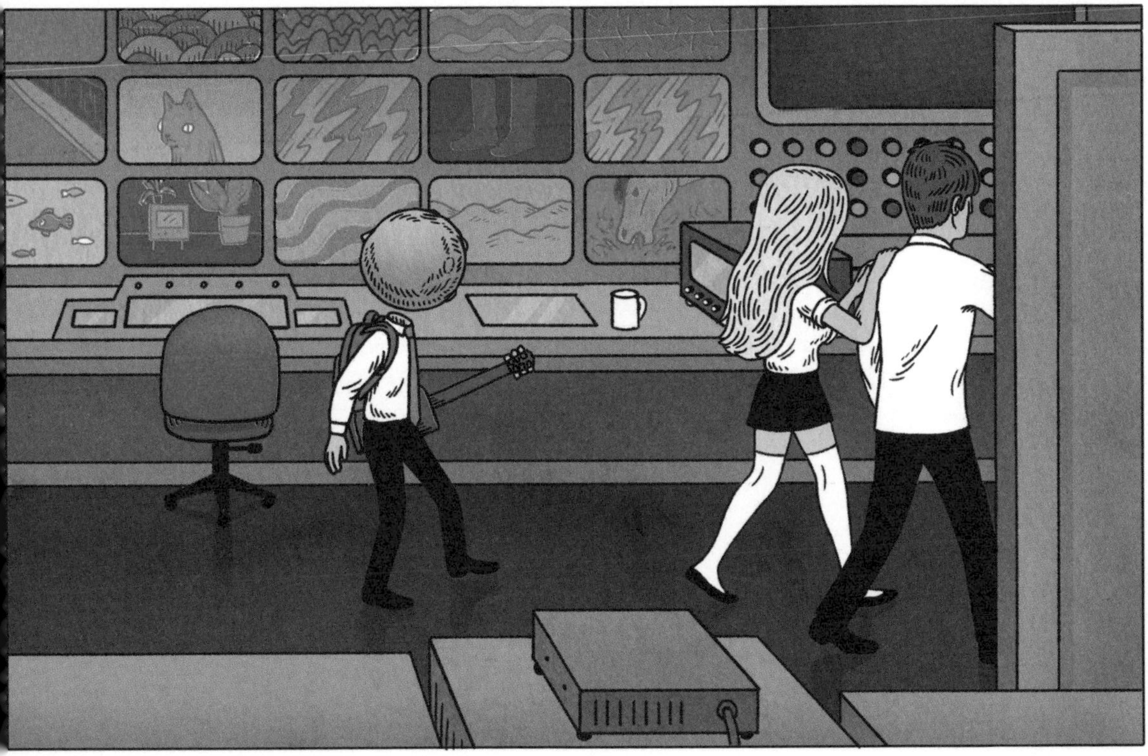

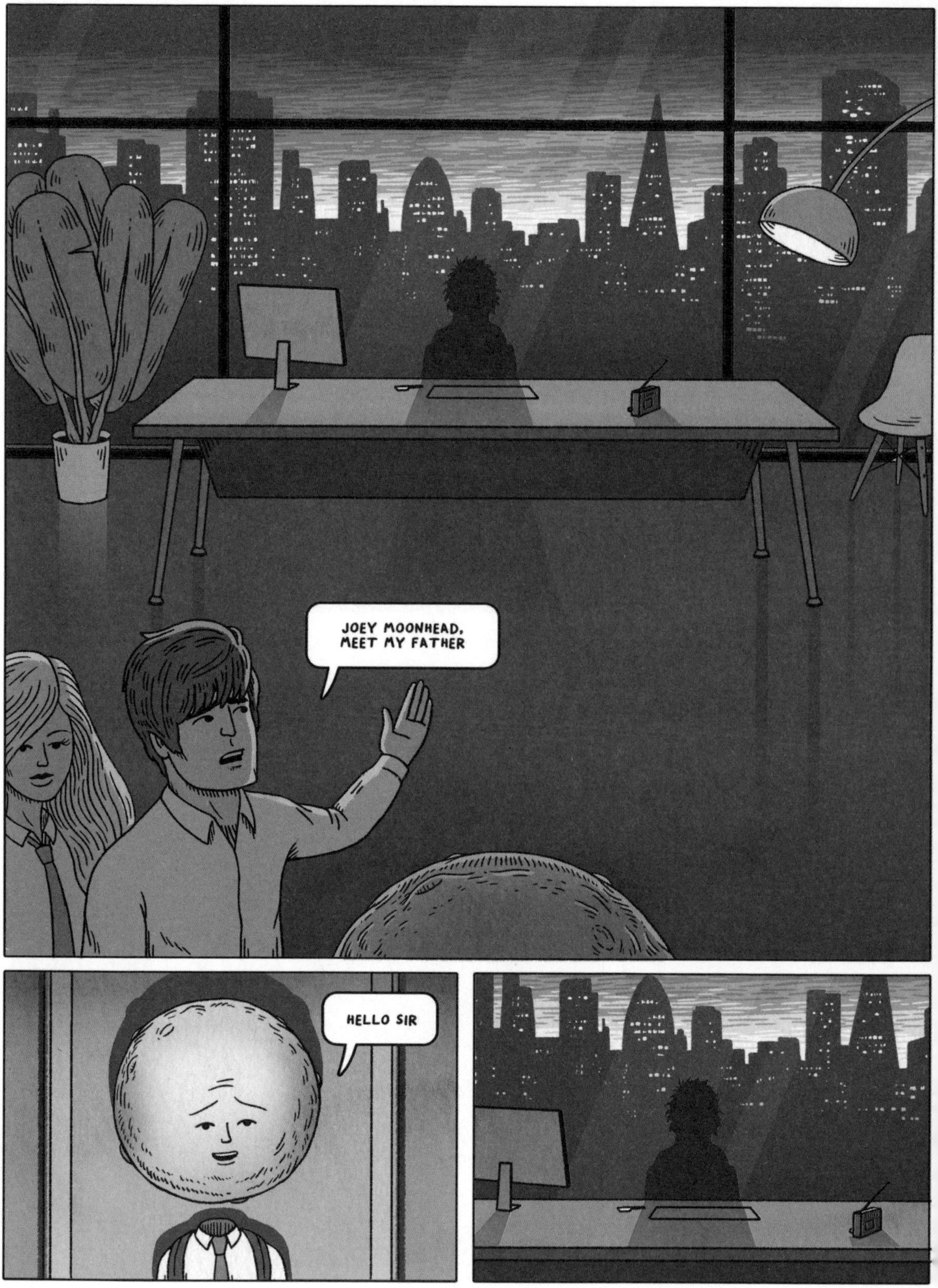
JOEY MOONHEAD, MEET MY FATHER
HELLO SIR

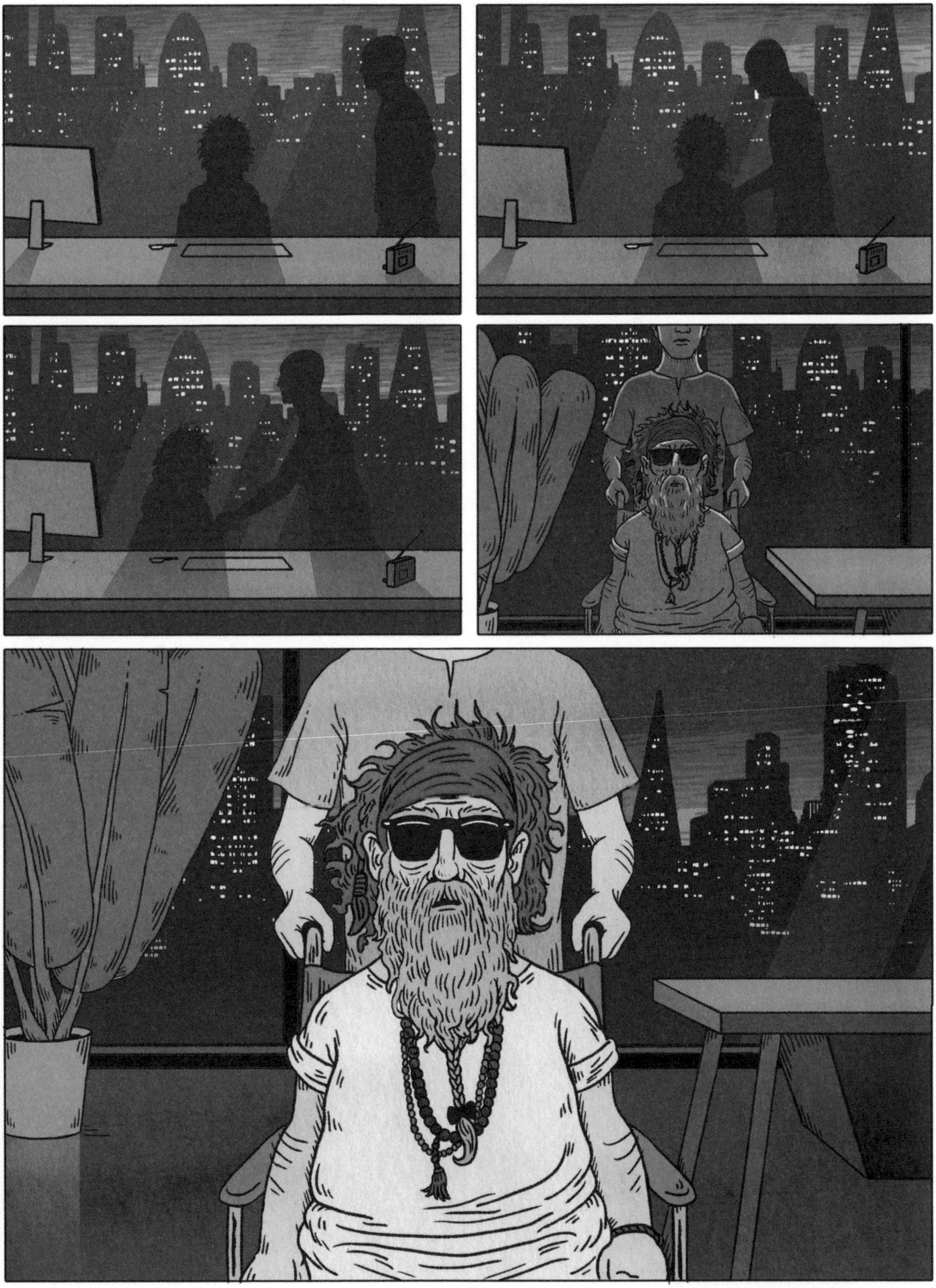

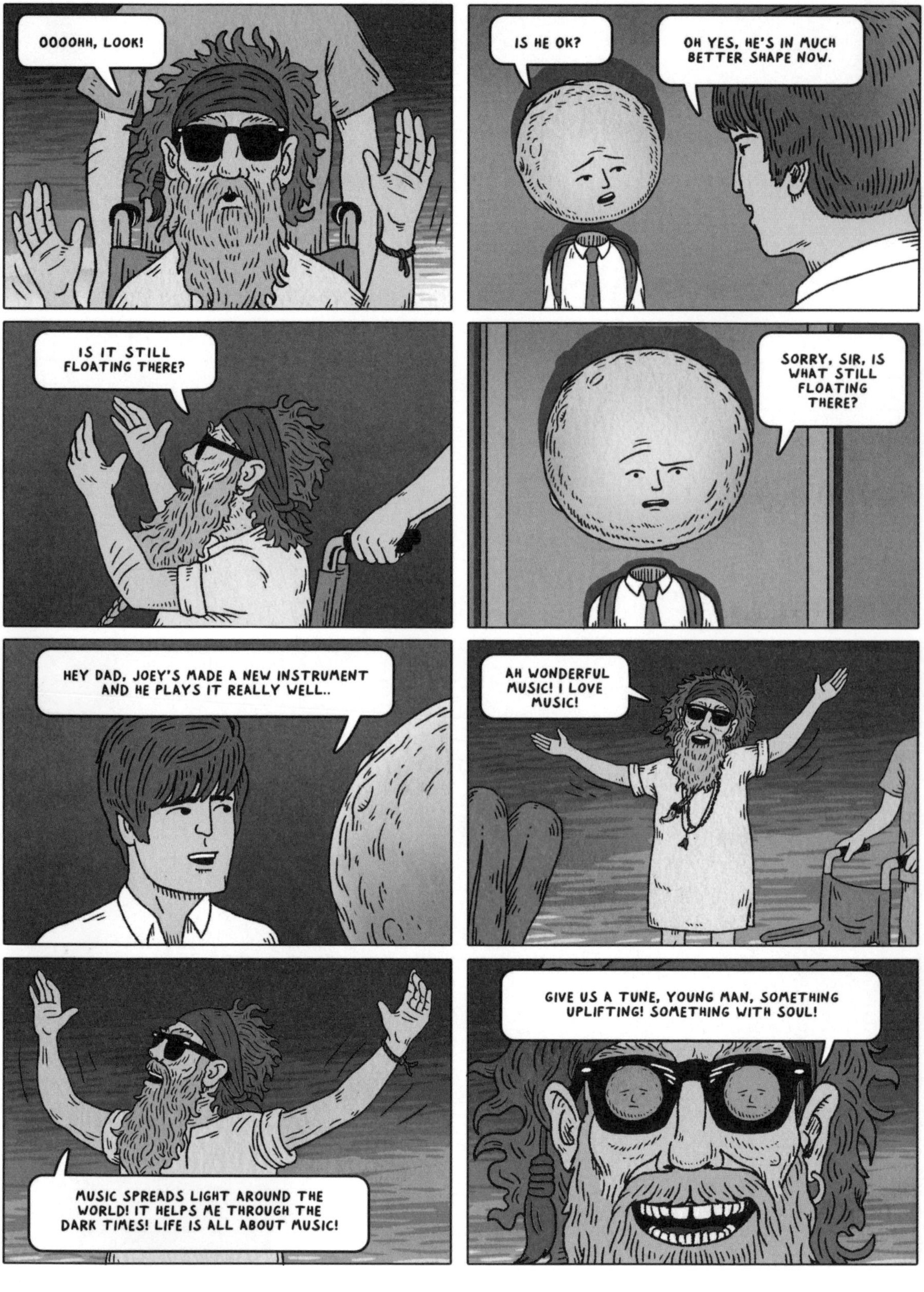

OOOOHH, LOOK!
IS HE OK?
OH YES, HE'S IN MUCH BETTER SHAPE NOW.
IS IT STILL FLOATING THERE?
SORRY, SIR, IS WHAT STILL FLOATING THERE?
HEY DAD, JOEY'S MADE A NEW INSTRUMENT AND HE PLAYS IT REALLY WELL..
AH WONDERFUL MUSIC! I LOVE MUSIC!
MUSIC SPREADS LIGHT AROUND THE WORLD! IT HELPS ME THROUGH THE DARK TIMES! LIFE IS ALL ABOUT MUSIC!
GIVE US A TUNE, YOUNG MAN, SOMETHING UPLIFTING! SOMETHING WITH SOUL!

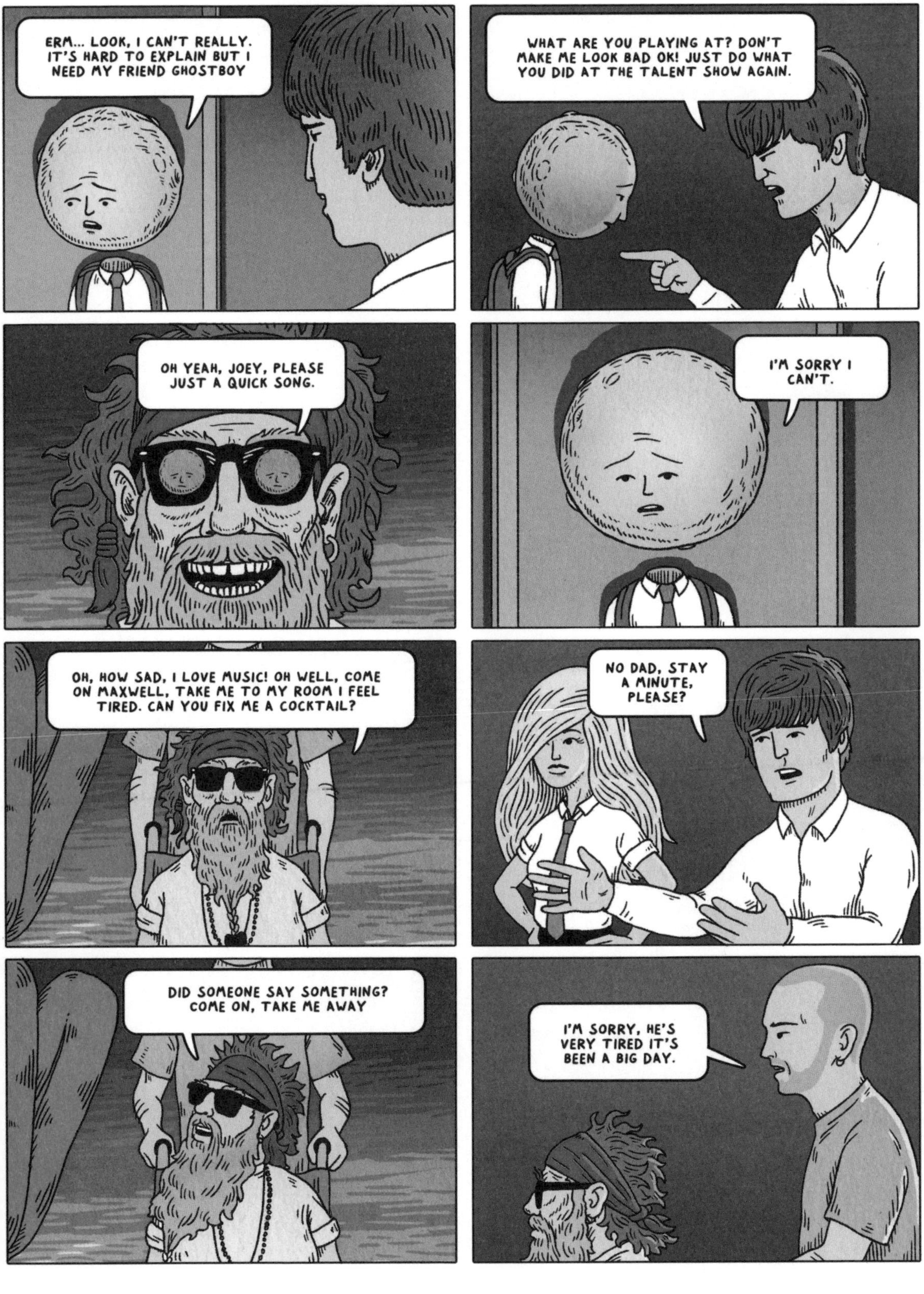
ERM... LOOK, I CAN'T REALLY. IT'S HARD TO EXPLAIN BUT I NEED MY FRIEND GHOSTBOY
WHAT ARE YOU PLAYING AT? DON'T MAKE ME LOOK BAD OK! JUST DO WHAT YOU DID AT THE TALENT SHOW AGAIN.
OH YEAH, JOEY, PLEASE JUST A QUICK SONG.
I'M SORRY I CAN'T.
OH, HOW SAD, I LOVE MUSIC! OH WELL, COME ON MAXWELL, TAKE ME TO MY ROOM I FEEL TIRED. CAN YOU FIX ME A COCKTAIL?
NO DAD, STAY A MINUTE, PLEASE?
DID SOMEONE SAY SOMETHING? COME ON, TAKE ME AWAY
I'M SORRY, HE'S VERY TIRED IT'S BEEN A BIG DAY.

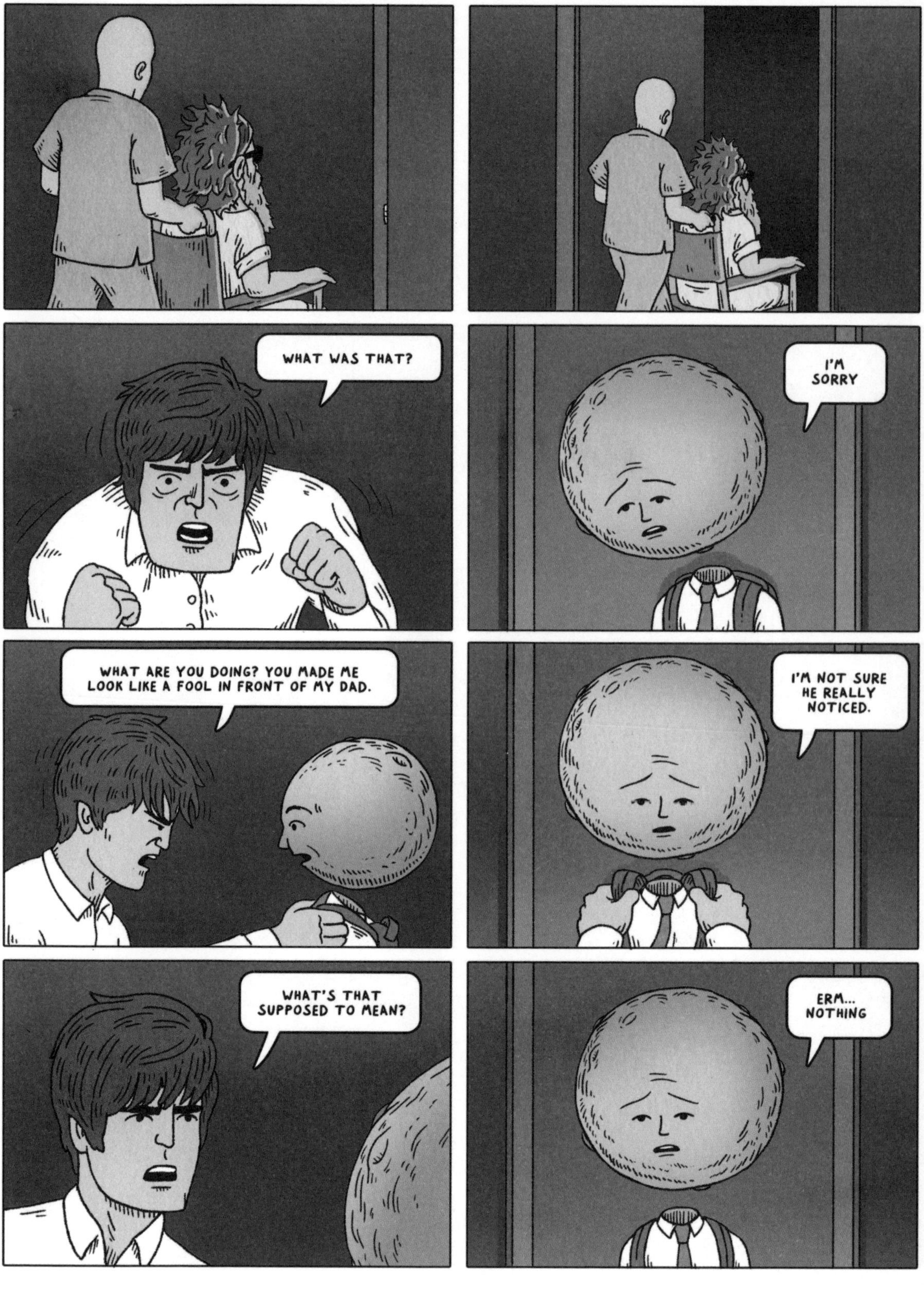
WHAT WAS THAT?
I'M SORRY
WHAT ARE YOU DOING? YOU MADE ME LOOK LIKE A FOOL IN FRONT OF MY DAD.
I'M NOT SURE HE REALLY NOTICED.
WHAT'S THAT SUPPOSED TO MEAN?
ERM... NOTHING

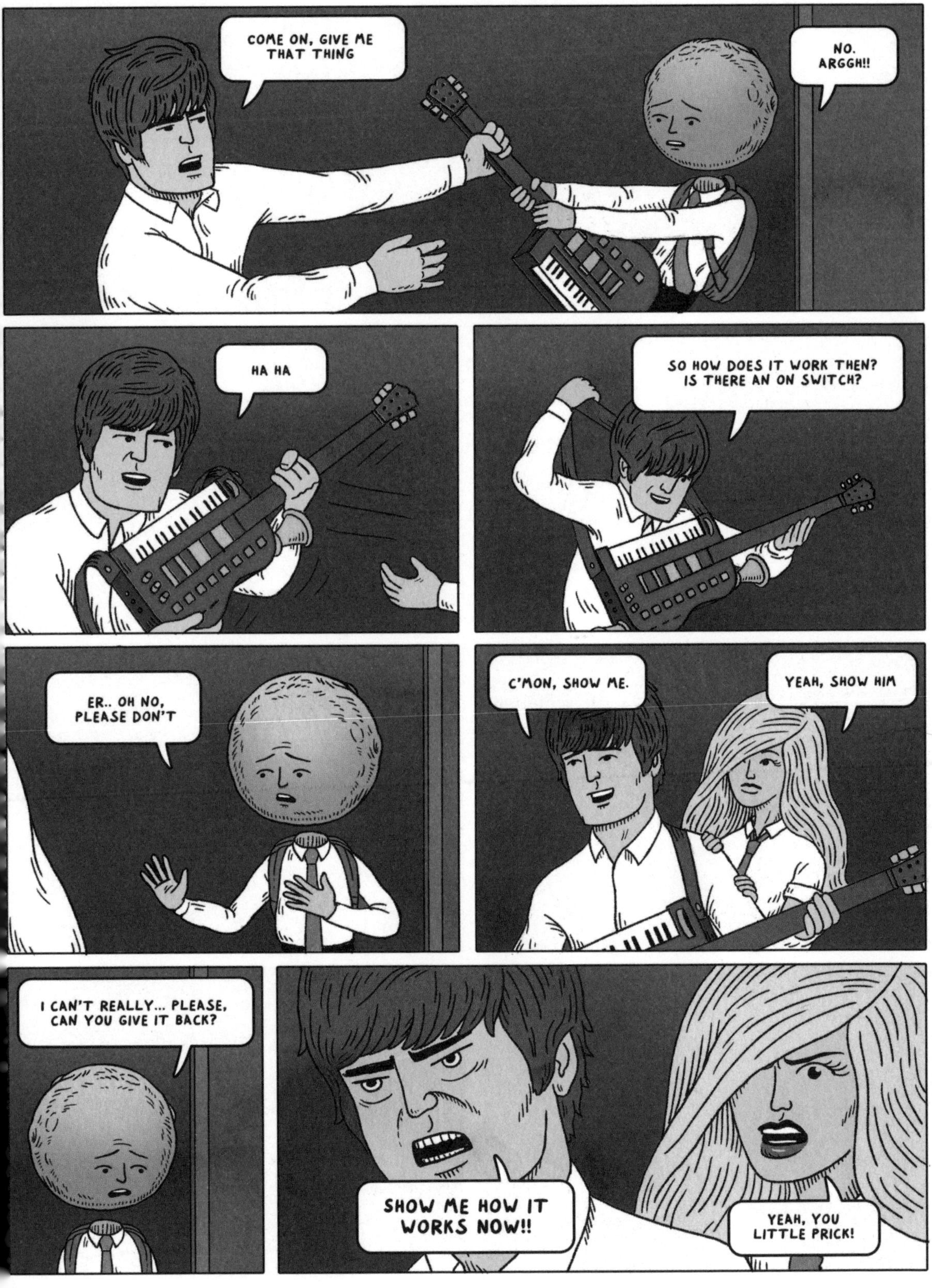
COME ON, GIVE ME THAT THING
NO. ARGGH!!
HA HA
SO HOW DOES IT WORK THEN? IS THERE AN ON SWITCH?
ER.. OH NO, PLEASE DON'T
C'MON, SHOW ME.
YEAH, SHOW HIM
I CAN'T REALLY... PLEASE, CAN YOU GIVE IT BACK?
SHOW ME HOW IT WORKS NOW!!
YEAH, YOU LITTLE PRICK!

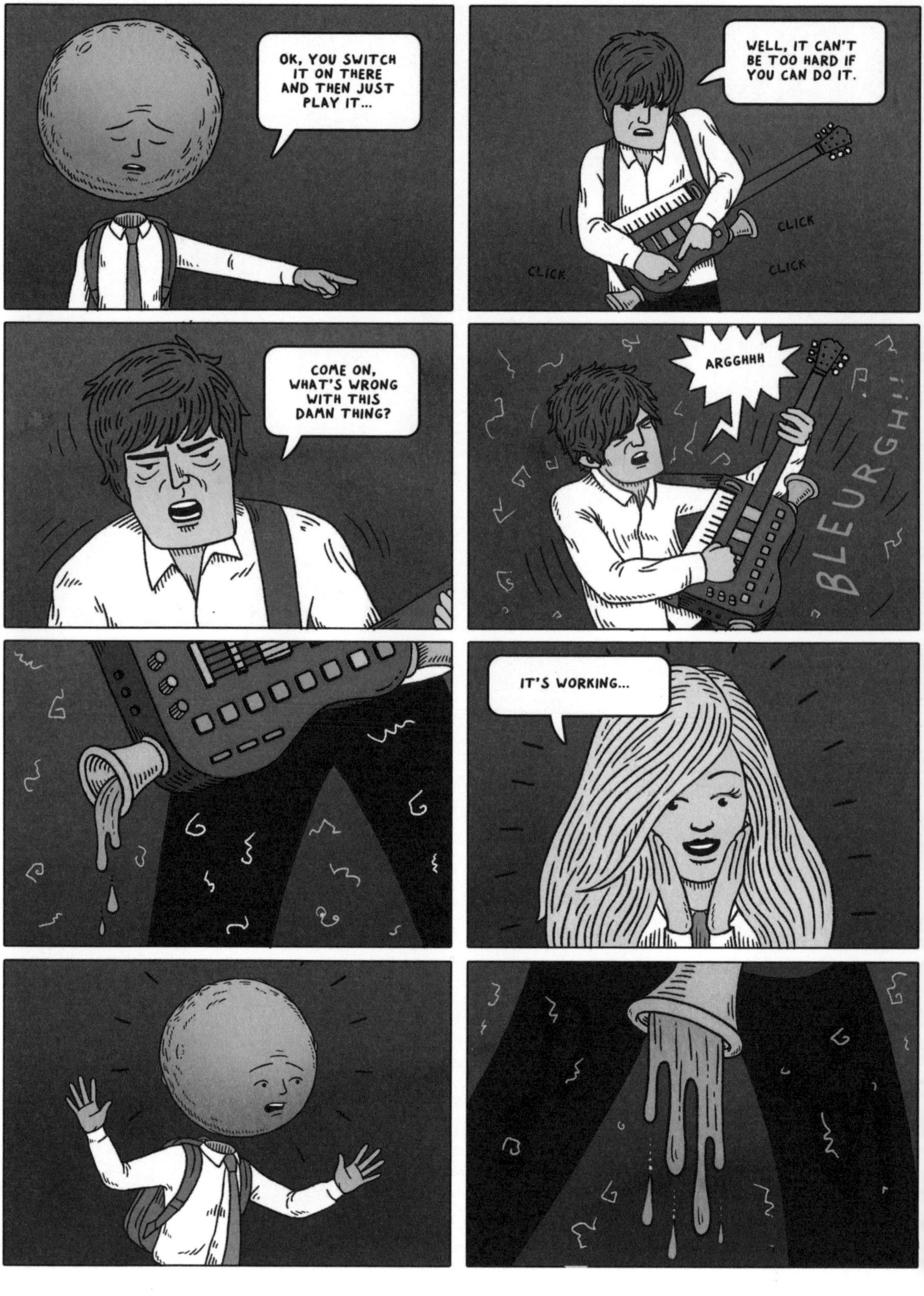
OK, YOU SWITCH IT ON THERE AND THEN JUST PLAY IT...
WELL, IT CAN'T BE TOO HARD IF YOU CAN DO IT.
CLICK
CLICK
CLICK
COME ON, WHAT'S WRONG WITH THIS DAMN THING?
ARGGHHH
BLEURGH!!
IT'S WORKING...

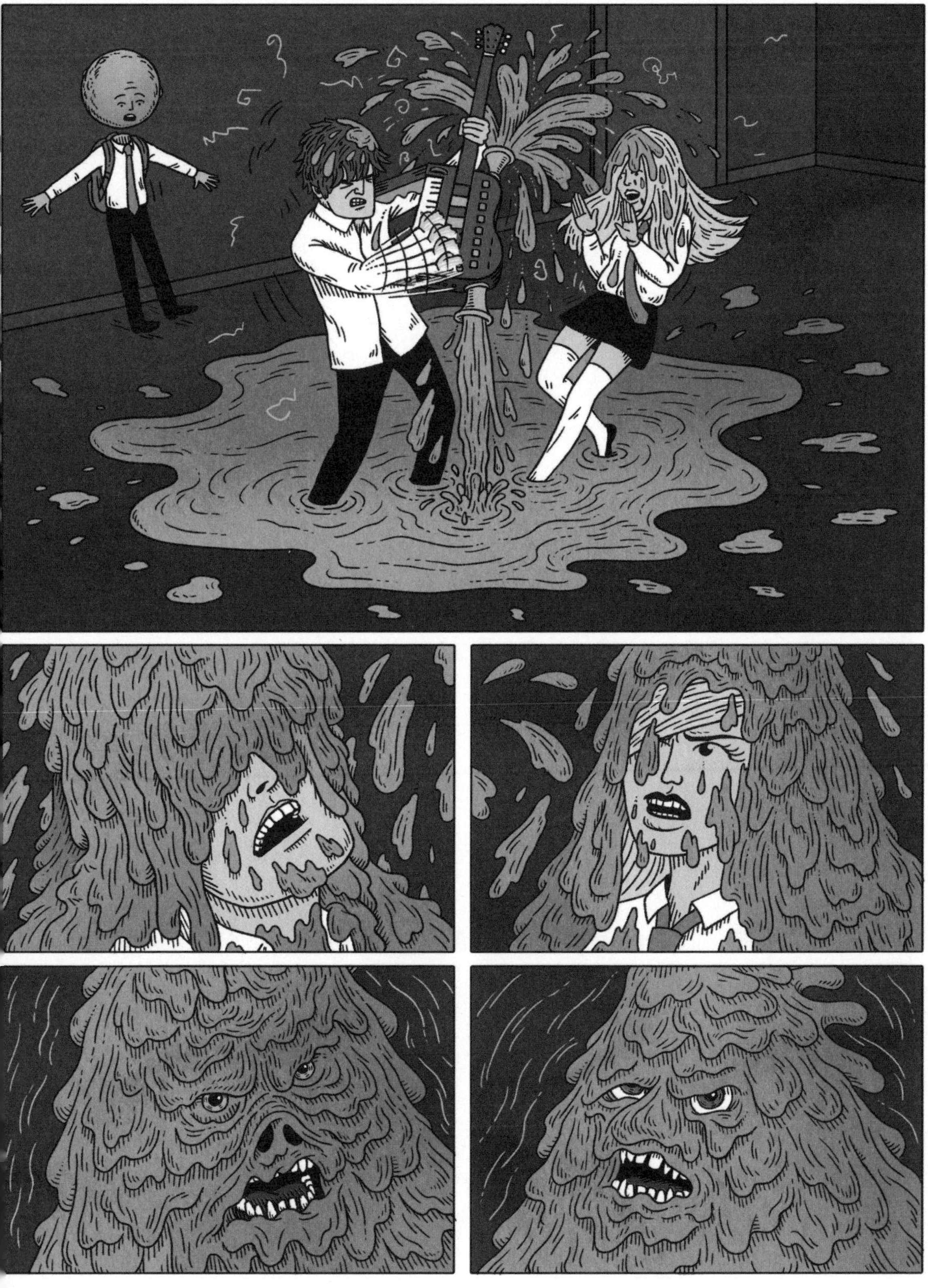

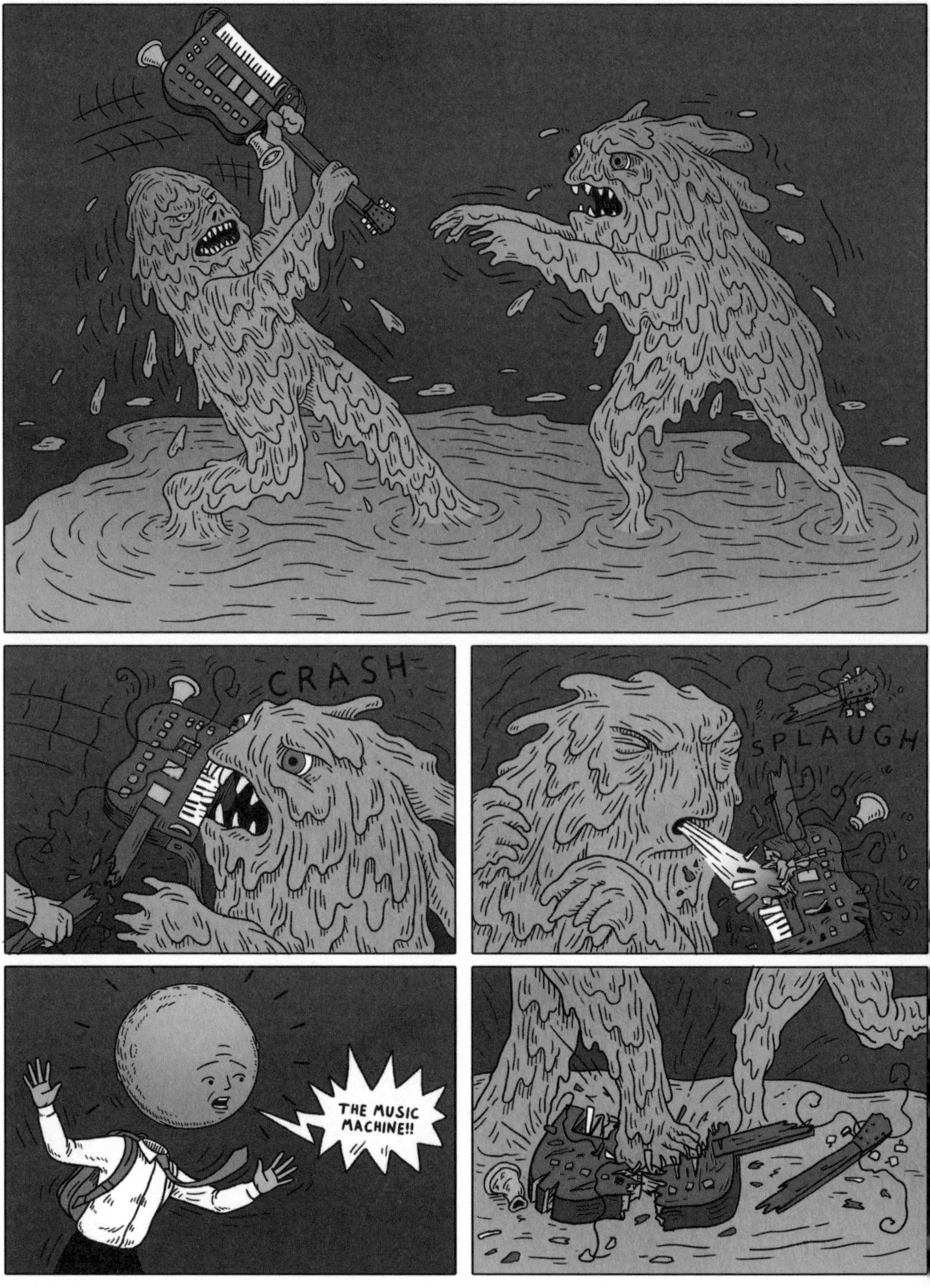
CRASH
SPLAUGH
THE MUSIC MACHINE!!

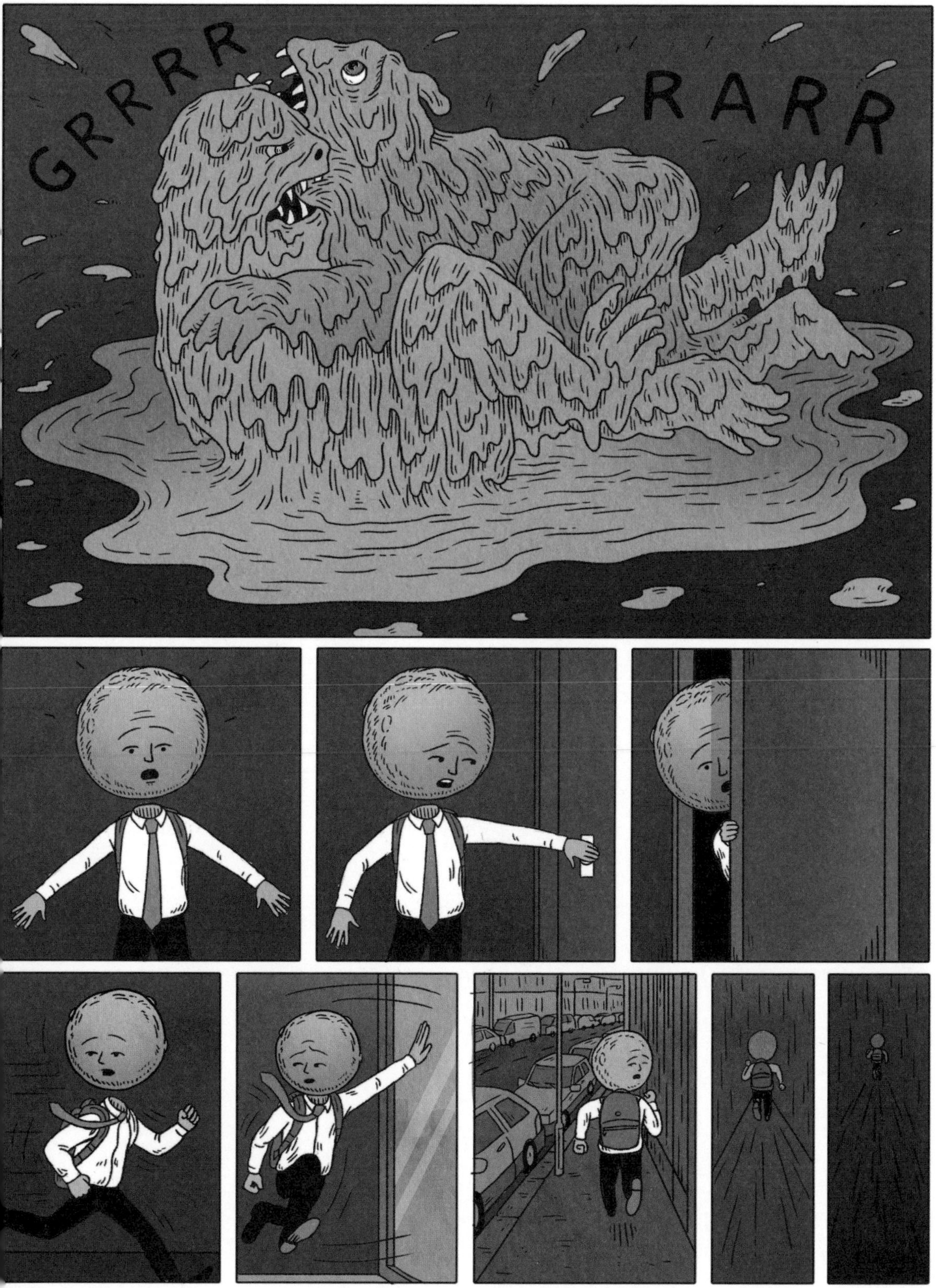
GRRRR
RARR

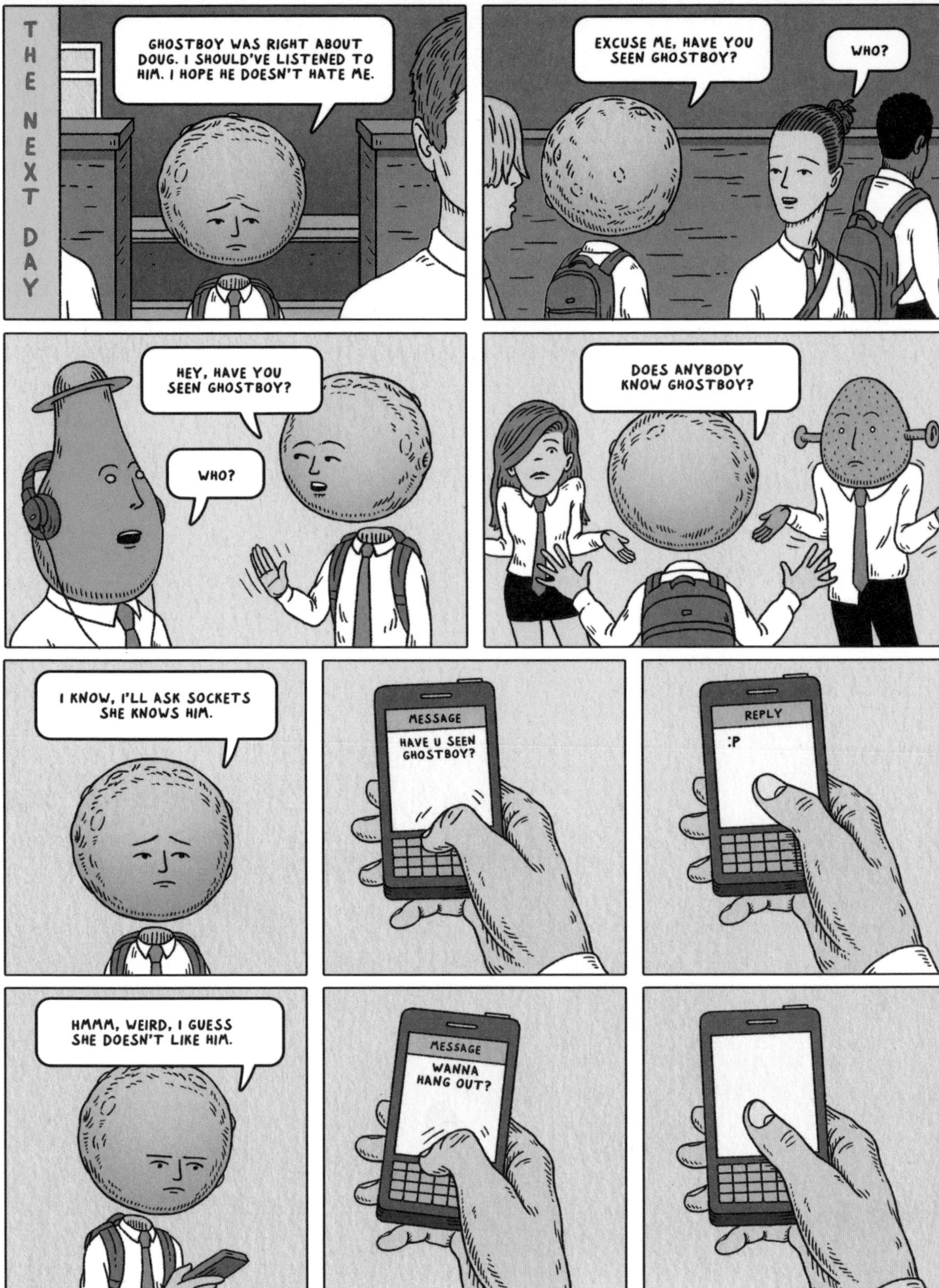
THE NEXT DAY
GHOSTBOY WAS RIGHT ABOUT DOUG. I SHOULD'VE LISTENED TO HIM. I HOPE HE DOESN'T HATE ME.
EXCUSE ME, HAVE YOU SEEN GHOSTBOY?
WHO?
HEY, HAVE YOU SEEN GHOSTBOY?
WHO?
DOES ANYBODY KNOW GHOSTBOY?
I KNOW, I'LL ASK SOCKETS SHE KNOWS HIM.
MESSAGE
HAVE U SEEN GHOSTBOY?
REPLY
:P
HMMM, WEIRD, I GUESS SHE DOESN'T LIKE HIM.
MESSAGE
WANNA HANG OUT?

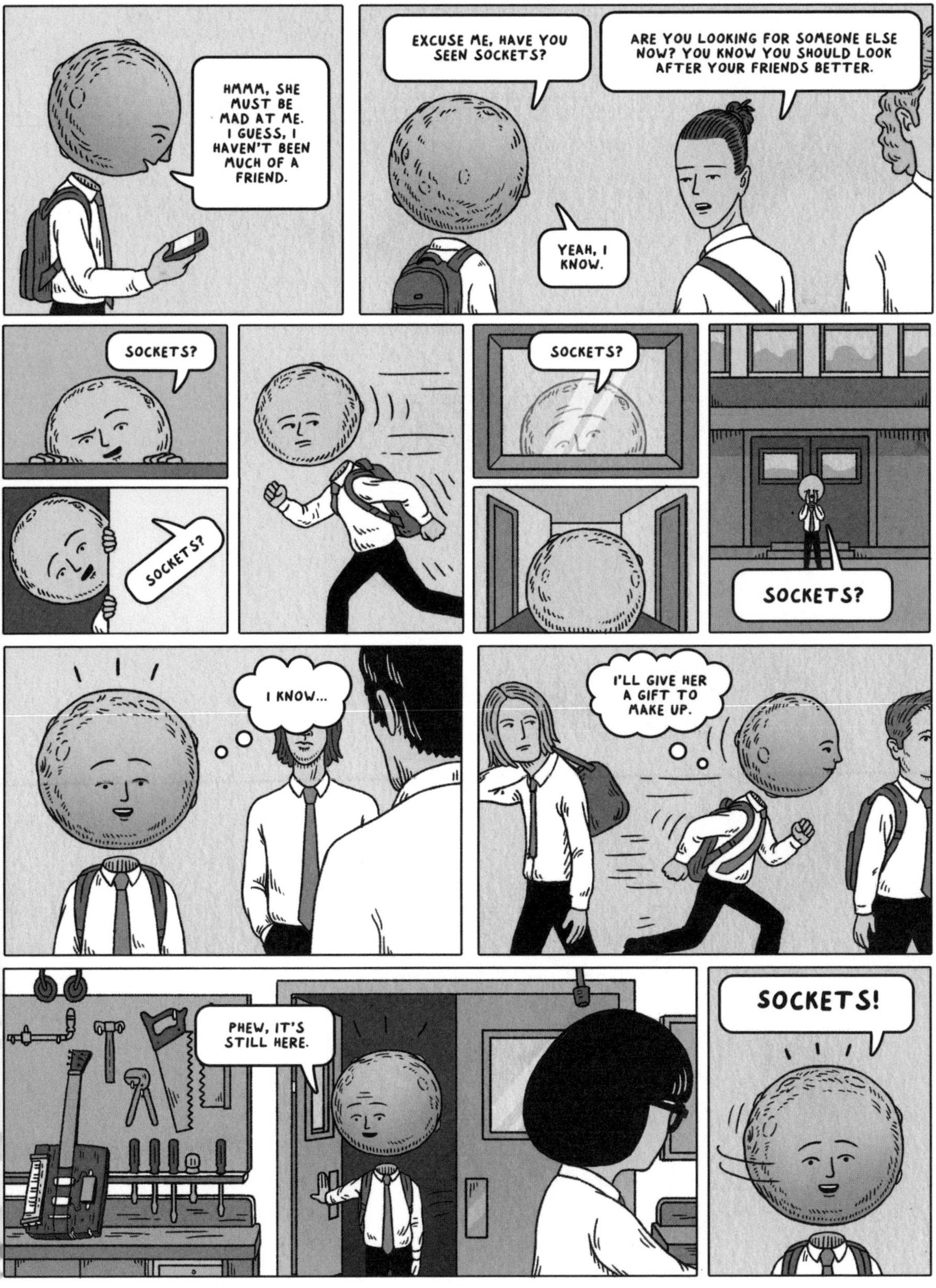
HMMM, SHE MUST BE MAD AT ME. I GUESS, I HAVEN'T BEEN MUCH OF A FRIEND.
EXCUSE ME, HAVE YOU SEEN SOCKETS?
ARE YOU LOOKING FOR SOMEONE ELSE NOW? YOU KNOW YOU SHOULD LOOK AFTER YOUR FRIENDS BETTER.
YEAH, I KNOW.
SOCKETS?
SOCKETS?
SOCKETS?
SOCKETS?
I KNOW...
I'LL GIVE HER A GIFT TO MAKE UP.
PHEW, IT'S STILL HERE.
SOCKETS!

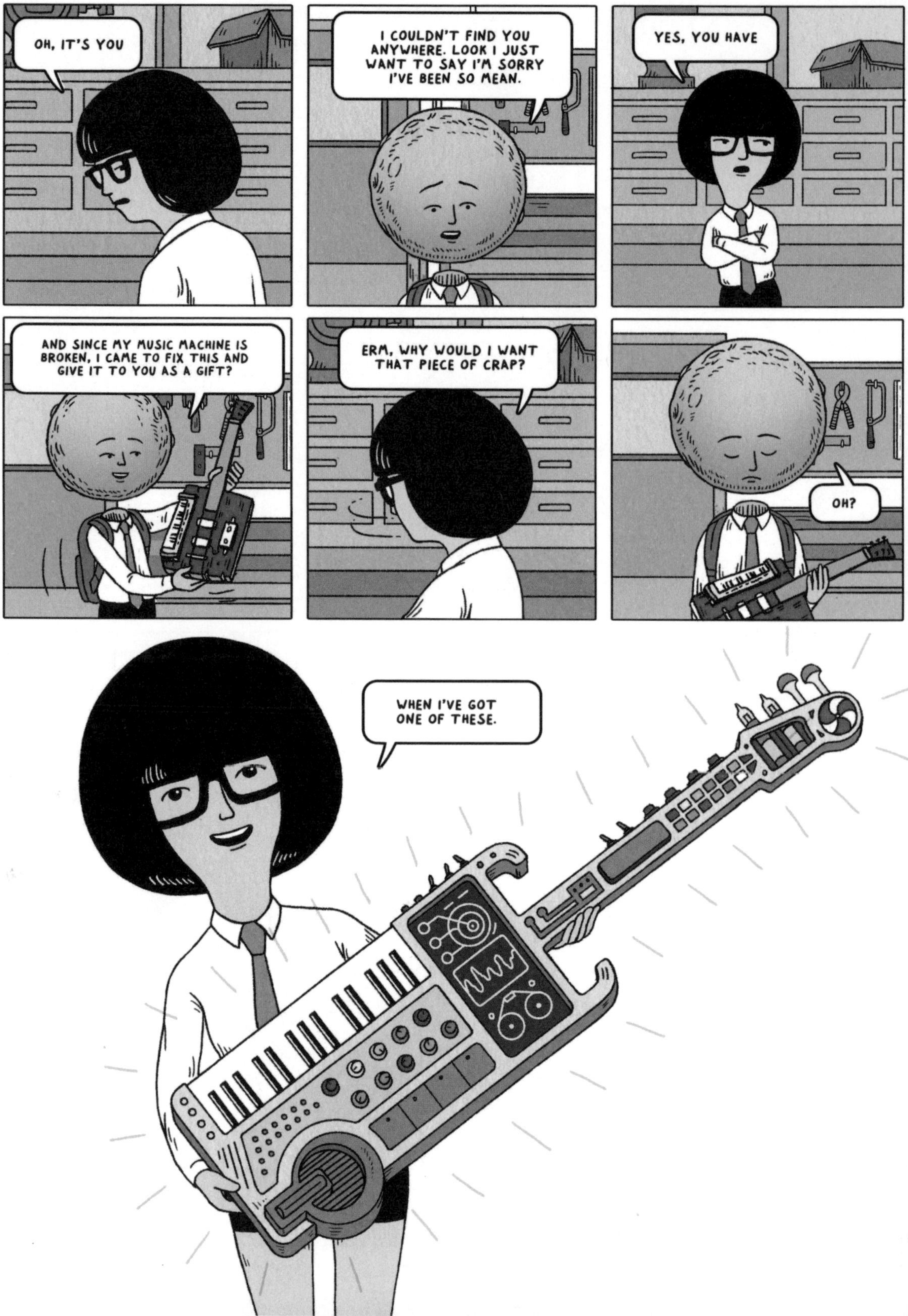
OH, IT'S YOU
I COULDN'T FIND YOU ANYWHERE. LOOK I JUST WANT TO SAY I'M SORRY I'VE BEEN SO MEAN.
YES, YOU HAVE
AND SINCE MY MUSIC MACHINE IS BROKEN, I CAME TO FIX THIS AND GIVE IT TO YOU AS A GIFT?
ERM, WHY WOULD I WANT THAT PIECE OF CRAP?
OH?
WHEN I'VE GOT ONE OF THESE.

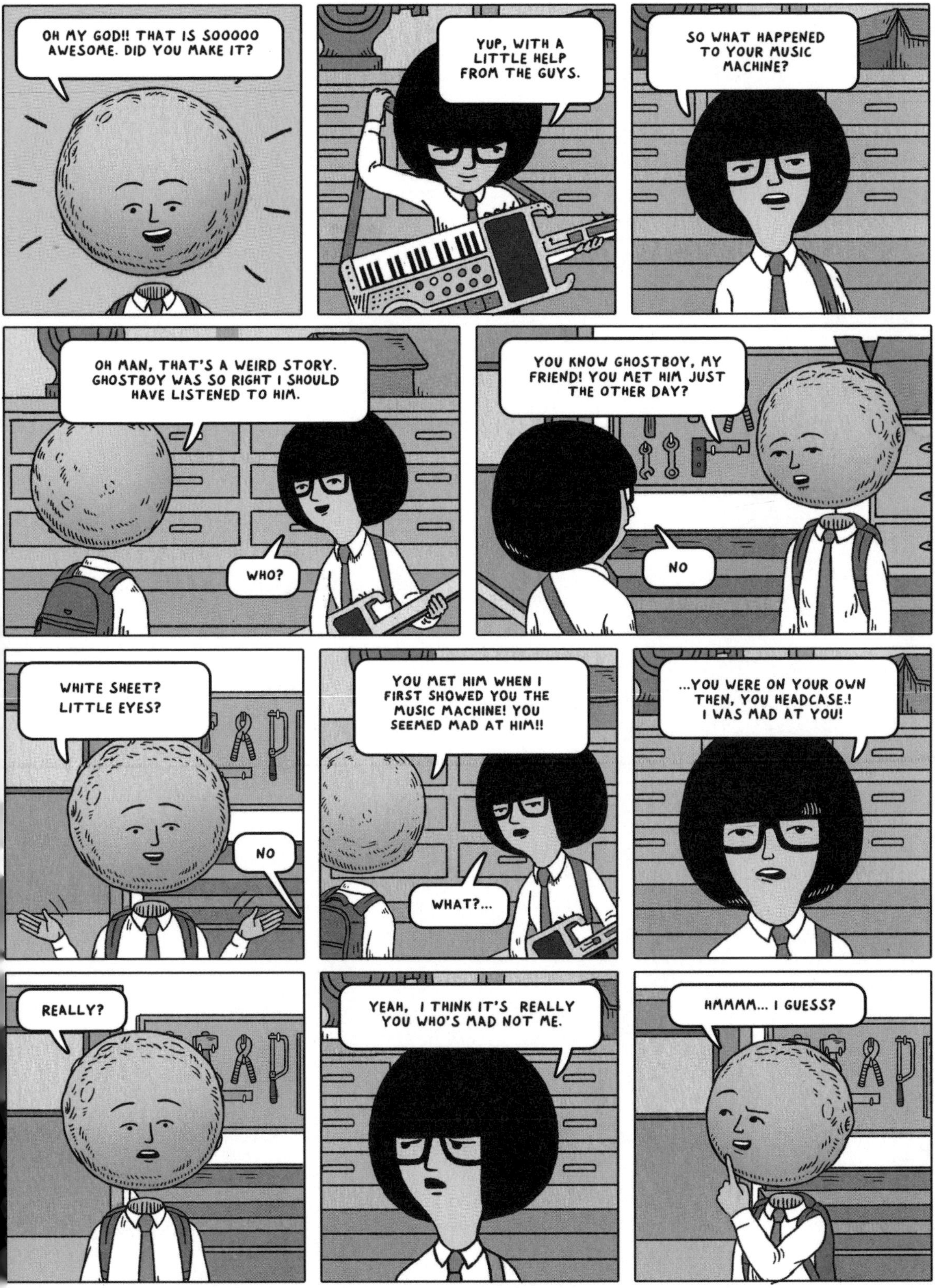
OH MY GOD!! THAT IS SOOOOO AWESOME. DID YOU MAKE IT?
YUP, WITH A LITTLE HELP FROM THE GUYS.
SO WHAT HAPPENED TO YOUR MUSIC MACHINE?
OH MAN, THAT'S A WEIRD STORY. GHOSTBOY WAS SO RIGHT I SHOULD HAVE LISTENED TO HIM.
WHO?
YOU KNOW GHOSTBOY, MY FRIEND! YOU MET HIM JUST THE OTHER DAY?
NO
WHITE SHEET? LITTLE EYES?
NO
YOU MET HIM WHEN I FIRST SHOWED YOU THE MUSIC MACHINE! YOU SEEMED MAD AT HIM!!
WHAT?...
...YOU WERE ON YOUR OWN THEN, YOU HEADCASE.! I WAS MAD AT YOU!
REALLY?
YEAH, I THINK IT'S REALLY YOU WHO'S MAD NOT ME.
HMMMM... I GUESS?

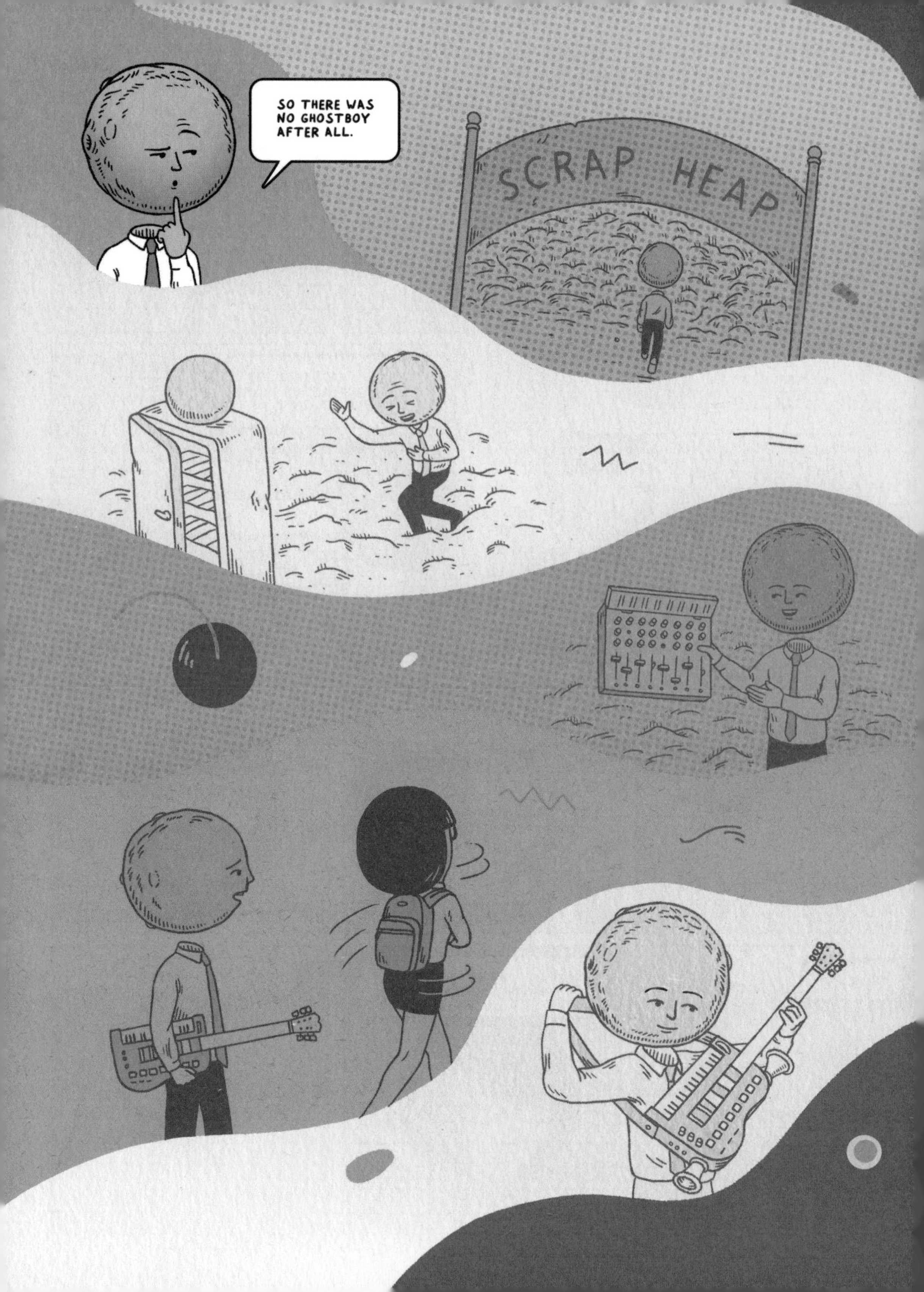
SO THERE WAS NO GHOSTBOY AFTER ALL.
SCRAP HEAP

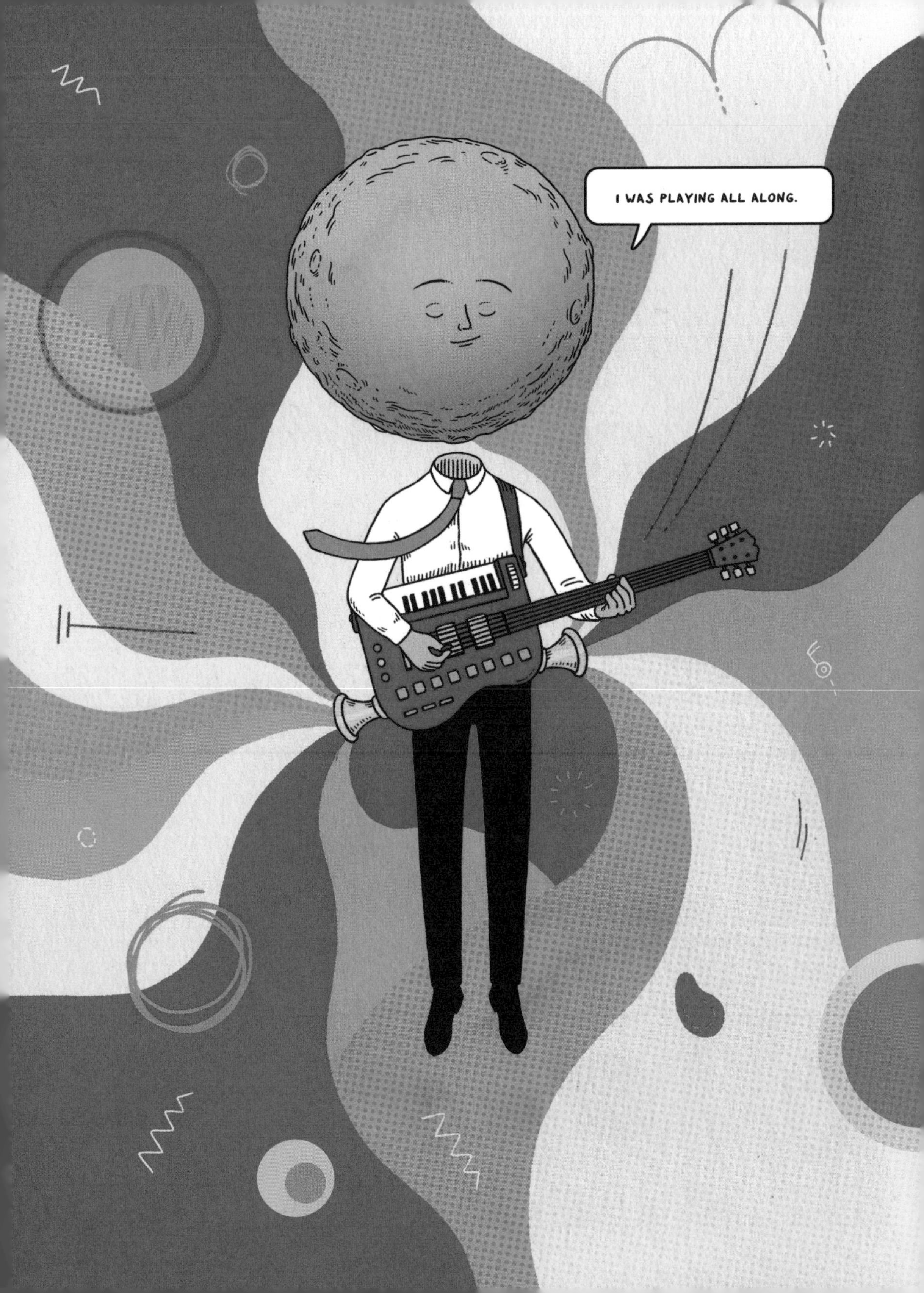
I WAS PLAYING ALL ALONG.

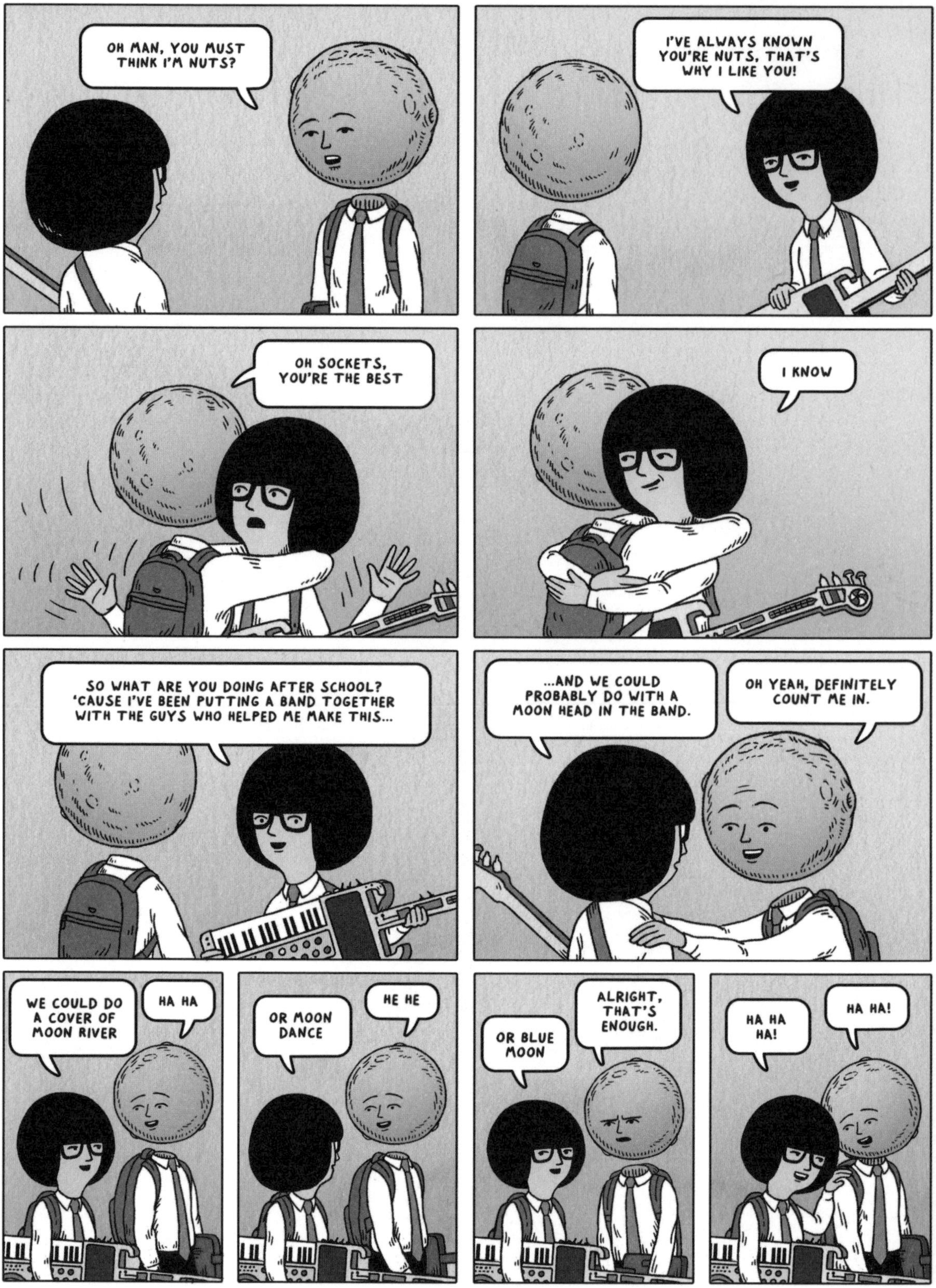
OH MAN, YOU MUST THINK I'M NUTS?
I'VE ALWAYS KNOWN YOU'RE NUTS, THAT'S WHY I LIKE YOU!
OH SOCKETS, YOU'RE THE BEST
I KNOW
SO WHAT ARE YOU DOING AFTER SCHOOL? 'CAUSE I'VE BEEN PUTTING A BAND TOGETHER WITH THE GUYS WHO HELPED ME MAKE THIS...
...AND WE COULD PROBABLY DO WITH A MOON HEAD IN THE BAND.
OH YEAH, DEFINITELY COUNT ME IN.
WE COULD DO A COVER OF MOON RIVER
HA HA
OR MOON DANCE
HE HE
OR BLUE MOON
ALRIGHT, THAT'S ENOUGH.
HA HA HA!
HA HA!

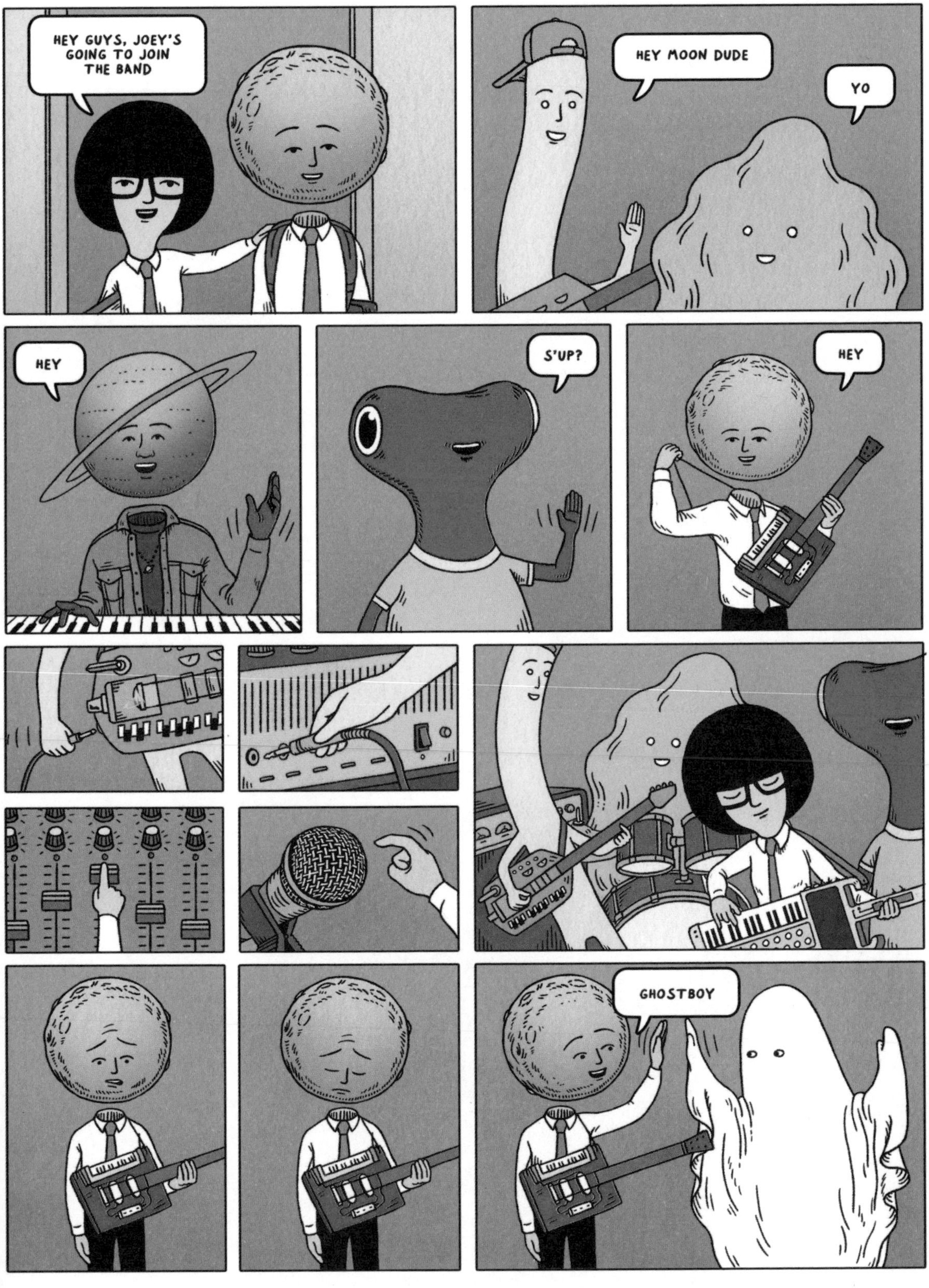
HEY GUYS, JOEY'S GOING TO JOIN THE BAND
HEY MOON DUDE
YO
HEY
S'UP?
HEY
GHOSTBOY

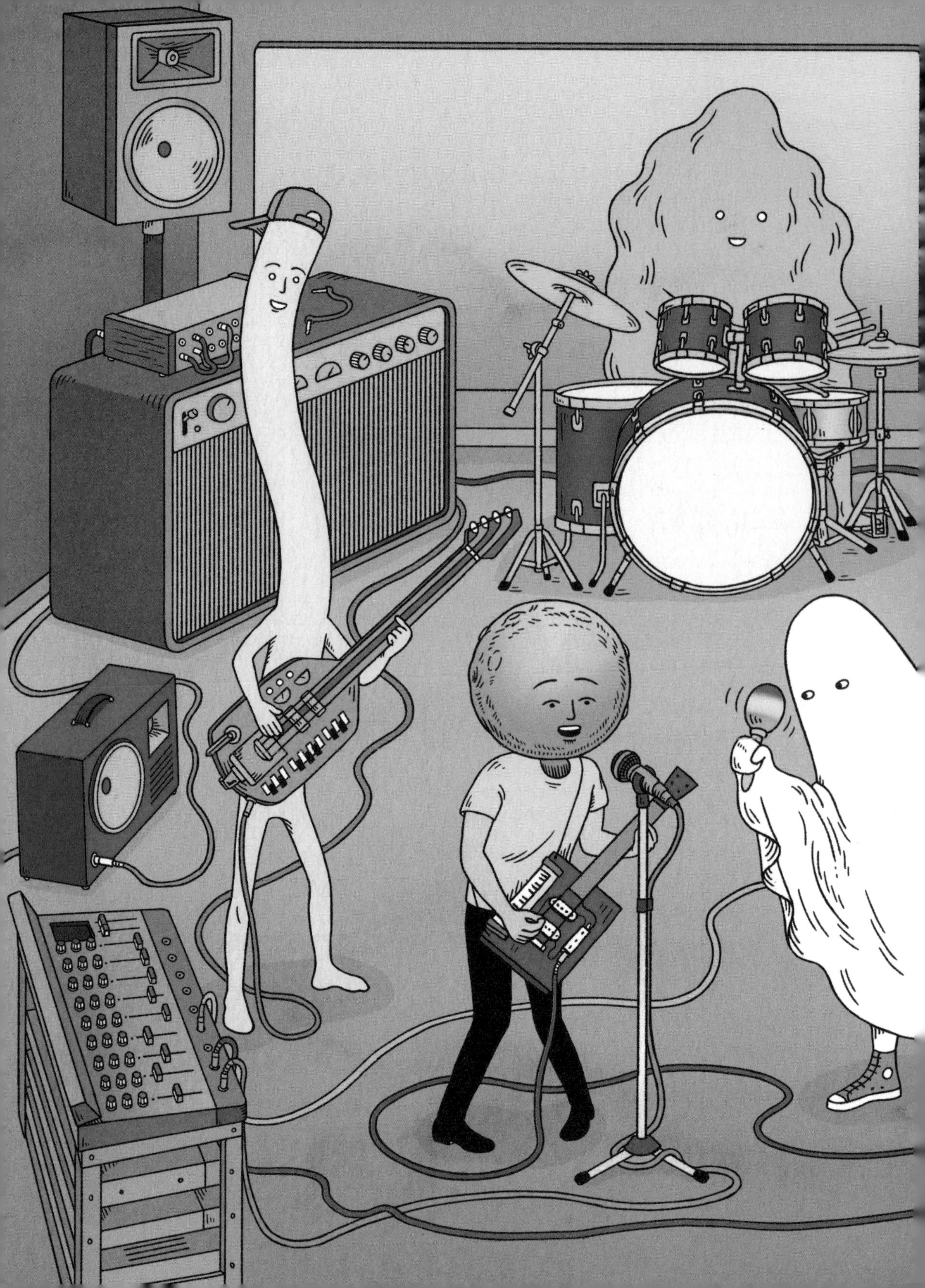

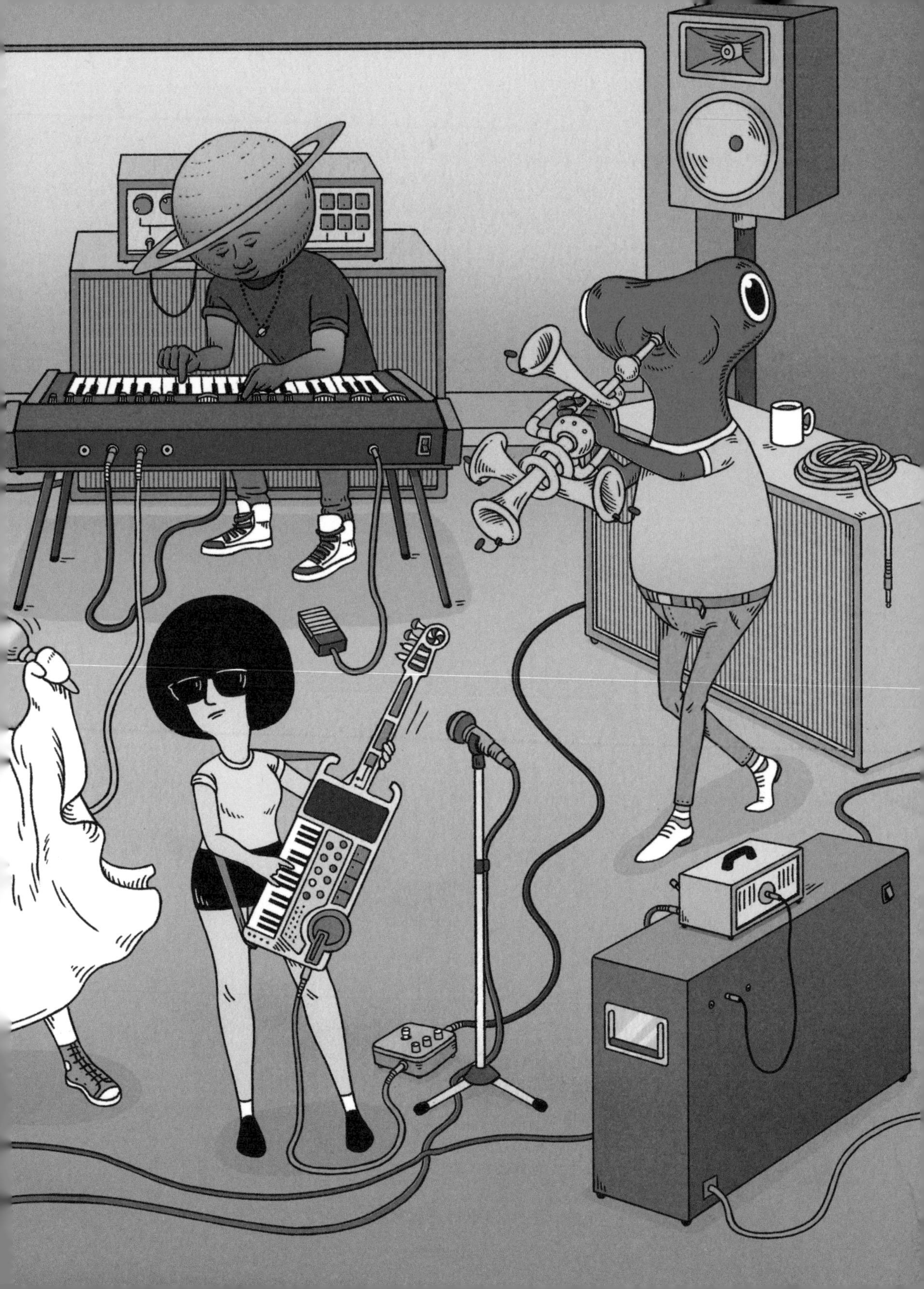

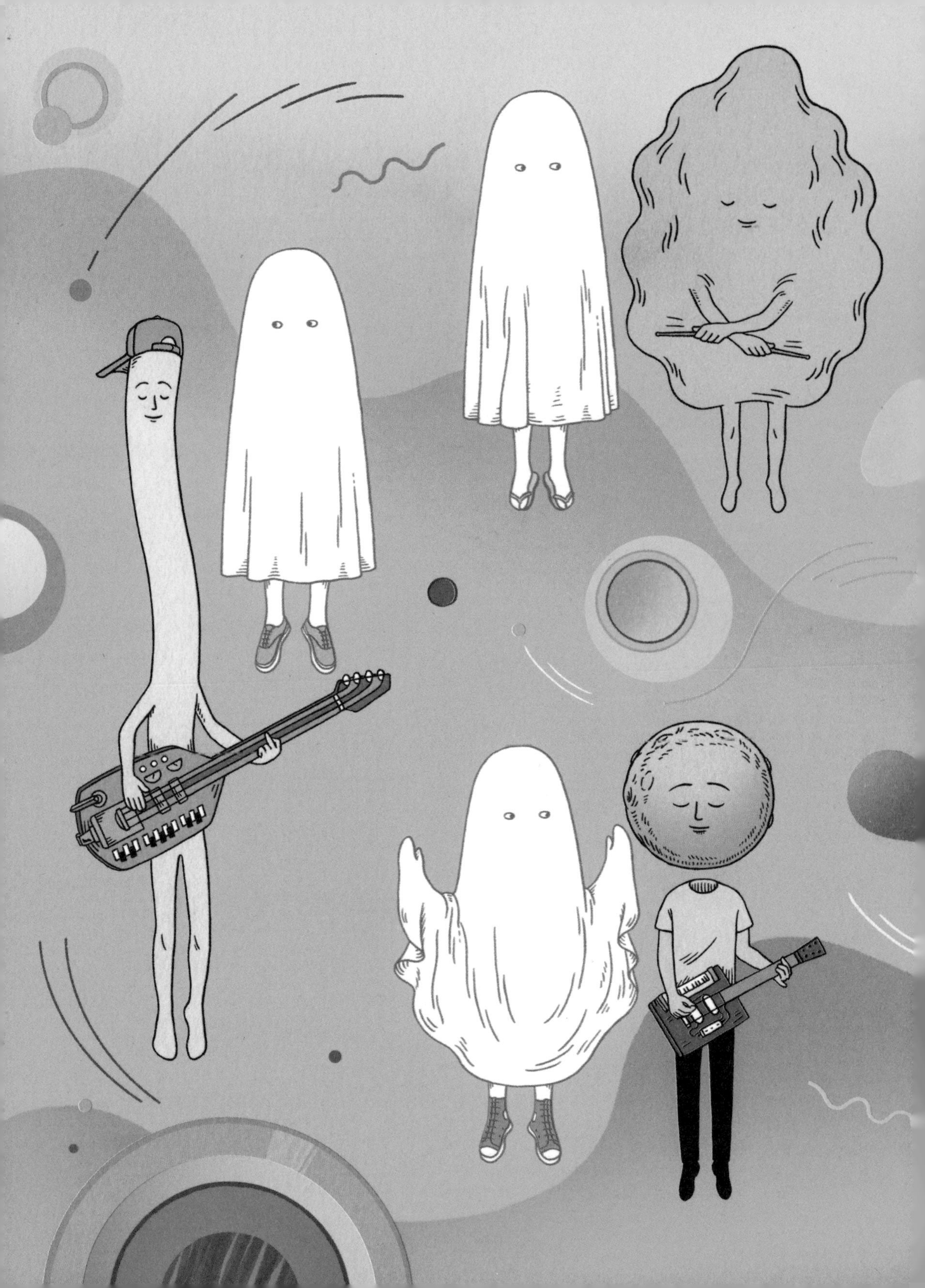

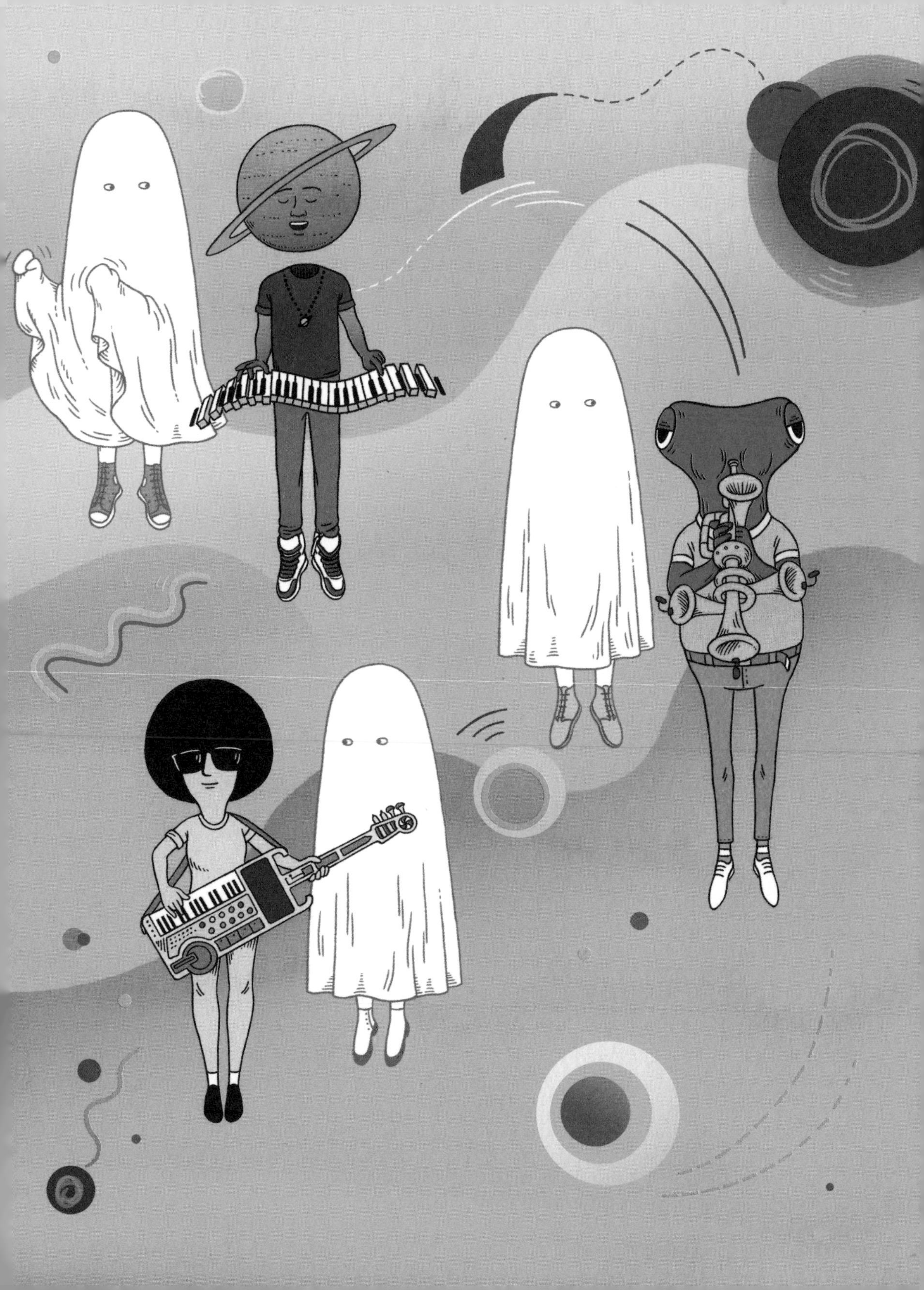

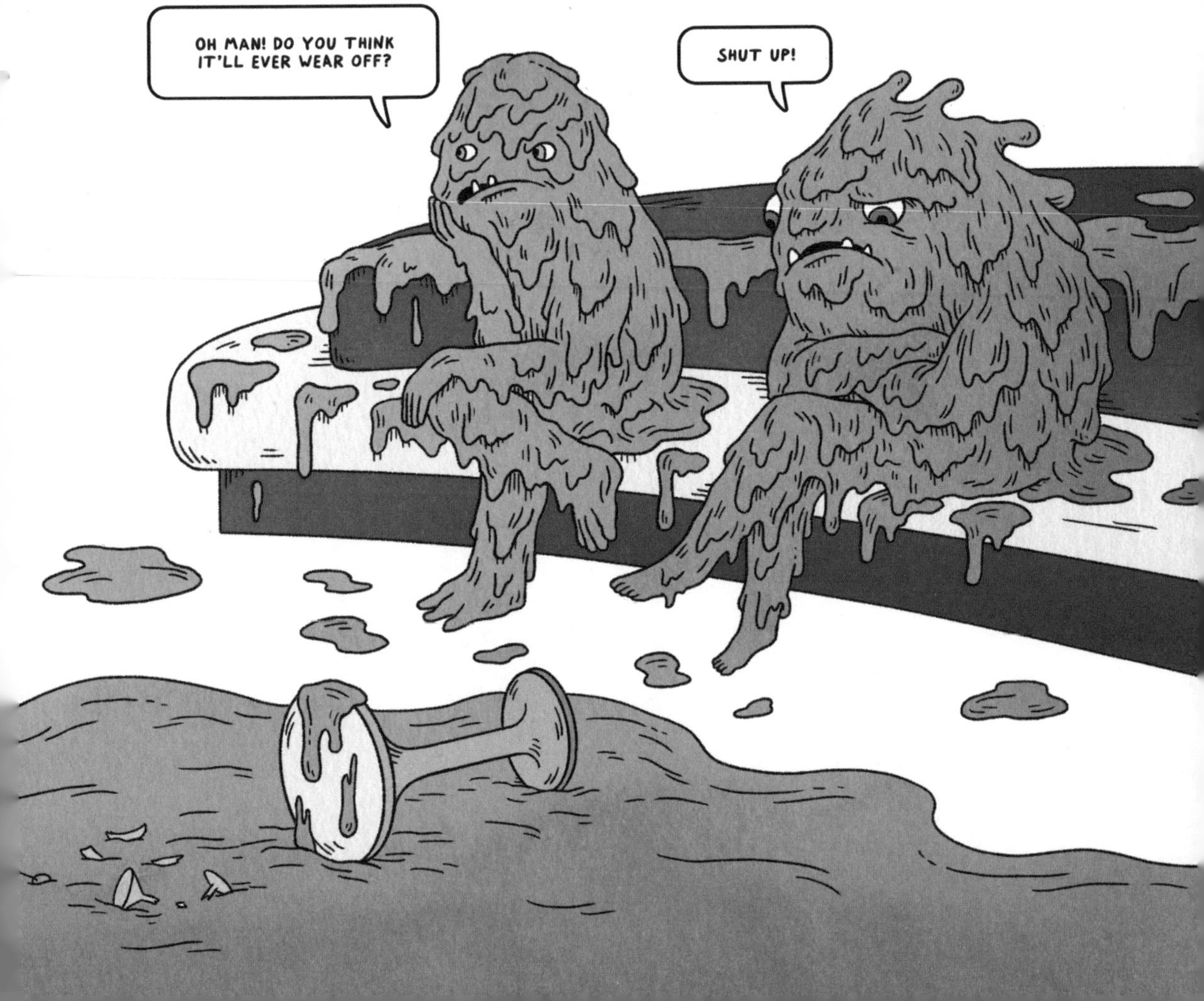
OH MAN! DO YOU THINK IT'LL EVER WEAR OFF?
SHUT UP!

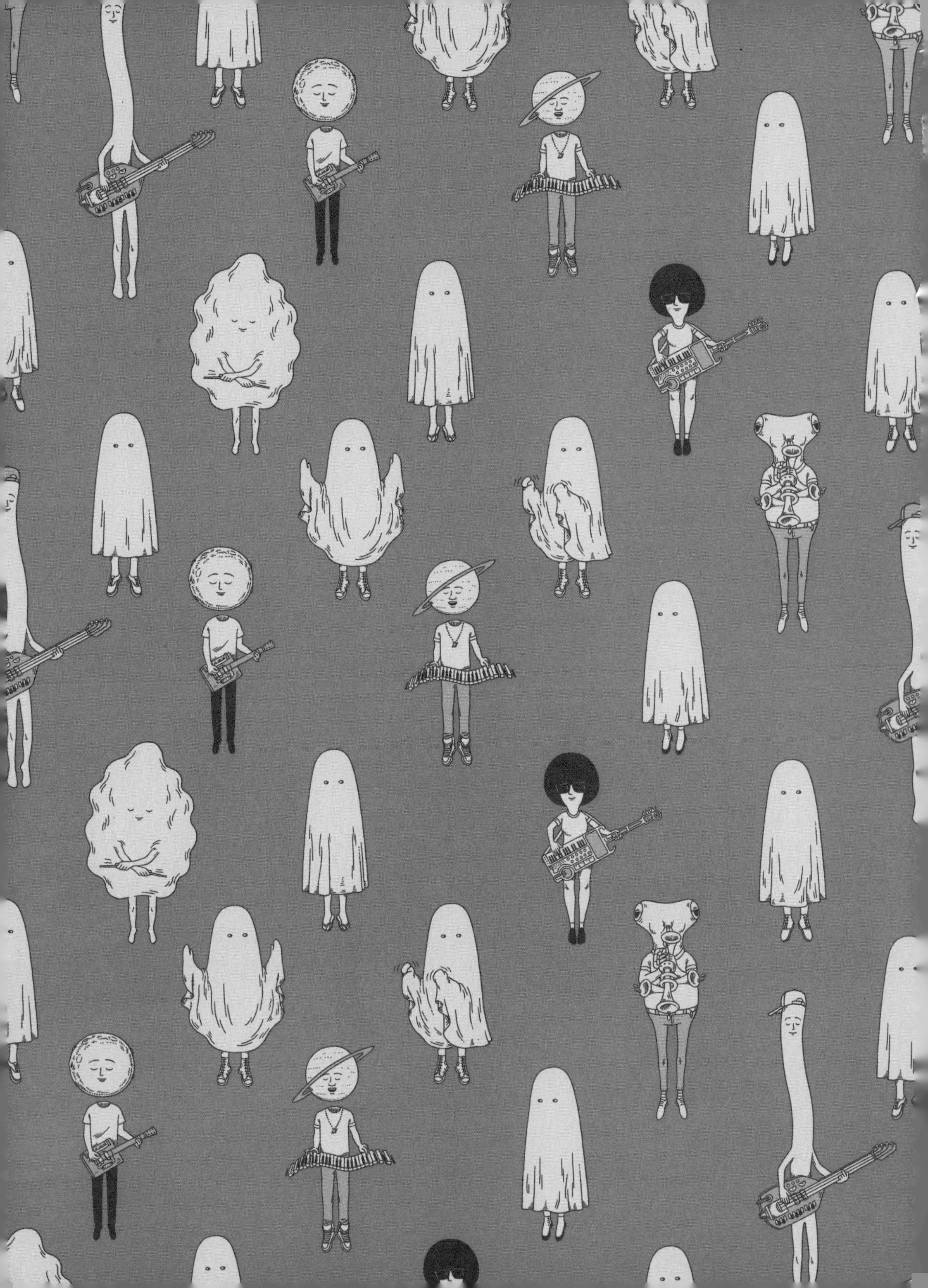